THE CHILDLESS ONES

the CHILDLESS ONES

TWO NOVELS
in STORIES
(?)

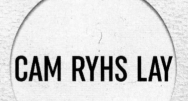

CAM RYHS LAY

Map Illustration by Daniel Hasenbos
Cover and interior design by Meg Reid
ISBN 978-1-7321035-0-4 (paperback) -- ISBN 978-1-7321035-1-1 (ebook)

Library of Congress Control Number: 2018907044

GOWANUS PRESS

to Sup

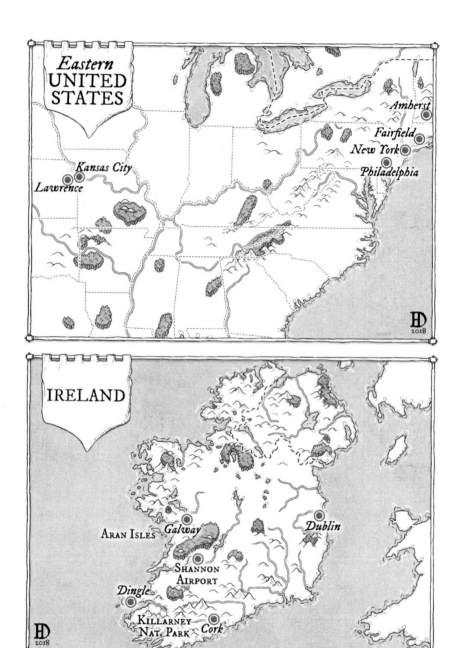

CONTENTS

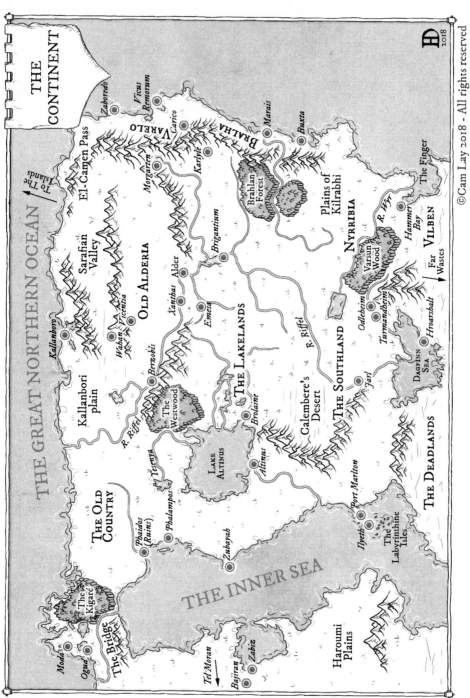

THE
CONTINENT

THE GREAT NORTHERN OCEAN

To The Islands

El-Camen Pass

Zaboredo

Vicus Remorum

VARELO

Carico

Morgarten

Karlyit

BRALHA

Marais

Busta

Brahlan Forest

Plains of Kilrabhi

NYRRIBIA

R. Wyr

The Finger

Hammer Bay

VILBEN

Far Wastes

Sarafian Valley

OLD ALDERIA

Xantbar

Alder

Brigantium

Ernia

Varsun Wood

Odlebeim

Turmanabeim

Hroarsibalt

DAGFINN SEA

Kallanboro

Vicentia

Waban

Berzokis

The Westwood

The Lakelands

R. Riffel

Calembere's Desert

R. Riffel

THE SOUTHLAND

Jarl

THE DEADLANDS

Kallanbori plain

R. Riffel

Brolaine

Altinus

Port Mariton

Ilyethi

The Labyrinthine Isles

Testyra

LAKE ALTINUS

THE OLD COUNTRY

Phaidos (Ruins)

Phalampos

Zubayab

THE INNER SEA

HAROUMI PLAINS

The Kigaré

The Bridge

Moda'n

Ogud

Tel Moran

Bajiran

Zabiz

CONTENTS

"The Singing Frog"

A man wearing rags walks into a bar and asks the bartender, "If I show you a good trick, will you give me a free beer?" The bartender agrees. The man reaches into his pocket and pulls out a mouse and a miniature piano. The mouse stands on its hind legs, stretches, and starts playing a jazz tune.

After the man finishes his beer, he asks the bartender, "If I show you an even *better* trick, will you give me free beers for the rest of the night?" Again, the bartender agrees. After all, no trick could be better than the first. The man pulls out the mouse and miniature piano again. The mouse stands, stretches, and starts playing a different jazz song. The man reaches into another pocket and pulls out a bullfrog, which begins to sing along with the mouse's music.

While the man is enjoying his beers, a stranger approaches from the other end of the bar. The stranger offers the man $100,000 for the bullfrog. "Sorry," the man says, "he's not for sale." The stranger increases the offer to $250,000, cash up front. "No," he repeats, "not for sale." The stranger again increases the offer, this time to $500,000 cash. The man finally agrees and gives the bullfrog to the stranger in exchange for a suitcase of money.

"Are you crazy?" the bartender asks. "That frog could have been worth millions, and you let him go for $500,000!"

"Don't worry about it," the man says. "The frog was nothing special. You see, the mouse is a ventriloquist."

ONE

THIS TIME WILL BE DIFFERENT
2013

Jack had seen the man earlier that evening—had noted his bright green eyes that he could, oddly, only describe as ... *magisterial*—but had only been moved to action this time around. Guilt, no doubt. But wasn't doing something good for the wrong reason better than not doing the thing at all?

The man wore what essentially amounted to rags: paint-spattered cargo pants slinking halfway down his backside, a crimson Temple sweatshirt with a rip in the shoulder. When he turned to ask a blond businesswoman, passing by in clattering heels, for spare change, Jack glimpsed a patch—about the size of one of those old JFK half dollars—at the back of the man's head where no hair grew and instead only pinkish scalp showed.

Jack caught the man's glance now. *Those eyes.* "Change, brother?" the man asked Jack, in a commanding, gravelly voice.

Jack handed him the Wawa bag. "It's Italian. I didn't know if you wanted mayo, so I had them put it on the side."

The man looked warily at Jack as he took the bag, peering inside as if to make sure it contained a hoagie and not a hand grenade. "Thanks."

"Sure thing."

"I'm Ben, by the way," the man said and stuck out his hand.

Jack took it. "Jack Ampong."

"It's good to know there are still decent people in the world, Jack Ampong."

Jack could have laughed out loud. "Good luck," he said and started on his way.

"You too," Ben said.

Jack walked briskly now. He was already late getting home. When he pulled out his phone to check the time, he realized it was still turned off. He held down the button to bring the thing to life. A notification box popped up telling him that in the last half hour he'd gotten four messages—all from Paul, his wife's kid brother.

"Jack," the first message played, "I'm with Sarah. We're at the University City police station. Call me." Jack stopped in front of a Starbucks and listened to the other three messages. More of the same. *Sarah. Police Station. Call right away.*

A debilitating dread blossomed out of Jack's stomach, spreading through his chest, head, arms, and legs. *Calm down.* He listened again to the four short (increasingly agitated) messages, as if doing so might somehow help him assess the truth of what was happening.

Jack called, and Paul picked up before the first ring had finished.

"Where've you been?" Paul said.

"My phone was off. What's going on?"

"It's Sarah."

"What about her?"

"She was...attacked."

"What? Where is she? Is she okay?"

"She's safe. She's talking to the police."

"Hold on...'attacked?'"

"I don't know. Someone followed her into my building when I buzzed her in. She didn't see him coming. When she didn't come up after five minutes, I walked down to see what happened. I guess the guy heard me coming down the stairs and ran off."

"Sarah didn't tell me she was visiting you tonight."

"Well, she was."

"Did you see him?"

"The guy? Only for a second. I chased him around the block, but he got away. I wish I'd caught the little fuck."

"Do you know why? Why he...Did he take her purse?" Jack hoped it was just this: a robbery.

"No. She still had her purse, I think."

"Did he *try* to take it?" He couldn't utter the other potential motives, less in doing so he introduce the possibility to the universe.

"I don't know. Everything happened really fast," Paul said. "Just get down here, okay?"

Jack hung up and sat down on the curb next to a parked car.

I deserve this, but she doesn't. I deserve this, but she doesn't. The sentence repeated endlessly in the talk track of his mind.

"Hey," a voice called, and Jack swiveled around. It was Ben, pushing a shopping cart of his belongings up the street. Based on Ben's eyes alone, Jack was almost moved to unload all his troubles on the man, to tell him everything. An absurd notion, to be sure. "Thanks again for the sandwich!"

Forty-five minutes earlier, Jack had been in an apartment off Sansom Street, lying naked on a firm mattress with only a sheet on top—a young Korean woman who called herself Coco astride him: her crotch against his, her skin—except on her face where makeup covered a trace of acne—soft and smooth and flawless. When he hadn't come after a few minutes, the woman bent forwards and leaned on his well-built chest, her lips brushing the microscopic hairs of his ear. "Doe-ggy?" she said in her broken English, the smell of cigarettes on her breath.

He repositioned himself behind her, starting off slow and gradually picking up the vigor of his movements. He turned to the mirror on the wall, undoubtedly mounted so customers could enjoy the view. What a surreal, ridiculous scene this was: he, a married man who *loved* his wife—his tan barrel chest heaving as he grunted behind this tiny woman to whom he'd hardly spoken two sentences.

When it was over, she kissed him on the cheek, not unlike how an older aunt might, he thought, and used alcohol wipes to clean her hands and between her legs.

"You want to shao-wah ba-by?" she said to him. He agreed and was led by the hand down a dark hallway to an industrial-looking bathroom where a shower head jutted from the wall and a drain sat in the middle of the floor. She gave him a towel and disappeared. Jack turned the water on as hot as he could bear and scrubbed copious amounts of cucumber-melon shower gel over his body. He couldn't seem to escape the feeling that an invisible filth covered his body, his face, his groin.

After he dressed, Coco re-materialized and guided him to the door.

On the way out, she slipped him a business card with the nonchalance of someone who'd just given him a haircut. The reverse of the card was a series of boxes, one of which had been filled with a pineapple stamp. "Buy 5, get one 50% off," it read. He pocketed the card out of politeness and made a mental note to throw it out before he got home.

"See you next time!" she said, and a moment later Jack was back on the street headed home.

A block away, he saw the homeless man with the green eyes again, still panhandling on the same corner. Jack stopped, turned back the way he'd come, and went inside a Wawa to buy the man, who would soon introduce himself as Ben, a sandwich.

He'd never been to a police station, except once to have his fingerprints taken as part of his substitute teaching application; that had been out in the suburbs, where the police stations were, if not inviting, at least calm and sterile, with upholstered chairs in the lobby. Here in the city, the station buzzed with chaotic energy, and there was a dinginess to the place that evoked hopelessness. He told the man at the desk he was looking for his wife, Sarah D'Albero-Ampong. The officer buzzed him in past a bulletproof glass door and motioned him to another seating area in a small corridor. The overhead fluorescent lights hummed like those things meant for killing mosquitoes. Here the walls were lined with bulletin boards of wanted posters and sketches: a thirty-five-year-old white male who killed his girlfriend with a kitchen knife, an unknown suspect who held up a liquor store and shot the clerk in the face at point-blank range, a Hispanic male wanted for sexual assault.

I deserve this, but she doesn't.

That morning Jack had woken up early to cook breakfast—a peace offering following the previous evening's fight. He made a mushroom, pepper, and cheese scramble and rye toast (with olive oil, which she preferred to butter). Sarah had been unusually quiet that morning, contrite even, which was unlike her. He had been prepared for a fight but, instead, she'd given him cold politeness.

"You want to talk, Sar?" he'd said.

"Not really." Her half-smile was a sharp, sarcastic dagger.

It all had made Jack uneasy—like something both important and terrible was about to happen. And it could have been his last memory of them together: eating breakfast like strangers sharing a table at a crowded restaurant.

He couldn't even remember what their fight had been about. Or, more precisely, he couldn't remember what the catalyst had been. Regardless of the superficial "topics" of their quarrels, they were all about one thing: his job. Or rather, how two years before he'd quit his well-paying job as an analytics manager at a marketing agency to write and substitute teach. Eventually, Sarah would come to some permutation of the argument that he was being selfish or irresponsible or both. Jack would accuse her of caring too much about money. "If we don't do what we love," he'd said, "then what's the point?"

"You think I love going to work every day making *sports collectibles*? Is this what I've been dreaming of?"

"Don't do it then. Quit."

"*Quit?* Quit, he says. I'm trying to have a life. Maybe have a little saved for our kids' college, if we can even have kids. Someone's got to make money around here, especially since you're so 'uncomfortable' getting any help from my parents, who literally just want us to be happy."

She had a point, but this only had the effect of making him more upset, more desperate, a cornered animal with nowhere to go.

When he'd first quit his job, she'd been mostly supportive; she bought him an antique rolltop desk at an estate sale in Manayunk—one of the models with a hundred little drawers and compartments—and she'd had it set up for him in the spare bedroom. Above the desk, she'd hung a framed calligraphic rendering of a Samuel Beckett quote that, although he'd never actually *read* any Beckett, was one of his favorite sources of inspiration:

Ever tried. Ever failed. No matter. Try again. Fail again. Fail better.

Months passed and Sarah's support waned. Jack could hear it in how she asked him about his progress on the book—in how she made little side comments about money being tight, bills being high. They might be walking past a real estate office with listings in the window, and she'd make a passing comment. "Wouldn't it be great if we could afford a place like *that*?" she'd say of a quaint-looking brownstone in Fishtown or of a newly built loft in the Northern Liberties.

Jack's book had been something he'd been mulling over for twenty-plus years. Ever since reading *The Lord of the Rings* in the sixth grade, he'd dreamed of one day writing his own series of fantasy novels. Through adolescence and early adulthood, he began to piece together the plot, characters, and setting of his imagined books—drafting up journals full of appendices, faux historic documents, and academic articles related to his fantastic world. He drew a massive map across thirty-six pieces of paper that combined to form a six-by-six grid, tracing the coastlines of various real-world maps to form the imagined continent on which his novels would take place. From here, he noted—in painstaking detail—the location of every city, town, hamlet, country road, forest, mountain, river, stream, abandoned mine, ancient ruin, and dragon's lair.

In college, when Jack started reading a lot of "real literature," he decided that rather than write a novel, he would tell the story of his fantastical world in a series of interconnected short stories. "Like *Dubliners* crossed with Tolkien," he'd say. The premise revolved around a medieval world controlled by a giant, bureaucratic empire. The world was populated by peasants and nobles and knights, yes—but also by elf-like beings (the Tolkien, not Keebler, kind) whose memories were passed down through a near-extinct variety of tree and where a small smattering of the population, called *the Cree*, had the ability to tap into mystical powers to perform amazing feats.

During this time, Jack happened across an article on fantasy world-building that argued any time a fantasy story employs magic, the use of the magic ought to come at a cost. Perhaps the practitioners of magic lose a limb every time they cast a spell, or else maybe *someone they love* loses a limb. Jack disliked both of these examples but thought the concept of magic "coming at a cost" was compelling. He toyed with several ideas, but only decided the cost for magic in his world when Sarah and he had married and he'd started writing in earnest. *The Cree*, Jack decided, would pay for their power by also being cursed with sterility. And so, they were faced with a sort of existential crisis—they were gifted with great power and a prolonged lifespan but had no hope of offspring and, therefore, their lives held no real "meaning."

Eventually, writing became his obsession; at lunch, he'd sneak away from the office to write at a nearby café or while sitting in Rittenhouse Square. He thought a lot about quitting his job. Finally, after completing more than three hundred manuscript pages, Jack—on an impulse and without consulting Sarah—went through with it. He was surprised how his boss, Michel Chowdhury, who he secretly despised, reacted.

"Good for you, Jack. I'm happy for you," he said and gave him a warm handshake.

That night when Jack got home, Sarah was understandably upset. "You can't just unilaterally make decisions like that," she said. "We're partners—a team. We need to talk these things out."

"You're right. I should have told you," Jack said. "I guess it's just I was afraid you might talk me out of it."

�֍

Jack had been waiting at the police station for half an hour when Paul came out of an adjacent hallway. Paul, dressed in jeans and a Penn Lacrosse hoodie, looked taller and broader than Jack remembered. His face resembled Sarah's so much that, if not for the near ten-year age gap, one might think the two were twins.

The two men shook hands. Jack noted the firmness of Paul's grip. He was no longer the scrawny teenager who'd been one of Jack's groomsmen. "How's she doing?" Jack said.

"She's just got a couple cuts and bruises. But I'd guess she's pretty shaken."

"Where is she?"

"They told me they're just finishing up some questions and that she'll be out in a bit." Now Paul came close to Jack as if to confide something in him. "I should have gone down sooner."

"What are you talking about?"

"It doesn't take five minutes to walk up three flights of stairs. I should have known something was wrong."

"It's not your fault. You need to get that out of your mind. Feeling guilty isn't going to help anyone."

I deserve this, but she doesn't.

They waited for another hour. They tried to talk—going over the details Paul knew of what had happened and then trying to make chitchat—but this lasted all of three minutes. After that, the two sat, mostly silent.

Jack knew he had betrayed his wife, and now she had been "attacked." If he hadn't been with a...a *prostitute*...maybe, somehow, he would have been there to protect her. He imagined the scene: a faceless assailant attacking Sarah and Jack coming to the rescue at precisely the right instant and tearing him to shreds. Sarah would see what a good, loving husband she had: one who would do anything for her—even tear some faceless motherfucker to shreds.

But he *had* been with a prostitute. She *had* been attacked. Even as he intellectually knew these two facts had little to do with one another, he viscerally felt that they had everything to do with each other.

Seeing escorts had been a gradual process. At first it had just been the occasional "body rub" or "sensual massage" where some young, cute woman would take off her clothes, rub up on him, and jerk him off at the end. It wasn't behavior he would advertise, but after a little moral and mental gymnastics, he could come up with an explanation as to why it was permissible. He was just fulfilling a biological urge, de-stressing, managing the rough patch in his marriage. He couldn't really afford the two hundred bucks a session given the pay cut he'd taken when he quit his job, but that was beside the point.

The first time he had sex with one of these girls had been a kind of accident. She was a young Russian girl…twenty-one, twenty-two max. It was the third time Jack had seen her. She was blond like Sarah, but that wasn't what he liked about her. He liked how she blushed when he paid her a compliment and how she responded to his every caress with an erotic bite of her lower lip. She had smiled, genuinely, he thought, when he walked into the back room that time and had called him by name.

During the first two visits, she stood to the side of the massage table as she finished him off with her hand. But this time, once she really got him going, she climbed up on top of the table, straddling his upper thighs. Jack rubbed her with his fingers. She closed her eyes—pleasure showing across her face and in the curvature of her mouth—and moved in rhythm with his hand. "I wish I was inside you," he said. It was true, but he'd said it only because he thought it wasn't a possibility. But then the young woman grabbed a condom from the nearby side table and put it on him.

Afterwards, wrapped up in the young woman's arms, the thought crossed Jack's mind that in another world, another life, he might ask her to dinner. No, that wasn't quite right. He didn't yearn for another life—only to live this one a second time. Like, if only he could fall in love with Sarah all over again, he wouldn't feel the need for all this.

Later, when the guilt set in, he swore to himself that he would never sleep with anyone other than his wife again. He wouldn't even get body rubs anymore. For a while he held true to his promise. Then a day would come when he was bored or lonely in front of his computer, and Sarah wouldn't be home, and he would end up on some website where girls posted their ads. He was just looking, he told himself. And most of the time, this was true. But every so often, the compulsion would grow and he would find himself on the phone calling one of the numbers, his heart pounding with excitement.

The whole process had given him an increased understanding of the nature of evil. Evil, or doing bad things, was an *acquired* taste. And we were all much closer than we wanted to admit. No one set out to do wrong. Evil was just a series of increasingly bad compromises, no single one that much worse than the last. If a man could betray his wife and if a man could say "I promise" before all his friends and family and then disregard that promise, why couldn't a man do other things? Why couldn't a man stab his girlfriend with a kitchen knife or shoot a liquor store clerk in the face or attack some woman as she entered an apartment building because he liked the way she looked?

An oddly cheerful man in an ill-fitting brown suit who, Jack thought, bore an uncanny resemblance to the actor David Schwimmer, came through a door down the corridor. He walked with a limp and, when he reached them, introduced himself as Detective Bergfalk. "We're taking Mrs. Ampong down to the hospital to get some tests," he said. "You guys can meet her down there. Just tell them who you're there to visit, and they should be able to take you right back."

"Can I just see my wife?" Jack said. "I've been waiting for over an hour. All I want to do is see my wife." But the detective shook his head.

Jack and Paul arrived at the hospital and were directed to the emergency department. Through the open door of one of the hospital rooms, Jack spied two male orderlies attempting to subdue a red-faced man of middle age.

"Sir, calm down," one of the orderlies said. "Calm. Down." But the man didn't. His arms and legs flailed, and he caught the other orderly in the chest with a kick.

"Don't touch me, you fucks!" he screamed.

A woman in a white coat walked purposefully into the room and closed the door behind her. Jack could just barely hear the commotion for a moment before that too subsided and was drowned out by the other sounds of the hospital. Jack and Paul exchanged a look.

A hospital attendant approached and, after Jack told her who they were looking for, he and Paul were led to a secluded wing in the emergency department. They turned left down another hallway and there, thirty feet away, Jack saw Sarah talking with a female doctor holding a clipboard. The hospital attendant left them, and Paul started walking towards his sister. Jack grabbed his arm.

"Would you mind?"

Paul nodded. Jack took a few steps in Sarah's direction. He didn't call to her, instead allowing himself the opportunity to observe her for a moment.

Her smeared eyeliner streaked down her cheeks in two black lines. Her chin had a two-inch gash on it. Her neck: a large, fish-shaped purple bruise. He inhaled once and held his breath, as if to experience what it must have felt like having the man's forearm around her throat. "Sarah," he said now. He was only vaguely aware of Paul some fifteen feet back, watching them.

They embraced. "How are you?" he whispered.

There was no doubt: he didn't want to lose her. Why was he such a fuck up? *I deserve this, but she doesn't.*

"Hanging in there. Looks like my modeling career is over though." She bared her teeth, displaying a large chip in her right front tooth.

"We'll get it fixed."

"There's no way our shitty dental insurance is going to cover this."

"We'll figure it out," he said. "If we have to, I'm sure your dad would help."

Paul joined them now and gave his sister a hug.

After Sarah got her chin stitched up, Detective Bergfalk came by and offered to take Jack and Sarah home in his squad car. Paul and Sarah looked at one another; Sarah nodded. They hugged again and then Paul turned to Jack.

"Take care of my sister," he said.

Paul left. Only now did Jack notice Sarah had a duffel bag with her.

"What's that for?" he said.

"It doesn't matter," she said.

"So, unfortunately," the detective said, as they made their way out to his car, "regulation requires you guys sit in the back. It's not the comfiest, but you guys don't live far, right?"

"No problem," Jack said, and they got in.

The squad car pulled away from the hospital. By now it was past two a.m., and the area around the hospital and campus was quiet. The car drove east on Spruce back towards Center City. They sat silently, Sarah curling up against his arm. If it weren't for the hard seats and the bars on the window separating them from the detective, Jack could have almost imagined they were going home in a cab after a night on the town. They didn't go on many proper "dates" anymore.

Two years ago—before Jack left his job, before things started to deteriorate—they would go on dates all the time. Like that one when they had made plans to each independently go to the Sofitel hotel bar and pretend they didn't know each other. They both dressed up for the occasion. Jack wore a sharp-looking blazer and a button-down with French cuffs. He added a handkerchief artfully peeking out of his jacket pocket; he personally thought it looked asinine but knew Sarah would appreciate it. Sarah donned a short black dress that clung to her waist and hips and stockings, that Jack hoped were held up by a garter belt. He approached her and asked to buy her a drink. After a little prodding and playful flirting and "I don't know if I should because I'm waiting for my husband," Sarah accepted, "but just this one." Five drinks later they were in a cab, their drunken mouths kissing and his heart exploding with how much he loved this woman who was his wife, but tonight was not. And when they were out of the cab, they kissed some more and grabbed and groped their way up the steps to their apartment. In the bedroom, Sarah pushed him on the bed and told him to wait just a minute so she could go to the bathroom. When she came out she was in lingerie and—surprise, surprise— that *was* a garter belt underneath that dress. She teased him with her fingertips, her tongue, until he couldn't stand it any longer and they made love recklessly, throwing in a couple of stupid positions that were more for show than actual pleasure. And that night when they went to bed, the last thought that crossed Jack's mind was how great his marriage was and how two people had never been so in love and never would be and damn they were lucky.

They arrived home and said goodnight to Detective Bergfalk. Jack carried Sarah's duffel bag; it was heavy and he wondered at its contents. When they entered the apartment, Sarah went into the bathroom and closed the door.

"Sar," he called after a minute, but all he got back was the crackling of their shower turning on. He lay on top of their unmade bed and closed his eyes.

A few minutes later, he returned to the bathroom door and knocked. "Sarah," he called again. All he heard was the water. He imagined the worst: empty bottles of Tylenol rolling around on the counter, blood flowing irretrievably from slit wrists down the shower drain. He was almost surprised when he turned the doorknob and it clicked open: unlocked.

Steam greeted him. He pulled back the shower curtain and saw his wife standing with her eyes closed, letting the water flow down her hair, her face, her breasts, her stomach. The bruise on her neck had darkened. She opened her eyes. "Hi," she said.

"I just thought I'd check to see if you needed anything."

"No, I'm fine."

"Okay. No rush." He turned to leave.

"Hey. Are you going to shower later?"

He had showered earlier in the evening, but another shower would do him good. "Probably, but take your time."

"You want to just come in with me? For efficiency?" she said, an inside joke, an excuse they used to make to fuck around in the shower, although he was positive that *wasn't* what she meant this time.

"If you want privacy, I can wait."

"No, come on."

He undressed, placed his folded clothes on the counter, and stepped into the shower.

"Can you soap me?" she said. He obliged, making sure to get every inch of her. Normally, he might playfully linger as he soaped her small breasts or between her legs, but this time he went over those areas without lust—like how he might imagine washing a child. Sarah rinsed off and offered to reciprocate, holding the bar of soap, a question, in front of Jack. He shook his head "no" and took the bar from her.

"What happened?" she asked. Three fingers of her left hand traced a trio of parallel scratches from his right shoulder down and across his chest. He hadn't noticed these before but knew how he'd gotten them.

"I don't know," he said and started soaping himself, scratching out the marks and making sure to scrub hard around his crotch.

After they dried off and dressed for sleep, they lay in bed for a while with all the lights off, except for the reading lamp on Jack's nightstand. There was so much that he wanted to tell her but knew he couldn't. "We didn't really talk about what happened," he said, "and that's okay if you don't want to talk about it. But if you do . . ."

She exhaled. "What is there to talk about?"

"I don't know. It wasn't very long...before Paul came down. So there probably isn't anything. But if there is, you can talk about it... I mean...did he? The guy?"

"No," she said. "I don't think so. Definitely nothing major. I couldn't breathe. He had me by my throat. I passed out for a second. But I don't think there was time for anything."

"That's good," he said. "But even if there was, we would get through it. Together, I mean...I mean, I'm here for you is all."

He meant every word but felt like a hypocrite.

"Yeah," she said. "Can you call the dentist tomorrow and see if I can get an appointment?"

"Yeah. Okay."

"You can tell him I got mugged."

He waited a while before he spoke again.

"Are we okay?" he said.

Her only response was the sound of her breathing.

"Are you asleep?" he said in a whisper, in case she was.

"No."

"I know it's a stupid question," he said. "I know we're not…But I was thinking…maybe we could try to start over a little, *wipe the slate clean*. You know, sometimes I think back and wonder if it's just nostalgia and remembering everything through rose-colored glasses, but then I stop and it's like, *no*. It really was that way. Remember how great things were? When we met in Ireland and for a long time, really . . ."

"I remember."

"So?"

"So tonight may not be the night to talk about this," she said, kissed him on the cheek, and rolled over so that her back was facing him.

When Jack was sure she'd fallen asleep, he got out of bed and went to the kitchen. He made toast. He usually took butter but tonight ate it with olive oil like Sarah did. Somewhere a car alarm was going off.

Shortly after they'd met in Ireland and then returned to the States, Jack took Sarah to dinner at the Rose Tattoo Café near the art museum. They'd sat up in the balcony overlooking the old-style bar area, and Sarah had talked at length about her art and all the illustrators she loved. Later, he'd driven her back to Princeton; in her apartment she showed him books of all the artists she talked about from the "Golden Age of Illustration." Jack was superficially familiar with a few of the artists—Maxfield Parrish and N.C. Wyeth—but most of the names were new to him. More than the art, what Jack remembered was the passion with which Sarah talked about it.

He grabbed his notebook and brought it back to the kitchen table. What Sarah never understood was that he didn't write in spite of their marriage but, in a way, because of it. At first it had just been about the world he'd thought up, but now it was different; the writing had become about something else.

He was at a critical scene in the longest of the stories, where one of the main characters in the collection learns his wife is pregnant. Since the man is a *Cree* though, he cannot possibly be the father of his wife's child. This revelation embitters the man and leads him down a destructive path—it turns him into a villain of sorts. Jack hadn't figured out all the details yet, but it was his plan that—by the end of the book—this character would be redeemed somehow.

In stories, there could be heroism and great deeds and redemption.

In the real world, there was just . . . *life*.

He started writing. For some reason, in spite of everything else that had happened, his mind drifted back to the homeless man, Ben, and his brilliant green eyes. He filled up five pages in forty minutes. Eventually his hand grew cramped and he stopped. He washed dishes, dried them, and put them away in the cupboard. He looked around his apartment for some task to fulfill. In the bathroom, he saw he'd left his pants and shirt folded on the counter. He went to put them away when he remembered the card the Korean woman had given him. It was in his pants pocket, precisely where he'd left it. Seeing the thing gave him a disoriented feeling—like he was learning for the first time about his own infidelity. *Why am I this way?* He took one last look at it before tearing it up, releasing the specks of paper above the toilet bowl, and watching them rain down like little pieces of confetti onto the still surface of the water.

He stood there, looking down into the toilet, when he heard footsteps. "What are you doing?" Sarah asked, sleep in her eyes. He had not been a good husband, he knew. He had done unforgivable things. He hadn't done right by the one person who he ought to have done right by. He needed to do better. But how many times had he said "never again" only to repeat the very actions he had sworn off? Why would this time be different and last for any longer than a week or a month or until the wretched feeling in his stomach was quelled and the events of the night subsided into some less immediate past? *Because this time will be different*, he thought. *It just will*. But how many times had he said *that*? Any objective person would conclude there was no good reason to believe things would be different this time. And yet he wanted them to be—more than anything.

"Nothing," he said. He pulled the handle and watched the little pieces of paper whirl down the drain.

"What was that?" she said.

"Nothing. A note. To myself." The words cracked in his throat.

"A note?" she said.

"Tonight's not the night to talk about all this, remember?"

"You're right."

"Come on then." Jack took Sarah, the woman he loved, by the hand. She squeezed, and—though she might not have meant anything by it—he felt reassured, consoled, hopeful, from the gesture.

From the journals of K. R., recovered by Master Padgett in 603 YAF

A Year Amongst the Mandrakhar of the Westwood

Three days after the Summer Solstice, 556 YAF

In all my travels since I left the South, I have seldom stayed in any location more than a few weeks—certainly never more than a month. And yet, somehow, as of today, I will have found myself here in the Westwood for a full year. I do not suppose I can stay here forever. Though I know not in what precise way, I believe that, sooner or later, the premonition, as I have written about extensively in these pages, will catch up with me. Yet, for the time being, I am enjoying this respite from the troubles of my life.

In earlier entries, I have written at length in regards to both the nature and culture of the Mandrakhar, as well as my life here amongst them. Howsoever, it is only now that I feel a sufficient comfort with their language that I can write with any authority on the topic.

To begin, the sound of the Mandrakhi language, especially when spoken by a native speaker and not my butchering mouth, is a marvelous thing to hear. Something about how the rhythm of the words mixes with the quick, melodic voices of the Mandrakhar gives the language a quality that rivals beautiful music. Even before I could much understand anything of Mandrakhi, I could spend hours sitting in one of their meal houses, eavesdropping on Mandrakhar conversing in, what was to me, sounds no more intelligible than a bird's song.

In recent months I have obtained, if not fluency, at least proficiency in the Mandrakhi language; I have discovered that the tongue is remarkable, not only sonically but grammatically and syntactically as well. I am no expert on matters of language, but I will try to explain some of the interesting aspects I have discovered.

One of the first things that a student of the language learns is that in Mandrakhi the verb "to be" does not exist. Rather than say "I am *Cree*," someone speaking Mandrakhi would say "I belong to the *Cree*" (or possibly, but less common, "People know me as *Cree*"). Rather than say "Benedictus is the son of Olwyn," one would say "Olwyn gave birth to Benedictus," or "Benedictus climbed from Olwyn's darkness."

I have hypothesized that such linguistic idiosyncrasies, when compared to other tongues across the Continent, might be a function of the Mandrakhar's very unique relationship to memory and self (which I have previously written about). None of the Mandrakhar themselves seem to know the origins of their language's unique qualities.

Another, perhaps less fundamental, difference between Mandrakhi and most other languages is its dealing with the feminine and masculine. Take, for example, the word pairings in the Common Dialect of "man" and "woman" or "male" and "female." In both cases, the masculine is always primary, with the feminine being some secondary syllable added to the primary male noun. There exist countless more examples of male linguistic dominance when examining some of the other languages of the Continent, including the use of verbs in Eyasu, the Islander tongue, or the masculine default of all Kallanbori nouns.

On the other hand, it is the feminine that is usually dominant in Mandrakhi. Take, for instance, what speakers of Mandrakhi call themselves: the word "Mandrakhar" is used to describe people of that race generally but also when referring to one or more females of the race. If the person or people in question is/are solely composed of males, then the word "Mandrakh*ir*" is used instead. The generic is the female, whereas the male is thought of as "the other."

There is, of course, a great deal more to write regarding the Mandrakhi language, particularly the syntax, but for now, I am told it is supper time at the meal house. Perhaps I will get to such topics in a future entry.

TWO

THE MEMORY TREE
606 Years After *The Fall*

Autumn was Corinne's favorite season, and were Erlan not dying, she would have been quite happy walking down the hill to the Center Road amongst the reds and yellows of the ancient trees. As it was, the crisp air against her skin, the sound of leaves rustling whenever the wind blew, failed to elicit their usual joy; now they just served as reminders of things irretrievably lost. She couldn't dwell on any of this though. She had to focus on the tasks before her: reach the settlement, get the herbs, return to her husband.

By the time she reached the southern entrance, it was past midday. The journey would have taken three hours instead of six were Miranda still alive, but Erlan had had to put the horse down six months ago when she fell on the trail and broke a leg.

She knocked hard on the tall wooden gate, and the gray-skinned guard slid open the window to look upon her with his violet eyes.

"*Gilmani kilbathur,*" she said, the standard expression of salutation and one of the few things she could say properly in Mandrakhi. The expression essentially had the connotation of "hello" but literally meant, "the day stretches long."

"Greetings, *Golemen*. What business do you have with us?" he said. Like all Mandrakhar, he spoke quickly. Over the years, Erlan had learned to slow down his speech for her sake.

"I come to trade."

"Have you any coin? I don't see any goods about you." She pulled a pouch of silver from her satchel and showed it to him. His eyes narrowed with suspicion. The Mandrakhar here were cautious—perhaps with good reason. Many humans hated them, thought them the spawn of the Demon, and would just as soon see them gone from the Westwood. Still, usually whoever was guard—seeing that Corinne was a woman traveling alone—would open the gate without too much hassle. "What do you come to trade for?"

"*What do I come to trade for?* What business of yours is it? Should I also tell you that I plan on having tea and a meal and using the latrine?"

"I care not if you eat or whether you use the latrine. But I stand sentry, which makes it my duty to ask questions. I wish to know what you come to trade for. You need not answer—only if you wish to enter."

Corinne was tired, in a hurry, fed up.

"Fine," she said. "If you must know: moonroot. I have come to buy moonroot."

He gave her a triumphant glance, as if he'd caught her in a lie. "Moonroot? What need does a human woman . . ." he stopped speaking as it dawned on him. "You . . . I know you . . . they talk of you."

"*The Whore of Sleeping Giant?*" she said, as if it were a title of great distinction. "Yes, that's me. Now open the gate."

The settlement was built in the oldest part of the Westwood. Many of the trees were the width of Corinne's cottage and it was said that most were nearly a thousand years old. The buildings at ground level were made from bricks of baked mud and straw. Even the gate and the wooden buildings up in the trees were made only from branches that had fallen on their own. The Mandrakhar revered trees and considered it an unthinkable act to cut one down unless it was blighted.

Fifteen years had passed since Corinne had first come to the settlement, yet she still remembered the day clearly. She had twisted her ankle on the journey through the mountains, and so Gareth had carried her on his massive back. She was only a girl then, but even had she been full-grown, he would have had no problem bearing her. They had been walking for days with little food, but as they reached the northern gate, a sense of wonder fell upon them and they forgot their hunger, their wounds, the war. Darkness had descended on the forest; yet within the settlement, lantern bugs filled the air, flying in irregular patterns, illuminating the trails. The actual buildings of the settlement were modest compared to those of the cities and towns Corinne had seen on the way south—most little more than huts. And yet the trees, the gods' own towers, held a magnificence that was unmatched by even the most ambitious of man's architectural achievements. And then, in the very middle of the settlement, *Saloryn Bai*, the Memory Tree. It was not the tallest tree, but it was a sprawling, massive thing with an endless network of roots and branches, many themselves the thickness of tree trunks. The leaves of the Tree each emanated a faint, golden glow.

Corinne hadn't seen Gareth and Saleya for more than a year now. They'd been the closest thing to parents she'd ever had if you didn't count the Sisters in the orphanage—and she did not. Their own son, Joram, named in honor of Corinne's grandfather, would be nearly five now.

The village where Gareth and Saleya lived was only a few miles from Corinne and Erlan's cottage, but it was hard for Saleya to travel since she didn't walk well. As for Corinne visiting, ever since the other villagers had learned of Erlan, she wasn't much welcome in the village. *Depraved elf slut*, they called her. *Abomination. Tree harlot.* This last one made her laugh.

She made her way through the settlement to the herbmaster's shack. A few of the Mandrakhar stopped and stared at her. Corinne assumed they knew who she was. Unlike Gareth and Saleya's fellow villagers, the Mandrakhar said nothing, but Corinne saw the same spite in their eyes. Not so long ago she had been welcome amongst them—not simply another *Golemen*, foreigner, but someone who was accepted, loved even.

But then she committed the greatest sin of all: she married one of them.

The Mandrakhar staring at her from near the well—with her long black hair tied back, exposing her acuminated ears—was Pelaeus's granddaughter. When Corinne had first arrived, Pelaeus appeared to be only a few years older than her, and now her granddaughter looked only slightly younger. In another ten years, the granddaughter would be old and withered, whereas Corinne would still be of childbearing age.

Gareth had first tried to explain it to her back when they first arrived here. The war was still on then, and Gareth, Saleya, and Corinne, along with forty other refugees, had been allowed to stay in a small encampment just inside the gate, amongst some of the largest trees in the settlement.

These trees are over a thousand years old, Gareth had said. *They experience the years different than us. The seasons to the tree are a blink of an eye—a decade of our years like a single season to them. To the Mandrakhar we are, in a way, like the trees. A generation of theirs will pass before you are a woman. And yet, while the Mandrakhar are a young people, they are also—the ones who live in this settlement, at least—very old. It is said that when one of them dies, their bodies are brought to the Memory Tree and all of their life, their memories, are preserved in it. Then when their young come of age in their fourth year, they are connected to the exposed roots and all the memories of all the Mandrakhar who have died and contributed to the Tree are passed on. And so, in a way, these Mandrakhar all live forever.*

But a person is more than their memories, her nine-year-old self said. *If I die, even if my memories live, I am still dead.*

In a way yes. But also in a way no.

So I will hardly be grown up and Pelaeus will be an old woman.

He nodded.

It seems very terrible to me.

A lot is terrible in the world. But this is no more terrible than the fact that we too— myself, Saleya, and even you—must one day pass from this world. You cannot be sad for them. The trees, after all, do not weep for you or me.

And why did you say 'the ones who live in this settlement'? Are there other Mandrakhar?

Yes, there are other settlements. And long ago, each had its own Memory Tree. Yet over the centuries the other Trees have sickened and died, whereas this Tree remains—the last of its kind.

Most Mandrakhar didn't talk about the Tree. Even Pelaeus, who'd been Corinne's best friend, would change the subject whenever Corinne asked. "I have difficulty explaining," she'd say. Erlan was the only Mandrakhar who'd ever spoken directly to Corinne about the Tree and the memories he'd received from it. According to him, the memories from the Tree— or *yulthanispel,* as they called it—weren't the same as one's own memories. They were partitioned off in the mind. It would be difficult to function if one couldn't tell what had actually happened to them versus someone else hundreds of years before. Also, these memories were vague and distant and lacking context. Think about how much of one's own life is lost to forgetfulness. The memories of the ancestors were far cloudier.

"And will this Tree one day die as well?" she'd asked her husband once.

"I suppose," he'd said. "Hopefully it is long from now."

"And why couldn't you plant another?"

"Though we have the seeds of *Saloryn Bai*, the skill needed to get them to sprout—if we ever knew it—has been lost to the centuries."

✤

Flynn, the herbmaster, was one of the few in the settlement who showed any goodwill towards Corinne. Perhaps he was predisposed to kindness, or else his trade made him acutely aware of what Corinne was going through with Erlan. Whenever she visited, he would prepare a warm cup of tea for her and would share with her some of the unleavened bread that was a staple amongst his people. The stuff was bland and tasteless but nourishing, and it gave her energy for the walk back to the farm.

When Corinne entered the dimly lit shack, she found Flynn talking with a human merchant who must have been traveling either to or from one of the cities to the east. From the style of the merchant's high-collared, dark-blue coat, Corinne pegged him as either an Alderian or one of those Provincials who hoped people would mistake him for an Alderian. Corinne waited as the man haggled over the price of spices with Flynn in a combination of the Common Dialect and broken Mandrakhi. Finally, they struck a deal, and Flynn called his two Mandrakhir boys from the back to bring in the goods from the Alderian's wagon. On his way out of the shack, the merchant tipped his black triangular hat at Corinne and looked at her for some acknowledgement of their shared racial heritage. She looked away as the merchant walked out the door.

Corinne approached the counter and tried unsuccessfully to craft a smile on her face.

"How fare you, friend?" Flynn said. She noticed the deep lines under his eyes. Even Flynn was nearly to middle age now.

"The walk was fine. A little muddy from the rain yesterday."

"And Erlan?"

"You've seen it enough, I'd guess."

"Mmm, yes. Too much of the wasting sickness, I've seen."

She said nothing.

The sickness had changed Erlan's grayish skin to a very pale, almost translucent, blue. It had all happened so quickly. A year ago…he hadn't been young for a Mandrakhar then…but he'd been strong, with taut skin and long, wiry muscles that never seemed to tire as he worked on their small farm or made love to her in the meadow next to the cottage. They had last made love only two weeks ago, when he had, for a day, been up for it. Nowadays the act felt increasingly empty, a tribute to something gone.

"You come for moonroot?" Flynn said.

"Yes." There was no cure for the wasting sickness, but the tea of the moonroot slowed its progression, although it was getting to the point that even the tea would soon be ineffective.

"The sickness has lived in him for some time," Flynn said.

"He has a strong will to live."

"Yes. But even will cannot overcome the design of the Forefathers."

The Mandrakhar worshipped the Forefathers; in the North, during Corinne's childhood, the Sisters in the orphanage had spoken of gods. Yet when had either—Forefathers or gods—helped with anything?

He put the moonroot in a leather pouch and pulled out another smaller cloth pouch, which he placed on the counter. He opened this and showed her the dried red flowers inside.

"Do you know these?"

"No," she said, even though she knew exactly what they were. She'd seen them given to Pelaeus.

After Erlan was expelled from the settlement, she'd often hoped for Pelaeus to visit; yet her old friend never came. So instead, after hearing Pelaeus was gravely ill, Corinne returned to the settlement just in time to see her best friend die. The Mandrakhar shunned Corinne and referred to her as *Kuntstel,* "whore," but it had been Erlan, not she, who was actually forbidden to enter the gates of the settlement. On her deathbed, Pelaeus had been too sick to speak, but Corinne would later tell herself she'd seen understanding, love, in her friend's eyes.

"Dragon flowers," Flynn said. "When the time comes, boil a tea and give it to him. He will drift off to sleep. No more pain . . ."

"No," she said and slid the pouch back towards him.

"I understand. But you should have it just in case. Sometimes it gets very bad."

On her way out of the settlement, Corinne saw the merchant from earlier loading a few crates into his wagon. Two adolescent boys were hitching up the horses. When the merchant noticed Corinne glancing in his direction, he bowed with a flourish. She pretended to not see him, but it was too late.

"Hello," he said, walking towards her. "Hello!"

She kept walking. "Hello," she said in as unfriendly a voice as she could manage. But he kept stride beside her.

"Are you in a hurry, m'lady?"

"Yes." She kept walking.

"I see. I only meant to ask what a lady like you is doing here amongst these . . ." he looked around to make sure that none of the Mandrakhar were within earshot, "these gods forsaken *elves*?"

Inside Flynn's, the merchant's rounded, boyish face had made him appear younger, but now, at this close distance, she saw the gray speckled through his hair, the lines under his eyes and guessed he might be forty-five or more. He was handsome, but only in a soft sort of way. "There are Mandrakhar who would not hesitate to shove a dirk in your gut for calling them that."

"That right?"

She nodded. "Now if you'll excuse me, I must be on my way."

"It was not my purpose to offend; it's just I'm not used to seeing fine women like you on the lonely road westward."

"And if you did, I'd hope you wouldn't try to woo them with lines like that."

"Beauty *and* wit," he said.

"I have a husband."

"Is it a crime to speak to a married woman?"

"To answer your original question—not that it is your business—my *husband* is ill and I came to get him herbs."

"Ah, I see. I suppose if these bloody elv— err, *Mandrakhar*…are good for something it's cooking up potions and ointments and teas and what-all."

They were almost to the gate now. "Yes, well, I should be getting back home now. Farewell."

"Are you headed south?"

"Not your concern."

"I only ask because if you are headed south along the Center Road, you might ride with us for a time. We are headed in that direction ourselves, and I do imagine our wagon is a bit faster than your two feet."

"Maybe I have a horse."

"Do you?"

The idea of sitting for two hours in a wagon with this Imperial blowhard was not particularly appealing. But a wagon *would* be faster than walking, and that meant she would get back to Erlan sooner.

She stopped walking. "I will take you up on your offer," she said. "Just know that if you have any but honorable intentions . . ." She lifted up her tunic slightly to show her dagger sheathed in its leather scabbard.

He whistled as if impressed. "Understood. It will be so nice to have better conversation than the two louts who I travel with, even if just for a little while. I am Percel Callowsway, by the way, and the lads hitching up the wagon are Jon and Lenny."

�֍

The two boys took turns driving, as Corinne, Percel, and whichever of the two wasn't up front remained inside the covered wagon.

"Up until the war—the Uprising, that is," Percel said, "I didn't just have this little shit operation you see here today."

They'd been traveling for about an hour, and the merchant had been talking almost non-stop since they'd left the settlement. Jon was driving, so Lenny was inside the wagon taking stock of some of the herbs they'd picked up at Flynn's. "I had as many as two-hundred-twenty-three men in my employ running over-land trade routes west of here and as far south as Jarl and the Dagfinn Sea. And ships too. Traveling up and down the Riffel, through Brigantium and to the ports on the Great Northern. And this whole operation—this wasn't something I inherited, but something I built with these two hands." Percel displayed his palms to Corinne. By the expression on Lenny's face, it was clear the poor boy had heard all of this on more than one occasion.

"Is that right?" Corinne said. She kept telling herself she would be back to Erlan sooner this way.

"And looking back…it was a terrible life. Where was the adventure in sitting around in a magnificent Phaidonian mansion—four floors tall and with a statue of yours truly out front—getting fat and rich? Yes, I had the finest food, the finest jewelry, the finest women…the *finest* women! I could see the palace from my bedroom window, but who cares? Now I have the fresh air, the road, seeing the world—not from atop a jeweled rickshaw but as the world truly is, from the eye level of the common man!"

"Lenny!" Jon called from the front of the wagon.

"Boy, you're interrupting my conversation. And Lenny's got work besides."

"Sorry, sir," Jon said poking his head into the wagon. "It's just that . . ." and now he turned to Lenny and lowered his voice as if Percel wouldn't be able to hear him. "I think I see the castle. The one that the miller's daughter was talking about in that village yesterday."

"Really?" Lenny said.

"Are you still talking about this nonsense?" Percel said.

"The miller's daughter swore on it, told us that her brother had met him," Jon said from the other side of the canvas partition that separated driver from passengers. Lenny nodded his head in agreement.

"Oh, shut up about the miller's da—"

"What are you talking about?" Corinne said. It couldn't be less interesting than what Percel had been rambling about.

Jon reached over to the side of the wagon and pulled back the covering so Corinne could see. They had been traveling steadily uphill and had reached a clearing where you could look out to a valley to the west, beyond which were a set of wooded hills.

"M'lady, you see that castle out there in the distance," Jon said.

"Gods, Lenny. Don't trouble the lady with your *stupid* tales."

"No, it's fine," she said. "Yes, those are just old Phaidonian ruins."

"May be m'lady, but word is there's a sorcerer lives there now. One of them Cree. They say he's more than a hundred years old and has all sorts of strange and terrible powers. Can light a man on fire...tell the future."

"Do you believe everything whispered by the campfire?" she said to him.

"Someone with sense," Percel said.

"I don't m'lady. It's just that the girl's own brother had seen him. And I didn't take her for a liar. He was traveling a few days west to one of the villages on the Yesenya. On his way back, he and his fellows been attacked by bandits. Every one of the travelers but the brother was killed, and the he *barely* made it away. He was in bad shape on account of the bandits using Mandrakhi poison on their arrows. And he wouldn't have made it, but the sorcerer found him and used his power to burn the poison out. No one survives Mandrakhi poison, m'lady. But this man, the miller's daughter's brother, did."

"The *miller's daughter's brother?*" Jon yelled from the front of the wagon. "You coulda just said the miller's son."

"What's the difference?" Lenny said.

"It sounds better."

"Fine. The miller's *son*. Point is, he saw this sorcerer—said he was a darky with one eye, seven feet tall, hands a foot long and a voice like thunder. And he had powers, *healing* powers. And he told the miller's son he could heal anything save death itself."

She parted from the three men where the road met the narrow dirt trail that went up the mountain to the farm. The mountain was called The Sleeping Giant because someone had once thought that the contours of the earth resembled one of the giants of old resting on the ground.

Much that was said of sorcerers was complete nonsense, yet not all of it. When she was a child, Corinne believed she'd seen one. It was during the war, up near Vicentia. One night after the minstrel's show, a gray-cloaked man took the stage. The large tent was packed with onlookers, townsfolk and refugees both, but Gareth put her on his back so she had a clear view. The things the man did—bending light to create wonderful images in the air, floating, half the height of a man, off the surface of the wooden stage— had no other possible explanation. *Starseed,* Gareth had told her, *the gift and curse of the Forefathers,* who came down from the heavens and walked the earth when men still dwelt in caves, in the time before *The Fall.* She was never sure whether Gareth believed in such things or had just been kidding.

So if that sorcerer could do the things he did, then why couldn't one of them stop Mandrakhi poison? And if he could heal a man from poison, what else might he be able to heal?

Hope, she knew, was a dangerous thing—a weed that could flourish on the scantest water and light if she didn't pluck the thing from its roots. Erlan would die; the wasting sickness would take him. Such had been the case with every other Mandrakhar. Better to savor the days remaining than fight against the inevitable.

She crested the top of the hill and reached the clearing where the farm was. During her adolescence, Corinne never would have thought she would find joy in farm work; she'd assumed she'd eventually travel to the capital, or at least a city like Altinus or Brolaine, and take up some kind of vocation as a scholar or archivist in one of the Imperial libraries. She had learned to read as a child, and even during the war—even as she fled from city to city, town to town—she still read whenever she could get her hands on a book. Yet after she married Erlan, she came to love the mindless physical exertion that gardening and farming entailed. There was a meditative quality to the labor that brought peace to the anger that often gathered inside her.

She opened the waist-high wooden gate and walked past the rows of vegetables. Much of their current crop needed to be harvested and would rot if she didn't get to it soon. With all of the work caring for Erlan, there had been little time.

The cottage where they lived was a small two-room building that Erlan had built when they first left the settlement. It would be imprecise to say those days had been completely happy. They had been cast out, shunned by human and Mandrakhar both—yet there was a kind of freedom, an alive-ness, she felt at finally having an identity, knowing where she stood in the order of things. It was her and Erlan against the world, and she had embraced this role—that of the rebel. She wondered how things would be when Erlan died. What would she be rebelling against? She would just be another widow, living alone in a house built for two.

She entered through the unlocked door. Inside, it was hot. Even though the weather was still mild, Erlan had the stove roaring. Should she be encouraged because he'd been able to build a fire or discouraged because he'd felt cold enough to warrant needing to? He sat at the table, slouched over, sipping some of the soup she'd made in the morning before leaving. Dark rings hung heavy beneath his amethyst eyes; his hair, the white of freshly fallen snow, seemed wispier than yesterday. He looked up, a smile of resignation on his lips.

"You're back soon. Did you run up the hill or have I lost track of the time?"

"I was eager to see you." She kissed the drooping skin of his cheeks. She didn't want to tell him about the merchant. Not until she had everything straight in her head.

"No trouble at the settlement?"

"No. Flynn was very helpful."

"He was always a kind boy."

"He's not a boy anymore."

"No. I don't suppose he would be. You know . . ." He trailed off, and his eyes appeared as if he was looking at something distant. "His great-grandmother used to have the loveliest voice. When she sang, you felt it through your body—shaking in your chest, tingling in your hands and feet. She played the harp too. Her fingers were so thin and delicate, but strong-looking also. I can see them so clearly . . ." He closed his eyes and plucked at the air.

"Did you ever meet her or is that the *yulthanispel?*" she asked. As the sickness progressed, Erlan increasingly found difficulty separating his own memories from those of the Tree, the border between the two becoming porous. Generations ago felt like yesterday, his own memories felt far off. This was normal enough, she'd been told.

"Of course I met her," he said, but then hesitated and looked out the window at a woodpecker cracking rhythmically on a pine tree. His face was a mask of confusion. "Actually, that can't . . . I knew his grandsire . . . I don't know. I'm not sure."

"It's okay. Don't trouble yourself."

"I feel tired," he said and stood up along with the blankets wrapped around him. "I should lay down." He picked up his bowl to set it away from the table. His hand trembled, and the bowl slipped from his grasp, landing with a clatter, its contents spilling out onto the table and floor.

"I'll get it," she said. Her voice had an unintended sternness to it.

"I'm sorry. The mess . . ."

She didn't care about the mess. She cared about what it meant that he couldn't hold a bowl of soup. "No. Don't worry. I didn't mean it that way. I'll clean. Go rest."

He nodded and turned towards the bedroom. Not two moments later though, his legs buckled. A quick, panicked grunt escaped his mouth before he crashed on the floor.

She rushed to him and helped him to his knees. His temple had already begun to swell; a trickle of blood had started from a gash above his eye.

"Perhaps I didn't eat enough today," he said. Corinne gathered herself, got him back on his feet, and helped him to the bedroom. When he was safely lying down, she returned to the main room to clean up.

It was only a matter of time now. She'd be returning from picking vegetables or from getting water from the well. She'd go to wake him from bed and, this time, he wouldn't stir. She would stand over his body until that first wave of grief washed over her. She would go to the settlement and three or four Mandrakhir would come in a horse cart to fetch his body and bring it back to the Tree, just like they'd agreed. Erlan had been banished, but in death all was forgiven with the Mandrakhar.

The dread was the worst part, she thought. Not knowing when the sword would fall.

She had to try something, foolish as it might be.

She figured they'd need three days to reach the ruins—much longer than one might expect based on how close the ruins looked when standing on the road. As the raven flies, the place was only a few leagues from where she stood; yet there was no trail that directly crossed the valley, so the journey would necessitate them weaving southwestward through a series of small canyons and creek beds before curling back north along a trail.

She'd never actually been all the way to the ruins, but years ago—on one of the long treks she took out into the wilderness with Pelaeus—she'd crossed the valley to the foot of the mountain that the ruins were perched upon. It was the longest excursion she and Pelaeus ever took. Pelaeus was well into adulthood then, with nearly grown children and a seat on the council that governed the settlement. This had all been before Corinne moved back into the settlement and fallen in love with Erlan. She was still living with Gareth and Saleya then, and—although they worried about her being away—Corinne was seventeen, a woman, and could make her own decisions.

Pelaeus had been a tireless walker and it was for Corinne that they'd had to take breaks. "Slow down, you merciless bitch!" Corinne begged as they traveled up a steep incline through one stretch of the valley.

"I can't," she said, looking over her shoulder but shortening her strides. "Mandrakhar don't have enough time to slow down." Even in youth, Pelaeus hadn't been beautiful—either by human or Mandrakhar standards—yet by her middle age, her angular features had matured into a visage that belied her strength of character and quick intellect. Corinne had never met royalty, but when she imagined a woman of such a lineage—a queen or empress from one of the old tales—she'd always assumed they'd look how Pelaeus did in her middle years, without the ears, of course.

It took them two days to make it to the base of the mountain where a high waterfall emptied into a deep pool and sprayed a cool mist upon their faces. A paradise, the two friends agreed; they spent another day and a night there, diving into the water from the rocks halfway up the waterfall, swimming, lying in the sun. That last night, they sat talking around their campfire until the early hours of the morning, holding each other beneath their blankets to ward off the night's chill. Though the two had known each other for years, it was the first time Corinne had ever spoken to her friend about her childhood—the orphanage, the great desert that surrounded her town, her grandfather.

Pelaeus had been dead three years now, but Corinne hardly saw her friend at all in the two years prior to her death. Now it was Erlan's turn to pass from her life. Unless this sorcerer…

Corinne assumed they could make it to the pool in two days again, but that it would then be at least another day up the mountain to the ruins, if one could find a suitable way up at all. There was no chance Erlan could walk such a distance, and Corinne certainly couldn't carry him. She could hope to travel alone and bring the sorcerer back, but even if she could convince him to come, they might be too late for Erlan.

There was only one thing to do: she would go to Gareth's house, beg his help, and with luck they could leave in the morning.

She boiled the moonroot tea and brought it into the bedroom. Erlan, lying in bed, mumbled to himself in Mandrakhi, a common occurrence now that the sickness had taken hold. Those memories again. She nudged him and he snapped to attention.

"I have to go for a few hours," she said. "I've left the tea here."

✤

It was dark when she reached Gareth's small, nameless village. Though she approached the cluster of forty-some-odd small, wooden buildings from the northeast and Gareth and Saleya's house was on the village's southern edge, Corinne took the long route around the perimeter of the village rather than cut through its center. Whereas the Mandrakhar showed their disapproval of Erlan and her marriage by issuing cold stares in her direction, the young men of the village would rather hurl insults or rocks or sic their under-fed dogs on her. If Gareth weren't twice the size of any other man in the village, they probably would have burned her at the stake long ago.

From outside the house, she saw raven-haired Saleya cooking through the window. Even as she'd gotten older, the woman—who had once been Corinne's caretaker—still had an understated elegance about her. She saw Gareth too, reading by candlelight. Though a few years younger than his wife, Gareth too was well into his middle years. Still, he was no less powerful than he had been as a younger man. The only signs of aging he showed were a little gray in his beard and a belly grown to rival his massive chest.

"Corinne!" he said, when he opened the door to her. "What a treat!" He spoke warmly, but she could hear concern in his voice. She gave him a hug and was engulfed by his hulking arms. She went to Saleya and kissed her on the cheek.

"Auntie Corinne!" said the dark-haired boy, Joram, bursting from one of the other rooms. Gareth and Saleya had given up on having children—thinking Saleya too old—when she suddenly became pregnant with Joram. A miracle child, they'd called him.

Corinne herself loved children, but she'd known when she married Erlan that children weren't a physical possibility—his seed was no more compatible with her womb than if she were a horse.

She knew if she didn't say why she'd come immediately, she might not ever get to the matter. She told them the story she'd heard earlier that day in the wagon and how she'd made up her mind to seek out this supposed sorcerer for help. When she was finished with the story (which, admittedly, sounded ridiculous when said aloud), Gareth stroked his beard and looked at her with a combination of alarm and pity.

"I am sorry about Erlan," he said.

She nodded. She was a little embarrassed about the story and didn't meet Gareth's gaze.

"But you know that this sorcerer likely does not exist."

"Yes."

"And even if he does, he likely cannot help Erlan."

"I know that as well."

"And even if he *could* help him, there's nothing to say that he *will*. Sorcerers don't necessarily have a reputation of being agreeable."

She nodded again.

"And the journey might be dangerous. If there are bandits on the west side of the valley, we shouldn't want to get anywhere near there. The truth is, those lands aren't as safe as in the old days of the Lunarises."

Saleya, who stood behind Joram, holding the boy by his shoulders, spoke up now. "But there's still a chance. Don't you have to try *something*?"

"Sometimes, there's just nothing to be tried, dear."

"And sometimes there is, but people are too stubborn to do it."

Gareth muttered something underneath his breath.

"You really want to do this, Corinne?" he said.

She looked up at him now. "Yes."

"Very well. We can take my cart as far as we can and I'll carry him the rest of the way. When were you hoping to leave?"

"Tomorrow," Corinne said, "and thank you."

Walking the path home, Corinne felt a strange lightness. The odds were against her; Erlan's condition was likely hopeless. Yet the fact she was doing *something*, that there was a plan—futile as it may be—filled her with excitement.

Some hours later, when she entered the cottage, her husband was still in bed, moaning in discomfort. He appeared not to have moved since she left.

"Is that you?" he said, his voice strained.

"Yes, love." Inside the bedroom, the smell of urine filled her nostrils. She lit a candle from the dying embers in the main room's fireplace and saw Erlan's clothes and the bed were soaked through. This wasn't the first time this had happened. "Gods. I'm sorry I was gone so long."

"Don't worry," he said. She brought in a pail of water from the other room and began cleaning. She stripped Erlan's clothes from his body and helped him get out of bed and sit in a nearby chair. She removed the blankets and did her best to scrub the urine out of the mattress, although she knew the stain wouldn't completely come out. Afterwards she wiped down Erlan's frail legs and buttocks before putting him in fresh clothes.

"Thank you, my love," he said and lay back down on the newly made bed.

Corinne felt tears building in her eyes but wiped them away with her sleeve. "Rest up," she said. "Tomorrow we're going on a trip."

"A trip?"

"Across the valley. There's someone who may be able to help you."

His eyes replied, *there's no one who can help me*, but he didn't say it. He would play along. For her.

Day had only just broken when Corinne heard Gareth's cart clatter up the path. She was still finishing the packing of food and supplies but went outside to greet him. A light mist, sure to be burned off by mid-morning, clung to the air.

Gareth wore a coarse brown cloak and held a lit pipe in his mouth. "Suppose you haven't changed your mind about this," he said as he brought the horses to a halt.

"What do *you* think?"

"That you're one of the stubborn-est, headstrong-est people I've ever known." He hopped from the cart and the ground almost seemed to shake with his landing. "Can I help you with bags?"

"You can help with Erlan," Corinne said.

Gareth grumbled something and went inside. Two minutes later, as Corinne was loading her supplies into the cart, Gareth exited the cottage carrying a semi-conscious Erlan in his two arms as if he were Gareth's bride.

They made good time, and by noon of the first day were off the road and following a dry creek bed that ran southwestward. Eventually they'd veer to the northwest along some of the Mandrakhi hunting trails, but for now the terrain was easy and the ride smooth. Erlan's pain had grown worse, so they spent extra time at their midday meal so Corinne could brew more moonroot tea.

"You ever think about the North?" she asked Gareth that afternoon as Erlan was napping and the wagon continued along the creek bed.

"Not much. Sometimes maybe I think about some of the people. Your grandfather, for one. He made his share of mistakes, but underneath it all was a kind man."

"I never knew him too well," Corinne said. "Only a little before the end."

"Those were bittersweet days, I suppose," Gareth said.

"What about *your* father? You never talk about him much."

"My father was a good steward. But I think he spent every moment away from his work either asleep or drunk. He wasn't an angry or violent drunk, at least."

"Would you ever consider going back?"

"Thought about it," he said, "but don't see there's much reason for it. My father was the last blood I had, and he died years before the Uprising. Otherwise...never liked cities much, and a village here is pretty much the same as a village there, except for there's more trees and less heat down here." He pulled the cart to a stop to move some medium-sized rocks in the road. "Besides, a move wouldn't be so easy on Saleya, and she and Joram are happy here. You?"

"Erlan is here."

Gareth nodded.

The next morning, they left the creek bed and made their way along the overgrown Mandrakhi hunting trails. They came upon few other travelers that day. Early on there was a toothless fisherman who'd come from a town over on the Yesenya River to sell smoked fish. Later in the afternoon, a suspicious pair of cloaked riders rode quickly up on them until catching a glimpse of Gareth and turning back the way they'd come.

"Bandits or other thugs by the look of them," Gareth said under his breath, gripping his woodchopper's axe. Since the Galsworth Ascension and the end of Imperial expansion, there were fewer soldiers to keep the peace, and the lands this far west of the capital were more dangerous than they'd once been. It was a bit ironic, Corinne thought, how countless thousands had died during the Uprising to topple the Lunarises, yet it had been an ordinary case of the sweating sickness that finally accomplished what all those Islanders failed at.

By sundown on the second day, they'd reached the waterfall at the foot of the mountain below the ruins. Erlan's condition continued worsening; taking a deep breath or moving seemed to cause him pain now. The moonroot tea helped less with each cup. While Gareth fed the horses and Erlan rested, Corinne walked from their camp towards the pool, trying to find familiar places from her trip with Pelaeus those years before. After some exploration, she found the spot—a small patch of whitish sand leading to the pool—where they had taken their meal, laid down their things, undressed, and entered the waters. She sat on the ground and skipped a few pebbles across the still surface of the pool. Taking off one of her boots, she dipped her toe in. Colder than she remembered.

Erlan came down with a fever that night. Lying beside him in the wagon, Corinne removed his blankets, exposing him to the night air. "One more day," she said into his ear in a whisper so faint it was hardly more than just her moving lips and thinking the sounds. He didn't respond, but over the next hour, his fever subsided.

After a breakfast of bread and cured pork, Gareth did his best to hide the horses and wagon in a clearing off to the side of the water; one could only see it from directly across the pool. They laid out ample food for the horses and packed up their other supplies. It would be Corinne's job to carry the packs up the mountain since Gareth had to carry Erlan. They couldn't count on Erlan to keep his grip on Gareth's shoulders so they were forced to tie the two together using ropes they had brought on the journey.

It didn't take them long to find the trail up the mountain, an endless series of switchbacks that wove back and forth, up and up and up.

A day of slow hiking uphill, stopping to rest and starting again, eventually brought them to a final rise, beyond which they could see the ruins a mere two hundred paces away. Gareth, exhausted and soaked through with perspiration, untied Erlan and laid him in the dry grass before collapsing to his hands and knees. Corinne, who had been carrying forty pounds of supplies, not another person, could barely stand herself—the muscles of her legs fire, her feet throbbing from her ill-fitting boots.

But they'd made it.

Her triumphant feelings at having arrived dissipated almost instantly as she studied the ruins. A crumbling stone wall—that once might have been white but was now weather-beaten, mud-spattered, and overgrown with moss—encircled all the ancient buildings. A large gap in the wall where a gate once stood afforded Corinne an unobstructed view of the grounds beyond. The main structure within the compound was a decrepit, blue-gray stone palace. A line of crows sat along the edge of the roof. Half of the palace's facade had collapsed and not a single one of the fifty or so windows seemed to have glass remaining in it. A few smaller granite buildings were directly adjacent to the palace. All these, like the palace itself, looked long abandoned, completely uninhabitable. No sorcerer lived here. No one did.

She shouted an obscenity to the sky and her voice carried in the breeze.

"Easy, Corinne," Gareth said.

"This was a stupid idea," she said.

Gareth, who was still on knees breathing heavily, said nothing now.

Erlan tilted his head up towards her. He hadn't said anything all day, but now, in sight of the old palace, he started speaking quickly in Mandrakhi.

She kissed him on the forehead. It was warm against her lips. "I'm sorry, love."

"I remember..." he said, now in the Common Dialect, "I remember... The palace at night...illuminated...so many torches...seemed almost day..."

Gareth gave Corinne a look as if to ask if this was normal.

"And the parties...the parties...banquets...more food than you have ever seen...beautiful ladies dancing on shiny marble floors...we used to perform...how the crowds would cheer . . ."

"There couldn't have been parties here for three hundred years," Gareth said.

"It's the memories. The *yulthanispel*," she said and Gareth shrugged.

They rested for a while longer on the grass. Erlan continued reminiscing, his speech sometimes drifting back to his native tongue.

They set up camp under a large elm tree and made a bed for Erlan out of blankets. Corinne built a fire and brewed more moonroot tea. When Erlan was comfortably resting, Gareth and Corinne went to survey the ruins. It was unlikely they'd find anything, but they'd come this far, so they might as well take a look. To cover the most ground, they split up. Gareth would search the palace itself and Corinne would look through the ruins of the adjacent buildings.

There were four other buildings surrounding the palace. The largest, and first Corinne explored, was rectangular in shape and consisted of a single large room with small, high windows circling the building. She tried to imagine what the building had been used for, but it was hard to tell since any furnishings had long been removed. All along the walls, stone slabs jutted out; Corinne thought they might have been used for beds. Perhaps the building had been a barracks or living quarters. There was no sign of a seven-foot-tall sorcerer.

The two smallest buildings were now little more than a few opposing walls and no roof, and Corinne could tell from afar that there was no chance of any person being within. The last of the four buildings, and the one furthest from the palace, had a large triangular roof still intact and seemed to be a chapel or temple. Inside, approximately twenty rows of pews faced a dais. Lining the walls on both sides were a dozen or more life-sized stone statues of men and women. Each had been decapitated, the head smashed on the floor directly next to its body. Other than a solitary bird, there wasn't a living thing inside. Corinne walked up to the dais and stood looking out upon the empty pews. "Thank you all for coming," she said to nobody, imagining speaking to an ancient crowd.

She walked down the center aisle and back towards the entrance. "If you're here, tell us," she called in a near shout, and her voice seemed to momentarily echo around the room. "We aren't dangerous. We just want your help." As if on cue, the bird flew from its perch through the door and was gone.

She returned to their camp. Gareth was already back and was feeding wood to the fire. Erlan sat huddled beneath his blankets, whispering to himself.

"Didn't find anything either?" she said.

"Not even any sign of bandits or hobos taking shelter there."

"Same where I looked."

"I did, however, manage to catch this with my sling shot," he said, gesturing to a bloodied rabbit laying in the grass by his feet.

"I'm not hungry," she said. "It will be good for Erlan to have meat though."

"Come," Gareth said. "We will share. You will need strength for the return trip." She nodded noncommittally and sat down next to Erlan. *The Return.* It was the name the Mandrakhar gave for when they connected the bodies of their dead to the Tree. Of course, Gareth hadn't been referring to this.

"How are you, love?" she said to Erlan. He was shivering. He stopped talking for a moment and looked at her. There was no sign of recognition in his eyes.

"Dreya wore the most beautiful dress I have ever seen. Five hundred diamonds laced into the gown . . ."

Her first inclination was to try to shake him out of whatever memories he was lost in. But then again, what was the point? She'd play along, listening to these memories that had been a part of him for so long, but that she had never been privy to.

"Tell me again, what were you doing in the palace?"

"Performing, of course. Our troupe was the greatest and most famous of all the Mandrakhar. We were known as far east as Vicus Remorum, north to the sea, as far south as the Dragonlands."

"Aren't no Dragonlands anymore," Gareth interjected from a few paces away as he was preparing the rabbit. "Seeing as there aren't no dragons."

"Of course there are dragons," Erlan said. Gareth shrugged and placed the now-skinned rabbit on a makeshift spit.

"Tell me more," Corinne said. "How was it to dance before a king?"

"The greatest experience of my life," he said. "At the coronation, we performed every night for a week."

"And where did you stay? Was there a town here?"

"No town, but the lower levels of the palace had more than a hundred rooms. If you made a wrong turn you could be lost for hours."

"Lower levels?"

"They were built in case the Bridgelanders ever came. Down below they'd get lost in a maze of corridors and the king could escape."

Corinne turned to Gareth. "When you were in the palace, did you notice any underground rooms?"

Gareth gave her a look of disapproval.

"Did you?"

"I saw one old stairway to a cellar or something, but it was caved in. No way down there and definitely no one lives there."

"Maybe there's another way down."

"It's getting dark already," he said. "We can't go looking all over the place on account of memories that are three hundred years old."

She looked at him.

"To the Demon with it, Corinne. Let's at least eat this rabbit first."

They all went together. Erlan might be able to help lead them to the underground chambers, and if Erlan were going, he'd need Gareth to carry him. Before setting off, Corinne walked back to find a couple green branches on the path up the mountain where the trees thinned out. She wrapped these in old cloth and coated the cloth bulges in tree resin to make torches. By the time she returned, Gareth had loaded Erlan on his back.

"We'll light one at a time," she said. "Between the two we probably have an hour."

Corinne held the torch and led the way back to the palace with Gareth bearing Erlan a few steps behind. Gareth directed Corinne over to where part of the palace wall had collapsed so they could enter.

Just like with the other buildings, anything of value in the ruins was long gone. There were no tapestries on the wall, no goblets of silver. The crumbling remains of a few particularly large pieces of furniture were all that suggested anyone had ever lived here. Soon they came upon a large room, maybe a ballroom, with a stairway that led downward. As Gareth had warned, the ceiling was caved in after the first few steps. There was no way down.

"See," Gareth said.

Corinne walked around behind Gareth so she could speak to her husband. "Do you remember any other ways down to the lower levels?"

He seemed to understand and closed his eyes. "Borlan, yes...No silly, this way...There is...there is...a hall connected to...to where? Over here...the kitchen," he said. "All servants, and that includes you performers, should come up this way...don't you ever forget it..."

They returned to a room they had walked through on the way to the ballroom; with its enormous stone oven, it must have been the kitchen. There, around a barely noticeable corner, they found a narrow staircase. At the bottom of the staircase, there was not even moonlight to help illuminate the way. If not for the torches, they'd have been completely swallowed by darkness.

They found themselves in a corridor that opened into a wider hallway at least a hundred paces long. The hallway was then bisected by three other hallways. At equal distance along the wall were a series of identical doorways, each leading, as far as they could tell, into identically sized, empty rooms. Corinne tried to keep track of how to return to the stairway back to the kitchen, but after a series of left turns down yet other identical corridors, she was hopelessly lost.

They lit the second torch as the first one waned. Corinne had started worrying they'd lose themselves in the dark when they came upon a non-identical feature in the passages. After yet another left turn, at the end of yet another hallway, moonlight filtered in through an oval window of colored glass. This part of the underground complex must have reached the edge of the cliff. They walked towards the window. As they approached, a faint orange glow, not just moonlight, could be seen on the adjacent wall. Corinne ran ahead and turned the corner.

They were inside some kind of library, and windows similar to the one they'd initially seen lined one side of the room. Down at the far end, a solitary man sat at a table reading a leather-bound volume by candlelight. He was dark skinned—although perhaps a shade lighter than those from the Northern Islands or The Bridge. His head was shaved; an ugly scar and an empty space marked where his left eye should have been. Otherwise, he seemed the complete opposite of the man who had been described. Rather than a seven-foot-tall behemoth, the man was slight, with a body resembling a twelve-year-old boy.

He looked up from his book. "Hello," he said in an accented, high-pitched voice. He pulled an eye patch out from his pants pocket and placed it over the missing eye. "A bit unsightly if you're not used to it, Corinne."

How did he know her name? She held the torch in front of herself like a shield. She sensed Gareth behind her, untying Erlan and lowering him into one of the chairs.

The man closed his good eye and the torches and candles around the room burst to life. Gareth stumbled back, startled.

"Nice trick, sorcerer," he said.

"Please...my name is...well, it would be hard for you to say, so you may call me Padgett. That's what most call me anyway. And you are . . ." He looked as if he was trying to remember something. "Gareth! Anyhow, I have grown to dislike this word. *Sorcerer...Doer of sorcery.* What is sorcery but all those things that men cannot understand?"

"If not *sorcery* then *Starseed*," Corinne said. "You have it."

"Starseed...*the gift and curse of the Forefathers*...a nice story that I'm afraid isn't completely accurate. And I should know! I've done quite a lot of study on the matter."

He rose from his seat and stepped towards them. The top of his head only came to Corinne's nose. "Perhaps instead it would be most useful for us to just think that I have a certain rare set of talents. Some people have a talent for languages; others have a knack for cooking. Gareth, I would imagine, can move large objects with his hands. Me, I am good at none of these things. It took me years to master the Common Dialect and, even now, my terrible Southland accent remains. The soup I prepare for myself is bland, and as you can probably guess, I would not win any competitions of strength. Yet I can do the things that I can do, you see? For instance—"

"You can heal people," Corinne said. It was in this brief moment that she let hope bloom in her heart.

"Why, yes," he said, "I do have a talent for that." But then he stopped and looked closely at Erlan. His expression changed; he looked at his feet. "Oh my."

"What? What is it?"

"Your friend...No, your *husband.* He is Mandrakhar. It is the wasting sickness that afflicts him."

"Yes. You can help him, can't you?"

"Bring me someone who has a disease or wound or who is poisoned even. I can help. But the wasting sickness is no disease. It is his body attacking itself, and it is a fundamental part of being a Mandrakhar. I cannot change him from a Mandrakhar anymore than I could change myself into a bird."

It felt to her as if the room was spinning; she sat down in one of the chairs. "But will you try?"

"There is nothing *to* try."

"How can you be sure? You *must* try something."

"I'm sorry."

"Please!"

He shook his head.

All at once, something took hold of her—something that perhaps had been latent in her since before she married Erlan, before Pelaeus, before coming to the settlement, before the war. She sprang forward, drew her knife, and held its point to the sorcerer's chest. "Try! Just try! Or I'll kill you, I swear to the gods."

He didn't flinch nor was there any fear in his eyes. Yet there was... *something*. A look of recognition, a painful memory brought back to life, as he beheld the weapon in Corinne's hand. "Have you ever killed a man before?" he said.

"There's always a first time," she said. She could feel how easily the blade would cut through his robe and into his heart.

"True. But afterwards, there's no going back."

Gareth came up behind her now and grabbed her wrist gently. With a power that would be futile to struggle against, he pulled the blade down. She released the thing and it landed loudly on the stone floor. "He must try. Why can't he try? All I want is for him to try . . ."

There were extra beds in one of the adjoining rooms, so that night they all stayed within the palace ruins. Once they were settled, Gareth returned to the library to talk to Padgett and to give Corinne time alone with Erlan.

It wouldn't be long now. She lay down next to him for what very well could be the last time.

"We tried," she said. She squeezed his upper arm, kissed his unreciprocating lips.

"It was the most beautiful dress, I have ever seen," he said, in a voice that sounded utterly content.

You don't deserve this, she thought. *We don't deserve this.*

When Erlan fell asleep, Corinne returned to the other room to speak to Gareth and Padgett and apologize to the sorcerer for pulling the knife on him.

"It's nothing," he said. "I understand your grief. And besides, I don't think you would have gone through with it."

Corinne wasn't so sure.

For a while afterwards, they conversed with the sorcerer about their journey to the ruins and about their experiences living in the settlement.

"You know, there was a brief time when I too lived amongst the Mandrakhar of the Westwood," Padgett said. "I was interested, amongst other things, in whether I could help them manage the ancestral memories better, rather than the memories simply coming and going of their own accord. I never did have much success."

"When was this?" Gareth said.

"Long before you ever arrived. I am older than I appear."

When Gareth excused himself to use the privy, Corinne tried to make small talk with the sorcerer.

"You mentioned you studied the history of the Forefathers?" Corinne asked.

"Indeed," Padgett said.

"Is that what that's about?" She gestured to the book on the table in front of him—the one he'd been reading when they arrived.

Padgett picked up the book and examined it, turning it in his hands as if trying to decipher the thing's use. "I suppose in a roundabout way this *is* about the Forefathers," he said but then stopped to think a little further. "It's complicated."

Corinne blinked a few times. She'd just noticed it: embossed on the book's cover was a seal upon which the name *Benedictus* was inscribed. She wiped her eyes. There was no mistaking it. *Benedictus.*

She and Gareth had known a man by that name. When she was a child in the North. She wondered if Gareth had seen the inscription when he'd been sitting with the sorcerer.

"What's wrong?" Padgett said.

Foolishness. It was a common enough name.

Besides, all that was far away and long ago. "Nothing," she said.

It was a common enough name. And she had Erlan to worry about anyway.

The next morning, they departed from Padgett and made the descent back to the pool and the horse cart. It was a long walk, but both Gareth and Corinne fared much better going down than up. When they reached the valley floor they found the horses and wagon undisturbed. Gareth unloaded Erlan into the cart upon a bed of blankets.

All throughout the afternoon and early evening, Erlan moaned in pain. His temples pulsed with fever. Corinne reached into her pack and found she'd been using so much moonroot that she'd gone through a two weeks' supply in a matter of days. She wasn't looking for moonroot now anyway.

If she thought about it too much—if she made ceremony of it—she wouldn't do it.

She boiled the Dragon flower in the kettle. The tea smelled sweet. She let the cup of hot liquid cool before giving it to him.

Erlan drank and then said something in Mandrakhi that Corinne didn't understand. His voice trailed off into silence.

Afterwards, Corinne would try to remember the sound of those last words and she would ask Flynn what they meant.

"I'm sorry," Flynn would say. "You must have misheard. Those aren't Mandrakhi words."

When she was sure he was gone, she sat silently for a long time. She had dreaded this moment for so long that now that it was here she felt a small sense of relief. This, in turn, made her feel even worse.

Gareth and Corinne rode for much of the next two days in silence, all the way back to the settlement. There was one small stretch when they spoke at any length.

"What did you and Padgett talk about that night?" she said. "When I was with Erlan." She thought now about that name she'd seen inscribed on the book, though she didn't bring it up.

"I asked him what he was doing living alone in a place like the palace ruins."

"And?"

"He told me he wasn't living there. That he had been looking for something. According to him, there were more tunnels below the ones we were in that were built long before the Phaidonians ever set foot on the spot. Apparently when the Phaidonians arrived they just built right over the site that was already there."

"What was he looking for?"

"Some scepter related to the Forefathers. He showed the thing to me: this sort of long, white stick with a red jewel at the end. Anyhow, after he showed it to me, he started going on about how the Forefathers weren't angels or spirits or gods as most have assumed, but just a different kind of being. Just like how the Mandrakhar are different than us."

"Oh."

"One more thing...I almost forgot," he said, reaching into the pocket of his coat and producing an envelope sealed in wax. "He gave me this to give to you."

Corinne took it. "What is it?"

"I don't know, a vision or something, he said. Who knows with these sorcerer types? He told me not to give it to you until we got back to the settlement, but I don't see any harm in giving it to you now."

"Should I open it?" she said. Gareth shrugged. She broke the seal and removed the contents of the envelope: a single piece of parchment.

Do not despair. The two of you will meet again.

"What does it say?"

"Nothing. Nonsense."

Gareth offered to stay with Corinne in the settlement in one of the travel houses, but Corinne knew he was eager to get back to Saleya and Joram. Besides, Flynn had offered to put her up.

That night, the Mandrakhar in charge of the Return allowed Corinne to stay with Erlan's body as he was wrapped in the roots of the Tree. Within a day those large roots would sprout into a million little capillary-like branches that would slip beneath Erlan's skin and begin the process. A day after that it would be complete and the roots would retract. Erlan's body would be burned, and all that was left of him would live in this Tree.

Corinne herself had decided that she would leave the farm to head east to the capital, not back north. To be honest, she didn't feel much like going anywhere or doing anything, but life, she knew, had to be gotten on with. And perhaps she might even get a job in the Imperial Library like she'd imagined when she was a child. She was still young.

She sat for several hours and watched the barely noticeable progression of the roots around Erlan's body. This was truly the end. Still, part of her couldn't help but think of the sorcerer's note, and she wondered whether, were she to return fifteen years hence, if all of the Mandrakhar—now with a piece of Erlan and Pelaeus inside of them—would look at her with kinder eyes, knowing, feeling, how much she had loved and been loved by two of their own.

Fairfield girls basketball crushes Trumbull

Sarah D'Albero leads strong showing as one-loss Whalers beat Thunderbirds.

FAIRFIELD — Never was the value of Fairfield High School sophomore Sarah D'Albero more evident than in Monday night's victory over Trumbull. After sitting out last week's loss to Western with flu-like symptoms (the first loss of the season for the Whalers), the five-foot-ten forward thoroughly dominated every aspect of the game. Early on the formula was simple: let D'Albero take advantage of her match-up by posting her up against smaller defenders and spacing the floor to let her take larger defenders off the dribble. In the second half, Trumbull resorted to doubling D'Albero, but this failed to slow down last year's conference Freshman of the Year. D'Albero, time and again, picked apart the defense by finding cutters and open shooters behind the arc. Fairfield never trailed in the game and ended up winning by a score of 74-48.

D'Albero finished with 29 points, 13 rebounds and nine assists, coming just short of the rare high school triple double, as the Whalers ran their record to 5-1 in County South and 17-1 overall. Trumbull fell to 14-3 overall and 4-2 in conference.

D'Albero—who was All-Conference Honorable Mention last year during her freshman campaign—seems to have added several new wrinkles to her game this year, including an improved handle and a reliable three-point shot.

"All summer I was shooting a couple hundred threes a day with my tutor, Chris," Sarah said, referring to former Sacred Heart University shooting guard Chris Hanes, who worked with D'Albero over the off-season. "So where last year my range was probably seventeen, eighteen feet, now I feel a lot more confident pulling up from behind the line."

Fairfield coach Lawrence Donahue echoed these sentiments: "Sarah put in a ton of work on her shooting during the off-season. The result isn't just that she can now hit deeper shots, but there's a domino effect where the threat of the long ball opens up the whole floor and really helps our spacing."

D'Albero and senior point guard Jenna Daly have formed the backbone of the team that—along with three-point specialist, junior Kara Tarnowski—led the Whalers to the state tournament last year. They're on the same track this season, albeit with a different supporting cast.

Fairfield next faces Stamford's Provisions High this Friday.

THREE

WHAT SHE WOULD'VE TOLD HIM IF SHE TOLD HIM THE TRUTH

Mostly 1996-1999

Tell me a story, he said, I've been talking too much.

It was maybe their fifth date—she's no longer sure exactly but something like that. Somewhere after three it blends together now and she doesn't remember what was fourth or seventh or twelfth. Even if her memory were better, it's unclear how to count things since they'd met on vacation (did the whole week in Ireland count as one?). Point is, it was early: that phase where everything was new and they simultaneously wanted to freeze time to stay in the moment and fast forward it to see what came next. Her early twenties had been an emotional desert of bad setups and ex-boyfriend nonsense and she was excited to be here now: lying on his IKEA bed, a little rickety from one too many re-assemblies, overanalyzing every word or incidental touch of their ankles beneath his red and brown flannel sheets.

The years have made her forget most of the details, but she *does* specifically remember thinking he had nice arms; she could make out the shape of his triceps despite the fact he wasn't flexing. A relic from his days playing football, she guessed.

He'd just told her about a book he was writing: a side project, a fantasy novel. She was surprised. She liked the idea of him doing this, but she was surprised is all. She'd thought *she* was the dork in this duo.

Like *Harry Potter* or something, she'd asked, but then immediately wanted to take back the question because it felt reductionist. No, he said, this wasn't for kids really. He described a part he was working on about these beings: human-like, except they experienced time differently. They would grow up in a few years. The longest any of them would live would be until they were fifteen, twenty maybe.

She was twenty-five; he was two years older. So we'd both be dead, she said to him. A shame. We never would have met.

But maybe, he said, we would have still lived full and wonderful lives and grown old with our great-grandchildren at our sides. Or maybe we would have still met...some way. Maybe those would be *our* great-grandchildren.

She gave him a look that said, *slow down, this is only date number five or four or seven or twelve,* even though she didn't feel that way—she didn't want him to slow down at all.

When she asked him how he'd thought of all this, he relayed an incident some years ago when, while in a Starbucks in Haverford, he watched a fly slam itself over and over into the immaculately windexed pane of the window. He didn't think much of it until a week later when he was at the same Starbucks and there was, as far as he could tell, that same fly again. The sound of the fly's body hitting the glass made the tiniest of sounds. He thought about how long flies lived and how much of this fly's life might have been spent wasting away against the glass and how this fly's whole perception of time must be so different than our own.

A little depressing, she said.

What she didn't say was that maybe this was one of the things she liked about him: the darkness around his edges, his ability, like her own, to tap into *that* side of things. She kissed him, after which he asked for that story.

A story, she repeated.

Yeah, a story: tell him about a day of her life, any day, she'd like to live again and again. Like in that movie with Bill Murray.

Why would she be living this day over and over? Just to experience it again or to change things?

Either. Both.

Present company excluded? She wanted to make sure he wasn't fishing for compliments.

Present company excluded.

She wasn't sure what to say.

It was a warm evening and the AC unit was busted, so they had just kept the windows open, hoping for the breeze that never came.

At last she told him about a day from her childhood—before her brother was born and before Emily died. It was one of their "Indian Days," a non-politically-correct name they gave to a few days every summer; their mom and the two of them would go into the backyard, dress up like (and otherwise culturally appropriate) Native Americans, paint their faces, and do nature activities. They each selected their own names; she was *Hops with Rabbits*, Emily was *Running Deer*. She can't remember her mother's alias. Come the evening, they'd grill on the barbecue, pretending it was their campfire and they'd sleep out back in their "teepee," a neon green Coleman they'd picked up at Sam's Club.

When she was through, he told her thank you for sharing and does she think about her sister still? She told him sometimes and he kissed her with practiced tenderness.

She looked at him intently, but ever since he asked for that story she couldn't get a different person out of her head. A person she could no longer even really picture, so what floated around in her mind, in place of a face, was just a fuzzy idea—like the mental image one might hold for a character from a book when no one's made it into a movie.

No, be present, she thought to herself. *You're in love.* Only she couldn't fully convince herself. And then a sentence formed in her mind. It was something she already knew, but hearing the words in her brain made it all much worse:

Everything I've just told him is a lie.

Not the event. It all happened as far as she could remember, but it wasn't the true answer to his question. It wasn't the day she'd relive over all others. She knew this when she said it and she knew this two years later when they got married on the beach in Westport and she continued to know it as their marriage went down the tubes and she couldn't help but think that this lie contributed to everything that went wrong.

Here's what she would've told him if she'd told him the truth:

It's fall of Sarah's senior year in high school, the day after her seventeenth birthday; she and Chris are driving down the Merritt Parkway as they have on so many evenings. Chris is acting different, distant, and it feels to her like things between them—like the trees, whose early autumn branches stretch overhead—are about to change. The air rushing in through the window of Chris's Corolla tosses her long, brownish-blond hair. She wonders if the two of them, just hours earlier, had sex—no, made love—for the last time.

That R.E.M. song, "Nightswimming" is playing on the radio and Sarah has the overly romantic, teenage urge for the two of them to find a little pond or stream somewhere and strip down, jump in. Despite the unseasonably warm weather, it isn't *that* warm. The water will be cold at first, jarringly so, but their bodies will eventually acclimate. When they come out shivering, Chris will wrap her in a fluffy towel, like the kind from a nice hotel, and kiss her closed eyes. They'll get in the car and turn the heat up all the way and everything will be perfect, as only brief moments in time can be.

They go to a cute café on a country road near Danbury and have coffee and a piece of pecan-date pie. Before Chris, she never drank coffee and she still gets one of those frou-frou drinks that's more sugar and cream and syrup than anything else. Chris drinks his black. When he goes to pee, she looks around, incapable of being still with her thoughts. A small child, the son of the owner, is at a table in the corner playing with his matchbox car. She imagines what Chris and her own caramel children might look like— not that it will happen, not that she'd be anywhere near ready for that kind of thing.

When he returns, Chris has an expression like he's been preparing to tell her something. Maybe he stood in front of the bathroom mirror just now and practiced. "You know I think you're special, right? And that I really care about you?" he says and she nods. She is a little hurt by his, undoubtedly conscious, demoting of his feelings for her from *love* a few weeks ago to this rather more flaccid, more ambiguous, *care*. She knows what will come next and something inside her clenches in preparation.

He rehashes everything he said before: that it's his fault and that he shouldn't have let things go on this long. It's not just that he's nine years older, it's not just that he could get in trouble, but it's that this isn't *right*. Years down the road, who knows? But for now, this can't continue.

She tells him she understands. She does. Really.

He says he's glad she can be so mature about things. Also, if she doesn't want him to be her coach he accepts that and he'll just tell her parents it doesn't work with his schedule anymore.

She tells him she can't imagine anyone else coaching her and that she wants him to stay in her life. As a coach, as a friend.

He says he'd like that.

It would be fair to ask why she'd choose this as her day to relive. If she was going to pick a day with Chris, why not an earlier one when neither of them showed signs of wanting to end things? She guesses the answer is that she's always found herself happiest when she was on the brink of despair. That somehow the abyss brings out the light by contrast.

Also, she regrets what happened afterwards.

In high school, Sarah was a tomboy and a serious basketball player. This was a departure from how she'd been as a younger girl when all she cared about were dolls and pink everything and sewing kits. Those were the things Emily liked and, up until Sarah was eleven, she desperately wanted to be just like her older sister. There are photographs of the two of them as little girls where Emily would be smiling for the picture but Sarah, rather than looking at the camera, would be staring expectantly at her sister.

The morning after Emily died from leukemia, Sarah took safety scissors and cut up all the old cross-stitch projects she and Emily had done together. She hid her tap dance shoes in the back of a closet so she didn't have to go to lessons. If she could no longer have her sister, she would throw out all the other parts of her old life too. The only activity she kept up from before Emily died was drawing—and that had been something, the only thing, she had done *without* her sister.

She took up sports. She was tall and hit her growth spurt early, so at eleven she towered over the boys in her sixth-grade class. Everyone, predictably, suggested basketball.

Between seventh and eighth grade, her family moved from California to Connecticut. Her father had gotten a new job—finally the CEO gig he'd been aiming for all his professional life. The fact that Emily had passed away made the move a much easier decision for her parents than the previous move from Ohio. Maybe getting away from California would help all of them start anew. Her dad had the architect add a regulation-size, indoor half-court to the design of their new house. Sarah would shoot around for an hour every day. Soon she was the star player of both her middle school and travel teams.

When Sarah's parents saw how much their daughter was taking to basketball, they hired a private coach so she could continue to work on her game during the off-season. She had already far surpassed most of the girls she played with on a regular basis.

As a high school freshman, when Sarah's then-private coach moved to New London, her dad hired Chris as a replacement. Chris had played at Sacred Heart University and was teaching history at a high school in Milford. During that off-season, he'd show up twice a week and put her through a string of drills: ball handling, defense, shooting, finishing around the basket with either hand, off one foot or both. Chris was a good coach: he pushed her hard but had a sense of humor about it that kept things fun. Also, he was handsome—tall and wiry with light hazel eyes that looked exotic contrasted against his coffee-colored skin. He wore his black, curly hair in little twists on his head that seemed to Sarah simultaneously intellectual and fashionable.

She worked with Chris through the summer after her freshman year and by the tenth grade, she was inarguably the star of the varsity team. Rumor had it that Coach Donahue, the head coach at the high school, had something against underclassmen starting on varsity. But by sophomore year, Sarah's work with Chris had paid off and it was undeniable that she was the most talented girl in the school. Chris and Sarah continued working together once a week on Sundays.

That fall Chris took Sarah to a UCONN women's game in Storrs. Chris's twelve-year-old niece was supposed to join them on the excursion, but the night before came down with a cold and couldn't attend. Chris called and asked if Sarah still wanted to go.

"Of course. Why wouldn't I?" she said.

"Are your parents okay with it?"

"Yeah, for sure."

"Do you want to ask them?"

"Trust me, it's fine."

The next afternoon, it took Sarah an hour to decide what she was going to wear to the game. Her Rebecca Lobo jersey was definitely going to be part of the ensemble, but should she wear something underneath it? On top? What pants would look good? Sporty but cute but also effortless was what she was going for. Her best friend Stacie came over and helped her do her makeup in a way that was pretty without being noticeable.

The whole evening, Sarah felt so anxious sitting next to Chris—cheering next to him when a good play was made, brushing her hand against his when she reached for a nacho—that she could hardly pay attention to the game. By the time it was over (a UCONN win, as always), she was so exhausted from the nervous energy she'd expended over the previous three hours that she fell asleep for the entire hour and a half ride back to Fairfield.

"We're here," he said, and she felt his hand on her shoulder. She opened her eyes to the familiar three-car garage at the end of her driveway. To tell the truth, she wouldn't have minded just staying put, ensconced in the warmth of his passenger seat, all night.

They began to occasionally hang out socially. Chris would swing by and they'd get ice cream at Nob's Creamery downtown after one of her games or grab lunch at the Beach Shack after their Sunday workouts. It was all harmless—like she was gaining back an older sibling after losing Emily.

Though they joked around during their workouts and Chris tolerated Sarah's mild flirtations (the occasional pat on the butt, a mischievous smile when their warm bodies pushed up against each other's during post practice), he kept things professional with how much of his personal life he'd reveal. Sarah might casually ask whether he was dating anyone and he'd deflect the question by telling her it was time to get to the next drill. Once, when Chris had to cancel one of their sessions because he was going to a wedding, it was revealed he was bringing his girlfriend. Sarah needed to know everything about her. Was she tall or short? How old was she? How'd they meet? Was she white or black or Hispanic or what? Pretty? Chris didn't say much. "*I* think she's pretty," he said.

As for Sarah's own romantic life, she had her share of interested suitors at school. She was tall—but not freakishly so—and thin and pretty enough and there was a certain segment of guys who thought it was cool that she was into basketball or art or both. She didn't have much interest in boys her age, though. They all seemed like little kids to her: scrawny and unsophisticated and more concerned with crude jokes and scoring weed than anything of substance.

In January, she lost her virginity to Remy Tarnowski in the guest cottage of his parents' house. That weekend the Tarnowski's were away at such-and-such forum in Davos, Switzerland, and this meant Remy was having a huge party with multiple kegs, all his dad's top-shelf liquor, and more flavors of Boone's Farm than Sarah knew existed.

Sarah had been vague acquaintances with Remy since middle school, when her family moved to Connecticut. She had then gotten to know him a little better that school year in both her world history and honors English classes, as well as through his older sister, who played with Sarah on the basketball team. Remy was one of the smarter kids, but he was also a bit of a douche. The majority of kids at her high school came from privileged backgrounds, and many had families that were flat-out rich. Remy Tarnowski, however, was guilty of being completely unaware of his privilege and flaunting it in numerous tacky ways.

Just the previous summer, he'd been over at Kristen Macgregor's party when her parents were out of town. As the story went, Remy had convinced Kristen to let him take her dad's hundred-thousand-dollar Mercedes for a joy ride, despite the fact that he only had his learner's permit. When, not a half hour later, Remy returned with a large gash on his forehead, having somehow managed to wrap the luxury automobile around a beech tree down the block, Kristen freaked out. Remy's response to Kristen's hyperventilating was a reportedly calm and cool: "I don't see why you're upset. I'll just buy you another one."

Sarah held no illusions that Remy was the man of her dreams, but nothing was going to happen between her and Chris. So that night, in the fifteen minutes between when Remy asked her drunken self if she wanted to see the pool house and when, in said pool house, she, with Remy's assistance, took off all her clothes, she decided she was tired of being a virgin. And since, especially in her inebriated state, she wasn't looking for a long-term boyfriend, Remy checked all the boxes for what she wanted in a sexual partner: at least moderately attractive, a nice body from all the swimming he did for the water polo team, and most importantly, being in possession of some sexual experience. If her first time wasn't going to be emotionally rewarding, it should at least be instructive.

The next day, when Sarah fully realized what had transpired the night before, she kept waiting to feel different. Something momentous had happened in her life, right? However, other than a little soreness, she didn't feel much different at all. Remy cooked her a surprisingly competent breakfast of scrambled eggs and rye toast with salted olive oil instead of butter (which Sarah found quite good). They ate, mostly in awkward silence, at the large island in the kitchen amongst an obstacle course of half-empty Solo cups and beer bottles from the night before. After breakfast, he drove Sarah to Stacie's, and Stacie drove her home, preserving her cover story that she had been with her friend all night.

That evening, as she wrote in her diary, Sarah decided that, while sleeping with Remy hadn't been the magical experience some girls dream about when imagining how they'd lose their v-cards, neither had it been terrible. Remy had been mostly gentlemanly about everything, and Sarah was happy to have gotten that whole awkward virginity thing out of the way.

The party was on a Friday night, so it was only a day later that she saw Chris. She remembered feeling they were now more equals—both adults.

"What are you in such a good mood about?" Chris said when he caught her giggling to herself between shooting drills.

"Nothing," Sarah said and smirked.

Of course, Sarah's feelings about her first sexual experience changed that Monday at school when she began hearing people whisper *pescado* any time she walked by them in the halls or in the cafeteria. Since Sarah took French not Spanish, she had no idea what this meant, but she sent Stacie out to inquire (she was also in French class), and she informed Sarah the word meant "fish." Apparently, Remy had described sleeping with her as being with a *cold, dead, floppy fish*. "Yeah, you can put your dick in it," he was reported to have said, "but it just sorta lies there." When any of this was translated into Spanish was anyone's guess.

The next morning, Sarah told her mom she was sick and stayed home. This was a big deal because it was a game night against the cross-town rival, and school policy was that if a student didn't show up for class on a particular day, they weren't allowed to play in the game. Sarah's team lost by twenty and fell out of first place in the standings.

When Sunday came around, Chris again noted Sarah's mood but this time observed how down she looked.

"I'm just feeling a little sick still," she told him. But then, while working on drop steps from the left block, Sarah—like a water balloon that'd been filled just a smidgen too much—burst. Chris, taken off guard by Sarah's sudden display of emotion, stopped practice.

"Let's take a break," he said and they drove to a nearby coffee shop. He bought her hot chocolate; she told him everything.

Afterwards, as he often did, Chris drove Sarah home. Just before she got out of the car to walk up to the house, Chris reached across the gearshift and hugged her tightly. "Keep your head up, girl."

Sarah was slightly taken aback. He'd hugged her before, but it had always been of that athlete, pat-on-the-back, good-job variety. This was the first time he'd hugged her with any emotion—even if that emotion was just sympathy. By the time Sarah made it up the long path to her front door, she was already feeling better.

By spring Mrs. D'Albero began showing a little concern at how much time Sarah and Chris spent together. "Shouldn't you be looking to spend time with boys your age?"

"What do you mean?" Sarah said, indignant. "Chris has a *girlfriend*. We're just friends." By then Sarah had met Chris's girlfriend on a couple occasions. Her name was Nadine and she was a petite Korean girl with skin like porcelain and every time Sarah saw her it seemed like she'd just gotten a manicure. She was pretty, but in a way that Sarah found annoying. Here Chris was this down-to-earth coach who was tough and always preaching hard work, and yet his girlfriend looked like she belonged in a wax museum behind a velvet rope and a sign that read *Please Do Not Touch the Sculptures.* And even though Sarah had met Nadine, Chris still didn't like to talk about their relationship. Any time Sarah asked Chris about how things were going, he would clam up and give her a noncommittal "you know."

Mr. D'Albero liked Chris and would occasionally invite him over to play poker and smoke seventy-five-dollar cigars with some of his friends and business associates. The way Sarah saw things, having Chris around made her dad feel progressive and hip. As if somehow, even though he was a middle-aged, fiscally conservative, white CEO, having a strapping, athletic, young black man around was a testament to how he could still let loose, have a good time, be cool.

That summer Sarah and Chris were up at Mohegan Sun catching the Third Eye Blind concert when she again asked him how things were with Nadine. She wasn't sure why she bothered. She'd never gotten an interesting answer and wasn't expecting one now. She nearly dropped her Dr. Pepper when Chris replied. "We broke up."

"Oh, are you okay?" she said. She tried to hide her excitement, her utter, complete joy.

"Yeah, I'm fine," he said. "What do you think of the band?"

Particularly at night lying in bed, in the still, dark moments before consciousness left her, Sarah liked to imagine what it would be like to have Chris as a boyfriend—or a husband even. She'd picture, in her mind's eye, what her name would look like with his last name replacing her own; she'd wrap her arms and legs around her body pillow, pretending it was him lying beside her.

You've really grown into a beautiful young woman, he'd say.

She'd blush, bite her lip to stifle her growing smile.

Thanks, I guess, she'd say coyly.

The first time anything "happened" was during Sarah's junior year. *Shakespeare in Love* came out in the theaters that year, and Sarah talked Chris into going with her. They had gone to movies in the past, but since this was a "romantic" movie, and she didn't want to take any flak from her mom, she told her parents she was going with Stacie. In truth, she *had* seen the movie with Stacie only the week prior but had been so moved, so emotionally wrecked by the film, that now she wanted to watch it with Chris.

That night after the movie, Sarah and Chris sat in his car and talked about how sad it was that William Shakespeare didn't end up with Gwyneth Paltrow. Chris admitted he'd liked the film more than he'd thought, and might have—just maybe—teared up a little. Sarah laughed and leaned in to hug him.

Did he kiss her or vice versa? He had tilted her head upward towards his, she thought. But whose mouth closed the final distance, those last three inches? Did it matter?

They didn't talk much on the drive home, but when he stopped in front of Sarah's house (he didn't go down the driveway on account of Sarah telling him that she'd told her parents she was with Stacie), Sarah was about to get out of the car when he grabbed her wrist.

"I like you," he said. "You're an awesome girl, really. But what we did today was a mistake. And we can't do that anymore," he said.

Chris didn't mention the kiss the next time they met at the gym. He did mention how he'd gotten three Knicks tickets from a friend and that he'd be happy to take her if she wanted to bring Stacie. Sarah would have jumped at the opportunity to go anywhere with Chris but was especially excited about the Knicks that year since they'd just gotten Latrell Sprewell, her favorite player when she lived in the Bay Area, from the Warriors. Sarah begged Stacie to come along so her own parents would give her permission. Stacie agreed and the two hatched a plan.

A week later, the three of them—Chris and Sarah and Stacie—drove down to New York. After the game, as Stacie and Sarah had agreed beforehand, Stacie abruptly left, saying she was going to stay overnight with her cousin who was a freshman at NYU. Alone now, Chris and Sarah walked through the wintry New York streets, down Sixth Avenue and eventually to Washington Square Park. It was there, near the large stone arch that was frequently featured on her favorite television show, *Felicity*, that she kissed him again. When their lips parted, she looked at him. Underneath his flimsy mask of feigned surprise, Sarah could see he'd been waiting for her to do it—that he couldn't bring himself to initiate, that that would be implicating himself, but now that she'd pushed things beyond the threshold, his conscience was sufficiently at ease to wriggle out of its self-imposed caution.

"This isn't right," he said weakly.

"I'm not a kid anymore."

"I know, but . . ."

"You know that in Connecticut the age of consent is sixteen," she said. She wasn't sure if this was true but thought she remembered someone at school saying this.

"Whoa! Consent? That suggests a lot more than this," he said, gesturing to their two mouths.

"What, you don't want to? You don't think I'm pretty?" she said.

"I'm your coach."

"Not really. Coach Donahue is my coach. You're like a tutor. I mean . . . I tutor some seniors in French."

They hardly spoke on the ride home, but when they were fifteen minutes from Sarah's house, Chris got off the highway in Norwalk and pulled into the parking lot of the Best Western. "Stay here," he said and got out of the car to go to the reception area. A few minutes later, he got back in the car and pulled it around back where he parked again. This time when he got out, he turned to her. "You coming or what?"

Soon the season was over, which meant Chris and Sarah were scheduled to increase their weekly meet-ups back to twice a week. Tuesdays they'd have their drills and basketball, the same as always except maybe Chris would sneak in a kiss when they were in the car. On Thursdays however, they'd steal away to some inexpensive motel to fuck for ninety minutes, shower, and have Sarah home in time for dinner with Paul and her parents. After a few weeks, the motel rooms were getting expensive, and they started just going to Chris's apartment instead. They were wary at first since Chris had a roommate, but his roommate Bill, who seemed to be perpetually high, either didn't notice how young Sarah was or didn't care.

Time passed, and Sarah's perception of her relationship with Chris changed. At first, she'd felt she was doing something illicit; despite the argument she'd presented to Chris in New York, she *was* sleeping with her coach. Increasingly though, she started to think of Chris as her boyfriend. She thought she saw the same change in him: he started to love her as an equal, a normal girlfriend, not some weird Lolita fantasy. Of course, Chris never used the word "girlfriend." Even when they were completely alone he could only speak about what they were doing in code. Sex was just "hanging out," and he would seldom directly admit to having romantic feelings for her, instead just telling her she was "special."

They continued through the rest of Sarah's junior year, and, for the most part, things were great. There were little things that bothered her about the relationship, not the least of which was that she couldn't tell anyone about it (Stacie was her sole confidante). Also, Chris would do this thing where when some subject would come up—usually regarding something that happened in the late seventies or early eighties—he'd say, "Oh, that was before your time." She hated this. Just because she was a little kid in the eighties didn't mean she didn't know who the fuck Jimmy Carter was.

They hiked a lot. It was safer to spend time together out in the wilderness where they weren't going to run into anyone. Chris bought a book detailing forty different hikes in Connecticut and they hit up all the spots within an hour's drive. One of their favorite trails was at this place called "Sleeping Giant" near Quinnipiac University. Sometimes they'd find little spots off the trail and set up a lunch picnic. They'd bring sandwiches and Wheat Thins and cheese, and sometimes Sarah would bring her sketchbook and draw while they were eating.

Spring semester Sarah's grades slipped a little, which caused concern in the D'Albero household, but she was still above a three point five and was happier than she'd ever been. She teased Chris a lot about him taking her to junior prom. This seemed to bother him. She ended up taking her gay friend Lucas Gagnon to the dance but, as soon as the event was over, drove straight to Chris's place. Chris made a big show of unzipping the back of her purple sequined dress, kissing each of her vertebrae as he pulled the zipper down, down, down.

Sarah was gone for the majority of that July and August on a family vacation to France and Scandinavia. A larger conglomerate had acquired her father's company, allowing him to take six months off before starting to think about his next job.

Towards the beginning of the trip, Sarah sent Chris a couple postcards with coded language and routine pleasantries that were parent-safe in case they read them, but she quickly grew tired of sending these censored correspondences, especially since she wasn't being rewarded with any word back. She managed to send him a single email, but those were the early days of the internet, and the only way to get access was in one of the few internet cafés scattered around Oslo and Paris. It wasn't until late August, when Sarah got back to the States, that she heard much from him.

When she finally saw him at the gym during their first training session after her family trip, Sarah sensed something between them had changed. Gone was any playfulness; when she'd make an attempt at flirtation, he'd pretend not to notice. He made a specific effort of avoiding excessive physical contact when they were doing box out drills and they were both trying to rebound the ball.

Nearly a month had passed, and the school year had started before Sarah got Chris alone away from the court and could ask him what was wrong.

He told her nothing was wrong. They were getting coffee after Sarah had begged him at least a half dozen times.

"How can you say that? Something's obviously wrong."

No. Nothing. He'd just been really busy is all.

That night Sarah cried for an hour before falling asleep.

In the weeks that followed, Chris kept finding excuses as to why he couldn't spend time with her, and the only time they made love was one night when Sarah went over to his apartment unannounced and found that Chris had been out drinking in Stamford with Bill. When Chris saw her at his door, she told him she was just in the neighborhood and thought she'd stop by. Inside his room, he told her he was tired and that maybe they could grab another coffee real soon. When she kissed him though, put her hand on his semi-erect cock, he didn't push her away.

Afterwards, as they lay in bed, a considerably soberer Chris told Sarah that he loved her, but they needed to stop this. *Really* this time. This absolutely could not happen again.

His words were bittersweet; he'd never told her he loved her before.

"Okay," she said. She'd seen it coming. She felt pride in how adult she was being—how she wasn't overreacting and was, in fact, accepting what Chris was saying. Almost before she could finish mentally patting herself on the back, she remembered her birthday was coming up. She made a request for the two of them to spend time together just once more. A "birthday present."

He reluctantly agreed and Sarah, with a license now, drove herself home.

Sarah's birthday was at the end of October, right around when she would begin practicing with the school team and when her sessions with Chris would go back down to once a week anyway. That would be as good a time as any to make a clean break from their off-court activities.

Over the days leading up to her birthday Sarah talked with Stacie a lot and she'd started to feel better about everything. In the last year, she'd grown so much and was wiser and maybe now was the right time to find a boy her own age for once or just be single for a little while.

"And ready to mingle," Stacie interjected.

"You're stupid," Sarah said.

She couldn't spend her actual birthday with Chris because her parents wanted to have a family dinner. Instead, Chris and Sarah planned to spend the following day, a Saturday, together. The night of her birthday, as Sarah and her family were preparing to leave the house, Sarah started getting suspicious because of how erratic her little brother Paul was acting. Sure enough, when they arrived at the restaurant, Stacie and a bunch of Sarah's other friends were there for a surprise party. Sarah wasn't sure if Chris had been invited, and she immediately swiveled her head around looking for him. When she got Stacie alone, her friend told her Chris had said he was busy and couldn't make it.

The next night, after Sarah returned from spending the evening with Chris, she went up to her room, locked the door, and sat alone in the dark, letting her tears flow freely. It had been a good night—a wonderful night, but it was over. She told herself it would be okay; she accepted that she and Chris couldn't be together. Still, it hurt knowing she'd been with him for the last time.

She heard her mom coming up the stairs and asking how her night with Stacie at the movies was. Sarah straightened herself up and told her it was great, but she just remembered she'd left something at Stacie's.

"It's already late, Sar," her mother said. "Can't it just wait until tomorrow?"

But she was already running past her mom, putting on her shoes, getting her keys. "I'll only be gone for a little while," she said.

She shouldn't be doing this, but it was still the same night, so maybe she was within her rights? She would just hug him and kiss him once, savoring the taste of his mouth, and be on her way. She didn't have much time anyway. The drive to Chris's apartment was further than the drive to Stacie's, so she had to hurry to not raise any suspicion with her mom.

At Chris's place, there was an unfamiliar car parked in the driveway, but Sarah assumed Bill had maybe gotten a new car or had someone over. She was nervous walking up the path to the front door because she was worried Chris might be upset she was making him go through all the goodbyes again. When she got up to the porch and was about to ring the doorbell, Sarah looked through the blinds of the kitchen window and saw Nadine sitting at the table with Chris. They each had half-empty glasses of wine in their hands and were talking and smiling. Chris looked so happy.

Sarah couldn't decide whether she wanted to ring the doorbell or run away. When Chris inadvertently turned his head in Sarah's direction, the smile on his face dissolved. He said something to Nadine that Sarah couldn't hear and came to the door. Sarah started back in the direction of her car.

She could hear the door opening behind her. "Sarah," he called out to her. "Sarah!"

She spun around, giving him the briefest moment to say something that would alleviate the pain in her chest.

"It's not what it looks like," he said, which was the worst possible response, a bad cliché. She turned back towards the car.

Chris ran after her in his bare feet and grabbed her arm.

"Don't touch me!"

"Listen," he said, not letting go, "she was just over to talk."

"Oh, she just stopped over? You didn't know she was coming when you were with me... *hanging out?*"

"Well, she told me she wanted to come and talk but—"

"But you guys are just totally friends. Just pals, chums."

Chris hesitated, the words caught in his throat. She could see Nadine standing on the porch with a concerned expression. Sarah pushed past Chris back towards the house.

When Nadine saw Sarah approaching, she went back inside.

"Hey, Nadine," she said.

Chris grabbed her shoulder. "What are you doing, Sar?" he said.

"Make sure he washes the sheets before you lie down in his bed because he just fucked me there, okay?" Sarah didn't wait to see Nadine's reaction but ran back out to the car.

"Hold on, Sarah."

She again pushed past him, got in her car, and locked the door, nearly slamming the thing on Chris's fingers. He stood beside the car but didn't try to stop her from driving off.

She took a circuitous route home to let off some steam and had been gone for an hour by the time she returned—far longer than it should have taken her to get back from Stacie's. She pulled up the driveway without her lights on and tried to sneak in the side door so she could pretend she'd been home for a long time; however, her mom saw her from the kitchen going up the side stairs and followed her to her room.

"Where have you been?" Mrs. D'Albero said.

"Stacie's."

"I just called Stacie's, and her mom said she never saw you. Stacie isn't even home."

She tried to think up another lie. Maybe she met Stacie elsewhere, or maybe she was actually sneaking out to see a boy, albeit a boy her own age. But Sarah no longer had it in herself to deceive anyone.

Her mother put her arms around her, got her a Kleenex, and Sarah thought about those times right after Emily died when they would hug for hours at a time. And so, feeling safe and so loved in her mother's arms, Sarah divulged everything—more than everything, really. In fact, she consciously told the story with Chris in a manner that would make him sound as monstrous as possible without telling any outright lies. No, he didn't rape her, but he coerced her, manipulated her, pretended he loved her when he was just trying to get between her legs. And perhaps this was the truth—a kind of truth. And Sarah thought for many years about the story she told that night and how much venom was flowing through her veins as she told it and whether or not Chris deserved it. For that night at least, she just wanted him to suffer.

She was very clear to her parents that she didn't want any kind of charges filed. It would be too painful for her to deal with the police. That said, she did, if not encourage, at least tacitly allow her parents to punish Chris to the fullest extent of their, not insignificant, influence. He, of course, was no longer employed by the D'Alberos as Sarah's coach, but Sarah's parents went further, going to the district Chris taught in to make sure he was fired there as well. He never taught again as far as Sarah knew, and he moved out of the area a few months later.

Some years later, when social media became widespread, Sarah learned that Chris and Nadine had ended up getting married. She wasn't sure what he told Nadine about that night—if he told the truth, or his version of it, or else if he lied and said that Sarah was a psychotic little rich girl.

For years after, past college and through her twenties, Sarah never stopped thinking about what happened with Chris. On nights when she didn't have any plans and when there was nothing good on TV, she'd sometimes flip through all of her old sketchbooks and look at the things she'd drawn. Most of the images were of trees and leaves and birds, but quite a few of them were of Chris: Chris holding a basketball, Chris in his car from her vantage point in the front passenger seat, Chris sitting across from her on an outspread blanket during one of their hikes at the "Sleeping Giant."

If they had accidentally been found out and Chris had received the same punishments, she doubted she'd feel so conflicted. Rather, it was that she had broken the trust between them and had done so out of jealousy. She couldn't escape the knowledge that she had *tried* to ruin Chris's life—had partially succeeded—not because he had done something terrible, but because he had the gall to want someone else after telling her they couldn't be together.

It was difficult for Sarah to talk to people about Chris because they would immediately assume she'd been victimized and that her insistence that she had not been victimized was further proof of her victimization. She might have been a naïve teenager, but even with a decade of distance, she didn't feel she'd been manipulated, taken advantage of, raped. She could acknowledge that Chris had done wrong by her, but she'd done wrong by him too.

She wondered where he was, if he ever thought about her, if he'd forgiven her.

Not long after Sarah's thirtieth birthday, she ran into Chris at the Stewart Lenard's in Norwalk in the produce section. She was home for the weekend and had gone to pick up some groceries for the meal that night. She recognized him immediately. He was still in pretty good shape but had a little gray at his temples. She was anxious as to how he'd react to seeing her, but she couldn't attribute all of her nervousness to that.

There was pain in his eyes when he saw her but also warmth. Seeing this, that she had mattered, gave her dual jolts of joy and hurt.

She told him she was married, happy. This was half true.

I'm glad, he said.

She asked him, what about him, was he married? She didn't mention she knew about Nadine.

"I was," he said. "But, you know."

"Yeah, life," Sarah said.

Life.

The things that happen to us.

But we soldier on because that's all we can do.

He didn't try to hug her or even shake her hand. He just smiled a little, told her to take care, and pushed his cart on towards the frozen food aisle.

When, a few days later, Sarah returned to Philadelphia from visiting her family, she kept thinking about Chris. By now, it'd been years since she'd lied to her now husband about the day she would live over again—more than enough time for one of his mythical beings to go from birth to full adulthood and more than enough time for her lie, combined with the problems they already had, to join together and become their undoing.

From The Introduction to *Padgett's Rise and Fall of the Alderian Empire*, **published 613 Years After** *The Fall* **on the quadricentennial anniversary of the Alderian Empire**

Throughout the four-hundred-year history of the Alderian Empire, there have been numerous periods of expansions and contractions, from its establishment in 213 YAF, when the City-States were brought under Alderian rule with the marriage of Silas I and Princess Casta of Brigantium, through the present day. The most prolific and protracted period of expansion, which lasted up until the death of Emperor Kaleb in 601 YAF, can be said to have begun with the reign of Emperor Patrin I (438–482 YAF), the second emperor of the Lunaris dynasty. The long-lasting support and success of this expansion can undoubtedly be attributed to the fact that Patrin supported his military endeavors with moral, rather than solely practical justifications, which in turn kept support for expansion strong amongst the populace. Central to these moral justifications was the *Doctrine of Continental Unification*. While, even contemporary to its practice, there was much criticism of the philosophical underpinnings of the doctrine, not least of which were how it infringed upon the sovereignty of other nations and was in no small part the catalyst to several armed conflicts, an objective person cannot deny that even today there remains some moral persuasiveness to the doctrine's arguments.

The doctrine states that in light of the many bloody and costly wars that took place prior to and during the ascension (and tragically short reign) of Patrin's father, Tomasis I, the only way to ensure a lasting peace was through the collapsing of political boundaries of nearby nations into the formation of a single political, military and economic entity, which would unite the Continent under Alderian rule. Creating such an entity would certainly necessitate armed conflict; however, the end goal would justify the means. The doctrine goes on to lay out a series of complex mathematical calculations with assumptions around population growth and expected "happiness scores" for the peasantry, aristocracy, etc. that make a compelling, common-sense case for Unification and "prove within any reasonable set of assumptions" that Continental Unification was in fact the *only* morally permissible path.

According to the doctrine (which was followed closely by subsequent emperors), the Unification of the Continent should not happen in a short period but rather should take place over several generations of Imperial expansion in a way that minimized casualties and maximized human utility. Although other sovereign states might be conquered, it was the moral imperative of the Empire to "conquer responsibly," in a manner that minimized civilian death while still maximizing the deterrent to future opponents from resisting annexation.

To these ends, for most of the more than 160 years preceding Emperor Kaleb's death, whenever the Empire went to war, they had a very exacting way of following the doctrine's suggestions. After each successful military campaign, the Empire would calculate all of its expenses—including compensation for their widows, loss of productivity, etc. These expenses would then be repaid, with a market rate of interest, from the conquered nation via reparations. After reparations were paid, the annexed territory would enter the Empire as a province in good standing. This policy served the Empire's military and political goals in two ways:

1. The Empire would nearly always recoup the cost of their wars (with a fair return). The importance of this is not to be minimized. The economic damage that multiple armed conflicts can have on a nation has been, throughout history, one of the factors that has led to many nations' collapse or near collapse (for example, the Lanzhenese dynasties of the 300s, the Phaidonians, etc.). By making sure that all armed conflicts subsequently led to economic gains, or, at the very least, economic breakeven, the Alderians prevented themselves from falling into this trap, which was yet another reason the military campaigns of the Empire, for the most part, remained popular amongst the citizenry.

2. The mathematic precision with which the Alderian Empire enacted
their reparations on the nations it warred against provided an
incentive for those nations not to fight to the bitter end and instead
to work towards brokering a peace, which would inevitably include
annexation. In the end, the opponents of the Alderians knew that
since they would likely lose in the end anyway, any damage done to
the Alderians was, in essence, damage done to themselves in terms
of longer periods of servitude and greater payments of natural
resources upon the end of the fighting.

For generations, conventional wisdom was that, whether one
agreed with the expansions of the Alderian Empire or the idea of
Continental Unification, they could not deny the efficacy of the
Empire's doctrines and strategies in making expansion an ongoing
military, political, and economic success. It was not until that
cataclysm we have come to call The Great Uprising (590–593 YAF)
embroiled the Continent in the worst conflict in recorded history that
public sentiment around Imperial expansion changed in earnest. As I
will detail in the section of this book devoted to those terrible years,
and which most contemporary readers of this volume know all too
well, the war between the Alderians and The Northern Alliance laid
waste to much of the northern half of the Continent. What is less
documented is how in the years following, the war's destruction finally
swayed public opinion against expansion. In turn, when Emperor
Kaleb finally succumbed to a case of the sweating sickness in 601
YAF, the conditions were set for the end of expansion and the first
substantive change in Alderian military policy in two centuries.

FOUR

THE RED RIDER

590 Years After *The Fall*

Despite talk of war in the daily assembly, all Governor Joram could think of was how he'd managed to forget the girl's damned birthday. Some grandfather he was. The others had just left the council chamber, and Gareth and Joram had moved to the private quarters when the chamberlain brought up the subject.

"Given the news from the North and how busy you've been, Lord Governor, I went ahead and had a suitable gift purchased." Gareth offered up the proposed item. The doll looked minuscule in his massive hand.

"Gods damn it!" Joram said.

"I'm sorry. Did you wish to select Corinne's gift yourself? We can probably still make it to the market before closing. Or we could go tomorrow before your visit."

What else was he forgetting? His wits and memory were pretty much the last useful things he had. If they'd gone, he'd have truly completed his transformation into a useless pile of flesh. To top it off, he was in a foul mood from the heat. They were deep into *autumn*, yet the air felt more like the inside of a smithy than two weeks before the winter solstice. Over thirty years and he still couldn't get used to this cursed desert climate.

A knock sounded on the door. Joram bid whomever it was enter. One of the guards walked in, panting and out of breath from running up the hundred and twenty-six tower steps.

"Lord…Governor…A rider…approaches from the north," he said and saluted.

Joram shuffled over to the north-facing window—the usual stiffness in his ankles and knees, a chafing where the perspiration from his inner thigh rubbed against his scrotum. Gareth pulled the magnascope down from its mount and handed it to him. Joram took the bronze cylinder, but his hand, as it was wont to, shook involuntarily as he held the thing. He stared disgustedly at his trembling, frail hand, trying to will it into stillness. It was no use and, after a few moments, he gave up and walked to the window.

Using this device from here atop the keep, which travelers called *The Oasis Obelisk*, one could see a man's face from a league's distance. Down the hill past the sandstone walls of Wahan town, beyond the wooden shanties surrounding the market and the lightly fortified outer wall, Joram saw only the golden-brown of the vast desert baking in the afternoon sun. Far to the north the red mountains rose up like flames from the earth, beyond which lay Kallanboro, nestled against the sea.

"I don't see anyone," he said before breaking into a fit of coughing. This recurrent cough hadn't broken for three months despite everything the healers had tried: the elixirs, the potions, the herbs, the leaching, the needling, the burning of mugwort, the attaching of glass cups, the flushing of nasal cavities, the breathing in of medicinal steam. Often at night his bouts would be so violent he'd taste blood in his raw throat.

"Spittoon," he said, and Gareth brought it to him. He dredged up a darkish green something and spewed it into the porcelain bowl. "Now where . . .?" Before the guard could answer, Joram saw him: a solitary rider cloaked in Imperial red atop a black destrier, now a mile or so from the outer wall.

"Ah, there," he said. "One of ours. But just one."

"Perhaps he rides ahead of a host from the capital," said Gareth.

"He rides from the north," Joram said. Much of Wahan had been built directly into the northern-facing cliffside and could not be approached from the south except by skilled climbers with ropes. Yet anyone traveling from the capital would undoubtedly approach from the west after circling around the cliffs.

"There's been word of sandstorms outside town," Gareth said. "A large army may wish to avoid such dangers by way of a more circuitous route."

The chamberlain was forever the optimist; Joram on the other hand, was too old, had seen too much, for optimism.

He turned to the guard. "Tell Constable Selbaird to have the rider escorted here. And Gareth, have the servants bring bread and wine…And wrap up that doll."

Gareth and the guard hurried down the stairwell. In his younger days, Joram would have just as soon gone to talk to Selbaird and the servants himself; he wasn't born into nobility and took no pleasure in being waited on. But given the condition of his legs—his gnarled, yellowed toes; his knees, which ground like rusted door hinges when bent—he had little choice. Sometimes he had half a mind to just set up makeshift quarters in the library downstairs. It would be easier to get around, not to mention cooler. Yet, as Gareth liked to remind him, it was "unbecoming" of a governor to sleep in the library. Imperial pomp and circumstance! Who was working for who here?

Gareth had been the Governor's chamberlain for three years. Like his now-deceased father and predecessor, Gareth was a serious, dutiful man and a good chamberlain, which was lucky because he would have been terrible at anything else. Although the boy was strong as a bear (and nearly as big) with massive tree-trunk legs and an extra head's worth of height on any other man in town, he was clumsy and couldn't hold a smith's hammer, much less a sword, worth a turd. When he was young the other boys in town used to torment him. *Gareth Half Giant,* they'd called him. Gareth was twenty-six now: the same age Thom had been when he'd left.

While Joram awaited Selbaird and Gareth's return, he busied himself with signing all the documents they'd put before him at assembly. The builders would be ordered to begin constructing additional fortifications. The smiths and the fletchers were to work overtime to craft an ample surplus of arms. Requisitions for additional water and grain and wood would go out immediately to the surrounding oases. And all of it would be paid for, not with silver, but Imperial certificates. Joram was going to have a lot of displeased citizens on his hands. Better displeased than put to the sword.

Merchant caravans first brought news of the events to the north a month ago. At first, they paid the stories little notice. But as the second and then third reports came in, they couldn't be ignored. A terrible army had come from The Islands—no, from the lands beyond the sea, flying under the banner of a clenched fist and terrorizing the villages and farms outside

Kallanboro. Those who resisted were butchered and the rest were made slaves and sent back over the water. Or so went the rumors.

Over time the accounts became more troubling and bizarre. Some spoke of riders atop enormous beasts whose hides couldn't be punctured by arrows. Others told of sorcery and fire and rock raining down from the sky. Perhaps these were all exaggerations. But even exaggerations are based on some small piece of truth. In Joram's own soldiering days, far in the West, he'd seen too much that to this day he couldn't explain. Then a fortnight ago, he saw firsthand the ragged group of refugees who'd arrived from out of the desert: skeletal children missing limbs, men burned all over their bodies. A few of them had stayed in town, but most continued on as soon as they'd eaten a meal and refilled their skins. Finally, ten days ago news came from Kallanboro. The city was under siege.

No further word came after that.

Joram hoped this army would have little reason to travel here, a barren trading outpost in the middle of nowhere. Yet if these fiends were willing to brave the desert, this was the most direct route south—if that's where they were headed. He'd written letters to the capital beseeching aid. Otherwise, all they could do for now was prepare and wait.

The sun was starting to set, but the heat would take another few hours to subside. As Joram finished signing the documents, he ate grapes from a silver platter that had been left for him earlier and sopped up sweat from his brow with his kerchief.

The sound of footsteps echoed up the stairwell. Joram went into the council chamber. The servants were laying out wine and bread, and Gareth stood in the doorway looming over Constable Selbaird and the red-cloaked rider who they'd seen from afar.

Gareth gestured to the rider. "As you've requested, Lord Governor."

"Lieutenant," Joram said, recognizing the rider's rank from the insignia on his chest. His blood-red cloak had turned clay brown from the sand and dust.

"Lord Governor," he said and bowed. "You are one of us then?" Something about him was very familiar, although Joram was certain he'd never met him before. The tanned skin on his face was taut—not a wrinkle—but he didn't look young either. He was clean-shaven, as were all Imperial officers. And then Joram realized what it was. His eyes. He had the same powerful, bright green eyes—the same shape even.

"Long ago." Joram gestured to the old sword and breastplate on the wall above the hearth.

"Once the Order, always the Order," the lieutenant said, the motto. There had been a time when Joram gave a shit for sayings and honor and what-all, but like his youth and his continence and the dark hair that grew from the top of his head, those things were all long gone.

"And your name?"

"Benedictus," he said.

"Benedictus. A good Alderian name," Joram said.

"Do we not all live under the banner of the Empire?" he said.

"For now, at least. You go by Ben?"

"If you prefer."

"I don't. Benedictus, then. Sit?" He beckoned to the rectangular oak table.

The four men sat. "Tell me," Joram said, "is it too much to hope you're a front rider from the capital and that your host will be arriving shortly?"

"I ride from Kallanboro," Benedictus said.

"So the siege has ended," the constable interjected, unconsciously pulling at his gray-speckled black beard. The constable was always pulling on that blasted beard and leaving hairs all over the place.

Benedictus didn't say anything at first. "In a manner," he said then, under his breath.

"Speak plainly," Joram said. He took a swallow of the warm water in his goblet. It was said that during the summer the rich in the capital would drink cold glacier water from the mountains. In another life, perhaps he would be a rich man in the capital.

"The city has fallen."

"*Kallanboro* fell?" Selbaird said.

Shit. Shit. Shit.

Kallanboro, "Jewel of the North" and home of those famed Kallanbori cavalry archers, was one of the most heavily fortified cities in all the Empire. Joram tried not to visibly react. A panicked leader breeds panic.

"Ten days past, two others of my order, seventy or so refugees and I all fled the city when the walls were breached. A few ships outran the blockade. I do not know what happened to the others who stayed behind. We escorted the refugees, most on foot, up the highway to the east. I departed from the group at The Crossroads three days ago and come this way only to give warning on my way back to the capital."

"Your group made it from Kallanboro to The Crossroads in seven days on foot?" said Selbaird. Such a journey would require over ten leagues of marching a day, more than half through mountains and desert.

"Not all the refugees survived," Benedictus said. His voice seemed to strain with the memory of it.

They sat for hours listening to the lieutenant's story. When it grew dark, Gareth had the servants come in and light the wrought-iron candelabra scattered around the room, and they spoke long into the evening.

After a few early skirmishes in the grasslands to the west of the city, the Kallanbori had retreated behind the city walls. Afterwards, nearly twenty thousand of the enemy laid siege, many mounted on horse or camel or other manner of beast that the lieutenant hadn't seen before. They brought timber on ships and built siege engines: towers and battering rams and trebuchets, which they used to launch boulders from a nearby quarry and diseased parts of men they had captured and killed. A blockade of enemy vessels prevented anyone from sailing in or out of the port. Still, the city's defenses held up well and supplies were plentiful. Then, a week into the siege, the walls were breached. Whether by tunneling or scaling or treachery, the enemy had gotten inside and opened one of the side gates. From there it had been a massacre. Thousands perished, soldiers and civilians both. The Kallanbori cavalry archers had earned their reputation on the plains outside the city, not fighting in city streets and side alleys.

"And what do we know about their motives or identity?" Joram said then.

"Little, Lord Governor. When first they arrived, their emissary, dressed in green like all their lot was, demanded unconditional surrender but refused to treat with us further. Some of the attackers appeared to be Islanders, and from what I know of my history, the Islanders have plenty of reason to dislike the Empire."

At least a dozen peoples—throughout the Continent and beyond, victims of near two hundred years of aggressive Alderian expansion—had reason to hate the Empire. "Whoever they were," Benedictus went on, "the Commander refused their terms, the walls of Kallanboro being strong as they are."

"And what of the rumors of sorcery?" said Selbaird.

Benedictus seemed to hesitate now. "I know nothing of sorcery," he said, "but I will tell you that this army was not like any I have seen. The boulders their trebuchets threw over the walls exploded with fire. And when the city had fallen and we battled in the streets, it was as if an unnatural despair attacked us from within, whilst the green clad devils attacked from without. This was not the normal fear of battle, but something darker, heavier."

Exploding boulders. Unnatural despair. Shit. Shit. Shit. This lieutenant didn't seem like an exaggerator and that made Joram nervous.

The hour was late and the governor had a headache. He adjourned the meeting. There would be much to do the next day. He ordered the constable to send riders out to all the homesteads beyond the outer wall and give warning. If those living outside Wahan wished to come to town, they'd make accommodations for them. Also, his men should make sure those residing between the inner and outer walls be ready, if necessary, to move inside the town proper. In the event they had a siege, they didn't have near enough men to guard the outer wall in earnest; instead, they would give up the outer wall and burn everything between it and the inner one. They couldn't have an enemy building siege engines out of their houses.

"And Gareth," Joram said, before everyone was dismissed, "make sure the lieutenant has a room suitable for his rank."

"Yes, Lord Governor," he said and bowed. As everyone rose to leave, Gareth turned to Joram and said under his breath, "The package we spoke of. It is wrapped and in your chamber." Joram nodded. He'd completely forgotten. Again.

Gareth left with Benedictus. The servants from earlier were waiting outside the chamber. Gareth told them to bring the lieutenant's dinner to his room and one of the servants followed them down the stairs. "Will you still be taking your meal, Lord Governor?" the remaining servant, the young woman, asked. He nodded.

Selbaird stood up, "My men will begin fortifying our positions on the wall at first light. I will send scouts further north. If this army is headed here, I should like to know ahead of time."

"Good," Joram said and the constable exited the chamber. The servant girl laid the meal out: roasted chicken and the earthy dirt-tasting bread that was native to the region.

"Anything else I can get you, Lord Governor?" she asked.

"No, that will be all." Her name was Saleya, or so Joram believed. She hadn't worked in the castle for more than a few months.

Her hand shook as she filled the Governor's cup from a ceramic pitcher. "You've got my affliction," he said.

"I beg your pardon, Lord Governor?" she said.

He picked up his cup and showed off his trembling hand to her.

"I'm sorry, Lord Governor."

"For me or for you? Either way, don't apologize. What's the matter?"

"Nothing, Lord," she said, but he gave her a disbelieving look. "We were waiting outside for some time."

"And you heard talk of battles and sieges?" She nodded. "Not much chance they'll come here, I think. We're being cautious."

"I am from Kallanboro, Lord. My brother and sister live there still."

Gods. Poor girl.

"The lieutenant said some escaped," he said.

"Yes. I will pray for them," she said but went on, more to herself than to Joram. "After my mother died, I cared for them like my own children."

Joram never knew what to say at times like this. "I'm sorry," he mumbled.

"Thank you, Lord Governor." She looked around the room and then out the window. "Look," she said, "it's raining."

She was right. Clouds had gathered overhead and by the moonlight, one could just barely perceive the shape of a downpour. In his younger days down south, rain was a common occurrence, but out here, every time it rained, it was a small miracle. The shower wouldn't last long—they never did—and the water would be swallowed up by the parched earth as soon as it landed. Still, it was welcome.

That night Joram dreamed of his wife, as happened more and more the last year—a sign, he sometimes thought, that he was nearing his own death and preparing to rejoin her in whatever afterlife the gods saw fit for them. The dream was ordinary enough: the two of them sitting in the two-room cottage they had shared with his mother before Thom was born—before moving to the capital and then north. Kellah prepared breakfast: eggs and the spicy mutton sausage that was native to her homeland. They talked as they ate; he put his hand to her cheek. He closed his eyes and let his fingers feel her face change into a smile. A sensation rose in his chest—something he hadn't felt for a long time. A lightness.

That was all.

Kellah had been dead for more than twenty-five years. Dysentery. Her last days had been a nightmare of vomit and shit and wretchedness and then she died. Joram still remembered the look on his son's face—standing solemnly by without tears—as he watched his mother's pyre go up in flames. It was neither Joram's way nor the way of his wife's people to burn the dead, but they'd adopted the customs of the people they lived amongst, and so she burned. Here in the desert it was thought of as a great sin to bury a body in the few patches of fertile land that the small oasis offered, and only a fool would attempt to bury a body beneath the shifting sands. At the time, Joram mistakenly took his son's stoicism for strength. But now looking back, he thought a piece of him—the best of him—burned up in that fire with Kellah.

Joram had met Kellah in the West when he was a young soldier during The Troubles. She used to wear her hair in a single long black braid that went down to her waist. She was the only woman he was ever with. That first night after they were married—just before Joram was to return east, Kellah naked in his tent, light from the flickering fire outside illuminating her skin—he remembered thinking how wondrous a creature a woman could be, a gift from the gods.

In those early days, Joram was the model of a doting husband. But time passed. Their small family—Kellah, Thom, and himself—came north and, after a short apprenticeship, Joram assumed the role of governor. The stresses of his new role changed him. He grew short-tempered and, although he never struck his wife, harsh, perhaps even cruel, words were never far from his lips. The love and passion he had felt so ardently for her cooled. After their daughter, Marielle, died at birth, Kellah lost interest in the physical aspects of marriage and there came a point when they seldom talked, much less touched, much less laid together.

The next morning, Joram woke early; it was still dark. A thin crescent of sun had peeked up over the dunes. After he dressed, he grabbed the parcel Gareth had prepared the day before and began his descent down the tower stairs. Gareth insisted he ring his pull-bell whenever he wanted to come down so that someone could accompany him. Gareth even offered to personally carry the governor. The shit with that. He made his way down slowly, gripping the railing. When he was finally downstairs, he stole into the kitchen to fetch some freshly baked bread and then walked across the dusty ward and out the side entrance of the castle, grabbing an inconspicuous cream-colored cloak so that he could limp about unnoticed.

Many of the preparations he'd discussed with Selbaird the night before were getting underway. Next to the castle, the mines, which burrowed through the cliffside, had been sealed. By the end of the day, guards armed with halberds would be posted at the entrance. While it would be impossible to bring an army or even a single mounted rider through the mines, a man on foot might navigate the tunnels and make his way into Wahan from the south. Better to be cautious than dead.

Further through town to the inner wall, everywhere Joram looked, men were beginning their work. Horse-drawn wagons rumbled down the uneven street, hauling wood from the keep, which would be used to reinforce and close the side gates. Shirtless men, a sheen of sweat already coating their sun-darkened torsos, had undertaken the complex task of re-assembling the onagers at the center gate, now the only way through the inner wall. In the outer crescent of town, between inner and outer wall, ox and ass painstakingly moved all the well water to wells or tanks in Wahan proper. Should an invading army come and they be forced to abandon the outer crescent, the waterless desert would be their surest weapon.

By the time Joram arrived at the main gate at the north end of the outer wall, day had fully broken. An old farmer who brought a cart of grapes in to market from another oasis stopped at the gate and Joram heard the watchman tell him that everyone was being called into town in case the invaders came.

Joram continued north to the top of a small dune a few hundred yards from the outer wall. It was a painful effort for him to make it so far on his own, but he also cherished the feeling—being alone, on his two feet, his knees and feet aching, a reminder they still belonged to him. North across the desert, no army could be seen bearing down on them. Instead, there was just sand and desolation and, far off, the mountains.

He'd been beyond those red peaks to Kallanboro just once in all his years here. The city had not impressed him. It was large but painfully pragmatic, not architecturally beautiful like the old Phaidonian cities to the south. Not that those cities were paradise on earth either.

He picked up a handful of the dark sand. It was cool in his palm although by midday it would be hot enough to burn skin. He released the grains into the air. A hot breeze blew from the north.

He went back into town and to the temple, his original destination. He wasn't a pious man, and if he had been, he'd have probably worshipped the gods of his own countrymen, not these northern gods. But he didn't go to the temple to pray.

One of the Sisters, who'd been lighting candles in the chapel next to the main temple hall, greeted him. He removed his cloak and bowed out of respect. He never remembered this one's name. She had an awful scar on her face that went across her forehead and down through her right temple before ending at a mangled right ear.

"You've come to see the girl, Lord Governor?" she said.

The Sister accompanied him through the orphanage that was adjoined to the temple and then over to the mess hall. Corinne wore the blue woolen dress he'd brought her the last time he'd visited and was cheerfully eating breakfast beside a ragged-looking girl missing a patch of hair the size of a coin at the side of her head. Corinne's hair had been pulled into a simple braid with ribbon woven in. She'd grown since he'd last seen her. She was starting to look like her mother: the sandy hair framing her dark skin, the aquiline nose. She had Thom's green eyes though. Joram thought of Benedictus.

"Corinne," the Sister called and the girl looked up, "the Governor has come to pay you a visit. Hurry and finish your breakfast." Corinne turned and glanced at Joram, the smile on her face vanishing.

"Lord Governor," she said. "Pardon me a few minutes and I will be ready for our visit."

Joram waited alone in the annex next door. *Lord Governor*, she'd said. He wondered whether she understood that she was his only flesh and blood left on this earth and he hers.

Gareth had suggested he could hire a governess, but he'd always responded by telling him the castle was no place for a small girl. Perhaps true, but not his real reason. But would anyone understand if he said it was just a feeling she stirred up in him? That, through no fault of her own, she acted as a reminder, when all he wanted of the time he had left was to forget.

His son…Thom…He didn't know where things had gone wrong, what he had done or not done to turn him into the man he became. Thom was never the same after his mother died, but does there not come a time when a man must be his own man and not simply a slave to his past? This is what Joram told himself.

As a boy, Thom had been a sensitive soul—gentle, like his mother. He used to sit in the arboretum, picking flowers: irises, geraniums, desert orchids, and whatever else grew there. Sometimes Joram would ask him what he thought about while picking flowers, but the boy would just run away to Kellah.

After a few minutes, the girl walked in. "Lord Governor," she said and curtsied.

"Come here," Joram said. She embraced him, but it felt like she did so out of obligation and respect for authority, not affection. He kissed her on the forehead.

"You've been doing well in your studies?"

"Yes, Lord Governor."

"Please. Call me Grandfather, or call me Joram, just please not this *Lord Governor*."

"Very well, Joram."

On second thought, he didn't like her calling him by his given name either.

"Tell me more about your studies. What do they teach you here? Weaving perhaps?"

"I do not care much for weaving. I have started to learn my letters. Once I learn my letters, the Sisters have promised I will be taught to read."

"*Read?* That's magnificent. I couldn't read until I was nearly a grown man. Of course, you're probably much smarter than I was," he said. "I have something here for you: a present for your eighth birthday." He gave the girl the small bundle and she slowly unwrapped the cloth, uncovering the doll underneath. She showed no emotion as she examined it.

"It is very generous of you, Joram," she said, as if she were a foreign diplomat the governor was receiving, "I thank you greatly for this gift."

"But do you like it?" he asked. "Does it please you?"

"Yes, it pleases me greatly," she said coldly.

Corinne's mother, Mari, was the daughter of a farmhand who worked at one of the vineyards two leagues west of town on a nearby oasis. Joram had met the man on occasion years before as he'd often accompany the vineyard's wine into town when it was brought to market. He was of an olive complexion, like most of the locals but seemed to permanently wear a vacant, unsettling expression, which gave one the idea that he was bearing some terrible burden. Mari herself, at the age of thirteen or so, had been sent to live in town as the servant for one of the wealthier merchant families. She had actually served Joram on one occasion as he dined at the house of her employer. She was quiet; one could hardly hear her when she spoke. *What would you like to drink, Lord Governor* were the only words, frightened and nearly inaudible, that Joram heard her speak that night.

She was fourteen when she began showing signs she was with child. At first, she refused to name the person who had impregnated her, but after several beatings from her father, she'd identified Joram's son. Thom denied any responsibility until the innkeeper's wife testified she'd seen the two of them together behind the slaughterhouse. He'd been drunk, Thom said then. Mari was a temptress. Joram demanded Thom marry the girl, but instead he rode off one night, to Vicus Remorum in the East, Joram later learned. Or at least that's where he was when he died.

Mari was the kind of girl you just knew would never survive a child. She was such a lithe, fragile thing. She bled to death when Corinne was born. Her funeral took place at the vineyard. As Joram watched her pyre burn to the ground, he noticed Mari's father looking hatefully in his direction. The man hated Thom—and Joram by extension. Yet Joram was governor; there was nothing a farmhand could do. He died of a fever a few months after that. When Joram learned of his death and that Corinne was being looked after by one of the other farmhands, he sent Gareth's father to bring the girl into town.

The next day in the afternoon, the lieutenant visited Joram in the castle. Joram was sitting in the library beneath the wind tower going through the inventory of supplies. Some of the provisions they'd requisitioned had arrived; if a siege were to be laid they'd be able to withstand it for some time.

The lieutenant wore a tunic of the rough-spun gray wool that was ubiquitous amongst the townspeople. Even in these common clothes there was something very remarkable-seeming, *magisterial*, about him.

"The temperature in this room is quite astounding," Benedictus said.

"A marvel of the local architecture. Cool air is pulled up from tunnels underground and flows up through the wind tower," Joram said and pointed upward to the sets of large, arched windows on each side of the rectangular stone tower overhead.

"Quite ingenious."

"I don't know why they couldn't have built one of these for my chambers. The keep is like an oven. Come sit. Have some wine." He poured the lieutenant a glass from the carafe on the desk. As he poured, his hand shook, rattling the pitcher against the glass.

"So, what news?" Joram said.

"I have been in counsel with the constable as to the fortifications. All is going according to plan."

"Excellent. And from the scouts? I haven't seen the constable all day."

"Nothing yet."

"I suppose no news of an army bearing down upon us is a good sign," Joram said. He took a long drink. "Tell me, where are you from? You don't have the look of Kallanboro about you."

"What do I have the look of then, Lord Governor?" he said.

"To tell the truth, there are aspects of your appearance that remind me…that remind me…of my son." Something in Benedictus's gaze made

Joram feel at ease but also as if his eyes could peer inside his mind, his heart. "His mother was from the West, beyond the Inner Sea, so I thought perhaps—"

"Before Kallanboro I travelled around for some years. I lived for a time in the capital. My family was from the South though. Past Hammer Bay."

"Hammer Bay...The *far* South then. I can't say I've ever been. A lot of wild country down there, I hear. They say there are still dragons."

"If those dirty beasts the size of gulls are dragons, then there are dragons. Hardly the creature of legend though."

"Stories have a way of growing as they travel. But you've seen one? A dragon?"

"Not in my village but once or twice when traveling. In my youth, I was a fisherman and, at times, we'd go nearly all the way to the Wastes."

"The Wastes? You are a remarkable man. It seems as if you've already lived the life of three or four men."

Benedictus smiled. "You know dragons are often spoken of as if they are flying lizards when, in fact, that couldn't be further from the truth. They are closer to bats, with a fine fur coating that helps them with their navigation in flight."

"Really? Interesting. And how did you like the capital? Before they rewarded all my hard work by sending me into the desert, I lived there myself for some years."

"They say Alder is the most beautiful city in the world," he said. "That it is one of the first cities built by the Phaidonians—at least outside the Old Country—after the Forefathers died off. That Lionel the Great built the city with a team of sorcerers—of Cree, *the Childless Ones*—as tribute to his wife who died from fever and that the city's beauty reflects his love for her. Indeed, the palace grounds, the obsidian walls of the Capital Building, the limestone alleys of the Merchant District, the Gardens at Erith Bay, are all sights to behold."

"But . . ."

"But most of the city is a shit hole."

Joram burst into laughter, which transformed into another fit of coughing. His body convulsed with each spasm of his chest and he stumbled out of his chair to one knee.

"Lord Governor," Benedictus said and reached to help Joram to his feet. Joram relaxed and felt the wave of coughing pass. "Shall I call a doctor?"

"No, those idiots can't help." Benedictus nodded and placed his hand on the governor's back. Joram was probably just imagining, but it almost felt as if a tingling sensation emanated from the lieutenant's hand, seeping through Joram's back to his lungs.

"Did you just…What was that?"

Benedictus looked at the Governor, confused.

"Never mind," Joram said. He regained himself, sat in his chair, and took several deep breaths. Outside in the courtyard, the guards chanted along with the routine of their daily practice session. "So, what are your plans now?"

"I ride south to receive further orders."

"I see. That makes sense. Although, if this enemy is headed here, we could use a man of your experience. Selbaird is competent, but few of our soldiers have ever seen real fighting. You're battle-tested and you have the air of command. You could do a lot more good here than down south."

"I appreciate your confidence. But protocol requires my going south."

"Shit on protocol. I'll write a letter to General Belasmus. He'll understand. He and I served together in the West long ago."

Benedictus looked at Joram as if he were trying to measure what sort of man the Governor was. "Very well," he said. "I will take you up on your offer. Notify the general and I will stay here for the time being."

Joram was pleased with the lieutenant's decision.

They continued preparations. Excess food supplies were gathered and centrally stored in the main granaries near the keep. A team of workers went about digging a trench, the depth of which was the height of a man and the width twice that, down the inside length of the inner wall. They then filled it with thousands of wooden spears so that one could only come down off the battlements using the steps at one of the three gates. What able-bodied townsmen weren't actively building the defenses were conscripted into a reserve force of pike men and archers. In all this Benedictus was invaluable. He personally headed up the training of the pike men and his knowledge of siege defense was of great use to Constable Selbaird and the engineers. The scouts kept returning with no news of import. Twice one of the scouting parties found a squalid band of refugees wandering the desert, but these poor souls had no information other than what was already known.

Every night after Joram's evening meal, Benedictus would join him atop the keep for some of the spiced tea Saleya had recently introduced the Governor to. The two men tried to limit talk of the day's events and, instead, would reminisce about their past lives and travels. Joram enjoyed speaking with someone who'd traveled beyond this town, this desert. He'd lived in Wahan so long that it was refreshing to be reminded of the world outside this little oasis.

Joram found Benedictus to be a fascinating man. Before his time in the capital he'd traveled widely and claimed to have even spent time amongst the Mandrakhar in the Westwood.

"The Scriptures hold that the Mandrakhar are a holy people, *the chosen* of the Forefathers or some such thing, right?" Joram said. There was a time in his younger days when he'd aspired to be a learned man and read everything he could get his hands on.

"I am not overly familiar with the Ilyan Texts, but I believe they say something of the like."

"I ran across one or two Mandrakhar during my years in the capital, but they say the ones in the Westwood are different."

"They still live in the old ways and carry with them the memories of their ancestors. I'm not clear as to how it all works, but I can't imagine what it would be like to hold the weight of so many generations deep in your mind."

During one of their nightly talks Joram got to telling Benedictus about Thom—how he had been born not long after Joram returned from the West, how he and Kellah had brought him with them first to the capital and then to this place.

"I too had a son once," Benedictus said.

"What happened?"

"He drowned…in the seas north of Kallanboro." Joram thought to ask Benedictus more about this, but he could tell the lieutenant didn't want to linger on the subject.

A fortnight after Benedictus's arrival Joram dreamed again of his wife. In the dream, they were staying in a small hillside cottage overlooking the gray ocean. The two of them sat out front on a large divan beneath blankets, drinking tea and breathing the pleasant coastal air. All around were enormous trees, bigger than any Joram had ever seen; they were nearly the height of the keep. Snow lightly covered the ground in places. He'd only seen snow a few times in his life—all long ago in the West—seeing as it neither snowed in the capital nor, obviously, in the desert.

Thom was with them in the cottage—as was Mari, who was no longer the sickly teenager Joram remembered but had grown into the woman she might have become: confident and flowing with health.

It was afternoon and Joram was going down the hill to a village on the coast to buy fish for the evening meal. His legs had miraculously been healed and there was no sign of a limp in his step as he walked down the mountain trail. Halfway to the village, he heard a wrenching cry back in the direction from which he'd come. There was a great whooshing sound, like a sandstorm heard from within a shuttered house, and an enormous winged creature broke through the treetops. It was dark green, nearly black, and its fine fur shimmered in the afternoon sunlight. It dove back down beneath the cover of trees and up the mountain towards the cottage.

Joram ran back up the hill, but the pain in his legs had returned, and with each step a sharp jolt shot through his lower half. He bore the pain and kept climbing. As he approached the cottage, the air grew hot and smoke was everywhere. He turned around the final bend and there was the cottage, burning brightly in flames that were blue and green. He stumbled to the ground, overcome at last by the pain in his legs. The fire grew in intensity. A flaming figure burst out of the cottage door, writhing in pain. Mari. She was naked, her clothes having burned off. Her skin was charred and bleeding. She fell to her knees a few steps from him. They crawled towards one another.

She opened her mouth to speak, but her words caught in her dying mouth.

The next day, when Joram told Gareth of his decision, the chamberlain asked what had caused the change of heart.

"Dangerous times," was all Joram said.

Gareth made the arrangements. Saleya's serving responsibilities around the castle were lightened so she could attend to the child, who would stay in the guest quarters. Saleya had learned to read while in the employ of a wealthy merchant in Kallanboro, so Gareth and Joram decided she could serve as Corinne's tutor in addition to her caretaker. Saleya might not have been as learned as some other tutor they might have found, but Gareth suggested it probably best not to force the girl to get used to too many new faces all at once.

When Corinne first arrived at the castle, she sulked about missing her friends and wanted to return to the orphanage. To be clear, she didn't say any of this to Joram. To her grandfather, she maintained her icy courtesy. Yet sometimes Joram would hear her complaining to Saleya when she thought he wasn't in earshot.

"But isn't your bed more comfortable here at the castle, and are not the meals better tasting?" he heard Saleya say to the girl.

"I don't care about my bed!" Corinne shouted. "I don't care about stupid meals! I hate it here!"

Slowly though, the girl warmed up to Saleya and, after the first week, he'd sometimes catch a glimpse of the two walking hand-in-hand down the castle corridors. Not much changed with how she interacted with Joram. He accepted this though; he deserved it.

The scouts kept returning with no information. No enemy was in sight. Still, Joram decided they'd keep on preparing the town's defenses as best they could until they were sure they were safe. Some of the conscripted farmers grumbled about needing to get back to tending their crops, but the governor still had most of the townsfolk's' support.

Whenever Joram found time during the day, he would steal down to the library to watch Corinne and Saleya practice reading. Rather than announce himself, he'd watch through a crack in a door or from one of the upstairs landings overlooking the library. In the evenings, Corinne and Joram would have dinner together, mostly in silence. Sometimes Saleya would join them when she wasn't busy with her other duties. Either way, Joram looked forward to these meals.

After Corinne was put to bed, Benedictus would come up to the keep and the two men would continue their conversations until it grew late. Joram's cough had resolved, he was shaking less, and his legs were feeling much better. It was as if the threat facing them all had woken the governor's body out of some long malaise.

It was towards the end of one of his evening meals with Corinne, as he drank his third cup of wine and the girl was enjoying a raisin tart he'd had the baker make special for her, that he had a realization about his granddaughter. Her gaze was focused on her plate and she tore at the tart with her fork as if it were the last tart the world would ever see; Joram just observed her, undisturbed. And it was then that he had the revelation that all this time he'd loved and hated her only for what she represented, when in fact, she had a mind, a soul, of her own.

"Did you enjoy that tart, Corinne?"

She looked up from her licked-clean plate, and he caught the faintest trace of a smile on her lips.

Those few weeks were the strangest in Joram's life. They were under threat of war, had heard nothing from the capital, and any day a merciless army of Islanders and sorcerers and the-gods-knew-who-else might show up outside their walls. Yet Joram couldn't help but think that *this* was somehow happiness, that this was what he had been searching for since long before Thom rode south.

Mostly his granddaughter would communicate to him through Saleya, but little by little she began speaking more to him, especially in their time alone.

"Joram, can you tell me about my parents?" she said on the rare day when she met him for lunch downstairs in the dining room adjacent to the library. Saleya had gone to the mercer to see if she might obtain Corinne a new dress, so on this particular day it was just the girl and him.

He'd practiced his answer to this question, but upon finally hearing the words out of her mouth, he felt not unlike he had that day so many years ago when he met the newly crowned Emperor Kaleb Lunaris in the Great Hall of the palace.

"I didn't know your mother very well," he said. "I only met her once before she became pregnant with you." Corinne looked at him, searching for more. "I suppose she didn't have an easy life. You've had it much better—even at the temple."

"And what did she look like?"

Over the years, Joram had occasionally tried to call up Mari's image in his mind. Every time he did, he'd see the haunted expression of a girl to whom the world had not been kind. He didn't know what had happened to make her this way, but he suspected things.

"She was...beautiful," he said. "When I look at you, I see her so much. Only you are braver, I think."

"And she died when I was born."

"That's correct. She was very young. But I know that if she were still alive she'd love you very much." He turned his glance tableward and saw his right hand had been unconsciously gripping his dinner knife with all his strength. He released it to the plate where it landed with a clang.

"And my father?" she said.

"Thom—your father," he started. "He was a very kind...a very lovely...child."

The day after his mother died Joram found him again in the arboretum picking flowers. For once, Joram didn't approach him. During the funeral, when Thom thought his father was looking away, he'd thrown a bouquet of irises he'd hidden in his tunic onto the blazing pyre.

"He didn't take the death of his mother well. And perhaps I didn't help him enough. As he grew older he turned to...vice...drink, to escape, I think."

As far as Joram knew, after Kellah's funeral, Thom never went back to the arboretum. Joram never went in there much to begin with and years later, after learning how Thom's body had been found with his throat slashed in a brothel near the docks in Vicus Remorum, he made it a point to avoid the place entirely.

Joram looked at the girl and she had a concerned expression. "But that's all ancient history," he said. "You don't have to worry about any of that. You have a fine future ahead of you."

"But what if the bad men come and take me and turn me into a slave or one of their mistresses?"

"Where'd you hear this?"

"The guards around the castle all talk about it. That it happened in Kallanboro and that it will happen here."

"You will be safe so long as you are here in the castle," he said.

"But what about my friends? Dhala and Cat and—"

"So long as I am governor, I will not let harm befall any of your friends." Joram stood up and walked over to his granddaughter, placing his hand on her shoulder. "Now tell me, do you like flowers? Behind the castle we have a beautiful walled garden that your father used to love."

Joram had Gareth postpone his meetings, and he and Corinne spent the afternoon walking around the arboretum, taking breaks every so often to sit under one of the large trees, out of the merciless sun. The gardeners had done wonders in recent years and flowers of every color and variety overflowed on to the cobblestone walkways. Corinne wanted to know the names of each flower and bush, but Joram knew few of them so he just made things up as they went along.

He slept as soundly that night as he had in many years. It was as if the great load he had been carrying had been lightened, miraculously, by the hands of the gods.

This nearly lasted until dawn.

An hour or so before the sun was to rise a knock came at his door.

"Gareth?" he said.

"Lord Governor, it is me," said the constable's raspy voice.

There was only one reason for Selbaird to come to his chamber at this time of night.

❖

As day broke one could see them from atop the keep: row upon orderly row of infantry, clad in dark green and flanked on each side by long columns of cavalry. Scattered amongst their lot were perhaps a hundred standard-bearers each waving the same dark green flag emblazoned with a clenched white fist.

They finally stopped a half-mile from the outer wall, well outside of the range of Wahan's catapults and archers. In the town, an air of chaos was palpable, as hundreds hurried to bring their belongings within the inner wall before the center gate was locked for good.

Selbaird estimated the enemy's numbers at ten thousand. He guessed a third were cavalry or mounted infantry, horse and camel. How such a large number could traverse the thirty leagues from the mountains without being seen by the scouts, no one could guess. At least there was no sign of the large gray mounts described by some of the refugees. Maybe they'd been an exaggeration all along. Joram took little consolation.

Sometime around midmorning, a horn sounded and the enemy forces sent a single rider half the distance between their encampment and Wahan's outer walls. He wore a dark green cloak like all the others and waved the white flag of parley. Benedictus volunteered to meet the enemy, and both Joram and Selbaird agreed he would make the best negotiator.

Already high up in the keep, Joram grabbed the magnascope to watch the exchange. Ten minutes passed before he saw Benedictus riding out on his black mount. His Imperial garb had been laundered and now he looked like a great knight in his bronzed plate armor and crimson cape. The air was still and everywhere was quiet; Joram could hear the rhythmic crack of the horse's gait. Were it not for the large hood the enemy negotiator wore, Joram would have been able to see the man's face in perfect detail. As it was, the large hood shadowed the man's eyes and Joram could only make out his pale mouth. This one, at least, was no Islander. The negotiator handed Benedictus a scroll and said something, a smile on his lips. *The gall!* Joram doubted he'd smile with a sword shoved through those smug lips.

The two men, still mounted, exchanged a few more words. After a minute, Benedictus turned, his face a mask of anger. He shouted something back at the other man before the enemy envoy spun his horse around and rode back from where he'd come.

Joram descended the keep. Gareth wanted to help the governor down the stairs, but he pushed him away. No one would accuse Joram of being light on his feet, but he had been feeling better than he had in a long time. They convened at the foyer beneath the wind tower in the library. In addition to Gareth, Benedictus, Selbaird, and Joram, several of Selbaird's best men were seated amongst them dressed in full armor.

Benedictus unfurled the scroll and held it up so Gareth could read aloud to the room in his deep, booming voice:

"On behalf of the Northern Alliance, this announcement hereby requires your complete and utter surrender by midnight tonight. No conditions will be met. Howsoever, should surrender not be made by the ordained time, we shall take such refusal as claim that you are in an open State of War with the Northern Alliance and take action accordingly. No further parley shall be allowed between us and no extension to surrender shall be granted."

The room filled with a low murmur of voices.

"What can you tell us of these invaders?" Joram said to Benedictus.

"Not much that we didn't already know. Many of their soldiers appear to be dark, so Islanders would make sense. Others are of some other place. I would estimate their numbers at near what Selbaird did, which makes their advantage of soldiers about ten to one. Their advantage in mounts is far greater."

"But we have the clear positional advantage," Selbaird said. "Men have defended a fortified position against worse odds."

"More skilled men," Benedictus said. "In more fortified positions. Against lesser foes."

"What did the negotiator say to you?" Joram said.

Benedictus paused. "He promised mercy if we surrendered. Beyond that it was just the normal threats and blustering."

Selbaird burst out, "We cannot trust these invaders. We know what happened to Kallanboro."

"Kallanboro did not surrender," Benedictus said.

"For good reason! We must prepare for a siege and hope for reinforcements from the capital. The Empire crushed the Islanders once and we'll do it again."

"Perhaps. But these invaders are more than mere Islanders. And should reinforcements not come, what then? Shall we end up like Kallanboro?" said Benedictus. A few of Selbaird's men grunted in agreement.

"You advise surrender then?" Joram said.

"We cannot stand for long unaided, and I've no trust in the capital to deliver us. If news has reached there of what they are up against, they may hope to buy as much time as possible and then make a stand against the invaders at whatever location is of greatest strategic advantage. This town is not that location. The walls are too low, the men too inexperienced . . ."

"Then you would have us turned to prisoners or slaves? You would have our women raped or sold off?" Selbaird said.

"I would have us survive."

"Myself as well," Selbaird said and then turned to the governor. "But it's your call. What do you say?" All eyes turned to Joram.

He announced he'd think on the matter for a half hour and ordered everyone out.

The men left the room and for most of the next thirty minutes, Joram sat staring at his reflection on the still surface of his tea.

There was a time in his younger days when Joram, having let his success get to his head, was a prideful man. Those days were long gone; he cared nothing about glory or victory in battle and, had he trusted these invaders' word, would have opened the gates, their flags of surrender flying high from every battlement. But he had seen too much—had marched into too many towns a conquering soldier and had watched too much rape and pillage, despite agreements to the contrary—to be trusting. Nonetheless, he might have been inclined to still chance surrender had the promise he made to Corinne not been so fresh on his mind. Young girls did not often fare well when towns were sacked, and while he might somehow spare Corinne from violence should they open the gates, he still had to consider all the others—her friends, those sad little creatures in the orphanage who, like his granddaughter, possessed thoughts and hopes of their own. Against his better judgment, and perhaps to all of their doom, he made his decision.

"We're not going to surrender," Joram said when the half hour was up, and he exited the library to where the men were waiting. A few men cheered. One or two groaned. "Our men are untrained, but they are made of better stuff than Benedictus gives them credit for." He hoped what he was saying was true. "But I will need all of your help." He turned to Benedictus. "I know I am going against your counsel, but I still need your support. Will I have it?"

"Lord Governor…This is folly! We will end up like Kallanboro," Benedictus said. There was desperation on his face. His bright green eyes seemed to plead to the governor. "Think of your granddaughter, if nothing else."

"I am," Joram said. "Will I have your support, Benedictus?"

"You will," he said, with a sigh of resignation. "This is, after all, your decision."

❖

When the fires were lit and the last of the town's men were within the inner wall, the main gate was locked with a massive bolt, more than a foot and a half thick of iron. The great lock required two keys to open it; Selbaird carried the first and Joram, high up in the keep, wore the second on a string around his neck. Even if a few enemy troops got over or under the wall, it would be nearly impossible for them to locate both keys and open the gate from inside.

All night, everything between inner and outer wall, burned.

From the keep Joram watched the crescent of fire they'd lit slowly grow towards the inner wall. Even during The Troubles he'd never seen a fire like this. If it weren't people's homes, stores, stables, stalls being burned—if it hadn't been done to prevent their enemy from building siege tower, which they'd use to mount their walls and murder them—it would have been a beautiful sight.

He went down to where Corinne slept. They'd put her to bed before the order had been made to light the fire. Saleya sat in a chair overlooking the girl.

"How is she?" Joram said just before breaking out into another fit of coughing. He'd been coughing less of late; however, all this smoke was re-aggravating his lungs.

"Everything here is well. I started to tell Corinne a story and she fell right to sleep."

"Good. Let her sleep. Come into the other chamber with me."

They sat down on the two plush chairs in the other room. "You know, I had a daughter as well as a son. Long ago."

"She passed, Lord Governor?"

"Yes. At birth."

"I'm sorry to hear that."

"It was a long time ago. And the world is full of tragedies worse than my own."

She poured them both some wine.

"I want you to know that we'll do everything we can to protect the people of this town," Joram said.

"Of course, Lord Governor."

"And I'm still very hopeful that help will come from the capital."

She forced a smile.

"But no matter what happens I want you to know that I'm very thankful for your service these last few weeks and of how you've taken care of Corinne."

❧

There was little action the next two days as the outskirts of town finished burning and the smoke that hung above them drifted southward. Selbaird oversaw the final fortifications of the inner wall and anyone who lived within a hundred paces of it was relocated further into town. Joram had ordered Gareth to bring all of the girls from the orphanage, as well as some of the youngest boys, within the keep. The castle grounds, which had during Joram's governorship remained relatively empty, now filled with the voices of children. Even if they failed and all were put to the sword, Joram at least took consolation knowing he had tried to do right.

Since they'd abandoned the outer wall, the enemy had moved their encampment forwards another several hundred paces, and at odd intervals they'd send a deployment of archers forwards who'd launch a volley of arrows over the wall. A few of Selbaird's guards were wounded, one gravely, but mostly these attacks were little more than annoyances.

Joram knew the enemy wouldn't wait long to mount an assault. The little well water Selbaird's men hadn't manage to move from the outer crescent had been poisoned with rotting animal carcasses just as the invaders arrived. Even with the resources from the nearby oases Joram assumed the enemy had captured, their water supply wouldn't last long for ten thousand men and some nine thousand or more mounts. This was their great hope: that the desert itself might save them. As Joram predicted, when the smoke cleared the enemy began their advance. Joram watched everything from the keep. Saleya and Corinne were below, behind a locked door and away from any windows.

Joram thought the enemy might send climbers under cover of darkness; instead, they sent three traditional columns of infantrymen at the walls— one down the center with battering rams and two others with ladders and ropes to the east and west ends of town, where the cliff face met the wall. For all the invaders' cavalry, horse or camel would be of little use charging a wall. They needed to get over or through the walls, and Joram was resolved to make sure they didn't do that.

The center gate had been fortified heavily, and the onagers had been preloaded with rocks from the mines and arranged to beat back a direct attack. When Selbaird's men fired the catapults, the invaders' center column quickly scattered, many of the attackers retreating. Despite the triumph Joram felt watching the enemy's center assault falter, he couldn't help feeling a little sympathetic for these bastards. It's hard to hold too much against a man when he's bleeding to death beneath a rock.

The fighting on the east and west corners of the town was more contentious. Though the defenders had the advantage of position atop the wall, they were still outnumbered. Several of the Greencloaks (as the men had come to call them) made it atop the battlements and once they did, were ferocious fighters, often taking down several of Selbaird's men before being felled themselves.

Within a few minutes the defenses at the main gate were able to redistribute themselves to the east and west. These additional troops quickly beat back the invaders at the west end and, at last, there was only fighting on the eastern corner of town. Joram knew then that the fighting for the day would soon be over. He went down to check on Saleya and Corinne. Selbaird and Benedictus would give the governor their report when the day's work was done.

That evening Joram went to visit the wounded soldiers in the barracks. Many were hurt, but the morale of the soldiers was high. They'd only lost twenty men and had killed at least two hundred fifty of the enemy, many of whose bodies still littered the charred ground beyond the inner wall. The Greencloaks were excellent fighters when on level ground with their adversary, but they couldn't walk through walls and they bled and died just like everyone else. So long as they could hold the wall, the enemy's advantages in numbers, skill and cavalry didn't matter.

Joram became worried when he couldn't find Benedictus or Selbaird. Perhaps they'd been hurt in the fighting. His fears were allayed though when one of the soldiers reported he'd seen the two men talking together near the battlements after the fighting had ended. Joram would meet with them later. For now, he needed to rest.

When he entered the main room at the top of the keep, Joram saw that a few candles had been lit to illuminate the room. Benedictus was standing beside the large oak table looking out the window. He was dressed in one of the cream-colored outfits of the guards.

"Benedictus! I've been looking for you and Selbaird," Joram said, but the other man didn't turn towards him. "Why the glum face? There's still a lot to do, but today was a great vict—"

Joram's voice caught in his throat when he saw a glimmer of moonlight reflecting off Benedictus's unsheathed sword.

"The constable is dead," Benedictus said, matter of fact, like he'd just told Joram it was hot out.

"What? The men said they just saw you walking with him." Even before Benedictus showed Joram the key, the governor realized what was happening.

Joram remembered the feeling he'd had the day he received the news of Thom's death—like realizing there was no ground beneath his feet.

"So the attack today . . ." he said. His head rang with disorientation.

"If they'd wanted to attack the city in earnest, they'd have done so with all of their forces. It would have been a bloody business and they would have lost a lot of men, but it would not have been so large a challenge. You were expecting an attack, so you got an attack."

"I thought you were my friend, you treacherous little cunt." Joram grabbed an earthenware cup from the table and threw it at Benedictus's head, but Benedictus just batted it down and it shattered harmlessly on the floor.

"In another life, perhaps," he said.

Joram gripped the key hanging around his neck. On the periphery of his vision he eyed his old sword mounted over the hearth.

"How'd you know I'd ask you to stay?" Joram said.

"If you hadn't, I'd have found a different reason to stay."

"It all feels like a lot of work, Benedictus. Why heal me too? That is what you did, right? In the library? You're not a bad man."

Joram casually inched towards the sword. It was only a step away now.

"I didn't want things to come to this," Benedictus said. He turned away from the window and faced Joram. "I begged you to surrender!"

"Shut up."

"But you refused. And now there's nothing I can do."

"And so you've come to kill me."

"No. I come only for the key. Give it to me and have the soldiers lay down their arms. There could still be some hope. I will do what I can, but the Chieftains listen only to their own counsel."

"Who are you? *What* are you?"

"A man from the South, near Hammer Bay, with a drowned son. Just as I told you."

Joram lunged for the sword on the wall. No sooner had he wrapped his fingers around the sword hilt than Benedictus's blade came flying down at him. Joram attempted to parry the blow, but his deflection only slightly knocked Benedictus's swing off course. Rather than cutting Joram down the center of his skull, Benedictus's blade scraped across Joram's forehead and temple, opening a gash that spurted blood into his eyes.

Joram gathered himself and gripped the sword tight. If he died, he died.

Benedictus came at him again, and this time the old, former soldier parried him more successfully, countering with a stab towards the traitor's chest, which Benedictus easily dodged. Benedictus countered Joram's counter with a slash of his own, opening up Joram's sword hand and slashing deep into his leg. Joram dropped his sword and balanced himself on his one good leg, preparing for the next attack. Yet right then, though Benedictus was still several paces away, Joram felt a tug at his neck as the key floated, still tethered by its string, in front of his face. There was a hard pull, the string snapped, and the key floated into Benedictus's outstretched hand. After Benedictus pocketed the thing, he muttered a few words and Joram felt his body being lifted up towards the ceiling. Just before he reached the chandelier overhead, his body changed directions and he was sent hurling to the floor.

When Joram came to, Gareth and two guards were standing over him in a candlelit room. He was lying in his bed and hurt all over. He reached up to where the gash on his forehead had been and felt a bandage. Saleya sat in a chair in the corner of the room with Corinne on her lap and a concerned look on her face. It took a full minute before Joram remembered what had taken place and shot up in bed.

"How long have I been out?"

"Perhaps a half hour, Lord Governor," said Gareth.

"My key," Joram said. "Benedictus has both keys."

"Benedictus?" Gareth said.

"We must man the gates. Send reinforcements. Now."

Gareth turned to the guards. "Go. Both of you. Find the lieutenant." The two men ran down the stairwell.

A half hour had been too long. Two minutes later they heard shouting near the center gate and then the blow of a horn.

Gareth ran into the front room and looked out the window.

"It's hard to see in the darkness, Lord Governor, but there is fighting...the gate is open. The enemy is there now in numbers."

Joram got out of bed. Sharp pains shot through his skull and up his leg. He walked over to the window to look out into the darkness for himself. Torches danced back and forth. It was impossible to know which torches were held by which side, but it was clear that the majority of the tiny flames were pushing their way into the city, not pushing invaders out.

"Bar the castle," Joram said. Without the benefit of their defensive positions on the wall they were doomed. Barring the doors might buy them all an extra hour. Saleya started to weep. Joram's granddaughter sat, impassive, as if she'd known all along.

There was nothing else to do now. This was how it would end. Joram's mind searched for some plan, some other way. *Shit. Shit. Shit.*

"Mines!" Joram shouted at last. Gareth looked at him like he'd gone mad. "Gareth," he said, looking over his chamberlain's massive stature to assess whether he'd be strong enough for the task. "Can you get your hands on an axe?"

"There should be one down in the armory, although the little training I have is with a sword, not axe," he said and grabbed at the blade sheathed at his waist.

"Not for fighting," Joram said. "But to break down the barricade in front of the mines."

"Those tunnels are treacherous, Lord Governor," Gareth said. "In your condition, there is no way you will be able to make it through."

"Gareth, my boy...I may not have been a good governor, but I'm not an idiot." Joram limped over to his chest and his drawers and gathered what small valuable items he could find—some jewels, a few rings—and placed them into a canvas bag. Such valuable items might come in handy when they were on the road.

Joram sat and looked out the window. He imagined all the men who were probably dying in the dark streets below. It would be another twenty minutes before the enemy, that mass of tiny torchlights, breached the castle gate and fought with the few remaining guards in the inner ward. By now he hoped Gareth, Corinne, Saleya, and as many of the orphans as they were able to gather, were safely in the tunnels. With a decent head start, they might have a chance. You couldn't bring a horse into the deeper parts of the mines and why spend effort chasing orphans and a few castle servants? The trek out of the desert would be hard but not impossible. In time they might even rebuild their lives—move on from all this. That's what people did, right? Move on?

It wouldn't be long now before the enemy arrived in the stiflingly hot keep. *The Oasis Obelisk.* What a stupid name.

Joram shuffled to the hearth. Why would they build a hearth here in the hottest room in a castle in the hottest place in the Empire? Idiots. His leg was bleeding through the bandages. Once again, Joram was a gimp.

He took his armor down from the wall and put on his breastplate, his greaves, his gauntlets. He looked at himself in the polished copper plate that served as his mirror. Dressed in this armor he didn't look so decrepit, so old, so useless. He returned to the bedroom and barred the door. He held his sword and waited.

As Joram stood there with nothing to do, a powerful feeling washed over him. Hopelessness. Three decades ago, he'd come to the desert and brought with him everything he cared about and now it would all be ground to dust. His home would be burned to nothing. His children were dead, his wife was dead, and soon he'd be dead too. Perhaps Benedictus had been telling the truth about this "unnatural despair" after all. Fucking sorcery. At least there was Corinne.

He imagined how it would be when they came. The door would fly open and he would catch the first one by surprise. The cunt would fall bleeding to the floor. So much for how great of fighters these bastards were. If Joram were lucky, he might be able to drop another one before he was struck down.

A few minutes later he heard the clomping of footsteps up the stairs and then voices in some unintelligible tongue. Someone's hand tried the door on the other side. Locked. There was a momentary lull and then came a great beating on the door. Bang. Bang. Bang.

Joram held the sword up with both hands now, waiting for the door to give way.

< Messages   **Sarah**   Details

did you get the fm I left you the other day?

vm . . . stupid autocorrect . . . voicemail that is

Yeah I got it

Tue, Sep 16, 2:15 AM

??

sorry I didn't call you back. I've been really busy

Ok, np. But what do you think about what I said?

About us meeting up.

Tue, Sep 16, 8:59 AM

I'm actually not in town.

Oh. Where are you?

Florida

Your parents' place? Sarasota?

Y

Well maybe when you get back then?

I'm going to be down here for a while.

You're coming back eventually, right?

I just don't know if it's a good idea.

Can I just call you? It's really hard to communicate via text.

I'm actually in the middle of somethign.

K

Wed, Sep 17, 1:34 AM

hey sorry to bother you again

are you still going to be down in Florida next week?

I think so

I'm in DC right now and next Thursday I'm having a reading in Tampa

maybe we could plan to meet up then?

I think I might need a little more time before I see you again.

I get it. It's just.....you know with my dad and stuff......I just kinda want to talk to you...it would be a BIG favor

If you can't though, I understand.

Okay. Next Thursday I can do.

I can drive down to Sarasota after the reading. Should be 9?

No. I'll come to Tampa

great. I'll share the invite for the reading with you on fb

K

Wed, Sep 17, 10:14 AM

I know you may not want to hear this but I'm really looking forward to seeing you.

FIVE

Jack spent the week by himself on the southwest coast of Ireland in a stone house that George Bernard Shaw and William Butler Yeats used to frequent and is now driving around the countryside with an Estonian cocktail waitress he met in Dublin.

Her name is Leelo, or at least that's what she told him. He suspects this isn't her real name. They met at a stand-up comedy show in the attic of an old pub near Temple Bar. She'd taken the seat next to him because it was the only one left. When the warm-up guy on stage was having fun—messing with the audience, going from group to group—his eyes rested on the two of them, and he asked them how long they'd been together.

"We're not together," Jack said.

"How come?" said Mr. Warm-up Guy. She and Jack looked at each other. The crowd laughed.

"No, really. How come?" he said. "She's certainly cute enough. Is she your sister? Don't tell me she's your sister. That would be weird."

"We don't know each other," she said. Her English was a hodgepodge of impossible-to-disentangle accents.

"Oh, I'm sorry to have presumed. In that case, I'm Michael, and if you'd like to grab a drink after the show..." he said and winked at her. The crowd laughed some more. "Except I'm a stand-up comedian so you're buying."

Mr. Warm-up Guy moved on to another group in the crowd and Jack and the woman turned to each other again. *I'm glad that's over*, he said by the raise of his brow, the roll of his eyes. She shrugged in agreement.

She was attractive, with dyed-dark hair, pale skin and eyes that were vaguely Asiatic (which he wouldn't have expected in someone who was Estonian); the collar of her tight Ramones t-shirt had been cut to form a jagged, plunging neckline.

During the break between acts Jack chatted her up because it would have been more awkward for him to just sit silently next to her. She told him she was a bartender in Cork and that she'd come up for a weekend trip. "Two years in Ireland and never to Dublin," she said. She'd planned on taking the trip with a girlfriend, but the friend backed out at the last minute. The bus ticket had already been purchased though, the hostel stay reserved, so she made the trip alone.

When the show ended, he invited her to come by for a drink. He had a nice bottle of whiskey back at the apartment, which he'd been planning on bringing back to the States but now supposed he could just as well drink right here in Ireland.

The apartment he'd rented for his three days in Dublin was the ground floor of a renovated Georgian house facing Mountjoy Square. In the foyer, when one opened the door to the apartment, was a giant oil painting of a half dozen sheep grazing in a field.

When they were a quarter way through the bottle Jack and Leelo made an attempt at sleeping together; only by the time Jack was through fumbling with the condom, he was no longer up for the endeavor.

"I'm older than I look," he said. She didn't seem disappointed. A few minutes later she was sleeping, curled up like a child beneath the down comforter.

The next day Jack planned on driving out to the west coast of the island. Leelo was scheduled to catch a bus back to Cork, so he offered her a ride back in his rental car. It was a little out of the way, but he was in no hurry to be anywhere.

"Maybe instead you want me to come with you on your holiday?" she said.

"Didn't you say you had to get back to work?"

"It's a shit job anyway."

They drove by the hostel so she could pick up her things before they got on the M7 heading southwest.

❀

When Jack's ex-wife Sarah and he split, his book had just come out, its sequel just accepted for publication, so he had a little money from the advances—all of which she let him keep seeing as she came from money anyway. He stopped substitute teaching, stopped writing, and, as soon as the book tour he'd arranged was finished, stopped doing anything at all that might properly be considered "work." For the last year and a half he's been traveling aimlessly overseas or else catching up with family and friends across the States. Although his books have done reasonably well, Jack's sabbatical would have almost certainly led to financial ruin had he not received a sizable, though not extravagant, inheritance when his dad died right after the split with Sarah. Jack's father, who'd emigrated from the Phillipines and worked as a nurse for forty years, never made a lot of money; however, he'd pinched pennies and knew how to invest in the stock market, and that adds up over forty years. Jack wasn't close with his dad but neither was their relationship particularly dysfunctional; he grappled with what it meant that, when he received the news of his dad's passing, he didn't feel much of anything other than a vague emptiness at one of the people he knew best being gone from the world.

Jack rarely talks to people he meets about his books and when he does he usually avoids going into a lot of details regarding what they're about. Although it'd been his goal for many years to be a "published author," the books he had wanted to write didn't end up being the books he published. For what probably added up to more than a decade, he had worked, on and off, on an interconnected series of fantasy stories. Then one night three years ago when Sarah was away for the weekend, Jack—drunk off the six-pack of wine coolers he found in the back of the fridge, maddened by the impasse he'd reached in his writing, depressed with the impasse he'd reached with his wife—took all the printed drafts of his stories he could find around the house and placed them in the bottom of the barbeque they kept in the backyard of their row-house apartment. He picked up the bag of charcoal and scattered a few briquettes on top; when he squirted the copious amount of lighter fluid onto the heap, he held the bottle at his crotch as if it were his cock, the flammable liquid, piss. The instant the match touched the first soaked piece of charcoal, the entire bottom of the barbeque exploded in one terrible, cathartic fireball. When this was done, he went inside to the computer and started deleting files. He was surprised by how much work it was to destroy his manuscript. No matter how many files he sent to the recycle bin, more would reveal themselves. There were files on his hard drive, files on flash drives, files he had emailed to himself, files he had saved online. In his drunken state, he imagined his unfinished book a kind of kraken who, as soon as one tentacle was destroyed, would grow another. He was persistent though, and by morning the beast had been slain— nearly all traces of the manuscript erased from existence. Jack regretted his rash act of self-destruction almost immediately, and the next day he searched on his computer for hours to see if he might somehow recover his manuscript. A few early drafts of a few early stories had survived the massacre in the "Sent Items" of his email, but these were little consolation.

Daunted by the seemingly impossible task of re-writing his book essentially from scratch, Jack took the advice of a writer he had met at a conference a few years before to put his labor of love on hold and just finish a book, any book, to prove to himself that he could. "Write something formulaic," the writer, who had made a career of the formulaic, had said. "Something where you can just follow genre conventions: a coming-of-age story, a thriller, a detective novel, a chick-lit book. Then just follow the script and fill in the blanks." As a kind of joke, and to prove he didn't give a shit about the book he was writing, Jack decided to follow this advice and chose the genre he had absolutely the least interest in: the romance novel. He picked up a few books at the public library on how to write such a thing, outlined the plot from beginning to end, and *voilà,* three months later the novel that would eventually become *The Delicious Paradise,* the first of Jack's "Virgie Chapman novels," was born. Jack never did tell Sarah that he had destroyed the other book, instead just explaining that he was working on another project for a little while.

After the divorce, after his father's funeral, Jack decided to see how long he could make his money last. He visited old friends around the country and would stay with them until they tired of his couch surfing. He visited his mother in Michigan for a time; she had long been divorced from Jack's father but seemed to take his death hard nonetheless. He would go overseas whenever he felt moved to do so. Last year he spent three months in Patagonia, mostly on the Argentinian side in a small tourist village called El Chalten that was hours away by car from pretty much anything. In March he joined a tour group out to Xinjiang in western China where they rode a rickety bus for eight hours a day and visited historic sites along the old Silk Road.

For the last few weeks he's been traveling around Ireland. It's probably no coincidence that, just as he started to feel his worst about everything, he got on the first flight to the country in which he'd met his ex-wife. For the most part he's consciously avoided anywhere he traveled on that first trip nearly a decade ago. But perhaps, he thought, he might at least re-capture a little of that feeling he had back then—that sense of awe at how vast and wonder-filled the world could be.

After driving across the island from Dublin and spending the previous night at a bed and breakfast out on the Ring of Kerry, Leelo and Jack circle down to Killarney to check out the national park adjacent to the town.

"You want to walk around lake?" she asks, pointing to the map they received at the information booth.

"It looks like it's about seven or eight miles…twelve kilometers around. You up for that long of a hike?" he says.

"It's okay," she says and they head towards the lake on a well-kept pathway.

After a mile or so, they start talking about Jack's writing. Though Leelo had told him she didn't read much, she's been exceedingly interested in his books. The previous night after dinner he lent her the extra copy he had stashed away in his backpack and she started reading as he flipped channels before bed.

"I was wanting to know from where you get ideas for all characters in your stories," she says now as they walk alongside a horse drawn carriage.

"The characters aren't all that deep, so I just make up a lot of it. I suppose some are loosely modeled on people I know."

"Will you make character from me?" she says and he can't tell if she's flirting or if she's asking in earnest.

The trail's difficulty increases as they ascend some hills to the west of the lake, and Leelo gives Jack a defeated look when he tells her they're only a third of the way.

"I told you it was twelve kilometers," he says.

She shrugs and her purse-bearing shoulder slumps down. He told her to leave the purse in the car and now she refuses to vocally complain and prove him right. She pulls out a hair tie from her jeans' pocket and puts her long dyed-black hair into a ponytail. Based on her complexion he guesses she's a natural blonde. He wonders if the dye job was done as some form of rebellion, as a rejection of something. She has rebellion, defiance, in the way she carries herself, the way she swings her chin around when you call her name—like she's taken a little too much shit and is now overcompensating.

In the next half hour the clouds dissipate. It's late June but the weather has been chilly these last couple weeks. Although Jack is enjoying the sun, the warmer temperature only makes Leelo crankier.

The first time Jack went to Ireland was nine years ago this November and it pretty much rained the whole time. Back then he was working a corporate job he was good at but hated and had been involved in a string of increasingly shallow and pointless three-to-six-month relationships. He lived alone in an apartment outside of Philadelphia that he'd spent way too much money furnishing and decorating even though he didn't personally care about home décor and seldom had guests. Many nights he'd find himself waking up, anxiety ridden, at three in the morning from dreams where nothing out of the ordinary happened. His therapist suggested this might all have something to do with his relationship with his father. A nutritionist friend insisted he ate too much sugar.

When Jack, on a whim, decided to go to Ireland, met Sarah in a restaurant up north in Enniskillen, and fell in love within eight hours, it felt like the cosmos was paying him back for all of the angst he'd gone through the last couple years.

Not that he'd go so far as actually believe the cosmos gave a shit one way or another; still, it was funny how things could, even if governed by the uncaring hand of physics and chance, work out.

Sarah had been traveling with a pair of her old sorority sisters from college, one of which—a former pageant queen he'd later learn—would probably be thought considerably more beautiful than his ex-wife. Nonetheless, as Jack observed the three girls from an adjacent table in the restaurant, Sarah was the only one he was interested in. She was the quietest of the three, and there was something about how she stopped to think before saying anything that suggested to Jack that she had depth, that she'd experienced tragedy and had grown wiser as a result. But then, just as soon as he thought he had her pegged as a fellow tortured soul, she told her friends a ridiculous joke involving both a piano-playing mouse and a singing frog that had Jack biting his lip to control his laughter.

Later, whenever he'd try and retell that joke he'd always mess it up.

"I couldn't help but notice your guys' American accents," were the first words he said to her when Sarah's two friends left to go to the bathroom and Jack approached her table. Afterwards, he'd wish he'd said something cleverer.

He pulled up a chair without being asked; he'd read in a men's magazine that asking permission for stuff like that showed a lack of confidence. They introduced themselves. She told him that "Jack" sounded made up, considering they were in Ireland.

"It's actually a nickname."

"For John?" she said.

"No, 'Kojak.'"

"Like the bald guy?"

"Yeah, I know. I guess they played a lot of re-runs in the Phillipines where my dad was from. I don't know what the hell he was thinking."

The two friends returned and he learned that all three lived in New Jersey—Sarah in Princeton, only an hour from where he was living. They moved on to a pub three doors down from the restaurant. A few drinks in and feeling more daring than he had any right to, he asked Sarah and her friends if they minded if he tagged along with them on their travels. His flight wasn't for another five days and he'd be able to get from anywhere on the island back to the Dublin Airport without too much trouble.

By three in the afternoon, Leelo and Jack are back on the road. The hike was her idea, but he can tell by how she sulks in the car that she's mad at him for how long and exhausting it was. He turns the volume on the music a little louder than normal—REM's "Automatic for the People," in this case— so it's not awkward they aren't talking. Leelo seems fine with this. Eastern Europeans, he has discovered, love REM. He glances over at Leelo. The absurdity of the whole situation hits him hard. Him, a thirty-five-year-old man here with this girl who can't be much beyond college age.

When they turn onto the highway that runs along the coast to Dingle, he pulls over so they can stop for a look at the scenery. Up the hill to the right is a wide swath of the greenest green imaginable. Down to the left is the most insubstantial of guard walls and then steep yellowish cliffs that drop all the way down to the ocean.

"This whole country is like a damn postcard," he says, but Leelo isn't listening. She has one of those expensive digital cameras with the big zoom lenses, a gift from an ex-boyfriend she told him, and she's snapping pictures of *everything*. She's been doing this much of the two days they've been traveling together. This annoys him. He wants to tell her to put the camera down, to just soak it all in. Experience it. *Remember it.*

Once they reach Dingle they drop off their stuff at the inn and walk down a hill into town to find dinner. After several weeks in Ireland, he's sick of European/white-people food in general, particularly Irish food, and suggests they try Golden Phoenix Chinese Restaurant.

She looks at him, exasperated. "You are in *Ireland.*"

They walk into a nice-looking place that advertises locally caught fish on the chalkboard out front, but they don't have reservations and the wait is forty-five minutes.

"You know, it didn't look like there was a wait over at that Chinese place," he says.

"We'll wait at bar next door," she says to the hostess.

In contrast to most of the tourist-trap pubs, everyone inside the bar seems to be a local. The place has the look of a crappy corner store whose owner, just that afternoon, came up with the idea of transforming it into a bar by removing half the shelves. The remaining shelves hold a haphazard assortment of hand-knit scarves, salt and vinegar chips, laundry detergent, and small metallic-colored packets that promise men "maximum performance." Patrons are crowded around the bar drinking beer and trying to catch a glimpse of the soccer match playing on the twenty-five-year-old television set, which hangs from the ceiling by a jerry-rigged set of cables and pulleys.

They go up to the bar and order. Jack gets a beer and Leelo orders a scotch—the best they have. An older red-faced man at the bar turns to him. "Your girl has expensive tastes." Jack smiles politely. He doesn't mind paying, but it's a little tacky to order that kind of drink at a place like this.

Leelo makes small talk with the bartender. A younger man, almost certainly in his twenties, he is tall and well built with brown hair and a beard that borders on red. It's surprising how few redheads he's seen in Ireland. The bartender touches Leelo's hand casually, once, and then again thirty seconds later. Jack's not jealous, but *is* a little offended. *Who the fuck does this guy think he is?* Eventually the bartender catches Jack glaring at him and the two men introduce themselves to one another.

"Have you any Irish in you?" the bartender says.

"Don't think so." He didn't think he looked like he had any Irish in him either.

"It's just that with a name like that . . ."

"It's short . . . for Kojak."

"No shit? Like the detective."

"Like the detective," he says.

"You play football?" the bartender says, gesturing to the television.

"I used to play American football. A long time ago."

He grips Jack's bicep and whistles.

On the way out, Leelo goes to the washroom. Jack goes outside to wait. Despite being over two hundred pounds, he's a lightweight when it comes to alcohol, and after two beers, that feeling of mild hopelessness he gets when he drinks begins rising up in his face.

"Jack? Is that you?" he hears a woman, an American, say. She's just walked out of the bar, but he hadn't seen her when he was inside. He recognizes her, but the shock of unexpectedly seeing a familiar face has his head a little discombobulated.

"It's me? Neha?" she says. "You don't remember me."

"Of course I remember," he says, which right then is a lie but becomes truth a second later when his brain makes the connections. He sticks his arms out for a hug.

Jack had briefly dated her a few years after college, now more than ten or eleven years ago. It had just been a few months. She'd been a sweet girl and made the best pancakes Jack had ever had (her recipe required six different kinds of flour), but there'd never been that spark. When she got a job in New York, he visited her a couple times, and then things fizzled—less a breakup than two people just losing interest.

She looks good now. Age has given her a look of sophistication. She was an avid triathlete and yogi, and he can tell by her figure that she's kept up the habits.

"I was getting worried by the look on your face that maybe you weren't you," she says. Her wavy black hair is a little wild, and as she pushes it out of her face, he sees her wedding band. He thumbs his own non-existent ring, now long gone.

"Why would I *not* remember?"

"It's been a while."

"Not that long," he says. "So what are you doing here? Traveling for work? HR something or another, right?" The last time he saw her was definitely on that visit to New York. Of this he's sure now. But somehow he can't remember a single thing about the trip. Memory is a bitch. So much of our lives are lost through its faultiness.

"It does seem like there are tons of large corporations out here in rural Ireland that need HR consulting, doesn't it?"

"You have a point. So vacation?"

She points at him and makes a clicking sound. "This trip was mainly to visit my brother and his kids in Switzerland. The little jaunt here was kind of a *why-the-hell-not* while I was on this side of the ocean."

"That's right. Your brother was married to a Swiss girl, right?"

"Austrian...but whatever."

"So how're you liking your trip?"

"I've never travelled alone before, so that's a new experience. But overall, it's been great."

"It *is* beautiful here, isn't it?"

"The road coming here was amazing," she says.

Jack nods in agreement. "And where to next?"

"Well, tomorrow I'm going to Connemara and then to the Aran Islands, I think."

"I hear they're lovely. I don't think I'm going to see them on this trip. I'm headed up to Galway and then back down to fly out of Shannon."

"What about you? I saw you coming in with someone. Not that I've been creepily watching you or anything...Wife? Girlfriend?"

He'd forgotten about Leelo. "Who? Oh. No, I'm not married. Not anymore. We're just friends. We met in Dublin."

"Really?" Neha says and tilts her head down to look at him with upturned eyes.

"What does *that* mean?" he says. Just then, Leelo walks out of the bar. "Oh, here she is."

"I didn't know you are outside," Leelo says.

"Oh. I thought I told you...This is Neha. She's an old friend from...my younger days. Neha, Leelo. She's from Estonia but lives in Cork."

"Great to meet you," Neha says and sticks out her hand. Leelo looks at it for a second before shaking it. "I hear Cork is a great little city."

"It's nothing special," Leelo says and turns to Jack. "The table at restaurant is ready, I think."

"Oh yeah," Neha says. "Don't let me keep you from dinner."

"You wanna just go to the restaurant and I'll meet you there in like two minutes?" Jack says to Leelo.

"Whatever you want," Leelo says and walks away.

"So, she's...*cute*," Neha says when the other woman is out of earshot.

"It's not like that," he says.

"Like what?"

"Whatever you're thinking."

"I'm not thinking anything." They both laugh.

"Anyhow. It's really nice seeing you." They embrace again, for a little longer this time. "Where are you living these days? Still New York?"

"No, I moved out of the city a few years ago. I'm back near Philly, out on the Main Line."

"Wow, so close. We should catch up sometime," he says, but even as he does, he knows it probably won't happen. Something will come up. They'll get busy. They'll forget.

"Yeah, look me up on Facebook." She goes back into the bar. Jack takes his time walking to the restaurant.

The dinner is probably one of the best he's had in Ireland, but he can't fully enjoy it. Seeing Neha has stirred something inside of him. He wouldn't exactly call it regret but something like it. Not about her specifically, but about all the paths not taken—all the branches that would now be forever closed to him as time marched ever forward.

Two years after returning from Ireland, Sarah and Jack were married. They moved into a row house apartment in an up-and-coming neighborhood of Philadelphia with trendy coffee shops and brunch spots that boasted organic ingredients. Once a week they hosted game nights for couples they were friendly with. They were happy—not in the I-can't-believe-how-great-my-life-is way, but in the everyday, slow burn that is the foundation of a good life. Time passed. Slowly all those seemingly silly disagreements that people warned couples about started to pop up and even though they'd sworn they'd never be so petty, things started to fall apart.

They tried for about a year and a half to have a baby; Sarah quit smoking, they kept track of her cycle, and followed doctor's orders. She never got pregnant.

Shortly after they took a break from "trying," Jack went through a phase where he started being unfaithful with some regularity. An escort would occasionally be involved. He wasn't proud of it, but he'd done what he'd done. Later, when he'd had time to reflect, he concluded what he'd known intuitively all along: it wasn't the sex that compelled him, but rather what led up to it—the excitement, the nervousness. Like a watered-down version of falling in love.

Sarah never found out about any of this.

Back in the hotel room, Jack's dozing off when Leelo comes out of the shower and gets into the bed naked. She kisses him where his neck meets the back of his ear and slips her hand into his shorts.

Since the failed attempt at lovemaking back in Dublin they haven't done anything more than kiss each other on the cheek and spoon in bed with all their clothes on. Jack supposes there was something about her—a hidden fragility that he sensed, that made him not want to be too aggressive. Yet now, with her athletic body pulsing with sexual energy right before him, he doesn't care about any of that. He kisses her neck, her breasts, her closed eyes.

"Go get something," she says.

"Okay," he says, and he is about to go to his bag to retrieve it when her face changes. "What's wrong?"

"Nothing," she says right before she starts crying.

Jack puts his shorts back on and gets back into the bed with her. Her back is turned to him so he just drapes his arm on her shoulder and smells the back of her head. After a few minutes, Leelo gets out of the bed, wraps herself in the hotel bathrobe and goes out on the balcony to smoke a cigarette. Jack eventually joins her outside.

"You okay out here?" he says.

He kisses her on the cheek. As his lips touch her cold, slightly blemished skin, she closes her eyes. He's struck by great pity for this girl—although who the fuck's he to be pitying anyone?

"Can I have a drag?" he says. She hands him the burning nub. He takes it delicately between his fingers and inhales, the second cigarette he's ever smoked. Strangely, Jack likes the way they taste. If it weren't for how terrible smoking is for one's health, he'd likely have taken it up on a regular basis.

"I lied to you," she says.

Jack passes the cigarette back to her. "You're not Estonian are you? You're Lithuanian . . ."

"You are idiot. Lithuanian girls have no ass."

"And . . ."

"Don't *and* me," she says and slaps her rear. "Trust me, I am Estonian."

"Fair enough," he says. "It's your name then, isn't it? Your name's not Leelo?"

"Wrong again. Leelo isn't my birth name, but it is what my friends call me since when I am little girl."

"I give up then."

"It's my job."

"Okay."

"It is bar but not mainly."

"What is it then?"

"Fucking 'gentlemen's' club," she says and makes disdainful air quotes with her fingers.

He thinks about the significance of this. "Doesn't bother me," he says.

This is both true and not. "Why are you mentioning this now?"

"I don't know." She takes another drag of the cigarette, stamps it out on the balcony railing and throws what's left into the dirt of the planter that's out on the balcony with them. "It is shit place. Most of us live above club so even when not working we feel the boom, boom, boom from the stupid music. And guys are all cheap assholes. Like they expect to get hand job for twenty euro. I'm not that kind of girl."

Jack doesn't have anything to say, so he kisses her on the cheek again. The moment he does this, he has the strong feeling that this was somehow inappropriate.

"Last week guy comes in and we are in back room, and he wants everything for forty euro. I tell him I don't do that. Dance, yes. But not the other things. He says to me that last girl did and I tell him that I'm not last girl. So I leave and he complains because owner is friend and my boss bitches me out."

"I'm sorry. That sucks."

"Yeah. Sucks. Oh well."

Three men speaking loudly in Japanese approach the front door of the inn. Leelo and Jack watch them. "Well, thank you also for dinner," she says after the Japanese men are in the lobby. "It was really good place, yes? Aren't you glad we didn't go to Chinese?"

"It was pretty good. I'll give you that." He goes back into the room leaving Leelo outside.

When she comes in, she starts getting dressed. She tells him she's going back into town to have another drink. She doesn't ask him to join. He tells her to be safe. She nods.

As he lays in bed, Jack imagines her going back into town to see the bartender, running her hands through his reddish beard as he ravishes her right there on the filthy barroom floor.

The Cliffs of Moher are one of the touristiest destinations in Ireland; however, they live up to the hype. At their highest point, near where Sir Cornelius O'Brien in 1835 built O'Brien's Tower to impress a woman he was courting, the cliffs stand some seven hundred feet above the rocky shoreline below. As you make your way up towards the cliff edge, several signs seek to dissuade would-be suicides by offering a toll-free helpline and words of encouragement.

When Sarah, her friends, and Jack arrived at the cliffs, Jack had already been traveling with the three girls for several days, and Sarah had started staying in his hotel room at night—although they would only lay in their underwear and make out.

It was cold and raining steadily that day. After walking along the cliffs for thirty minutes, Sarah's friends wanted to head back to the car to warm up. Sarah, though, continued on. Off to the south was another tower, probably a mile's distance.

"Let's see if we can make it out there," she said.

Jack's coat wasn't waterproof and his socks were soaked through, so with every step they squished beneath his cold, pruned feet. He would have followed her anywhere though.

This second tower was much further than it had initially appeared and, after twenty more minutes, it hardly looked closer. By now they were so far removed from the visitor's center and parking lot that they seldom saw anyone else around.

When the rain slowed for a minute they stopped to share a granola bar. While Jack finished his half, he watched Sarah stand on a rock and swivel around, her hands up near her face, the thumb and index finger on each forming inward facing brackets.

"Whatcha doing?" Jack said.

"Mental snapshot," she said. "So I'll remember."

"Not a bad place for that."

"No kidding. I mean, can you even believe that a place like this exists?" she said and gestured to the cliffs and water and rocks and everything. "When you see this, don't you just have to believe that it isn't just an accident? That this was *made*. Maybe it wasn't an old bearded dude sitting atop a mountain waving a wand for seven days and seven nights, but someone *made* this."

He'd been raised Catholic but had lapsed just as soon as he left home for college and had the chance. He wasn't sure what he believed, although he was pretty sure that no religion had gotten it right. "But if it *were* an accident," he said. "If we are here just on account of all the right random events lining up just so. And if our existence is just a blip, a mistake…isn't there a kind of magnificence in that too?"

Sarah opened her mouth and let a few raindrops fall in.

"Come here, help me," she said and walked down towards the cliff edge.

"Are you sure that's a good idea?"

"I want to look over the edge."

"It's dangerous. Be careful."

"You'll make sure I don't fall."

She went to the edge. "Here, take my hand," she said. He took it. She leaned over the precipice so that her body made a forty-five-degree angle with the ground. He gripped her wet fingers with all his strength.

Don't die. Don't die. Don't die.

After that, it started raining harder again. They never did make it out to that other tower.

It's been two days since Leelo and Jack parted at a train station in Limerick and Jack has three more days to kill here in Galway before his flight back to the States. The previous night he went on a pub tour and was at least a decade older than everyone else there. Six drinks in at the karaoke bar, he slipped away unnoticed and made his way back to the hotel.

When Leelo and he left Dingle, the plan was to drive north and stay for a night at a B&B near the moonscape plains of The Burren National Park, after which time they'd continue on to Galway for a few days' before Leelo caught a bus back south.

Over breakfast at their inn in Dingle, Leelo had seemed anxious. During their travels together thus far she'd hardly been a chain smoker, yet three times during their meal that morning she'd gotten up to smoke a cigarette outside on the large wrap-around porch. He'd asked her what time she'd gotten back to the room, how her drink was in town the previous night, but she only gave him vague responses.

They'd not been an hour's drive from Dingle, descending the treacherous curves of the Conor Pass road into an enormous valley, when she told him she wanted to go back to Cork.

Like today, he'd asked.

Like today.

Jack was so focused on managing the hairpin turns of the narrow road that he hardly glanced at her. He just barely acknowledged her request with a nod of his head. When they were back on more easily navigable roads, he thought to ask her if this decision had anything to do with what had transpired the previous night, but then he stopped himself. There was no point in stirring up trouble.

"At least let me drive you," he'd said, but she insisted she just catch a train from Limerick.

Two hours later, in front of the ticket gate, he kissed her goodbye, on the lips and with an open mouth, even though this felt like a sad attempt to pretend that nothing was something. He told her to take care of herself.

"You also," she said. "And if you write about me, don't make me asshole."

After that Jack decided to skip all the rural sightseeing and just drove straight through to Galway. Being among people, he decided, might provide him with the necessary distraction before he returned home.

This morning, after a greasy brunch of unfamiliar breakfast meats, he returns to his hotel because he's hungover and tired of walking around. He's sitting in his hotel's downstairs tearoom surfing the web when he sees he's received a Facebook message from Neha.

For a few seconds he just stares at the message on his laptop. He doesn't want to open it; he wants to leave it unopened so that he can forever believe in the promise it might contain. After another twenty seconds, this sentiment is overcome by curiosity. He clicks.

Hey Jack,

Greetings from lovely Connemara! Bet you didn't think you'd be hearing from me so soon. There is an abbey here that is on a lake that is ridiculously beautiful (sunlight literally <u>shimmers</u> off of it!), although maybe it's a little overrun by people with fanny packs and guidebooks. Anyhoo... today I am off to the Aran Islands. Right now I'm waiting for my ride to the ferry and they have surprisingly good Wi-Fi here, so I thought I'd just drop you a line and mention (again) how nice it was to see you. So many people pass through our lives that we then never see again, and it is sad in a way, no? I guess the other thing I wanted to mention (I don't know why I'm bringing this up, it's silly really) is that when I saw you the other night... Well, I am probably totally imagining things (I have a tendency to falsely read into things, did you know that? You do now!), but I seem to have gotten the impression that you were looking at my wedding ring (paranoid!). And not that it matters, because you've got your own thing going on (she was really cute! But you know that), and this isn't me trying to make a pass or anything, but I felt that if I didn't clear something up, then I would be misrepresenting things, and not that you're a gossip, but word gets around... So, yes, I was wearing my wedding ring, but the thing is that I'm not married (anymore). Gerard (my husband) and I haven't lived in the same place for nine months and it's only a matter of time before the paperwork gets processed, etc. So why did I continue to wear it? This is rather embarrassing, but I haven't necessarily told my family and so when I was visiting my brother, I just put it on again and forgot to take it off.

Sheesh! Now that that's all cleared up, I'll just say that I can't believe I typed all that and that hopefully you don't think I'm insane. I hope you enjoy the rest of your vacay and maybe we'll run into each other when we're back stateside.

Safe Travels,
Neha

PS: I read your book. I forgot to tell you. I can't say that it's the type of thing that I'd ever imagine you writing, but I still really liked it. I remember the stories you shared with me back when we used to date and how they were always so good.

The last day before Jack was set to return to the States, Sarah and he just stayed in bed most of the day talking and listening to the rain pitter-patter on the skylight above their hotel room. They were in Belfast but had grown weary of sightseeing and decided instead just to relax. Sarah's friends had looked up a local theater and were spending the afternoon watching the latest Hollywood blockbuster.

For a few hours straight Sarah and Jack took turns posing questions that each of them would answer. It was all so new and exciting—they were, each of them, explorers mapping out the new continent they'd just discovered.

What was your favorite vacation spot from childhood?

What was the class you hated most in high school?

If you had to take three books to a deserted island what would they be? What about three CDs, assuming you magically had a CD player with electricity on said deserted island?

Jack has no recollection whatsoever regarding either of their answers to any of these questions. What he does remember so vividly was thinking about Sarah's "mental snapshot" on the cliffs and trying then himself, in that moment, to take everything in: the green and white quilted comforter they lay under with a single round cigarette burn in it, the wood paneled walls in which someone had carved *slainte*, the aroma of bacon wafting up from the kitchen below, mixing oddly with the smell of Sarah's shampoo. And he filed it all away, thinking that if this thing with this lovely girl all ended up being nothing, at least let me have these few memories.

The tricky thing with the Aran Islands is that there are three of them and Jack has no idea which one Neha has gone to. He could reply to her message from yesterday and ask which island she's traveling to, but this would defeat the point. He doesn't want to meet up with her, he wants to chance by her again, even if that means he has to give chance a little kick in the ass.

He arrives at the ferry station and parks his rental in a field of tour buses. At the ticket counter, he asks the clerk, who wears a wool San Francisco 49ers hat and a green polo, which island he'd go to if he were looking for someone.

"What the hell kind of question is that, eh?"

"My friend said she's going to the Aran Islands, but I forgot to ask which one."

"You sure she wants you to find her?"

"Yes," he says, but his voice betrays his doubt. "Can you just tell me if there's an island that someone traveling here for the first time would likely go to?"

"Well, Inishmore is the largest and so is the most popular."

He buys his ticket; the next ferry leaves in twenty minutes.

From the pamphlet that comes with his ticket he reads that Inishmore would directly be translated as "Great Long Ridge" and is approximately nine miles long with a population of just over 800. When the weather is nice there might be twice as many tourists on the island as actual residents. After a bumpy half hour, the ferry docks in Kilronan, the only proper town on the island—although even it is just a smattering of houses and shops situated between the water and the hilly grasslands beyond.

Jack and his fellow passengers are herded off the boat along a narrow plank onto the pier. As they wait for luggage, red-faced buggy drivers hurry among their ranks peddling scenic tours. Right where the pier meets the land, giant signs for several bicycle rental companies compete for passengers' attention. How can he realistically expect he'll "run into" her? She easily might have gone to one of the other islands. Less popular, yes, but also more peaceful. And even if she *is* on this island, what's the likelihood of running into her? And even if he does see her, what then? *Hi, I'm stalking you.*

He resigns himself to the fact that he probably won't find her. Maybe it's a blessing. This island seems nice enough. A nice place to get some quiet alone time. He'll just stay here and look around for a couple days before heading back to the main island to catch his flight. If he sees her, he sees her. He's not holding his breath.

He books a two-night stay at a pale yellow guesthouse. His room is quaintly decorated and has a view overlooking the pier. He washes up in the room and walks back to the docks to rent a bike. After receiving some basic advice from the girl at the bike rental counter regarding the layout of the island, he hops on the bike and rides past most of the accommodation spots along the water in town—just in case. There's no sign of her.

He takes one of the roads that leads uphill and away from the shore, stopping by a small grocery store that is surprisingly well stocked to buy a sandwich. Roughly five miles away is Dun Aengus, an ancient stone fort and the island's main attraction. That, he decides, will be his destination.

He last saw Sarah eighteen months before in Tampa. He was having a reading at a Barnes & Noble in town at a strip mall opposite a Ruby Tuesday. The divorce had recently been finalized and Sarah was staying at her parent's winter house in Sarasota. When Jack texted her that he'd be in town and asked if she'd come to the reading, she agreed.

Tampa, it turned out, wasn't much of a hotbed for turn-of-the-twentieth-century historical romance novels. Not counting Sarah, there were four people at the signing. Jack's publisher had given him little help promoting the book, so he had gone on his own to schedule his "book tour." He'd hired a girl off Craigslist for ten bucks an hour to be his "assistant" and gave her a list of cities in which to schedule readings and signings. His thought, which turned out to be correct, had been that any author with an assistant would be viewed as sufficiently important to warrant bringing in to a store. The only flaw in this strategy was that just because he had a full schedule of events didn't mean anyone was going to come to them.

After the reading, he and Sarah left to have dinner at a "Vietnamese fusion" restaurant that mandated they valet park Jack's sub-compact rental.

The two of them hadn't seen each other for several months and, for most of the meal, they conversed as if they were two old—but never close—friends catching up. Jack had something on his mind but couldn't work up to broaching the subject until the end of the evening.

"I'm going away for a while," he told her after the dessert, a fourteen-dollar mung bean pudding that tasted little different than the tapioca Jack bought at Costco, arrived. "I've got one more reading in Athens, Georgia before I head back to Philly. After that I'm just going to travel for a bit."

"That's great," she said. "I think that will be really good for you."

"There's still a ton of paperwork for me to take care of with my dad's will, but I can probably do some of it remotely."

"Well, I'm happy for you." Sarah took a dainty spoonful of the pudding followed by a sip of her cappuccino. "This place is great, isn't it?"

"I'm a simple guy."

"You need to learn how to enjoy things."

"Maybe," he said, not wanting to re-hash old arguments. "So I'm going to go down to Argentina. To Patagonia." She didn't react so he went on. "You remember how we used to always talk about going there someday? *The edge of the world* and all that?"

"I remember," she said. "I'm sure it will be a great trip. A great way to get away from everything for a bit. You've been through a lot. You and I. Your dad."

"You know, you could come with me," he said. He'd meant for it to come across like a casual off-the-cuff comment, but it ended up sounding like a plea.

"I don't know why you'd even ask that." She put her spoon down and pushed the dessert towards the center of the table.

There was no more sense in being subtle so he just barreled on ahead. "What would stop you? It's not the money."

She rifled into her purse and checked the time on her phone. "It's getting late."

"What is it? Are you seeing someone?"

"No...What? That's none of your business. I've gone on dates...but nothing serious. That's not why—"

"You know, sometimes when I'm on the road or something I get to thinking about what if I die—like in a car wreck or something. And what I think about is what is the last thing I said to you and if I will regret it. And if you know how I really feel and how there's nothing I want more than to go back in time and do it all over again."

"Jack...This...What you're doing here...it doesn't make it any easier for either of us. There's no going back."

"I guess I was just thinking—"

"You have to understand. We can't go back in time. And even if we could, the truth is, I don't think I'd want to."

The village of Kilmurvey isn't really a village at all. It's just a few white thatch-roofed buildings that sit at the intersection of the dirt road to Dun Aengus and the dirt road back to Kilronan. There's one restaurant, a snack bar, and a few crafts stalls. Fifty yards from these lies an open field and an old stone house, which the sign tells Jack is a bed and breakfast.

Although he's just eaten a little over an hour before, the five-mile bike ride from Kilronan and the walk up the hill to Dun Aengus have made him hungry. He stops in the restaurant to get a bowl of parsnip soup and some soda bread. The place is run by what looks to be a family—the mother takes the orders and works in the kitchen and two teenage girls serve the food and bus plates. As Jack eats the delicious, nourishing soup, he imagines what it must be like to live and work on a remote island like this.

It's after he's paid and he's on his way out that, through the window, he sees Neha.

It doesn't quite make sense to say he's *surprised* to see her, seeing as she was the reason he came to this island in the first place. Still, a surreal feeling overtakes him.

She's wearing jeans and a cream-colored wool sweater like they sell at all the gift shops throughout Ireland. She is sitting on a low stone wall outside—the type that is ubiquitous on this island and gives the countryside a labyrinthine feel—thumbing through a guidebook and eating crackers from a Ziploc bag.

She looks sadder, older than before. Maybe it's just what she told him in her message about her marriage. He feels at once less attracted to her and more affection towards her.

He's spent some time thinking about what he might say if he saw her, but the question never entered his mind of *whether* he would approach her. Now the question hangs over him. Would going outside and talking to her be just another desperate attempt at retrieving the irretrievable, another humiliation in a long line of humiliations? All this traveling around...Leelo...The past is past; you can't relive it. He should know that by now. He can just slip out of here unseen and go back to the guesthouse and get on with his life. Tomorrow he can read all day and then take the ferry back the next day. And yet, what is one more failure when compared to the chance at...what?

He has just about decided on what to do when he's startled by a light touch on his shoulder. He wheels around. It's one of the teenage girls who work at the restaurant. "Excuse me, sir," she says. "Is something wrong?"

Excerpted from the lecture: *A Primer on the Nature of the Cree for the Alderian Military*
By Master Aron Vairn, 591 YAF

Over our near five centuries in existence, we of the Ilyan Brotherhood have established relatively little about our own nature, which is to say we know little about the nature of being Cree. However, through observation and a variety of experiments conducted at the Sanctum over the centuries, there do exist some few facts that are known. These "Tenets," as the Ilyan Brothers call them, are the foundational elements of our knowledge of being Cree and are taught to all new arrivals at the Sanctum in the first week.

To begin, some definitions: a Cree is someone who has the *potential* to do sorcery—regardless of whether or not they ever do it. The vast majority of those with the potential would never fulfill said potential without training. Those who do not ultimately end up ever performing sorcery are called simply, *unfulfilled.* Conversely, that minority who do sorcery without the aid of training are aptly called, *naturals.*

Generally, The Ilyan Brotherhood has accepted that the term *sorcerer* be used interchangeably with Cree, with the exclusion of those who are unfulfilled; however, they have rejected other commonly used terms such as *wizard, witch, warlock, conjurer, necromancer,* or *magician,* as these terms have historically been used to describe a number of individuals who, in the eyes of the Brotherhood, are little more than charlatans, con artists, or, at best, talented illusionists.

Naturals tend to, with an equal amount of training, have a higher potential at sorcery than do other Cree. Certainly there have been non-naturals who, through diligent practice, ended up as superior sorcerers to many naturals. In fact, some of the greatest sorcerers in the history of the Ilyan Brotherhood have been non-naturals. That said, it is clear that, on average, naturals have a higher aptitude for sorcery— especially as relate to some of the more challenging spells, which the Alderian military may have had the misfortune of encountering in the field of battle this last year, including mage fire, telepathy, and various forms of levitation.

No one is precisely sure what causes one to be a Cree (although there are no shortage of theories); however, it has been proven that being a Cree is at least partly due to hereditary factors.

Cree are incapable of having children. In all recorded history, there has not been a single verified instance of either a) a female Cree becoming pregnant with child or b) a male Cree siring a child. Over the centuries there have been numerous instances of male Cree claiming to be the father of a child, but, in most instances, these have all proven to be mistakes or outright deceptions. For these reasons, many of the stories about Cree have referred to them as *the Childless Ones.*

In most cases, the mothers of Cree offspring have difficulty conceiving additional children following the birth of their Cree child. In cases where they *do* conceive again (with the same father), that child has roughly a one-in-two chance of being a Cree, as well. Further, other family members of Cree (cousins, uncles, aunts) seem to have an increased likelihood of being Cree versus the general occurrence of Cree in the population, although the range of stated probabilities varies widely depending on which expert one asks.

It has long been difficult to calculate the percentage of the population who is Cree for the dual reasons that a) population figures across the Continent are often educated guesses at best, and b) since the majority of Cree do not (prior to training) manifest any readily identifiable signs of being Cree, it is thought that many go unidentified. In what limited studies there have been, when Ilyan Brothers adept in the ability of *identification* have gone on surveying expeditions, the frequency of Cree amongst the population has usually been found to be approximately one in ten thousand people.

Anecdotally, certain populations seem to have a higher likelihood of being Cree, namely some of the Western peoples like the Zabissians and the Lanzhenese and, as we have been made frighteningly aware, certain tribes of Northern Islanders. This has not been verified in any rigorous way.

Other species of humanoid creatures, such as the Mandrakhar, the Haroumi in the far west, or Melothani who reside in the Bridgelands, have not shown the capacity to be Cree in any way that fits our understanding of what the designation means. There have been reports of Melothani sorcerers, but it seems to be that these individuals—insofar as they existed at all—derived their powers from artifacts, talismans, and other mystical items, rather than from their own bodies, as is the case with the classical definition of a Cree.

According to those who have studied the nature of Cree abilities in detail, the source of these abilities is a series of invisible energy channels or "meridians," which all humanoid species contain (given that the Haroumi have six limbs rather than four, their meridians are slightly different). The meridians themselves are not unique to Cree; the Cree, rather, are unique in their abilities to utilize these meridians to perform a variety of, what most non-Cree would deem, "amazing" feats—including telekinesis, pyrokinesis, a kind of one-way telepathy the Cree call "gathering," accelerated healing, and more.

Excessive manipulation of the meridians by a Cree in order to perform any of the aforementioned feats will usually lead said Cree to feel physically weak and/or ill. In rare but extreme circumstances, coma or even death has been known to occur.

In addition to the "active" abilities described previously, there are also a number of "passive" abilities that Cree have. Chief amongst these seems to be a slower rate of aging. Most Cree tend to age up to "maturity" (late twenties or so) at approximately the same rate as regular humans. Those Cree who have unlocked their abilities (i.e. all those excluding the unfulfilled) tend to age at a much slower rate thereafter. The actual rate tends to vary from Cree to Cree (usually between two to four times slower), and it is generally held that those Cree of greater power tend to age at a slower rate. Other passive abilities that are sometimes attributed to Cree, but which are not consistently present amongst all Cree, include the ability to withstand very hot or cold temperatures, the ability to go long periods without sleeping (although if too much time elapses, long periods of hibernation may ensue), and the possession of extremely efficient metabolisms, which allow some Cree to function nearly at full capacity on virtually no food or water for long periods. One hypothesis as to why these passive abilities are not present in unfulfilled Cree is that the manipulation of the energy meridians by a Cree has the effect of somehow altering the inner workings of the Cree's body.

Many laymen, insofar as they have witnessed a Cree using his abilities, have labeled this act "casting a spell." This label is actually based on a misunderstanding of the mechanism through which Cree abilities are derived. Often times a Cree will chant or recite some kind of incantation as they are manipulating the meridians to various effects. Contrary to popular belief, this incantation is simply a way that the Cree focuses, as manipulating the meridians requires a high level of concentration. Witnesses of Cree performing sorcery have often made the mistake of thinking there was actually power in the words being said and therefore labeled the words as *spells*. In actuality, the words, in the mouth of a non-Cree, lack any power or significance whatsoever. Ironically, so ingrained has this idea of "casting spells" become that many Cree have adopted this terminology themselves when discussing the use of their abilities.

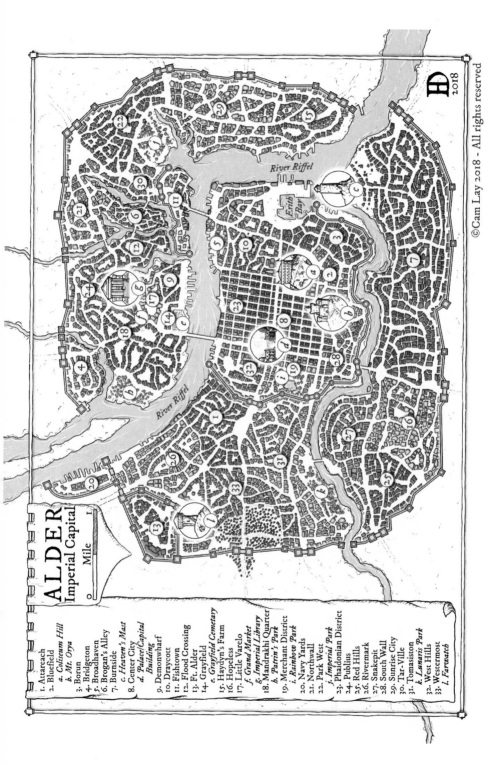

ALDER
Imperial Capital

Mile

River Riffel

Erith Bay

River Riffel

River Riffel

HD
2018

1. Attareach
2. Bluefield
  a. Coliseum Hill
  b. Mt. Orya
3. Borun
4. Bridgeton
5. Broadhaven
6. Brogan's Alley
7. Burnside
  c. Heaven's Matt
8. Center City
  d. Palace/Capital
    Building
9. Demonwharf
10. Draycott
11. Fishtown
12. Flood Crossing
13. Ft. Alder
14. Grayfield
  e. Grayfield Cemetary
15. Haydyn's Farm
16. Hopeless
17. Little Varelo
  f. Grand Market
18. Mandrakhi Quarter
  g. Imperial Library
19. Merchant District
  h. Patrin's Park
20. Navy Yards
  i. Rainbow Park
21. Northwall
22. Park West
  j. Imperial Park
23. Phaidonian District
24. Publius
25. Red Hills
26. Rivermark
27. Snakepit
28. South Wall
29. Sunrise City
30. Tar-Ville
31. Tomasiston
  k. Lamaris Park
32. West Hills
33. Westermost
  l. Farwatch

SIX

THE MAN WITH THE GOLDEN HAIR
599 Years After *The Fall*

Far from the alabaster spires of the Imperial Palace and the sprawling mansions of the neighboring Phaidonian district, across the green-black waters of the Riffel, and beyond the Demonwharf and Fishtown and the teeming crowds and pungent aromas that fill the Grand Market from dawn until past midnight, lays Brogan's Alley. While the origins of the locale's name have been completely forgotten (even the neighborhood's oldest residents couldn't tell you who Brogan was, and there is no single "alley" but a network of fifty or more narrow walkways and staircases that curve to and fro, between, beside, over and around buildings whose now-decrepit facades reached their aesthetic apex some two centuries earlier), the one thing anyone in the capital of the *greatest nation that ever was or will be* could readily tell you is that "the Alley," as locals called it, was dangerous.

The rough reputation of Brogan's Alley had not escaped Undersecretary Novik and, as he circled the neighborhood that morning in search of a very particular person at a very particular address, he anxiously fingered the small wooden club he carried beneath his coat. Under normal circumstances there would be no chance the undersecretary would traverse these streets without a retinue of guards to accompany him. However, this was a subtle mission and he'd been instructed not to draw attention to himself.

Even with the map he'd been supplied back at the IAO, finding the building he sought was seemingly impossible. The addresses of Brogan's Alley corresponded only to the neighborhood, not any of the specific walkways or staircases, and the ordering of these numbers seemed to completely defy any conceivable logic. Novik was seeking 728 Brogan's Alley; he had quickly found 727, but none of the doors either adjacent or across the walkway from this building were 728.

After two hours of searching and inquiring at no less than eleven different addresses, Novik was at a loss. No one, either on the street or at the doors he knocked upon seemed to know how to find the address in question. He was beginning to believe the place didn't exist. When he finally knocked on the sturdy, unmarked door across the street from one of the neighborhood's seemingly inexhaustible supply of alehouses, the undersecretary was almost resigned to the fact that this—like each of the near-dozen other doors he had knocked upon—probably wasn't the place he was looking for. To Novik's surprise, the light force of his knock pushed the door open.

"Hello?" he called, but no answer came. This probably wasn't the place; he should probably just move on. Still, there wasn't much harm in poking his head in.

On some level, the room wasn't unlike the living quarters of any other common house Novik had seen: on one side a table and four chairs, on the other a small hearth. Yet the room was in shambles. Empty bottles of every shape and variety were scattered about—ale bottles and wine bottles and mead bottles and bottles more suited for tincture or potion than drink and yet other bottles that the undersecretary could hardly imagine a use for at all. In addition to these, the floor was littered with what appeared to be children's clothing: here a small tunic, there a child's breeches. "Hello?" he called again.

He was just about to turn away when a gruff, yet also oddly refined, man's voice called from the other room. "Come in," the voice said and the undersecretary walked into the adjoining room.

This second room seemed to be a study or office. Lining the walls was a relatively impressive collection of leather-bound books. Not the type of thing one would expect to find in a ramshackle row house in Brogan's Alley. Sitting at a table in the center of the room was a man of middle years with a long gray mustache whose ends had been sculpted into sharp upward-curling points. The man appeared to be eating his midday meal and a large pile of picked-clean chicken bones gathered on the plate in front of him. A heavy odor of pipe smoke filled the air. Further into the room, a child, no more than eight by the size of him, lay face down on a mat. Novik might have been concerned were the child not making a deep snoring sound, which confirmed he was still alive.

"Excuse the untidiness in the other room. The main entrance to the office is over here," the mustached man said, pointing to a door to his right, "so you weren't supposed to see that. We've been meaning to clean up for some time now but just haven't gotten 'round as yet."

"No, please. Excuse my intrusion," Novik said.

The mustached man started eating his chicken again and spoke in between bites. "Now...how...can I help...you...good sir?" A small piece of meat clung to his lower lip.

"I don't suppose you can help me find 728 Brogan's Alley," Novik said.

"I can," the man said, still chewing.

"Really?" He exhaled a deep sigh. This was the first positive news all morning. "Wonderful! Perfect! Thank you!"

"You're welcome."

"So which way is it? I don't suppose you could draw a map? Finding my way around this neighborhood has proven itself to be quite dif—"

"Look down at your feet," the man said.

"Look down at my feet?" Novik looked down.

"You're there."

"I'm there." It took a moment for this to sink in. "I'm there! And this is Master Nicoletto's office?"

"And residence."

Novik studied the man sitting at the table with new eyes. Here was the man he sought: Master Nicoletto who, if the grand councilor was to be believed, was the shrewdest inspector in all the capital, if not the Empire, if not the world—apprehender of criminals, solver of the unsolvable, and finder of lost things. A number of years ago he had assisted Grand Councilor Kilroy with some sensitive and important matters—although the details hadn't been divulged to the undersecretary. Novik had to admit, he hadn't imagined Master Nicoletto would be quite so large and perhaps would have guessed him to look a tad more...*sophisticated*. Nonetheless, he was happy to have at last found his man. "It is so wonderful to meet you."

"Nice to meet you Mr. . . ."

"Novik. Undersecretary Novik. From the grand councilor's office."

"Ah, quite the honor then, Undersecretary Novik."

"Now if you don't mind, Master Nicoletto, I would love to get straight down to the reason for my—"

"Whoa there. I think you are mistaken. You see, this *is* Master Nicoletto's office and residence, but I am not Master Nicoletto. I'm Nob."

"Nob...I see. Well do you know when Master Nicoletto will return?"

"Master Nicoletto is here."

"Here?" Novik looked around. This floor of the building only seemed to contain the front room and the one they were standing in. "Where?"

Nob gestured to the mat where the child slept.

Novik turned back around and gave Nob a smile. Ah, a joke. Novik could appreciate a sense of humor in a man. "You are a funny one, Nob, you devil."

"Funny? I'm not sure I follow."

Novik was confused now. "Surely you aren't suggesting that Master Nicoletto is a child?"

"Master Nicoletto is no child, I assure you," Nob said and then stood up and walked towards the mat. He began shaking the child. "Sera! Sera! You have a visitor."

The child rolled over and, sure enough, it wasn't a child at all but a short, and rather stubby woman, with her reddish brown hair cut short and a streak of dried spittle pasted to her mouth.

"Wh...What do you? Nob, I told you not to wake—"

"You have a visitor," Nob repeated and she turned to look at the Undersecretary who, though still several paces away, could smell the wine on the small woman's breath. "Undersecretary Novik, may I present to you the famed inspector and the person you seek, Master Serafina Nicoletto."

I.

Sera made Nob and the undersecretary wait in the other room while she washed herself in the basin, changed into some respectable clothing, and ate the last remaining slice from a (now rather curious-smelling, if she told the truth) meat pie she'd bought the day before.

When she was ready, the three of them hired a coach near the Alley's western gate to take them to the Capital Building across from the palace. "My lady, please," the undersecretary said when the coach stopped. He motioned for Sera to get in first, extending his hand to help her and her short little legs get up the carriage's raised step. She ignored the offer, grabbed the step with her hands and climbed into the cab.

The ride was as pleasant as a dull blade shoved hard in the gut. Having a hangover was never fun, but through relentless self abuse, Sera's body had grown accustomed to the feeling; on the other hand, having a hangover while riding for miles over cobblestone streets—not to mention that shit heap of a bridge that crossed the Riffel—in a hot coach with two bum wheels was a form of torture she was experiencing for the first time. Add to this the undersecretary talking her ear off and Nob smelling like rancid chicken grease, and it was a surprise she was able keep that meat pie down.

The Imperial Administration Office was located in the Capital Building directly across the promenade from the palace. While the two buildings were designed in the same grand Phaidonian architectural style with a large dome at the center of each and spires at each of the buildings' four corners, they were otherwise complete inverses of one another. Whereas the palace was constructed of white stone, the Capital Building was of shiny obsidian; whereas the interior of the palace was (allegedly) all luxurious rugs and massive tapestries and golden chandeliers, the insides of the Imperial offices were decidedly more pragmatic—stone floors, bare walls, and only the most utilitarian furnishings.

After entering the Capital Building and walking through a series of nondescript corridors, they reached the grand councilor's office where Novik left Sera and Nob to wait. From Sera's few previous experiences with the Imperial administration, she suspected it was unspoken policy to make visitors wait at least an hour before conducting any business with them. She was surprised when the grand councilor himself came in after only a few minutes.

Sera had done work for Kilroy's office some years ago, but she'd never met the man. Now, with him there in front of her, she didn't see what was so *grand* about him. Take off those satin-striped robes and don't trim the beard for a few days and he'd look not so different from the smelly hobos who wandered the Alley begging for crust. Technically speaking, the grand councilor was the highest-ranking official in all the Empire, but there was a reason he was in a cramped office with her and Nob while old Emperor Kaleb Lunaris was across the way probably being fed grapes by a harem of naked beauties. The practice of the Alderian Council actually choosing the emperor had been strictly ceremonial for give or take a century and a half, and when the emperor died it was tacitly agreed by all that the council would appoint the emperor's heir as the next leader of the Alderian Empire.

The grand councilor sat down at the desk across from Nob and Sera.

"Master Nicoletto," he said in a voice one would use for a three-year-old, "it is so wonderful to finally meet you."

Sera's head was still pounding. She nodded.

"You have been described to me in the past," he went on, "but it is one thing to hear your description and quite another to see you in the flesh and learn that all the descriptions were true."

"All the descriptions of *you* I've heard have been sorely lacking," Sera said, resting her gaze on the wart covering the tip of his nose. "No one ever mentions how dashingly handsome the grand councilor is."

He laughed; he even laughed like an asshole. "Well, we are not meeting to trade compliments, are we now? Shall we get to business?"

"Works for me."

He poured himself a cup of water from the pitcher on the desk between them and took a long drink. Sera was surprised there were no servants in the room. In her experience, even the lowliest officials would prefer not to clean their own asses if it could be avoided. "I will preface everything by saying that this is a matter of the utmost importance—a matter of national security—and that it requires *absolute* discretion."

"I think you know from the previous work I did for you that discretion is not a problem," she said.

"Well...yes...of course..." His face turned a slight shade of pink. "In any event," he said, "for the past three days, the emperor's son has been missing."

She and Nob looked at each other. "The crown prince?" Nob said.

"No. Prince Marcellus." The emperor's second son was thirty or so and had a reputation of being sullen, unfriendly, and a bad tipper. Beyond this, Sera didn't know much about him. "He was last seen departing the palace in the evening three days ago with his coach driver. Both coach and driver have also gone missing."

"You're thinking kidnapping?" Sera said.

"We have not ruled out that possibility."

"Any chance the driver is involved?"

"We have no reason to suspect it but have not completely ruled that out either."

"This sounds like a job for the Imperial Guard or the Redcloaks, not us." Nob said, more to Sera than Kilroy. "Why would they want to get us involved?"

"Who is this man?" Kilroy said to Sera.

"This is Nob," she said, and Nob nodded. "He helps me in case any of my jobs get difficult."

"Lovely," Kilroy said. "To the question: neither Imperial Guard nor military has yet been notified, and we hope to keep it that way."

"Why?" Sera said.

"You see, the prince, well...he has many vices...not the least of which is the ameghemite powder, and, given the state of our empire—what with us still recovering from the conflict in the North—and the state of the royal family—"

"What do you mean, 'the state of the royal family'?" Sera said

"As you know, the emperor grows rather advanced in age. What is less known is that the crown prince has, in recent months, grown very ill. Gravely, perhaps. And since the crown prince is without a child—"

"Marcellus might be heir and you don't want it known he's a degenerate powder head," Nob said.

"Not as delicate as I might have put it, but yes."

"Still, you must have some agents who you can trust this job to," Sera said. "If you need to find a stolen jewel or who stole it...if you need to find out who your wife or, in your case," she lowered her voice, "your *friend* is rolling around in bed with...we can help. But political kidnappings aren't our cup of wine."

"We certainly haven't yet confirmed this is a kidnapping. That is one of the things we wish for *you* to find out. We have chosen you because, in addition to the competence and, how shall I say, *finesse* you have shown in your previous work, I was also hoping you might have the proper connections to help with this specific situation. As you undoubtedly know, much of the ameghemite trade is centered in your... Brogan's Alley, and Prince Marcellus was known to frequent the area."

"I don't make friends with powder merchants, if that's what you're implying," Sera said.

"You mistake what I say, my dear. You are *certainly* above associating with such vile characters." Sera wouldn't go so far as to say this, but she appreciated the sentiment. Other than Nob, Sera could count her friends on the fingers of a double arm amputee, but she was *acquaintances* with some pretty shady characters. It couldn't be avoided in her line of work.

"But perhaps," he went on, "you know someone who knows someone..."

Sera kept her mouth shut.

"...who knows someone?"

She couldn't put her finger on it, but something about this job stunk like a rotten fish on a ripe summer day. They could use the silver though. She turned to Nob, who shrugged his shoulders. "If you think I'm right for this, I'll do what I can," she said.

"Excellent."

"But first we have some questions."

"I'd expect nothing less."

"For starters, we're going to need to know what the prince looks like."

"I assumed as much," he said and stood up to grab something behind one of the side tables. It looked to be a large painting still wrapped in cloth. "I had them fetch this from the palace. It's the most recent portrait of Prince Marcellus." He placed the frame on top of his desk and began unwrapping it.

Whereas the emperor, before going bald, had had straight black hair, Marcellus's was curly and dark brown. He did have his father's distinctive hawk nose.

"What about the driver?"

"Regrettably it is not customary for us to paint portraits of our carriage drivers," Kilroy said. "However, he is known to have several distinguishing physical characteristics. Namely, he is bald and has a large purple birthmark on his chin."

"And what about any friends. Is there anyone we can talk to that might be helpful?"

"Prince Marcellus had few friends amongst the aristocracy. Those few who were known to associate with him on occasion have already been interrogated to no avail."

"Does that mean you're not going let us question them?"

"The only useful piece of information we gathered is the name of a woman—an 'Esmeraldah' who is said to reside in Draycott. We haven't been able to find her yet. But we believe her to be a... *woman for hire*, if you understand my meaning."

"*Esmeraldah?* Zabissian girl?"

"Regrettably the Zabissians seem to have become a permanent fixture in our cities. I sometimes wonder if we won or lost the fighting beyond the sea. Every time we win a war our streets fill with foreign filth. I suspect we shall be overrun with Islanders and Kallanbori before too long."

"Kallanboro has been part of the Empire since long before any of us were born," Nob said.

Kilroy gave Nob a look of disgust but didn't say anything.

"The only other open matter is that of our fees," Sera said.

"You worry the *emperor* will have trouble paying your fees?"

"Not at all. But I've found that whoever my client may be, it is good to discuss such matters ahead of time."

"We will pay whatever is necessary—although we won't stand for price gouging, if that's what you had in mind."

"I can appreciate a fair price as much as the next girl," Sera said. "But as I'm sure you would agree, this isn't a normal job. Eight crowns a day for Nob and me, plus fifty up front for expenses. In addition, I would propose a bonus . . . say five hundred crowns if we find the prince for you?" This last bit she threw in just to see what they could get.

"Done. And make the bonus a thousand," he said and Nob's eyes opened wide, "if you find him alive. A corpse is of little use."

II

Kilroy's assistant supplied them with an advance to cover expenses and paperwork that proved they were performing work for their office, although the nature of this work was left vague. Afterwards, Nob and Sera headed straight to Draycott to see if they could find this Esmeraldah girl. Draycott, directly adjacent to the river docks on the south side of the Riffel, was a different kind of bad neighborhood than the Alley but was bad nonetheless. Draycott had, at one time or another, been home to just about every immigrant group that made its home in the capital: the Lakelanders and the Lanzhenese and then the Jarlites and the Nyribbians and the Zabissians and on and on and on. Over the course of some years one group would slowly rise in status before moving out of Draycott to make room for whatever new group the Empire's tide of expansion washed back in. And whatever group had been in the city longer would view the newcomers as uncivilized savages deserving their spite. So it had been and so it would continue until the Empire ran out of new lands to annex or until the gods saw fit to wash this whole cesspool away.

On the way over Sera had the driver stop so she could pick up a fresh jug of wine. She wasn't going to get the kind of rest necessary to get past her hangover, so the only other option was to keep pouring poison down her gullet.

When they got to Draycott they swung by a few of the well-known brothels, but no one had any knowledge of anyone named Esmeraldah. In retrospect, it made sense that a prince with unlimited funds wouldn't be cavorting with your garden-variety hooker, but they had to make sure to run down every angle.

After an hour of touring the whorehouses of Draycott, both she and Nob were famished, so they decided to find something to eat. Nob was a big fan of some of the foreigner's food they served in the neighborhood, but it gave Sera the runs, so they stuck to the familiar—a meal house called

The Noble Cod where Nob knew the owner and Sera figured they stood a fair chance of getting free food.

The proprietor was an old-timer named Wynford Cluff who stayed in Draycott through every wave of immigrants and had around twice as many fingers as teeth—and he didn't even have all of his fingers since he mangled one gutting a carp in the kitchen. Old Wynford and Nob were pals from back when Nob used to run protection detail for some big-time merchant. Sera personally couldn't stand the guy.

"Ho, ho. The Beauty and the Scoundrel!" Wynford said to them when they walked in. He was serving a table of sailors and was perfectly balancing two enormous trays of food and drink.

"Ho, ho! But which one is which?" Nob said. Sera rolled her eyes. How many times could these two make the same idiotic jokes?

Over half the tables were open, but Sera chose one within earshot of a group of sailors. In her line of work, eavesdropping often paid unexpected rewards.

On Nob's advice Sera ordered the cod, but when the food came five minutes later, it crossed her mind that if this was what the restaurant was known for, she'd hate to see what they weren't known for. The wine at least was half decent.

Nob was telling her a story about a time he and Wynford fended off an attack by Bridgeland pirates outside Vicus Remorum when she heard the sailors at the next table talking about high-end whores who cost a week's pay. Sera raised her finger and gave Nob an urgent look in an attempt to discretely tell him to shut up. Somehow Nob mistook this for a sign she was choking. He leapt from his chair and, before she could get him to sit down, was behind her slapping her back and yelling for Wynford to bring water. Everyone in the establishment, including the sailors, stopped to stare at them.

"Sit down. I'm fine."

"Oh, it's just that look on your face…I thought—"

"Sit. Down." He sat down.

Wynford came from the kitchen with water and asked if everything was all right. "Keep the water, but you can refill my wine," Sera said. Wynford looked confused.

Since her opportunity to eavesdrop was gone, Sera stood up and went directly to the sailors' table. "Excuse me. I couldn't help but overhearing you fine gentlemen discussing expensive whores just now."

"I couldn't help but hear you choking on a fishbone just now," the biggest of them said.

"A misunderstanding," she said. "Now about these expensive whores…"

"What's it to you, dwarf-bitch?" another said. This one was lighter skinned and looked to be a Jarlite or other Southlander. He would have been handsome if not for his vacant eyes and crooked nose and bad skin and huge belly.

"Which establishment did you all visit?"

"The one on Percy Street," the first one said. "Now be gone with ya!"

"North on Percy Street?"

"Why you so curious? Looking for work?" the Jarlite said and they all laughed. "There are plenty of men like to fuck themselves a midget, I suppose."

Sera stepped towards the Jarlite and grabbed the space between his legs hard. "You won't be fucking anything, midgets or otherwise after I pop these grapes of yours."

The other sailors looked around, helpless and unsure whether to intervene. Sera was a woman after all. And a little person at that. There would be little honor in beating her. Besides, Nob was but a few steps away and carried a claymore that could sunder these idiots in two faster than they could say "dwarf titties."

"You are going to tell me *precisely* where this brothel is." She squeezed a little harder and, like those Southland dolls that squeak when you pinch them, the Jarlite started talking. He not only told her which direction to go on Percy Street (yes, north), but how far and what the nearest cross street was and the color of the building. She could have drawn a map of the whole neighborhood from such fine directions.

"That wasn't hard, was it?" she said. She started to release her grip and then gave one last squeeze just out of spite.

She and Nob paid their bill (no free food after all) and headed out. Sera didn't get a chance to finish her cod, but it wasn't that tasty anyway. Besides, she wasn't going to put anything in her mouth without first washing her hand.

III

It was a nice place as far as tacky whorehouses in a bad part of Draycott went.

The building had a fresh coat of red paint and there were no beggars stinking up the entrance. Out front a burly Kallanbori thug with a vest but no shirt on puffed up his chest to scare off the riffraff. A nasty-looking curved blade hung from his waist. Seeing as whorehouses were more up Nob's alley, Sera let him do the talking.

"Hello, good sir," Nob said as he and Sera approached.

"You a customer?" the thug grunted.

"In a sense," Nob said.

"We don't want no customers in no sense 'cept the normal one."

"And how do you know that isn't what I'm here for?" he said cheerfully.

"Well, yer friend for one," he said gesturing to Sera. She had to give him that. Generally a man who brings a little person to a brothel probably doesn't have "normal" intentions. "T'ain't no good can come from a man walks around with a she-dwarf."

Perhaps Sera had overestimated Nob's powers of persuasion. "Listen," she said. "We don't want trouble, we just want a little information."

"Them who's looking for information usually end up stirring trouble."

"Let your boss decide."

"Can't do it."

"We have silver," Sera said.

"How much?"

"Enough." She pulled out two crowns and pitched them to him. "A sign of goodwill."

The thug went up through the entrance and when he returned, they were led up a stairwell through a room kept dark by heavy red velvet drapes. They didn't see any girls, but through the walls they could faintly hear the dulled groans of the establishment's customers. Sera was going to need to wash more than her hand.

They were led to a small office. The thug stopped at the door and told them to go in. The sheer curtains let in a little light from the high windows, but the place was still quite dim. On the walls hung an assortment of large paintings of naked women in various compromising poses—on all fours, bent over, spread-eagle, various fruits and vegetables inserted into various orifices. In the corner of the room a grotesquely large woman sat half-reclined on a divan upholstered with expensive-looking fabric. She was seventy or more and her hair, like the paint job on the building, was an unnatural red. She wore a white robe, partly open, which displayed her pale, overflowing stomach.

"I hear you're looking for information," she said in a husky voice that suggested *blacksmith* more than *lady*.

"We're looking for one of your whores. Pretty girl—"

"You've come to the right place. They're all pretty," she said and laughed.

"Western girl. Maybe goes by Esmeraldah." Sera looked for any reaction, but the fat lady didn't flinch.

"Why are you looking for her?"

"Will that change whether you know anything about her?"

"Might."

"Just looking for her help in finding someone."

"How much silver you got?" she said.

Sera grabbed a small stack of crowns and placed them in the woman's pale, corpulent paw.

"She *is* a pretty one, that Esmeraldah. She didn't show up to her shift four days ago."

"No one checked in on her?"

"We figured she was quitting. Happens every day."

"Can't be good for business—losing your girls all the time," Sera said.

"Quite the opposite, actually. There are always more girls. And customers want fresh meat."

"Wonderful. You know where she lives, I assume?"

"I didn't say that."

"Well, do you?"

The woman stuck out her hand again, but Sera slapped it down. It wasn't Sera's money, but she had to draw the line somewhere.

"Oh fine," the fat lady said. "If you're going to be so tight with your silver…You read?" Sera nodded, and the woman wrote down the address of an apartment a quarter mile away. Sera put the small slip of parchment in her pouch.

Out of the corner of her eye, Sera spied Nob over by the wall. She turned and saw he was studying the paintings as if there were going to be a test at the end of the day. "Nob!"

"Sorry," he said and stood at attention next to her.

"Anything else?" the woman said, ready for them to go.

"One more thing," Sera said. "Did you notice any customers who took a particular liking to her? Perhaps a nobleman?"

"Now that *is* going to cost you more silver."

Sera wanted to tell her that the only thing more she was going to give her was a kick in that disgusting gut of hers but realized this wasn't going to help them move things along. She took two more coins and dropped them on the ground next to her divan.

"Well?" Sera said.

"There was a man who called himself Hethcliff, or so I heard. Probably a pseudonym as most of my customers don't much like using their real names. I personally never saw him and I don't know anything else about him."

IV

It was getting late and all Sera wanted was to have another glass of wine and go to sleep. Already being in Draycott though, they decided they might as well visit Esmeraldah's apartment so they could avoid another trip out there in the morning. Sera's instincts told her they wouldn't find Esmeraldah at home. She was wrong, in a manner.

The apartment was on the ground floor of a three-level stone building across from the public baths. The building's imitation Phaidonian facade was of the kind that had been of great popularity before the war. The ground-floor apartments are usually the largest and most expensive, and despite being in Draycott, the place was nicer than they'd expect from the living quarters of a whore—even a high-end one.

Nob found the door and knocked. No one answered so Nob stepped out of the way, Sera did her little trick with the locks, and the door opened.

From the smell—that foul, slightly fruity scent of death—Sera knew this wouldn't be a pleasant scene. She and Nob wordlessly drew their blades.

They made their way through the dark apartment by the moonlight that came in through the windows. Sera spied a dark shape on the ground in the adjoining bedroom and walked over to it.

Accounts of Esmeraldah's beauty had actually been understated. She was gorgeous, with perfect hair and big eyes that Sera could imagine some sailor paying a week's wages to stare into for a little while—to keep warm, to chase away the loneliness of the sea. Esmeraldah would have looked even better were her skin and lips not so cold, pale. Sera could almost imagine she was just sleeping peacefully—albeit with eyes open, albeit naked on the floor of the apartment—until she saw the knife plunged into Esmeraldah's chest and realized she was lying in her own blood.

Nob found a candle and went outside to one of the torches on the street to light it. By candlelight you could tell now what a mess had been made of the place.

"Nice looking girl," Nob said. Sera nodded. The kind of girl Sera wouldn't have minded cozying up to herself. The kind of girl someone might kill for. Sera had known a girl like that once, years ago, but that was another story. "Think our prince has anything to do with this?"

"Can't know for sure. A beautiful lady of the night living in an apartment that's a little too nice could be caught up with all sorts of things."

"But . . ."

"But it seems a coincidence that she'd go missing around the same time our prince did."

"Maybe he was with her and he was kidnapped," he said.

"Might be."

"Or maybe he did this and ran."

"But why run? You think anyone's making a fuss over a prince killing a whore?"

Esmeraldah was on her side, and Sera used her foot to turn her onto her back. Sera recoiled. Much of the side of Esmeraldah that had been against the floor was covered in horrific burns. In many places her skin had scabbed over with a strange greenish clot. "Gods," Sera said.

"But only half her body burned. Like someone put her out," Nob said.

"And then stuck a knife in her heart," Sera added. "And other than her skin, there's no sign there'd been a fire in the room."

"Maybe someone moved the body." Nob sounded unconvinced by his own words. There would have been blood everywhere near the entrance to the apartment if that had been the case. No, Esmeraldah had died in this room.

They looked around the apartment but didn't find much else. Esmeraldah had quite the jewelry collection—and not fake stuff by the looks of things.

They walked out, and Sera locked the door again before the two of them made their way to the nearest constable's office. They weren't getting home for a long time yet.

V

The constable on duty was a rotund, red-faced fellow with a long black mustache that rivaled Nob's for both length and ability to defy the laws of nature with its steep upward tilt. When Sera and Nob walked in the candlelit office, the constable didn't even look up from the papers on his desk, instead just calling out in a tired monotone: "Constable Behrfalden, here. How may I be of service?" It was only after he turned his gaze in the new entrants' direction, and beheld them—a curious duo consisting of a dwarf woman and a tall man who was a fellow member of the Fraternal Order of Stupid Mustaches—that he pushed himself up from his slouched seated position at his desk.

"Good evening," he said. He was intrigued with what this odd couple's business might be, and his curiosity only seemed to grow when Sera unfurled the papers from Kilroy's office and spread them out on the constable's desk.

"You mean *Grand Councilor* Kilroy?" he said.

Sera nodded.

"Did you actually meet the man?"

"He's not so impressive in person," Nob said. This was the first time Behrfalden had fully acknowledged Nob directly and he briefly gestured to his mustache and gave Nob an eyebrow raise of approval.

Sera told the constable about Esmeraldah's body and tried her best to describe the condition they'd found it in. She was sure to be as vague as possible regarding the reason they'd been looking into Esmeraldah and the constable didn't push the matter.

"Burned on half the body and her scabs turned *green* you say? And then stabbed through the heart?"

Sera nodded. "Have you ever seen or heard anything like that?" she said.

"Gods no. But maybe I'm not envisioning your description properly."

"It's probably best for you to see for yourself," Nob said.

"I don't know if I want to. Sounds dreadful," he said and made a dramatic exhale. "But such is my life. There's no getting around it, I suppose. If you give me the address, I'll gather a team."

Sera gave him the location of the house as well as their own address in the Alley. The constable promised to send them any information that came up in regards to the dead girl.

"One more thing," Sera said. "After your people have a look at the body and do the necessary paperwork, can you send it to an associate of mine?" This was a strange death and Sera knew a guy who specialized in the strange who owed her a favor.

"Such a request is not…typical, but seeing as you're working for the grand councilor, who am I to say no?" Sera removed a small slip of parchment from her pocket and used the constable's quill to scrawl a short note that would accompany the body to her associate, whose location she supplied.

"Best of luck to you both. And hopefully I shall see you again soon," the constable said as they were leaving.

It took Sera and Nob nearly an hour to get back to the office, by which time Sera was an exhausted, useless mess. Seeing as this Esmeraldah had, at least temporarily, proven to be a (pardon the wordplay) dead end, their focus needed to shift to the prince's powder habit. If Marcellus was wrapped up with the ameghemite merchants, their contacts in the Alley might have a lead of some kind. For now though, she just needed some sleep.

VI

Sylas Nottle's place was less than a ten-minute walk from Sera and Nob's office, but it was nearly impossible to find if one didn't know it was there. If a person were to walk past The Rusted Goose they would see a walkway on their left so narrow that a man who'd been eating too many meat pies would have his gut scrape both sides of the wall. Forget about fitting a horse through the space. At first glance, the walkway appeared a dead end; however, once a person reached the end of the walkway they would see that the ivy hanging from the alley walls obscured the fact that they could turn left again. Taking that left would lead one down another narrow walkway, which eventually opened up into a courtyard with a half-dozen connecting staircases that each spiraled upward to various landings and rooftops of surrounding buildings. If one took the third staircase on their right, came to a landing and went to the second door on that landing, they'd get to Sylas's.

In addition to being hard to find, the other thing about Sylas was that he was a lying, conniving, powder head, whom one could trust about as much as they could trust the sun to rise in the north and set at noon. Still, he was well connected, and if anyone could help figure out Prince Marcellus's business in the Alley, it was him. Nob seemed to have an especial disdain for Sylas, beyond just the normal disdain one might have for a lying, conniving powder head, and he didn't want to come along when Sera told him where they were going that morning.

"Can't you just come back by the office when you're done?" he'd said, but Sera told him she wanted him with her in case things got prickly.

When they got to Sylas's, Nob knocked once hard on the door and followed with three softer knocks, the sign they weren't coming to murder Sylas and that he should let them in. One of Sylas's flunkies opened the door a crack.

"Yesss. How can I help you?" The flunky's irises were a bright purple, a temporary side effect of the ameghemite powder.

"We need to talk to Sylas," Sera said.

"Sssorry…Sylasss isss not here."

"We don't have time for this," Nob said. He stepped in front of his partner and rammed the door with his shoulder, knocking the flunky back. Nob was making sure he wasn't going to have joined Sera in vain. They walked in and started making their way to the staircase that led to the main part of the building. When flunky reached for the dirk sitting on the table in the front room, Nob turned around and socked him in the nose with his gauntleted hand. Flunky collapsed to the floor, blood suddenly everywhere. They turned around and went down the stairs.

"Ssstop! You can't go down there!" he called, his words further muddled by the blood in his sinuses.

Sera turned to Nob. "What's crawled up your ass this morning?"

"What?" he said, innocent.

They found Sylas down in one of the main rooms of the house, which overlooked the fountain in Brogan's Square. He was reclining in a chair eating pomegranate seeds while his head rested in the lap of a girl who couldn't have been more than fourteen. He shot up out of the chair when he saw his new visitors.

"Sera," he said pretending she'd come alone and that Nob wasn't standing right next to her, "it's so nice to see you."

"We need to talk."

They heard the doorman skulking into the room from upstairs. His face was a bloody mess and his nose seemed to point in two directions at once. "Sssylas," he hissed. "I told them they couldn't come down here but thisss brute—"

Nob drew his hand back like he was going to strike the man again and he scurried away back out of the room.

"It's okay," Sylas called out and turned back to his uninvited guests.

"Nice eyes, by the way," Nob said, referring to Sylas's brown, and most definitely not purple, irises. "It's only a few hours until noon and you're still sober. What are people going to think?"

Sylas ignored Nob and looked at Sera. "What do you want?"

She sat down. "We're trying to find a missing person and we need information."

"What does it have to do with me?" he said.

"You claim to be the most well-connected man in the Alley, don't you?"

Sylas sent the girl away. "Okay. Details," he said once she'd gone.

"From what we hear, our man may have had a predilection for the powder. Last known contact was a high-priced girl in Draycott named Esmeraldah."

"And what did she have to say?"

"She's dead."

Sylas popped a few pomegranate seeds into his mouth. "I know a lot of people, but there are even more people who like the powder, and I can't keep tabs on all of them."

"Something tells me you would have heard of this one?"

"Why's that?"

"His name's Marcellus. As in *Prince* Marcellus."

"You don't look surprised," Nob said.

For once Sylas acknowledged Nob's presence. "Of course I'm not surprised," he said. "The emperor's son doesn't come to the Alley without me finding out about it. This bit about him being missing though? That's new."

"So what have you got for me?" Sera said and jingled a small purse of silver in front of him. He grabbed it and placed it inside his jacket.

"Unfortunately, not much," he said. Nob stood up as if to make a show that such an answer wasn't going to be acceptable.

"Hold on, Nob," Sera said. "Come on, Sylas. You have to give us *something* for the money."

"One thing then. Just a rumor."

"Do tell."

"Apparently he visited a whore while he was here and that afterwards she was really shaken up."

"Why?" she said. "Were his tastes . . . *eclectic?*"

"You must not know much about the whoring business do you, Sera? Perversion is run of the mill—the cost of doing business. From what I heard he didn't even touch her, just talked."

"About what?"

"Occult stuff, the Forefathers, some such nonsense."

"And do you know who the whore is?"

He gave them a name but then added, "But it won't do you any good looking for her. She's been missing for months now." He got up and walked to a small wall safe and placed the purse inside. "Now, if there's nothing else, I need to find my friend," he said, gesturing vaguely to the part of the house the girl had gone.

"Yeah, there is something else." Sera said.

"What is it?" he said, exasperated.

"Where is he getting his ameghemite?"

Sylas exhaled dramatically at the stupidity of the question. "The same person everyone gets their ameghemite from, one Thaddeus Lucke."

"No shit," Nob said, "of course that's where it *originates*, but which of the distributors is he contacting directly."

"From what I understand, he is going directly to the boss man himself."

On the way out Sera threw another silver piece at Sylas. "That's for your man," she said. "Maybe he can get his nose patched up."

"I've never known you to be the generous type, Sera," he said.

"I'm not. It's not my money, and if I don't use it, I have to give it back."

"Very well. Goodbye, Sera, and goodbye, cousin."

VII

Thaddeus Lucke controlled pretty much all of the ameghemite trade from the Northern Islands to the Dagfinn Sea and had his hand in a dozen other businesses—some legal, other less so. Still, during the Uprising, Lucke sent a good deal of his own personal army into the scrum, while also financing a lot of the war effort that he wasn't directly involved in. On account of this, the Redcloaks pretty much left him alone so long as he didn't disturb the nicer neighborhoods of the city.

As opposed to Sylas, Thaddeus Lucke was most certainly not hard to find. Technically he lived in a mansion in the Phaidonian district but was said to spend most of his time in his fortress-like compound that sat on the banks of the river inlet between the Alley and Tar-ville, directly to the east, so that he could more conveniently run his many enterprises. The problem wasn't going to be one of finding the man but instead of getting within a hundred feet of him without getting gutted like a pig by one of his bodyguards.

For the time being, all Sera and Nob could do was wait and watch. Sera reached out via courier to a guy they knew named Maris whose boys they'd used for a few surveillance jobs in the past. She gave descriptions of the prince and his driver, without mentioning who they were, and hoped for the best.

Two days later in the morning, having made no progress, Sera received a sealed envelope from the constable in Draycott via a messenger boy. Inside the envelope were several documents, the first of which was a note addressed to herself:

Master Nicoletto,

I hope this note finds both you and your associate Nob doing well. The other day I spoke true when I said I had never seen a murder like Esmeraldah's before. Howsoever, today, through diligent research, I learned that such a murder was not completely unheard of within the city.

Per the city death records, ten somewhat similar incidents occurred over a span of fifteen months a few years ago. I say "somewhat similar" because with these others, the bodies were all burned in a manner similar to the body you found; however, in all of these other cases, no knife was used. The other ten all burned to death. In all cases the victims had been women. In more than half of the cases, the women were prostitutes.

I have sent you an accompanying document, which lists all of these ten other deaths as well as what we know about their circumstances. Also, as we have agreed, I have sent the body of Esmeraldah, along with your note, to your associate.

Please let me know if there is anything further we can do to help in your investigation. Also, if in your work on behalf of the grand councilor's office you learn of any information that might assist me in this inquiry, I would greatly appreciate you forwarding it.

Sincerely,
Your Friend Constable Quoyle Behrfalden

On the other sheets of paper were a list of the ten women along with their ages, profession (if any), where each had lived, and a line or two describing each body as found. When Nob came in after breakfast Sera showed him the letter and the accompanying document.

"What do you make of it?" he said.

"I don't know. It may have nothing to do with Esmeraldah. These ten dead women all showed up within a one-and-a-half-year span and the most recent of these murders happened nearly two years ago. And even if they do have something to do with Esmeraldah, her death may have nothing to do with the prince."

"Do you really think that?"

"No."

"Me neither," Nob said.

"But *what* does it have to do with the prince, and why would Esmeraldah be killed differently?"

Nob shrugged his shoulders. Sera felt the same.

VIII

They agreed Nob would seek out information on the victims who'd lived on the north side of the capital; Sera would look into those who'd lived on the south. This would give Nob six girls to look into and Sera four; however,

Sera also needed to stop by the man to whom she'd sent Esmeraldah's body, and he lived at the southernmost edge of the city. She set off for the first address immediately.

Since all the murdered women had been prostitutes or poor, and some years had passed since the killings, finding any information on these girls proved difficult. People might have heard of the murders, but it was nearly impossible to find anyone who had personally known or interacted with the victims. This wasn't completely surprising. The capital was a waterwheel powered by the broken dreams of people foolish enough to hope for a better life. Especially amongst the lower classes and immigrants, people came and went from the capital at a startling rate—even more so since the Uprising. And they'd push the wheel for a time and perhaps even be lifted up by it, but sooner or later they'd get dropped right back where they started.

Sera spent half the day traipsing around the southern half of the city, learning essentially nothing of the first three girls on the list. In the afternoon, she caught a carriage south to the outskirts of the city, where all the abodes were one-story, hastily made wooden shacks, if not tents, to check in on Esmeraldah's corpse.

Believing in half the things she'd heard about Padgett would require her to believe in all sorts of things she *wasn't* prepared to believe in. As far as Sera was concerned, he was sort of a doctor, sort of a collector of curios, and sort of just weird. He specialized in helping people with rare ailments and gruesome injuries—a racket that could have been quite lucrative if not for the silly fact that Padgett accepted whatever donation his patients offered up. A sucker, if you asked Sera. Still, he was as good a candidate as anyone to figure out what was up with Esmeraldah's burns. Sera had helped Padgett some years ago recover a silver dagger that had been stolen from him, and, as a result, he owed her. Plus, he liked her—maybe because she was one of the few adults he knew that was actually smaller than him. Padgett was no dwarf, but he might have shit-near qualified if only he were a few inches shorter and his head were a little bigger. On this day however, Padgett was not happy to see Sera.

"She arrives at last," he said, when he opened the creaky door of his shack. His voice was high-pitched and he spoke in a muddled Southland-Lanzhenese accent.

"Hi, Padge." He walked back into the shack, but since he left the door open, Sera followed him in. On top of his worktable lay Esmeraldah's naked, smelly corpse, partially covered with a blanket.

"Yesterday I returned home from my evening walk to find two men from the Draycott constable's office insisting they unload a burned corpse on me."

"Did you get my note?" Sera said.

"Yes," he said and pulled out a piece of parchment from his pocket, which Sera assumed was her note, crumpled it up and threw it at her.

"What?" she said. "I thought this was right in your corner."

"First off, I work with the living, not the dead. Second, even if this were, as you say, 'in my corner,' you cannot send rotting corpses to my home, do you understand?"

This seemed reasonable. Sera nodded.

"So you will *never* do this again?"

She pointed to the silver dagger that was buckled to his side. The one she'd retrieved for him.

"Never," he repeated.

She promised.

"I assume you have come to talk about these burns."

"Yeah, so I'm working on this missing person's case—"

"To find Prince Marcellus and you think this murder may have something to do with his disappearance."

Padgett had a habit of knowing things without you telling him. Since Sera had seen him pull off this trick before, she didn't even stop to ask how he knew. He wouldn't have given her an answer that made any damn kind of sense anyway.

"Yeah," she said.

"I unfortunately can't help you find the prince, but I can tell you that whoever burned this woman was a Cree."

"A Cree? Like a *sorcerer*?"

He nodded.

"Really? You want me to believe in all that spooky crap?" A far-off look filled his eyes, as if his mind was somewhere else. "Padge?"

He returned to the world of the living and glanced back at Esmeraldah's beautiful, half-burnt face. "I know the look of mage-fire burns when I see them."

"*What* fire?" She shook her head. "It doesn't matter. Suppose I believe you for a second. Why would a sorcerer want to burn up a bunch of girls?"

"Why would anyone want to burn up a bunch of girls? Sorcery is but a tool used to serve the ends of its wielder, be they charitable or malicious, good or twisted."

"Fair enough." Outside, the late afternoon bells rang and Sera knew she had to get going to check on the remaining woman on her list. "I guess I'll just figure out if I can find this *sorcerer* then."

When Sera turned to leave, Padgett stopped her.

"You're taking this body with you," he said.

IX

It took a little extra time to find a carriage, but one thing Sera had learned is that if one was willing to pay enough coin, they could get a driver to take them around the city, even if they were lugging around a pungent, burnt corpse.

On account of the extra hassle, by the time she reached the last of the four addresses on the list, a single-story house in Burnside, it was nearly dusk. According to the information the constable had given her, this girl, Josia, had not been a prostitute but the daughter of a local weaver. Josia's body had been found not far from her father's house, floating in a canal and wrapped in old quilts. She, like all the others, had been strangely burned.

Sera arrived at the address and knocked on the rotting wooden door. After a second round of knocking, she heard someone come to answer. The door cracked open. Through the thin gap between door and frame, she saw a middle-aged woman with a knife in her hand. She looked at Sera and frowned, maybe because Sera was a wretched little dwarf or maybe because the woman didn't like visitors or maybe both.

"Good evening," Sera said, all politeness.

"What do you want?" Her voice was an angry hiss.

"Is there, by chance, a weaver who lives here?"

"Weaver's dead," the woman said and started to close the door.

"Wait," Sera said. "You kin to him?"

The door opened back up a crack. "What's it to you?"

"I'm looking into the death of his daughter. Of Josia." The woman's eyes opened a little wider in recognition of the name.

"Who are you?"

"My name is Serafina Nicoletto and I'm looking into the death of Josia and a number of other girls on behalf of the grand councilor's office." This technically wasn't true. She was looking into a missing prince on behalf of the grand councilor's office, but if the two were connected, she wasn't completely lying.

"You're too late." The woman started closing the door again.

"Wait! Please."

The woman swung the door open wide now. She wore a dirty, potato sack dress and the skin on her arms hung from the frame of her bones like a poorly tailored garment. Her face took on a look of disgust. "For three years we been trying to get someone to help give our daughter justice. My husband spent every free moment traveling around the capital asking people questions, trying to figure out who done it, begging the constables for help. And it was that…the not knowing…drove him mad, sent him to an early grave—and now you're coming around, a dwarf no less, from the 'grand councilor's office' to help? Bah!" She spat once and her phlegm landed an inch from Sera's foot.

"I'm sorry. I was only brought into this affair a few days ago."

"Well, you're too late," she repeated, "as I said: weaver's dead."

"Please," Sera said, "it's happened again. To a girl in Draycott."

"Why do I care about a girl in Draycott?"

"Because she has a mother about your age who loved her daughter as much as you loved yours." Sera didn't know a thing about Esmeraldah's mother.

The woman's name, Sera learned, was Saskia. She brought Sera into the two-room house, sat her down in an uncomfortable wooden chair and brought her a cup of hot water. "I'd bring tea, but I haven't got any," the woman said.

She didn't have much useful information either. Her daughter had been a "good girl" and had never gotten into any trouble in the past. And she was smart too. Even though she only worked as a barmaid in the local tavern, she had taught herself to read and sometimes made a little extra coin copying out books for a local academic.

When Sera asked the woman if it were possible that Josia had become involved with a man, the old woman shook her head. "I don't think so," she said.

"How do you know?"

"Like I said, she was a good girl. But she also kept a book. Wrote in it every day: what she did, who she saw. I told her it was a waste of money, all that paper, but she used her own wages to buy it and said she needed to practice if she was going to get a job as a scribe. 'A good job,' she'd said. She was going to buy me and her papa a nice house outside of this shit neighborhood." She laughed now—a bitter, painful laugh. "Anyhow, her father had the scribe take a look and there wasn't no mention of any man she was involved with."

"Do you have this book?" Sera asked.

The woman nodded, walked over to a cupboard, and pulled out a large stack of papers bound together by leather string. "Take a look if you like. I don't figure Josia would care now. I can't make any sense of it since I don't know my letters, but the scribe said there didn't seem to be nothing connected to her death in here."

Sera took the papers and, after a few more questions that led nowhere, thanked the woman and met her driver outside. The smell of his wagon had gotten considerably fouler. The driver told Sera he'd decided to significantly up his price for taking this body back to Draycott after dropping Sera off in the Alley. Sera didn't argue.

It was a long ride back to the office, so on the way back, Sera had the driver light a lantern for her and she started reading through Josia's writing. There didn't seem to be much of anything interesting here—just a lot of thoughts of a young girl. Sera was dozing off when her sleepy eyes, skimming through the carefully wrought penmanship of the journal, saw something that jolted her awake:

Today at work a man told me he'd give me a silver crown if I sat with him after my shift was over while he finished his wine. I had no plans so, when it was the hour for me to go home, I sat with him for a time. I usually would not do such a thing, but a crown is more than I make all day and besides, he seemed handsome enough. He had long golden hair that went down to his shoulders and very fine clothes.

Not a few minutes after sitting down, he started frightening me. I cannot exactly say why I was frightened for I hardly understood what he was speaking of. I hope he does not come by the alehouse ever again.

This passage took place roughly a month before Josia died and after this entry, the writing went on for another twenty pages with no mention of the golden-haired man. Still, the little voice in Sera's heart told her this was Josia's killer. When she got back to the Alley and met up with Nob, these suspicions were confirmed.

Nob had had significantly better luck than his partner. He'd found people who knew two of his girls. Both were prostitutes, and in both cases, people recalled the girls spending a lot of time with a rich, golden-haired man.

"So let's assume that the man with the golden hair is our killer," Sera said.

"And he's a sorcerer," Nob added as if to highlight the hopelessness of this case.

"What does this have to do with the prince, who has dark brown hair?"

Maybe the killings had nothing to do with the prince after all.

Nob went upstairs to get some sleep. Before retiring to her own room, Sera jotted a quick note, addressed it to the owner of Esmeraldah's brothel in Draycott, and left the office to slide it under the door of the local courier. It was a long shot but worth a try.

The next morning Sera was awoken by the sound of knocking on the office's front door. She pulled herself out of bed, descended the stairs, and answered.

"How nice to see you, Novik," Sera said to the undersecretary.

X

"While the grand councilor understands you must be given some amount of leeway to pursue this matter as you think best, he grows very concerned regarding reports you are investigating murders rather than finding the prince." Novik sat on one of the chairs in the office and Sera sat behind the desk. She'd called Nob down and he was standing in the corner.

"Why is Kilroy having us followed?" Sera said.

"It should be expected that certain countermeasures are put into place in a matter of this importance," Novik said.

"Well you can tell the grand councilor we think these murders have something to do with the prince's disappearance," she said.

"Do you think the prince may have been murdered?"

Nob started to say something, but Sera cut him off. "We're not sure. All we know is the girl your prince had been seeing turned up dead at the same time the prince went missing. And that some years ago a series of girls wound up similarly dead without a killer being found."

"And have you learned anything about these murders that is useful?"

"We think whoever committed them is of noble or at least wealthy birth and has golden hair," Sera said.

"Oh, wonderful. That narrows it down to just a few thousand aristocrats and merchants. Shall I round them up for questioning?"

"Could you? It would help."

Novik huffed. "Surely you must have more to go on than that."

"We think he's a sorcerer too," Nob said. Nob was Sera's best friend and she'd do anything for him, but sometimes she just wanted to slap him across that mustached face of his.

"A *sorcerer*? Why didn't you say that before?" Novik turned again to Sera with an exasperated look.

She shrugged her shoulders. "Listen," she said, "I think what you can take away from this is that we're looking under every stone for anything that might lead us to the prince. We understand the urgency and are confident we will have some results soon."

This last little bit seemed to satisfy the undersecretary, and a little while later they were able to get him on his way. In truth, she had no confidence they'd turn up anything, but she couldn't tell that to Novik. Still, every once in a while, one gets lucky, and that's exactly what happened.

That afternoon when Nob and Sera returned from some fruitless interviews with some of their other contacts in the Alley, there were two separate notes slipped under the office door. The first was from the proprietor of Esmeraldah's brothel and sealed in wax. Sera tore open the note and saw in a beautiful flowing woman's hand five words:

Hethcliff never wore golden wig.

Attached to the note was a small invoice asking for Sera to remit payment for the information. She threw the note into the fireplace. So much for that hunch. She looked at the second note and then cursed herself for not opening it first. This one was from Maris.

Boys found driver leaving Lucke's. Tracked to house in Bluefield across Dunfaldihr Bakery. —Maris

XI

Nob and Sera found Maris's agent, a boy of ten or eleven, at the street corner nearest the bakery in Bluefield, directly across from a large apartment building. The boy told them that Marcellus's driver had left the building earlier but had returned an hour before. From what the boy could tell, the driver was in the second-floor apartment. They thanked him and sent him off with some silver.

"What do you think?" Nob asked.

"Wait it out," Sera said. "We can't go barging in. We don't know how many people are inside and, if Marcellus is being held, we could end up with a dead prince."

They waited. With nothing else to pass the time, Nob recounted a story his old man had told him about his life as a soldier during the Troubles. It was an entertaining tale, although Sera was pretty sure it was bullshit. If she wasn't going to believe in sorcerers, she sure as shit wasn't going to believe some second-hand story about soldiers who are half horse and half man.

After an hour of waiting, they saw the driver (bald head, big birthmark) walk out of the apartment door. They agreed Nob would follow him and Sera would try to figure out if there was anyone else in the apartment he'd left. If there wasn't, she'd snoop around and see what she could find. First though, she went to the bakery.

Each floor of the building only had a single apartment, so when Sera reached the second floor she knew that the one door was where she needed to go. She placed her ear up to it and tried to hear if anyone was on the other side. Nothing.

She knocked. "Pastry delivery," she said. Admittedly, this was a pretty unimaginative ruse, but it was the first thing she could think up and time was in short supply. When no one answered, Sera put the small bag of pastries she'd bought down and took out her tools to start in on the lock. After a minute of working it, the knob turned, and the door swung open.

Most of the windows were drawn so the place was relatively dark. The apartment had only minimal furnishings: here a chair, there a small circular table with nothing on it, along the wall a shelf with a few decorative vases. The only color in the room was a rug that looked to be of Lanzhenese make. Those were expensive as far as Sera knew. Bag of pastries in tow, she tiptoed from room to room. No one was home. In the single bedroom was a bed, a desk, and a large chest. She unlatched the chest and found it filled with immaculately folded clothes. Nice clothes: silk and the softest, most finely knit wool. Too nice for a driver. Common sense would have dictated Sera stop looking through the chest and that she finish checking out the rest of the apartment, yet something compelled her to keep looking—to check every tunic and pair of small clothes and vest until she reached bottom. And then she found it: a fine, golden-haired wig.

It was real hair, she guessed. And yet the thing still felt ridiculous in her hand, a gag item for a costume ball. She had the sudden desire to smell it.

I've got your scent, you son of a whore.

Behind her came a click—a single boot heel coming down on the wooden floor. She turned. A cloaked figure stood at the end of the dim hallway. Sera reached for her knife but stopped when the man pulled back his hood, revealing the face—albeit a much more haggard version—of

Prince Marcellus. He looked like a man ready to give up on the world. He didn't seem particularly alarmed to find her there, only a little curious.

"Who are you?" he said and took two steps in her direction. Click-clack went his boots.

"Pastry delivery?" she offered. She tossed the bag of baked goods to him and he snatched it midair, looking inside. He had the faintest bit of the purple glaze in his eyes, as if he'd just taken the powder or else was coming down off it.

"These are from across the street, aren't they? A pretty terrible ruse," he said. Sera shrugged. He removed one of the pastries from the bag and took a bite. "Are you a thief?"

"No."

"Then what?"

"Kilroy sent me. He's worried about you. Your father is worried about you... Your Highness."

He laughed as if she'd just told him the Riffel was made of wine rather than water. If only. "Have you ever met my father?"

"Can't say I've had the pleasure."

"I will tell you then. It's more likely—far more likely—that you are a pastry delivering dwarf than that either Grand Councilor Kilroy or Kaleb Lunaris are *worried* about me. Maybe they are worried about the line of succession or Imperial expansion or the Lunaris dynasty, but—"

"Well, they hired me to find you."

"And what if I don't want to be *found*?"

"I guess I'll have to wrestle you down, tie you up, and bring you in that way. I don't suppose they'll much like me handling a prince like that, but a job's a job, right?"

He laughed again. "I like you. What's your name?"

She told him.

"And tell me, Master Nicoletto, what did you hope to find amongst my clothes?" He gestured to the open chest she stood before.

"To tell you the truth, I didn't know this was your chest." She'd guessed as much, but now she knew for sure. She tried to think up an escape plan if he started shooting lightning bolts out of his eyes.

"It is."

"In that case, what's with the wig? You seem to have a perfectly good head of thick hair."

"A prince does not always wish to be recognized—"

"When he's murdering girls?" Stupid, she knew. But she had a soft spot for snappy lines.

A dark cloud fell over him. Whatever joviality their banter had brought him vanished.

"It is not what you think," he said. He ran his hands through his dark hair. "I may have turned into a monster, but it's not my fault. Not all my fault, at least . . ."

Nothing's ever a prince's fault. That was one of the benefits of being a prince.

"I loved her. Did you know that?" he said.

"Which one?"

"Esmeraldah. We talked about going away. Far away. Getting out of this filthy city and—"

"Start a little family maybe?"

"You jest, but there's nothing I would have wanted more...if but for this sickness fate has bestowed on me. A *Childless One*. They call it *the gift and the curse of the Forefathers*, but it's been nothing but a curse for me."

Frankly, Sera was growing tired of this prince and his damned feeling sorry for himself. "What about the others?" she said.

"What?"

"The other women you killed? Were you in love with all of them too?"

"They were...I couldn't control myself ...You can't know what that's like. I thought I could control the urges, but . . ."

Sera had no idea what he was talking about. "Come with me and you can tell Kilroy all about it."

Downstairs Sera heard the sound of a door opening and closing. The prince heard it too.

"Are you alone?" he said.

She hoped that was Nob coming up. "Do you see anyone else?"

Marcellus took a deep breath. He appeared to be about to say something but then abruptly turned and ran. Sera gave chase, yet as she made her way to the front room the few pieces of furniture began, as if of their own accord, flying towards her. She dodged the chair as it crashed into pieces against the wall. The flying table clipped her on the ankle, but she was able to catch herself before falling.

Just as Marcellus opened the door to leave the apartment, two of the vases that had been shelved in the front room inexplicably flew through the air and smashed into Sera, one in the gut and another hard in the face, each shattering to pieces. Her legs stopped taking orders and she crumpled to the ground like a puppet whose master had let go of the strings.

As far as she could tell, she never fully lost consciousness and a few moments later there was a commotion in the hallway—a crash and what sounded like Nob shouting. Sera tried to get up but was too disoriented and weak.

A few minutes passed. She heard someone coming back into the apartment. She pulled out the knife strapped to her thigh, although she was in no position to protect herself. Her head was ringing something terrible and a tiny pool of blood had formed on the ground beneath her nose and mouth.

Nob stumbled in, sword in hand, and Sera put her knife away. He wasn't in much better shape than she was. There was a gash over his forehead and blood poured down into his eyes. His clothes were all singed black and the left side of his mustache had been burned to a few crumbling ashes. "You all right, Sera?" he said.

"Not really," she said. "How about you?"

"I've been worse." This was true (Sera had seen it), but it also wasn't saying much. Nob stumbled to his hands and knees right beside her.

"You get him?" she said.

"Nope."

"Why not?"

"For one: he shot fire out of his hands."

"Fire? Was it green fire?"

"More like a kind of bluish color. I don't know. Maybe it was green."

"What about that?" She gestured to the gash on his forehead.

"Wooden club."

"Did he shoot it at you or something? Like with sorcery?"

"Nope. Swung it with his hand."

"Oh."

Neither of them said anything for half a minute. Nob crawled over to where Marcellus had dropped the pastries, picked one up, and took a bite. Outside you could hear that someone was starting a livestock auction. *The finest tasting lamb this side of Zabiz,* the auctioneer shouted.

XII

It would have been nice and clean if they could have subdued the prince and brought him to the grand councilor's office tied up with a bow on top. *Here you go, Mr. Grand Councilor: not only have we found your prince, who, by the way, is a sorcerer, but we've also solved a bunch of murders in the process. A thousand crowns, please!* Unfortunately the real world is seldom so clean. Usually one, at best, only plays a small part in things. Maybe they're there at the beginning but not the end. Maybe they're in the middle but don't see how things start or finish. Nonetheless, Sera supposed she was happy about the part she played in this business. It's not every day one is able to reveal that a potential heir to the world's largest political entity is a deranged sorcerer with uncontrollable murderous impulses. On second thought, minus the sorcerer part, that description probably fits half of the rulers throughout the history of the Empire—the history of everywhere. Oh well.

After she and Nob peeled their bloodied, dazed bodies off the floor of Prince Marcellus's secret apartment, they stumbled over to the local constable's office, where Nob had brought the driver and had him shipped in chains over to Kilroy before returning to the apartment. They hired the first ride they could and made their way there themselves. She and Nob talked about cleaning themselves up, but thought it would make for a nice dramatic effect showing up this way. Maybe they'd even still give them part of that bonus.

Kilroy already knew much of what happened by the time they reached him. There couldn't have possibly been enough time for his people to interrogate the prince's driver yet, but Sera supposed one didn't get to be grand councilor without the ability to gather information. Kilroy knew that the prince hadn't been kidnapped, that she and Nob had confronted him, and that he was somehow involved in a bunch of murders. What he didn't know was all this business about Marcellus being a sorcerer. Still, when they told him, he didn't seem completely shocked either.

"How unfortunate," he said, shaking his head, as they sat before him in his office, their faces swollen and bloody. "Emperor Kaleb will not be pleased."

After an hour of talking to Kilroy, they were passed off to his inquisitors for further questioning. All in all, they questioned Nob and Sera, on and off, for the better part of three days, during which time they were prohibited from leaving the IAO compound and were subjected to countless hours of interviews and cross-examinations. At least they housed them in some nice guest quarters across from the grand councilor's office and not in the dungeon. True, there were bars on the windows, but one of those windows had a nice view of the square. Sera guessed the prince's driver was not given such comfortable accommodations.

At first no one from the grand councilor's office was very forthcoming with Sera and Nob about what the driver was telling them, but eventually they became a little more open, dropping nuggets of information here or there during their own interviews. Here's what Sera was able to piece together:

Some years ago, Prince Marcellus figured out that he had a talent for sorcery. The prince began collecting every book he could on the subject of sorcery and soon was practicing all sorts of stuff in secret.

Somewhere around the same time, the prince also started getting into the habit of secretly killing women—first it was just the whores he was seeing and then others as well. Was it the sorcery that compelled the prince to kill? Was his heart seduced by the ancient powers that coursed through him? Sera didn't feel qualified to judge. She'd certainly known of men killing women without ancient powers being responsible. Sometimes something much more mundane can set off a man: jealousy, a bruised ego, an unkind father.

Whatever the cause, the prince knew that what he was doing was wrong. He just "couldn't control his urges." The killing spree continued for about fifteen months. At some point, the prince discovered, by accident, that ameghemite powder helped him control his urges. The prince became a powder head, and the killings stopped. During this reprieve, the prince continued visiting whores; he just wasn't killing them any longer. And then he fell in love with a prostitute named Esmeraldah. He bought her an apartment and since he wasn't the crown prince, he was free to spend as much time as he wanted with her. He'd stopped wearing the wig too.

Then last week, for some reason, the prince couldn't get his hands on his normal ameghemite. The urges returned and Esmeraldah burned. In an act of mercy, perhaps, a knife was put through her chest.

The prince, distraught at what he had done, left with his driver—the man who had been his confidante for many years—and went into hiding.

Now that everyone was more or less clear on what happened, the grand councilor and the emperor were putting together a group of "experts" to track down the prince and bring him in. When Nob and Sera finally were set to leave the IAO compound and were getting paid for all their trouble (only a third of the bonus, but Sera would take it), Sera asked Novik what would happen to the prince when he was caught.

"The same as always," Novik said.

"How do you mean?" she said.

"Whatever Emperor Kaleb wants."

It was two weeks later, as Nob and Sera were enjoying a long overdue break from work, that they learned what that was. All throughout the capital it was being announced that Second Prince Marcellus was ill and that he was moving to a sanitarium in the far east on the sea. As a result, the Alderian

Council was changing the succession order. After the crown prince would come the emperor's second cousin, Lord Galsworth.

Seeing as everyone assumed that the crown prince would be ascending to the throne anyway, no one paid any attention to the announcement. Who cares who's second in line to rule an empire? Sera knew better though; she knew that the crown prince was sick and the emperor was old and a day would come very soon when the emperor's line would end and a Galsworth, not a Lunaris, would rule the greatest nation that ever was and ever will be.

Paul D'Albero
July 24

Hey Boston friends! Next Wednesday, August 1st, **Brookline Booksmith** is hosting a talk and signing with my sister, **Sarah D'Albero** for the children's book she just illustrated: Titus and Ronica's Escape from Magic-land. The book is a fun read/coming-of-age tale of a pair of siblings on a quest to save a magical realm. If you have kids or are just a fan of Harry Potter-esque stuff, you should definitely check it out. By the way, did I mention the illustrations are awesome? I'm proud of you, sis!

| AUG 1 | Titus and Ronica's Escape from Magic-Land Launch
Thu 7pm · Brookline Booksmith · Brookline, MA
92 People Going |

Like   Comment   Share

Sarah and 4 others Like This

Write a Comment

SEVEN

A HAUNTED HOUSE

2017-2018

The old carriage house was chilly that night and into the morning, but Sarah didn't mind. It was part of the experience—roughing it, an adventure, nothing a sweater or extra blanket couldn't remedy.

She loved old houses—the lived-in feel of them, the knowledge that they'd born witness to the little joys and sadnesses of so many years. For much of her early childhood she'd lived in Cincinnati, just across the river from the Kentucky border, in an enormous three-level Victorian that her parents bought when her father was promoted to division president.

She wiped away an arc of condensation from the cold windowpane. A thin layer of snow had fallen overnight but for now it was clear out.

Her running tights felt extra snug this morning—she hoped just on account of them being in the dryer too long. She liked to think she was in pretty good shape, especially for someone who wasn't twenty-two anymore— someone who, as of October was closer to forty than thirty. Of course, unlike most of her girlfriends of a similar age—from college or her old office—her body had the advantage of never having been transformed by the dual ravages of growing another human being in her uterus and ejecting it out her vagina.

She put on her running shoes and tied the laces extra tight.

Of a similar age…

When had she started thinking of her age in this way—not as a careless label that gave her license to do whatever she wanted (*don't worry, I'm only X years old*) but as a foreboding shadow, hinting at some terror in the distance. She *was* still young, relatively speaking, assuming the relative vantage point was that of her mother. But even if she performed the necessary mental gymnastics to label herself young, she would still have to admit that under any reasonable categorization, she was coming to the definitive end of her youth.

Most of the other residents were still sleeping so Sarah was quiet as she made her way down the groaning wooden steps of the house. Downstairs a fire had been started in the large stone fireplace. Someone else must be up early; Beth, the cook, didn't arrive until ten and Peter, who owned the house, was too frail to build a fire on his own.

Outside the ground wasn't too treacherous and Sarah's running shoes had good traction besides. She stretched her legs then ran eastward past the old white church and towards town. With every step came the crackle of snowflakes compressing together underfoot. The sun rose, orange and lethargic, from behind a hill of undisturbed snow.

Rather than run straight on to the end of town as in previous days, she turned left down a narrow, down-sloping road lined with similar-looking white houses. At the bottom of the hill, once she no longer needed to be so careful with her footing, she picked up her pace and broke into a sprint. There was something invigorating about pushing herself as hard as she could, her muscles pumping with energy, the chilled air lancing her face.

Her plan was to stay on another week. After that she'd return to Philly for a few days then fly to Florida for Christmas at her parent's winter place in Sarasota. Beyond that, she had no idea. She'd look for another office job, she supposed, although she still wasn't sure what she'd ideally be looking for.

Sometimes it felt like she knew less and less what she wanted every day. She'd thought the flexibility of being a freelance designer and illustrator these last months would make her happier. And yet, even though she'd kept herself busy with clients, the deep isolation of working from home had nearly driven her to a breakdown. Her personal life was in no better shape. Since the divorce, she'd been set up with friends of friends, "taken time for herself," gone on exhausting bouts of intensive online dating, taken up the guitar, tried to learn German, said to hell with men completely, filled her free time with classes and book clubs and volunteer work and trips to an archery range. None of it fulfilled her. One of her friends suggested she sign up to be a "Big Sister" in Center City ("the most rewarding thing she'd ever done") and Sarah had printed the application but, for some reason, couldn't bring herself to send it in.

Her dad, who'd earned more money than he'd ever be able to spend, had offered to give her, on several occasions, "a loan" so she could take time off—maybe spend more time in Florida and really figure out what she wanted to do. But idleness was the last thing she needed.

After another mile, she slowed to a walk, exhausted. On the right side of the road was an old cemetery and she went to take a look. Some found cemeteries creepy, but Sarah had always thought them beautiful in their tranquility. In middle school in California she used to cut through a cemetery on her walk home from school. Sarah had been a quiet child, but at ten, after her family relocated from Cincinnati to Northern California, after leaving behind all of her friends, and with her sister Emily constantly in and out of the hospital, she became especially withdrawn. Alone in the cemetery after school, she would meander around, looking at the tombstones, reading the epitaphs, and imagining what these people, long dead, had been like. She'd been fascinated with the tombstones of people who'd died as children, around her own age, around Emily's age.

Sarah tracked through the snowy cemetery grounds for a minute before stopping at one particular tombstone:

HERE LIES
JOHN PAUL ALLEN
who died of injuries received
while saving a child from
the fire at Bisby's General
December 28, 1858

I saved the Child's life
but lost my own

She dusted the snow off from the tombstone and traced her fingers along the top —coarse and bumpy. Everyone who had ever known John Paul Allen had died long ago. Who had the child been? She imagined a boy, although nothing specifically suggested that. Did he live a long and peaceful life, ever conscious of how close he had been to dying in the blaze? Did he have children and grandchildren and great grandchildren—perhaps who lived somewhere in town today—forever owing their existence to this John Paul Allen?

On her way back to the house she stopped by Hadley Corner to grab a coffee.

"Morning, Mrs. D'Albero. How was the run?" said the acne-scarred teenager behind the counter, the son of the owner.

"Good. A little cold but good." He'd gotten her full name that first day when she bought a bunch of small items with her credit card. *Mrs. D'Albero.* It sounded strange on multiple levels. For six years her last name had been different; now she wasn't a Mrs. at all.

"I have a strange question," Sarah said after getting her coffee. "Was this place ever called *Bisby's General Store?*"

"Not that I know of," he said. "My dad bought this place before I was born and I'm pretty sure the name was the same back then. Why do you ask?"

"No reason. Just something I read."

Nancy was in the living room, reading in front of the fire when Sarah got back to the house. Nancy, a writer and yoga instructor, was one of the other residents staying at the retreat. Two nights before, the women had sat together on the patio drinking wine Nancy had bought in Amherst and telling stories. Sarah had drunk too much but had enjoyed herself nonetheless.

She estimated Nancy was a little older than herself, but this was mainly on account of the gray hair that grew in streaks through the woman's frizzy brown curls. Nancy's figure, while not youthful, was thin and long, with wiry muscles from all the yoga.

"How was the run?" Nancy said.

"Good, thanks. You up early this morning too?"

"Not too early."

"When I came down the fire was already going. I thought it might be you."

"Nope. I figured it was *you.*"

Later, when Sarah was out on the covered and heated patio painting, a silver Volkswagen she didn't recognize pulled up to the house. Residents were on their own schedule here, and Sarah had seen several people come and go in the time she'd been here so she didn't pay the car much notice. The car pulled around back and was forgotten.

Sarah was finishing a set of watercolor illustrations for a children's book a friend had written; although perhaps "friend" was too strong a word.

Sarah had met Lindsay while attending a seminar at the Wharton School, which had been recommended by her dad's financial advisor. The subject of the two-day workshop was Managing Inheritance and the Family Business, which was euphemistic for "finding tax loop holes when you've got a lot of family money you don't know what to do with." Sarah's brother, Paul was supposed to have joined her at the seminar, but a last-minute work obligation had kept him in Boston. Lindsay, who lived in New York and whose own father controlled large oil interests in Texas, had struck up conversation with Sarah during one of the coffee breaks, and the night between session days, the women had gone together to a posh bar near Rittenhouse Square to talk about their respective divorces and try to get picked up by younger men. When no attractive younger men materialized, and when their divorces, as topics of conversation, had exhausted themselves, the two women chatted about their interests and endeavors. Lindsay, it turned out, was writing a children's book in need of an illustrator. Sarah worked as both a freelance designer and illustrator and had earned a degree in fine arts in college. A happy accident, they agreed.

That was the past spring. In the intervening months, the more Sarah worked on the illustrations, the more she grew to dislike Lindsay's book. It was such a banal story: a pair of siblings transported to a magical realm full of evil sorcerers, unicorns, and talismans. But Sarah had committed to the project.

A man wearing an expensive-looking blazer with elbow pads and a bow tie came from around the back, precariously holding several large paper grocery bags. He looked out of place, Sarah thought, in middle-of-nowhere Massachusetts dressed like he belonged on the set of *Downton Abbey*. Even his shoes were fancy—the kind that you kept those wooden things in whenever you weren't wearing them.

"Oh, hello," he said, struggling to open the patio door while holding onto his bags. Was he English? Welsh? Scottish? Sarah couldn't discern between various British accents.

"Let me help you," she said and stood to hold the door. He turned sideways in order to fit through with his bags. As he stepped in, his body came right up close to Sarah, his jacket brushing against her sweater.

When he'd placed his bags down inside, he returned to the patio. "Henry," he said and offered his hand.

"Sarah." She took it. His boyish face combined with his receding hairline gave him a confused look, young and old all at once. There *was* something quite handsome about him though—in a refined, soft-spoken way. Not at all like her ex-husband who had been a college running back and had a well-defined jaw line.

"Wonderful to meet you, Sarah. First time here?"

"Yup. Not yours?"

"I've been coming here for years. Since my early twenties."

"You're not *still* in your early twenties?"

He winked. "You won't tell anyone, will you?"

"Our secret," she said.

Sarah didn't want the conversation to end just yet. "I can see why you come back. It's a lovely place."

"Yes, *lovely*. All this nature around." He gestured to the barren trees, the snow.

"Just getting in today?"

"Last night. Needed to get some extra provisions," he said, pointing to the bags inside the door. "Speaking of which, I should go put my groceries away and say hello to Peter."

"Of course."

"I'll see you around."

She stood in front of the door for a little while.

Maybe it had been Henry who had started the fire . . .

A half hour later Sarah went inside to wash up. Beth was preparing lunch in the kitchen. "How's the painting going?" she said in her warm New England accent. Beth was short and sturdy with a face one might describe as "salt of the earth."

"It's going . . . I guess," Sarah said. "Whatever you have in the oven smells amazing."

"Vegetarian lasagna. And we have some organic quinoa salad and some green beans on the side."

"Sounds delicious. Let me help set the table." Even though the residents paid to stay at the retreat and there was a cook, the general ethos of the place was more of being in a family than a hotel and Sarah liked that.

"Looks like a new guest arrived," Sarah said while putting out the water glasses. "I think he said he's been here before."

"You mean Henry?"

"English guy?"

"That's him. He's been here plenty of times. Real sweetheart. He's a writer, and very talented. I bought his book online after the last time he was here. A novel about a French family living in the countryside during the German occupation in World War II. Really well done."

"He seemed nice," Sarah said.

"He's had some bad luck, but still he is just the dearest. A little eccentric, but all you artists are, right?" Beth finished washing the green beans and turned off the faucet. She lowered her voice. "He has a daughter. Six or seven. Pretty girl. He showed me a photo the last time he was here. But it's terrible what happened to the wife. She died. House burned down. Arson."

"That's awful." Sarah couldn't help but think back to the gravestone she'd seen that morning. What was the saying about all terrible things happening in threes? Or was it just deaths that happened in threes? She couldn't remember. The world was full of terrible coincidences; of this much there was no doubt.

Before lunch, Sarah walked out towards the main road to check her messages since the house had no service.

Her younger brother, Paul, had called earlier that morning, asking if she'd consider stopping by on her way back to Philadelphia. They could have lunch, the three of them: she and Paul and his wife, Kathy. She could see little Phillip. He was crawling now.

She remembered holding the baby when he was only a few weeks old—how she'd been struck by an alarming feeling she'd never before experienced. She loved the child so much—a startling, illogical amount. Little Phillip's head had rested against her breast and Sarah had imagined him suckling at her nipple, the warm milk flowing through her and into his welcoming mouth.

She and her ex-husband had never had children though they had tried for a brief time. Getting pregnant, it turned out, wasn't as easy as they claimed in eighth-grade health class.

She didn't call her brother back; she could do it later, maybe the next day. She hadn't brought her large coat out and was getting cold. Besides, lunch was ready.

Henry didn't come down for lunch or for dinner that evening. Instead Beth brought his meals up to his room.

"He likes to start strong and really get to work the first few days," Beth told Sarah when she asked.

She didn't want to admit she was disappointed by not seeing Henry again the rest of that first day or by the fire in the evening, where the other residents congregated to read or chat. Certainly he was an attractive man, but he wasn't George Clooney or anything—nothing to get too worked up about. Besides, she wasn't some boy-crazy nineteen-year-old. They weren't going to have some drunken liaison. This trip was about spending time with herself—with her art.

It wasn't until the morning two days later that she saw him again. The two were in the upstairs hall and Henry was returning to his room from a bath. His glasses were off and his hair was askew. He wore forest green, velvet slippers and a luxurious white bathrobe that looked like it had been stolen from the Four Seasons.

"Hello, Sarah," he said, a warm smile crossing his lips.

"Hi Henry," she said. "Have a nice bath?"

"Marvelous," he said and that was it. And they each made their ways to their rooms, the dual clicking of their two doors seeming like the final drumbeats of a sad song.

Sarah sat on her bed; she couldn't take more disappointment.

The painting went poorly. Despite however many hours Sarah spent sitting in front of her easel, whether up in her room or downstairs in the patio, the images on the paper in front of her always ended up different than the ones in her mind—not necessarily in how the image or scene actually looked but in how it made her feel. They were flat, lacking that certain indefinable something. The weather took a turn for the colder and, especially in the mornings, the watercolor took forever to dry. In the afternoon the temperature was a little warmer yet the lighting in either space was such that it was difficult for Sarah to discern color as finely as she would have liked. She trudged on though; one at a time the illustrations were completed.

Two days before Sarah was to leave, she woke up early, as usual, but decided she didn't feel like running. She found Henry downstairs sitting in front of the fireplace. The reflection of the few remaining embers shone in his glasses. He didn't seem to notice her approaching; his eyes were transfixed, as if hypnotized, on the glowing, charred scraps of wood before him.

"Morning, Henry."

He turned with a start. There was a look of wildness on his face before it returned to its normal jovial form. "Good morning, Sarah."

"You're up early."

He took a sip from the steaming cup sitting on the coffee table. "There is a kind of tranquility, a beauty, to the early hours of the morning, don't you think? So much possibility and hope . . ."

"You're an early riser I take?"

He laughed. "Not at all. If I had it my way, I'd stay in bed until noon every day. I just didn't sleep well."

"Sorry to hear. Bad dreams?"

"Just a little restlessness," he said. His eyebrows made a sudden raise as if he'd remembered something. "Would you like some tea? I made a pot."

"Tea, not coffee? How English."

"I love my tea. But I'm very particular. No Lipton's for me. I used to have to order it online from England, but then I found a place in SoHo that carries all my favorites."

"Well, if this is special tea then sure, I'll have a cup."

Henry went to the kitchen.

"You live in New York?" she asked while he was in the adjacent room.

"Yes, Brooklyn."

"And how long have you been in the States?"

"Quite a while. Fifteen years about? Not just New York; I've lived all over. Jackson Hole, Kentucky, a little island off the coast of Washington . . ."

He brought the tea and placed another log on the fire. As the intensity of the flames grew, their color shifted to a mix of nearly greenish blue and orange. "You know Peter's wife was an architect and she designed much of this house," he said. "The frame of the house already existed, but it was an actual carriage house before. Right here where we are standing . . . animals used to pass right through."

"I was wondering what actually made this place a 'carriage house.' It seemed far too big for what you normally associate with that word." The fire needed no further attention; Henry sat down on the couch facing it. Sarah sat in one of the large armchairs at a right angle to him.

"Yes, the bedrooms upstairs have always been there, but everything down here, the living room, the kitchen, the rooms in back where Peter lives, were all designed by Peter's wife, Barbara. She was a wonderful woman; although in the last few years she deteriorated quite dramatically. Towards the end she hardly remembered any of her life, hardly recognized Peter. It's strange to think how much we're defined by our memories. Like if you take them away, are we really the same people anymore?"

"*I'd* like to think so . . . that there's something else besides memories and the, you know, machinery of our bodies."

"A soul, you mean?"

"I guess, but it doesn't have to be."

"Anyhow, if you look out back by the oak tree," he said, gesturing through the window, "there's a plaque in her honor."

Sarah turned and looked at the tree.

Some years ago, she and her ex-husband had taken a trip to see the Angel Oak tree outside of Charleston. She wasn't sure why she thought of that. The two trees really didn't look anything alike. This tree was your standard issue, very big tree, whereas Angel Oak was a sprawling, massive thing with an endless network of roots and branches, many themselves the thickness of large tree trunks.

"So you met her, then? Peter's wife?"

"Many times. She wasn't a writer herself, but she was a very bright woman and would give me great advice on my work."

"You're a novelist, right? Beth mentioned really liking one of your books. Something about World War II."

"I've written a couple novels. But I also write essays and short fiction. Right now I'm working back and forth on two things simultaneously."

"Like what? If you don't mind me probing . . ."

"Not at all. One project is . . . Well, it's something quite different for me: a collection of what I am calling 'quasi-post-apocalyptic' short stories. I say *quasi* because they're not exactly post-*apocalyptic* but rather post disaster. And they focus on the characters much more than the big-picture scope of what's going on. Like what's it like being a homeless runaway in Seattle when a flu pandemic breaks out? Or what's it like being a single mother in Brooklyn when there's a nuclear attack somewhere else in the United States?"

"That's interesting. I can't say I read a ton of short stories."

"Don't worry. No one does—except other writers, I suppose."

"And what's the other project?"

"Well, I have a daughter and . . . her mother . . . my wife . . . passed away. So it's a memoir about that . . . about my experience as a single father."

Sarah tried to make an expression that was surprised, as if his daughter, his dead wife, were all news to her. "Oh," was all she managed to say.

"Her name is Maggie," he said and opened up his wallet to show Sarah a black and white picture of him with a young blond girl that looked to have been clipped from a photo booth reel.

"You guys are adorable." Based on the picture Sarah imagined the girl's dead mother had been very beautiful. "And so how *is* the writing going. We haven't seen much of you around the house."

"Writing is always slow work."

"It is, isn't it?"

"Do you write? I saw you painting the other day on the patio."

"No. My ex-husband was a writer—is a writer? He's not dead," she said, "but we *are* no longer married."

"Hence the *ex.*"

"Yes…This tea is quite good."

Henry laughed. "You should come sit over here," he said, referring to the couch. "It's nice to drink this tea and stare into the fire." He scooted over, although not all the way to the far end of the couch. She sat next to him and their two hips touched. From this position she could feel the fire on her face.

"When I first moved to Kentucky, I lived alone in a one-room house in the mountains. All I had was a bed, a desk, and a fireplace. That winter I didn't turn on the gas heat once. Even more than sitting in front of the fireplace, I love building the fire, giving it life."

"You sound like a pyro," she said, but as she finished the sentence realized it might be construed the wrong way and her tone drifted off towards an awkward, unconfident inflection.

"Well, I wouldn't say that exactly . . ."

"No, I didn't mean—"

"Of course," he said.

" . . . "

"Say, I was planning on going hiking later," Henry said after a time. "Just take a little break from all this writing. Would you be interested in coming along? The terrain isn't too steep and some of the trails are quite beautiful."

Sarah had always loved hiking.

II

On the final evening before Sarah returned home from the retreat, all the current residents—Henry, Sarah, Nancy, and another older woman named Karen whose hair was dyed an impossible shade of red— sat around the fire talking and drinking and eating Toblerone. The three women drank a bottle of Cabernet a previous resident had abandoned in the kitchen cupboard; Henry, who didn't drink, allowed himself only to smell the wine before making tea. When Nancy found an anthology of classic horror stories amongst the walls of books that surrounded three sides of the living room, she suggested they take turns reading.

"Ooh, fun. Horror stories by the fire," Karen said, taking a mouthful of wine.

Nancy went first, reading "The Monkey's Paw," and then Karen read something by Poe, which Sarah wasn't familiar with.

To be honest, even afterwards, Sarah could hardly tell someone what the story had been about. The entire time Nancy and Karen read, Sarah's mind was occupied with interpreting Henry's every movement—the crossing and uncrossing of his legs, how he leaned forwards or backwards at certain points in the story.

When it was Sarah's turn, she chose Ambrose Bierce's "An Occurrence at Owl Creek Bridge"; she wanted to read something that the others might not know. It had actually been her ex-husband who first introduced her to this story years ago on that weekend trip to Charleston.

"Who wants to see if we can find another bottle of wine?" Nancy said when Sarah had finished reading. Karen stood up and the two women went to the kitchen, leaving only Henry and Sarah in the living room.

The crackling of the fire seemed louder now.

"Productive day?" Sarah said.

"Moderately. You?"

"It was good."

"That's good. I liked the story, by the way."

"I'm glad."

Nancy and Karen returned with a half-finished bottle of Pinot Grigio they'd unearthed from the back of the refrigerator. "You're up, Hanky," Karen said, not really needing more wine.

Henry offered to skip reading altogether and instead tell a *real* ghost story.

"Is it a good one?" Nancy said.

"Guaranteed or your money back," Henry said, and he turned his chair away from the fire so he was facing the three women.

"How could we say 'no' then?"

Henry winked at Nancy and cleared his throat. "Now, I've never been one to believe in the otherworldly," he said, "but after this took place two and a half years ago, I started to change my mind about that.

"Most summers I rent a cottage in the countryside somewhere in Europe for Maggie and myself—usually France or Italy." As he spoke he made sure to turn his head and make eye contact with each of the three women. When Henry looked at Sarah, she couldn't help looking away.

He had kissed her out on the trail hiking, but so what?

She wasn't in seventh grade.

"Two years ago, I put things off until the last minute and the only house available near where I wanted to stay was this massive French country home that was far too big for Maggie and me. Now, I didn't have many options, and since the house was in a bit of disrepair, it wasn't all that expensive. So I went ahead and rented it."

The day before, Sarah and Henry had hiked to the top of the small mountain and were sitting on a large tree stump together drinking water when he did it. What had they been talking about? Sarah couldn't remember. No, on second thought, she was telling him about her childhood— about Emily, who had died when she was eleven and how she and her family moved around all the time as her father climbed the corporate ladder. How it had been hard, moving so often, not having permanent roots anywhere. And then he kissed her. Just briefly and then he backed away. She was worried it had been a sympathy kiss but then realized otherwise. "Is that okay?" he'd asked.

Yes, it was okay. He kissed her again. His lips tasted like vanilla lip balm.

Then last night he hadn't been at dinner. Something about needing to drive to Amherst and she wondered if that was code for *not wanting to see her*.

"The estate was a few hundred acres," Henry said, "and the closest neighbor was a half-mile away. Surrounding the house was a ten-foot-high stone wall and the only way in or out was through an eight-foot-tall iron gate. It was a bit of a chore because the groundskeeper insisted we keep the gate closed. When you drove up to the house, you had to get out of your car, open the gate, get in the car, drive in, get out of your car, close the gate, and then drive up to the house.

"I'd told the caretaker there'd only be two of us so a few of the rooms of the house were made up in a quite lovely way, but many of the others remained sparsely furnished. The caretaker was an old French man with a short white beard and very tan, leathery-looking skin. He had a nasty scar on his face that went across his forehead and down through his right temple before ending at a mangled right ear." Henry took his finger and dragged it across his face to demonstrate. "He was a very a gentle man though.

"Maggie and I get to the house and the caretaker leaves and the two of us are walking through the house and exploring everything and Maggie loves it because it is a great big place and it is an adventure to explore all of the rooms."

Sarah thought again of her childhood house in Cincinnati. She had thought it so wonderful that the house had a library with a swinging shelf that led to a hidden office, just like the *Scooby Doo* cartoons.

"And then, down one corridor we come to a room. It's normal enough except it's completely empty: no furniture, no decorations. The only object in the room is a rotary phone sitting in the precise middle of the floor with a long wire stretching from the phone to the wall. Now, it looked peculiar, and Maggie and I made a joke about it, but we didn't think much of it that first time. But the second evening we were at the house and, as I was walking past that room, the phone started ringing." Henry paused and, as if on cue, one of the logs in the fire broke with a loud snap. They all laughed; Nancy hummed the tune from *The Twilight Zone*.

"I pick up the phone, but there's only silence. I place the phone back on the receiver and start to walk out the room, but as soon as I cross the threshold of the door, the phone starts ringing again. I pick up the phone— again nothing. This happens two or three more times and I start to think something very odd is going on or that someone is playing a joke on me. This room is surrounded on three sides by large windows that look out on the estate and I try to see if someone is out there with a cellphone or something, but it's pitch black outside and difficult to see. As I peer out into the darkness, I have a very peculiar sensation, like something cold is crawling on me beneath my clothes.

"From there things get weirder and weirder. At night there are sounds: sometimes a knocking from up in the attic...Sometimes a squeaking noise on some of the windows like someone is cleaning them with a...What do you call those things you use to clean a window?"

"A squeegee?" Sarah offered.

"Yes. A squeegee," he said. "Once, after hearing these noises I went outside to look about and there was a raccoon, but mostly the sounds were inexplicable.

"As Maggie and I are getting ready to drive into town one morning, I see the caretaker trimming the hedges. I get to asking him about the history of the house. He tells me that, from after the war up until recently, the estate was owned by a single man who lived in the house alone. When the man died, he had no children so the property passed to a niece. The niece lived in Paris and didn't want to be bothered by the house, so she hired a management company to rent the place out, who in turn had hired the caretaker. I asked him if he knew who had lived in the house before and during the war and he replied that he had no idea, but that there had been a lot of fighting in the area during that time and if I looked closely at the wall I could still find bullet holes.

"That same night as I'm sleeping, out of nowhere, the smoke detector in Maggie's room starts going off. The rooms that were set up for us are quite far apart so I go sprinting down the hall, my adrenaline pumping. And all of my fatherly instincts are going off and I grab a kitchen knife and I'm determined to protect my little girl. I get to Maggie's room; only, there's no actual danger. No smoke, no fire, no intruder. Just the smoke alarm going off and Maggie with her hands over her ears.

"Another time during the day I went up into the attic to see if I could find out what was making all the racket, the tapping. I thought perhaps there was a raccoon or rat up there. Turned out there wasn't, but what I did find were piles upon piles of old toys: dolls and trucks and playhouses and one of those mini tricycles all strewn about. And I thought to myself that there hadn't been any child that lived here all those years."

"There's no way I would have stayed in that house," said Nancy.

"It was funny," Henry said. "During the day the estate was beautiful and we would just have such a lovely time that we would forget what a frightening place the house was until the evening. Maggie and I would drive to town and have croissants and hot chocolate at this charming café, or we'd go swimming in the lake, and the weather was marvelous.

"The final straw with the house was a few nights later. It was raining hard that night. I was sitting in the den in front of a fireplace very much the same as this. It was summer but chilly in the evening so I had decided to get the fire going. I was reading—I remember specifically—this fantasy/detective novel and Maggie was in the other room coloring. All of a sudden I hear, *BOOM, BOOM* on the window followed by this scraping. I can't rightly describe it; it was the most terrifying sound I've ever heard. I look out the window where it was coming from, but I can't see a thing—just the darkness and a faint outline of the rain. Then there it is again: *BOOM, BOOM, scrape, scrape.* I shout to Maggie but she doesn't answer. I still see nothing outside, but I just felt terrible, like I knew something bad was about to happen.

"I run over to where Maggie was. She was right where she should be, sitting at a table with her open box of crayons. 'Why didn't you respond when I called to you?' I say and I think I frightened her with how angry I was. 'Why are you mad, Daddy?' she says, but I don't think I even responded to her because I'm busy planning our escape—how I'm going to gather up Maggie and a few things for the night and run to the car. But then I remember the gate and know it will likely take another thirty seconds or a minute to open the outer gate and get in the car and in that time, whatever is out there, well…you know. So instead, I decide the only thing to do is to go into Maggie's room, which has rather small windows and barricade ourselves in there with all the furniture. *BOOM, BOOM,* the window goes and I grab a baseball bat that happens to be in the house and take Maggie. We go to her room and I don't sleep for one second the whole night. I'm holding onto that bat guarding the door. It was such a long night. Then the thought crosses my mind as I stand over Maggie with a baseball bat and the sun is starting to rise: how come there is a baseball bat in this house in France?

"The next day I pack up all our things and drive out to the caretaker's house. I tell him we're leaving early. He says in his thick French accent, 'I would like to say dzat I am surprised, but you are not dzeh first one to leave dzeh house early. Many people come to here and leave after just one night.'"

When everyone had gone to bed, Sarah tiptoed out of her room and knocked softly on Henry's door. The next day she would take a detour to her brother's place on the way back down to Philadelphia. The day would be full of driving, and she knew that all the time alone in the car would make her crazy if she didn't at least give this a try.

"Oh, hello," he said when he opened the door. Without a word, she kissed him on the mouth.

"Sorry," she said.

He smiled. "For what?"

"Am I keeping you up? I saw the light on under the door."

"Oh, no. I just got finished talking to Maggie on the phone. She was having trouble sleeping."

"Do you mind company?"

"No. Not at all."

She stepped in and shut the door behind her. They kissed again only this time he initiated. When they were undressed save for his boxers and her bra and panties (the "sexiest" pair she had brought, although still a little ragged since how could she have known?), they lay on the bed. His daughter's name was tattooed across his chest in large calligraphic lettering and she couldn't decide what to think of this. He kissed her neck; she ran her hands down his body. While Henry was thin, his body was soft, that of a man more accustomed to sitting at a desk than physical exertion.

"Was that story true... the one you told?" she said.

"Most of it."

"Which parts?"

"I'd tell you, but then I'd have to kill you."

The bed was too creaky so instead they lay on one of the oriental rugs covering the floor. Even through the rug Sarah could still feel the cold wooden floor beneath her.

III

Nine months later, Sarah was driving with Henry down I-71 through Ohio on the way to a wedding. Maggie slept soundly in the Volkswagen's backseat and classical music could faintly be heard beneath the drone of the air conditioner.

One of Henry's close friends was getting married in Northern Kentucky and Henry and Sarah had decided to make a road trip of it. The first day they drove from New York to Pittsburgh and stayed overnight in a bed and breakfast. This morning they woke early to make the rest of the drive.

After staying at the retreat, Henry and Sarah had started seeing each other. Sarah was still freelancing from home, so in March of that year, after two months of visiting Henry in New York nearly every weekend, she decided to sublet a studio in Brooklyn near where he lived in Greenpoint. It was crazy, she knew, to go so fast, to make life-altering decisions based on what amounted to being with a person a dozen or so times. But that's what she loved about it all—how she was, for the first time in so long, giving in blindly to her impulses.

After a few months, she abandoned the sublet and moved in with Henry and Maggie. Henry was apprehensive about how his daughter would take it, but everything went smoothly and Maggie and Sarah became fast friends. Even if, that May, Maggie wasn't quite ready to draw Sarah a Mother's Day card, she still loved having another female in the house—someone to play dress up with and teach her how to braid her hair properly.

"I hope you understand," Henry once said to Sarah when Maggie was away at school, "why I keep pictures of her in the house. She's still Maggie's mother after all."

From the very first time Sarah visited Henry's apartment, she'd noticed the photographs. Henry's wife looked nothing like Sarah had expected. She was plain-looking with broad shoulders and matronly proportions. While Sarah would have thought she'd feel reassured by learning she was far more conventionally attractive than Henry's dead wife, she actually felt the opposite. Given the woman's appearance, Sarah immediately concluded she must have had many amazing qualities that compensated. Perhaps she was a great cook or had a beautiful singing voice or was amazing in bed.

❖

When they were just outside Cincinnati a vague feeling of familiarity began creeping into Sarah although she hadn't properly lived in the area for twenty-five years. She knew if she didn't say something soon she'd lose the opportunity.

"Henry, do you mind if we take a little detour?" she said, and he asked where to, keeping his voice low so as not to wake his daughter.

"I thought it would be neat to go by the house I used to live in."

"That's right. I forgot you used to live here."

Ever since Sarah knew they'd be coming this way, she'd been ruminating over the idea of visiting the house, yet she'd resisted the urge to tell Henry. She was unsure how she'd react to seeing the place after all these years. But now, as she spoke with him about the house, she sensed the excitement in her own voice and knew she wanted to make the trip.

"There were so many hidden little spots and I was always hiding in them: oddly located windowless rooms with no apparent purpose, several separate attics. Once I hid in one of the cupboards in the pantry and when neither my parents nor Emily could find me for a long time, they got worried. I remember hearing Emily calling all over for me, 'Sarah. Sarah!' But the more panicked their voices, the more I just wanted to stay hidden.

"I don't remember why I didn't come out. I'm not sure if I was worried I'd get in trouble. My dad was a frightening man back then. He had a lot of stress from work. He calmed down a lot—especially after Emily died.

"I had a stuffed rabbit that I was in love with and I remember, there in the pantry, gripping it so tightly. And the weird thing is, even though I remember that incident so clearly, I don't actually remember ever being found or leaving the pantry of my own accord, although it certainly must have happened at some point."

"Maybe they never found you," Henry said.

"How do you mean?"

"Maybe you're still asleep in that cupboard and everything you think has happened since has been a dream."

"That'd be something, wouldn't it?"

It would have made for one long dream. So much had happened since then: her sister died, she grew up, got married, divorced.

"You haven't been back to this house since you moved away?"

"No, I was there one more time. I was visiting a friend back in Cincinnati and we were riding bikes in the old neighborhood and I really wanted to visit the house. Emily was gone by then. I remember we rode over and I rang the bell and a lady came and answered. I tried to explain that I used to live there and asked if I could possibly walk around the house again just to see it. I'll never forget how she looked at me—sort of perplexed—like how it was crazy that I'd want to visit this house, and she just had these accusing eyes even though she said it was okay that I come in. I walked in. Some of the walls were different colors, but overall they hadn't done much with the place. Still the house just *felt* so different, like all the memories I'd left there—the good ones, the bad ones—had been washed away."

"Are we almost to the hotel?" Maggie said from the back of the car, her voice clouded with sleep.

"Almost. But we're going to make a stop for Sarah first," Henry said.

"It's the house that I lived in when I was your age," she added.

"I didn't know you lived here," said the little girl.

"I did until I was ten years old. Then I moved to California. Do you know where California is?"

"Duh. It's where Los Angeles and San Francisco and Yosemite are and it's the most populous state and its capital is Sacramento."

Out front of the house was an ornate iron gate, but it was open. The old dirt driveway was cobblestones now.

"This is new," she said. "It looks like they fancied up the place a bit."

"Hey," Henry beckoned to a real estate sign, "it's for sale."

They continued down the long driveway and parked in front of the house. Just as Henry cut the engine, a middle-aged woman in a business suit came out of the house to greet them. She had a huge head of puffy blond hair, carried an iPad, and was clearly a real estate agent.

"Let me handle the talking," Henry said. He got out of the car and greeted the woman, but rather than tell her the truth, he explained he'd been transferred to Cincinnati from London and that he was a prospective buyer. Henry always overdressed and today wore a black blazer with a crisp, starched blue-checkered shirt underneath. He looked, at least, like someone who might be able to afford this house.

"Well I'd be happy to show you around," the real estate agent said.

"Oh, thank you so much," Henry said. "But if you wouldn't mind, could we just wander around a bit first and check things out for ourselves? We like to take unguided tours of houses first. It really gives us a better feeling for a place."

"We're typically not supposed to do unaccompanied viewings. You know, liability and all that."

"I understand. However, if you could make an exception, it would be so very much appreciated. My wife is weird this way and it would really make a difference... in terms of our likeliness of buying a place."

The real estate agent looked at Sarah and Maggie still sitting in the car. "Well, you don't look like you'll steal anything," she said and laughed. "You won't tell?"

He winked at her. "And I will add...we are looking to make a decision quite quickly and expect to be paying cash." It startled Sarah how wonderful a liar Henry was.

"Okay. Enjoy. It's a pretty big house, so if you get lost or something, just holler."

"Will do. Thank you."

"Oh, and one question," Sarah said, now out of the car and holding Maggie by the hand, "why is the house for sale? Did the owner just move away or . . ."

"She died actually," the real estate agent said in a low voice and then darted her eyes in Maggie's direction, "but not *inside* the house." Sarah gave the real estate agent an understanding look. "Not to be morbid, but some people care about that kind of thing when it comes to real estate. You know, worried that the house is haunted or something."

"Oh yes, thank you."

They walked inside through the main foyer. Right in the front was the large spiral staircase, directly below which Sarah's family used to place the Christmas tree. Emily had so loved breaking out that enormous box of ornaments from the basement and decorating the tree. To the left was the dining room, same as before, although the large crystal chandelier was new. The new wallpaper looked to be made of luxurious fabric. Sarah turned the other way, taking Maggie by the hand. Henry followed. They walked through the living room and down a short hall to the library. There the walls were covered floor to ceiling with leather-bound books.

"Wow, Maggie," Henry said. "Look at all these."

"They're very pretty, Daddy," said the girl.

"How'd you like to live here? Maybe we should buy this house and move out here."

"Yeah, Daddy, this house is beautiful."

"Although...what about all your friends at home? Wouldn't you miss them? And we couldn't get hot cocoa at Wynford's Chocolaterie anymore."

Sarah turned her attention to the garden. They had completely changed it. Her mother used to plant so many flowers out there and for her or Emily's birthday she'd make an arrangement.

"I used to love sitting here and reading," Sarah said. "Our books weren't quite so nice, but otherwise, this room was pretty much the same." Henry was looking through the books on the wall and took one down to examine it.

"I would sit right here on a little bench and look out the window to the garden while I'd read." Sarah realized that Henry was engrossed in the books so she was in fact just talking to Maggie.

"Henry, you ready to take a look at the rest of the house?" Sarah said.

"Okay…These books are amazing. Look at these woodcut illustrations." Henry took a large black volume and brought it over to Sarah.

"What book is it?"

"*Crime and Punishment,* illustrated by Fritz Eichenberg." Sarah could smell the book's cured leather binding. "When I was a boy I had a copy of *Gulliver's Travels* that was illustrated by the same man." Henry held the book open to an illustration of a man brandishing a small axe over the neck of an old woman seated in a chair. It had been over twenty years since Sarah had read that book. She couldn't remember if Raskolnikov used an axe to kill the woman.

"Those illustrations are very dark, very…I don't know…evocative," Sarah said. Henry nodded in agreement. She'd taken a hand woodcutting class back in college. She hadn't had much of a knack for it. Nowadays, you could set up woodcuts on the computer. "Are you ready to see the rest of the house?"

"Actually, if you don't mind, why don't you go ahead and I'll catch up in a minute. I just want to take a look at some of these books a little longer."

"Okay. Maggie, you want to come with me or do you want to stay with Daddy and watch him look through boring books?" Maggie grabbed Sarah's outstretched hand.

They walk-ed up the main set of stairs to the second floor. On the landing the walls were covered with oil paintings in gilt frames with special lighting, as if the pieces were in a museum. The paintings were mostly landscapes (an icy coastline on an overcast day, a medieval town in a vast desert, a scenic waterfall that emptied into a pool, a forest of enormous redwoods). Another painting was of a city—all of white stone—that sat on the ocean. Behind the city were a set of hills and atop the tallest hill was a giant castle with towers that shot up into the sky. Sarah guessed the painting was of Greece or somewhere like that, although the castle building didn't seem very Greek to her.

"Like any of these paintings, Maggie?"

The girl shook her head. "Not really."

They walked to the end of the hall to where Sarah's room had been. The door was closed. She didn't think anyone was home but she knocked anyway. When no one responded, she opened the door slowly and then, confirming no one was inside, walked in.

The room was perfectly made up with blue painted walls and curtains and linens to match. No child lived in this room. A guest bedroom was her best guess.

"This used to be my bedroom when I lived here."

"It's so big," Maggie said. "I wish I had a room like this."

"Yes, well, rooms are bigger outside of New York, Maggie. But when I lived here the room was decorated differently. The walls were light yellow and I had a white bookshelf over there and a dresser over there with all of my stuffed animals on top." She saw the walk-in closet and then remembered. "And over here was my closet. Let me show you something."

Sarah opened the door. Inside were extra sheets and towels, no clothes. The light bulb needed to be replaced, so the back of the closet was complete darkness. Sarah ran her hand along the wall until she found the latch. She flipped it back and the door swung open—a closet within a closet. When she was a girl, she often used to sit in here alone. Sometimes she'd bring a flashlight and write messages to herself on the wall. She wondered if any of her notes were still there, but it was too dark to see any of them even if they still existed.

"Maggie, come back here," she said.

"It's dark in there," Maggie said but then walked into the small enclosure anyway. Sarah, from her own kneeling position, reached out and guided the girl towards her.

"This used to be my secret spot when I was young."

Maggie didn't say anything. Sarah's arms were still around her. With the girl's head so close to her chest, her breasts, Sarah became aware of her own heartbeat.

"Are you going to marry my Daddy?" Maggie said. Sarah felt the little girl's breath on her face.

"Why are you asking that?"

"I've never been to a wedding before so I was just wondering."

"You're going to a wedding this weekend."

"I know. But it would be different if you married Daddy."

"That's true. But getting married isn't a small decision. You need to be very sure before you marry someone."

"Do you love him?"

"Of course. And I love you too, Maggie."

"Then why don't you get married?"

"Well, your daddy has to ask me first."

"Okay," she said. "Well, I think he's going to ask you."

"Is that right?" She assumed it was a little wishful thinking on Maggie's part.

"Yeah, I saw him putting a ring into his suitcase."

"Oh," Sarah said. She gripped Maggie tighter against her body. She might have expected feelings of overwhelming happiness at this instant, but instead she felt afraid. That's not right. She felt happy—and because of that, she felt afraid.

They sat in the dark a while longer until, finally, their time together was broken by the sound of footsteps coming up the back stairwell.

"Maggie!" Henry called. "Sarah! You guys up here?"

"We should go back to Daddy," Maggie whispered.

"Yes, I suppose you're right. But let's just wait a minute longer."

Excerpted from *The Travels of Mandel Longfellow* (published 460 YAF)

A Description of Ilyeth

Of all the places I have visited on my travels, the one I am most often asked about is Ilyeth. This is not entirely surprising; why would not people be curious about the legendary home of sorcerers?

Ilyeth is both the name for an island some twenty leagues off the southeast coast of the Inner Sea as well as the city built on the island. The island of Ilyeth is one of the largest of a group of more than a hundred islands called The Labyrinthine Isles, which were given their name due to the extreme difficulty inherent in navigating them. On most days, a thick, low-lying fog hovers over the Isles, making it nearly impossible to see more than a half dozen ship lengths in any direction. More than a few ships have been marooned or stranded in the Isles for this very reason.

For an Ilyan captain though (and as I mentioned, I was onboard with one such woman) who is accustomed to navigating the Isles, the process is simple enough. All that is required is a compass and the proper approach.

The day I arrived in Ilyeth the fog was so thick that the position of the sun was totally obfuscated. Had I not been told we would be approaching the city from the north, I would have had no idea of our bearings. Though we had entered the Isles due east of Ilyeth, the shape of the Labyrinthine Isles made the shortest path one that would be approaching from a northerly direction.

We were sailing along through the fog when suddenly, and quite miraculously, the fog parted; there stood the island of Ilyeth in all its glory, with a five-square-mile hole in the clouds directly over the island, which allowed copious amounts of glorious sunlight in. I was told that though the fog over the Isles is natural, it is through some feat of sorcery that the clouds are parted directly above the island. The island itself is roughly circular with a diameter of approximately two and a half miles. The actual city takes up only a third of the island and is made up mostly of tightly packed, white stone buildings of two or three levels. The streets too are made of a similar looking white stone, and this, combined with the fact that I was first visiting on one of the pre-ordained sunny days, gave the city an especially wondrous quality. Imagine the bright white city contrasted both against the glimmering blue sea below and the verdant green hills behind. My descriptions undoubtedly sell the place short.

In addition to the architecture, one of the most noteworthy aspects of Ilyeth was the incredible diversity of its inhabitants. About one half of the population is made up of the tan-skinned descendants of those who accompanied the first group of Ilyan Brothers who settled on the island over four hundred years ago. The remainder of the people seemed to descend from every corner of the Continent. It was not uncommon in my few days in Ilyeth to see people who hailed from Lanzhao or the Islands or even, one man claimed, some distant northern lands beyond.

Aside from the actual city proper, the remainder of the island is made up in roughly equal parts of farmland, which gives the island a manner of self-sufficiency, and hilly terrain, on which the Sanctum is built. The Sanctum, which, as is well known, is home to the Ilyan Brotherhood itself, is a massive three-sided structure, which in terms of sheer magnificence matches or surpasses anything in either Alder or in the West that I have beheld.

Each of the three sides consists of five large towers of equal height, with the five towers on each side connected both at their base as well as via stone walkways at the towers' midpoints. These towers represent the Twelve Acolytes of Ilya (the three towers at the ends of each side are counted on twice, making twelve, not fifteen total towers). At the middle of the triangle created by the three sides is the Great Tower, which is much wider than each of the twelve smaller towers and twice as tall. This tower then is said to represent Ilya himself. In the remaining space within the triangle are six large domes, three of which are made of colored glass and three of which appear to be of the same stone as the rest of the complex.

Legend has it that the original designs of the Great Tower go back all the way to the time of the Forefathers and were brought to the island by the last surviving Acolyte, a man by the name of Neva. As I visited the Sanctum's library I was shown a vellum-bound book that contained a copy of a copy of a copy (etcetera, etcetera) of what is said to be the original designs. The head librarian, who at the time was also acting as my tour guide, readily admitted to me that though the plans for the Great Tower were undoubtedly very old, whether or not they dated back to the Forefathers (or, in fact, whether the Forefathers themselves were more than the stuff of legend), was itself a subject of intense debate.

During my time in the Sanctum, my hosts were generally not keen on letting me wander around the compound or the nearby grounds unaccompanied. I could only guess as to the exact reasons for the sorcerers' reticence. Perhaps they held some secret they wished to keep hidden from outsiders. Or else perhaps some terrible danger lurked somewhere in the bowels of the place. I never did come to a definitive answer on the matter. Howsoever, on my one night inside the Sanctum I can relay that I had the misfortune of getting lost in the middle of the night while in search of the garderobe. Although I do not suppose I ever left a very small corner of the Sanctum, there was something about those dark, ancient halls (even so close to guest rooms) that stirred in me a fear like I had never felt in all my life. Luckily, after perhaps a quarter of an hour of aimless walking, I was found by one of the apprentices who escorted me, first to the garderobe and then back to my room.

When I told the head librarian of my nocturnal ordeal the next morning and asked whether there had ever been reports of the Sanctum being haunted, he simply laughed at me and told me not to be so superstitious.

EIGHT

DAGGER
560-603 Years After *The Fall*

He couldn't have known at the time. Any talents he had for premonition—for peeling back the foggy layers of his dreamlike meditations to reveal the probabilities, the potentialities, of coming events—wouldn't develop in earnest for many years. All the same, trusting the man called Benedictus would be, for many years, Pa-Zhe Tu's greatest regret.

Much later, it wouldn't escape him that there was an irony in how Benedictus had been, in a way, the seminal force of his life, molding him in absentia into the accomplished, some would say great, man he'd become. Indeed, when, at that distant point in the future, he sat on his small palfrey outside the abandoned inn he'd finally tracked his adversary to—flanked by a score of armored cavalrymen from the capital and a half dozen of his Ilyan Brothers—he would reflect on how much he owed Benedictus even as he hated him. He would try unsuccessfully to dispel these contradictory feelings for, as he clutched unconsciously at the dagger strapped to his side, he knew what must happen next.

But that's getting ahead of things.

⚜

Everything began nearly a half-century earlier when Pa-Zhe walked out of a frigid winter evening into The Slaughtered Calf in search of his father.

Lo Tu was a regular at The Calf, though he seldom drank; he didn't handle alcohol well and would become erratic after even a few sips. Instead, the elder Tu's vice of choice was gambling. Dice. Cards. Sticks. Betting on pugilist matches. Betting on arm wrestling matches. Betting on dog races. Betting on chariot races. *Lucky Lo*, who had in fact been given his nickname in the same spirit that a giant is called *Tiny*, loved any game of chance where money might be won (or in his case, lost). It was fortunate that the other thing he loved (and was good at) was making remarkable sums of money as a timber merchant; otherwise, the Tu family would have long ago found themselves destitute by way of its patriarch's gambling debts.

Pa-Zhe was little more than a boy then, thirteen years old. His mother had sent him out in the snow to fetch his father for the evening meal. That evening The Calf was packed with men. Until a day ago, it had snowed unceasingly for a week and the men in that part of the city had only just managed to dig their houses out from beneath the heavy blanket of whiteness. It had been too long since they'd been able to indulge themselves in drink and cards and, now that they finally had the opportunity, were coming out in droves.

Young Pa-Zhe navigated the pungent crowd of bodies blocking the entrance and found his father sitting at a table, cards in hand, across from a man dressed in a dark green riding cloak. A large, rowdy group gathered around. Pa-Zhe crossed to the opposite side of the table to find an empty spot from which to watch the proceedings. From this new vantage point, he could see the face of the man opposite his father. He was undoubtedly a foreigner but from where, the boy had no idea. His complexion was a few shades darker than that of the other Jarlites (nowhere close to the rich tan of Pa-Zhe's people); however, unlike the locals, with their hair of fire and light blue eyes, this man's hair was an earthy brown, his eyes a bright green. He wore no beard and was of indeterminate age. There was something both unsettling and impressive about him. Since the annexation it wasn't entirely uncommon for foreigners to pass through the city on their way to Turmandheim or the other Southland territories, yet even amongst the aristocrats and noblemen Pa-Zhe had seen riding in the streets, he couldn't remember ever seeing anyone who appeared so…dignified.

Two emperor cards lay face up in front of each of the players signifying a tie-breaker would be required to determine the winner.

"Final draw!" the burly bartender and makeshift dealer, Hegreb, shouted.

The crowd hummed with energy. Hegreb slid three cards face down to each of the opponents, who glanced at what they'd been given. "It's to you, stranger."

"Five crowns," the man said in such a deep, gravelly voice that Pa-Zhe could make out no discernible accent. The crowd gasped at the sum, which had nearly doubled the already rich pot.

Pa-Zhe's father tried to stare down his opponent, but the man remained impassive. Lo checked his own cards again and looked at the crowd of men staring at him.

"What's it going to be, Lucky?" Hegreb said.

"The Demon take you, stranger," he said, an expression of the Jarlites he'd adopted even though he believed in neither The Demon nor any of the other southern gods. He slid his money to the center of the table. The onlookers erupted in cheers, pounding their cups on the long wooden tables.

"Lucky! Lucky! Lucky!" they chanted. Somewhere a cup shattered.

"Whichever of you bastards that was is going to give me three *chopeks* a cup," Hegreb shouted. "Now will you all shut those smelly holes you call mouths so we can get on with this?" The noise settled to a manageable level and Hegreb pulled two cards from the deck with a flourish, holding them hidden in his large hand. "I present you, The Last Stand."

He slammed the cards on the table face up. Pa-Zhe stood on his toes to see over some of the men seated around the table. Seven daggers and a blood warlock: the kind of hand that offered a million possibilities for victory or defeat.

"Stranger. Your wager," Hegreb said. Without a word the man slid three more crowns into the center of the table.

This time Lo didn't hesitate before countering. "Up to six," he said, sliding his coins to the middle of the table. The chanting started up again. "Lucky! Lucky! Lucky!"

The green-clad man eyed his opponent. Then, for the briefest instant, turned and glanced in Pa-Zhe's direction. A chill shot through the boy's midsection and he looked away.

"Surrender," the stranger said, putting his cards down on the table. The crowd began whooping and shouting. Lo burst into laughter and slapped hands with anyone within reach—many of who despised him and on any other day offered him only the smallest modicum of respect on account of him being wealthy. Lo collected his winnings. "One round of drinks on me!" he said and the men cheered again. Pa-Zhe was relieved. His mother would have screamed all night if his father had lost fourteen crowns on top of whatever other losses he'd surely sustained earlier.

Seeing his son, Lo stood up, paid for the drinks and placed his remaining winnings in a small purse. "A pleasure playing with you, foreigner," Lo said to the man who had been his opponent.

"You and I are foreigners both, I would guess," he said and gestured to Pa-Zhe. "Your son?"

Lo nodded.

"A *promising* young man, I think."

"Promising, eh?" Lo said and spat. "No head for business and spends all his time with storybooks. Also, a weakling, practically a dwarf, despite my wife's efforts to fatten him up. Is that what passes for promise where you're from?"

"There is more to promise than skill in commerce or physical attributes, no? I, myself, could barely walk for the first ten years of my—"

"And look what you've become. A bad gambler. Ha! Forgive me if I don't put too much weight behind your advice, foreigner."

"Please. Call me Benedictus."

"Well, BEN-EH-DIC-TUS…I am Lo. And my wife awaits." He gave a half-hearted bow to excuse himself. "It was a pleasure taking your money. I will admit that you have quite the face for cards. No emotion at all. Still, I had a feeling you were bluffing me."

"Bluffing?" he said.

"Why else—" but before he could finish his sentence, the man called Benedictus picked one of his cards off the table and flicked it at Lo. The card struck Lo in the chest and he reeled back in surprise.

"Until next time," Benedictus said and walked out The Calf's front door. Lo picked up the card off the floor, placing it face up on the table. The Ice Warlock, which, regardless of whatever the man's other card, would have beaten nearly any hand.

Pa-Zhe's walk back through the snow with his father started off more pleasantly than would normally be the case. Most times his father's favorite pastime was picking apart everything the boy did and was. Why was he so small? Why did he let the other boys bully him? Why did he spend so much time with his sister? If he received the highest marks in school, it was only because his classmates were barbarian idiots. If only Lo had had a real son to be proud of, to take over the business. Yet today, Lo seemed uninterested in doling out criticism and instead walked through the snowy streets with a smile on his face buoyed by his gambling win. "As soon as the road north is cleared of snow, I will take a crew out to the woodlands. The viceroy's office is auctioning off leases to a few parcels northwest of the river come spring and we need to have our bids in order by then."

Pa-Zhe's father had told him a thousand times that the key to the timber business was not so much the ability to cut down and transport the wood—any idiot could hire men to do that—but was instead in one's ability to accurately calculate the yield and transport costs from particular parcels of land. Good calculations meant good bids, which meant profitable leases, which meant a profitable business. Pa-Zhe did well in the rudimentary mathematics classes taught at his school but struggled with the complex formulas of his father's business, a fact that infuriated Lo Tu to no end. Perhaps with sufficient effort and repetition Pa-Zhe might have become proficient at the mathematical intricacies of predicting timber yields, but in truth, the boy's real interest lay not in numbers but in books: the histories and stories and songs. The favorite book of both he and his sister, which they'd each read at least a dozen times, was *The Travels of Mandel Longfellow*, which detailed the exploits of the famous explorer of a hundred years past—from the islands north of Kallanboro to Tel Moran and Lanzhao in the west, from the uncharted territories of the Far Wastes beyond the mountains to Ilyeth, secret home to the Cree. Needless to say, Lo Tu felt all of this reading a monumental waste of time.

"Some of these parcels could be extremely profitable. The terrain northwest of the river is mountainous and those idiot competitors of mine still haven't figured out how to accurately gauge mountainous terrain."

"Father, I've been thinking. That man…Benedictus . . ."

"Who?" He snapped out of his good mood.

"The foreigner. At The Calf. Why did he surrender?"

"Who cares? A win is a win. Twenty-two crowns is twenty-two crowns."

Technically, his father had only won eight crowns, seeing as he'd placed the rest into the pot himself—even less once you subtracted the cost for all the drinks he'd bought the crowd.

"It seems strange. He had the Ice Warlock."

"Maybe he didn't really have one. Maybe it was just a trick."

"A trick?"

"How should I know? Or else maybe he was worried that I had an even better hand." This explanation also seemed highly improbable. Theoretically it was possible, but would have required that his father had two or more of the remaining three Warlocks in the deck. "Maybe if you spent less time asking foolish questions and more time with the business, you could take over one day."

❖

The Tu household was located at the end of a short street off one of the main thoroughfares of Jarl's prestigious Lantern District. By the time Pa-Zhe and his father returned home, the sun had fully set and the lanterns lining the road faintly illuminated the snowy streets. Their house was a three-story manor that was small as manors go and was said, by the man who sold the Tu family the property, to have been built during the days of King Ulf II, long before even the first Lunaris emperor ascended to the throne of a then-far-smaller Alderian Empire.

As soon as they entered the house, they could hear Pa-Zhe's mother, Na-Wei, screaming in their native tongue from the dining room. "*Why have you let so much time pass? Dinner is aging!*" Between his time at school and the fact that his father insisted on using only the Common Dialect of the Empire, Pa-Zhe took a moment to translate the Lanzhenese in his head.

"*Who is the chief of this house, woman!*" Lo yelled back. "*Don't loudly speak to me!*"

"*Chief of the house . . .,*" she said as if the phrase was poison. "*Chief of offering up gold as sacrifice to drunken barbarians!*"

"*I want that you should know that I victoriously received more than thirty crowns today!*"

"*Thirty crowns! Thirty crowns! You are the lord of sums and equations so, if it pleases the spirits, you tell me what part is thirty crowns of the four hundred you sacrificed last year?*"

Pa-Zhe was not privy to the inner workings of any other marriage yet felt confident his mother and father's was unusual. His parents' way of relating to one another vacillated between two, equally troubling extremes: verbal conflict which ever teetered on the verge of physical violence (hurling household items was a regular occurrence) or else behaving like the young lovers he read about in the stories. Countless times Pa-Zhe would be kept up late into the night with the eerily similar sounds of his parents' vigorous arguing or love-making—sometimes both in the same evening.

The shouting continued. The boy went upstairs to check on Mei-Fa. His sister was sitting in the window, brushing her long black hair and looking at the men shoveling snow on the street. Even upstairs, one could still hear their parents. "They're at it again," he said.

"Yes," she said, but he could tell her mind was elsewhere. Now she tied her hair up above her head to reveal her full, slightly flushed face, which contrasted her otherwise slim features. "Do you know that in the northern reaches of the Continent it never snows?"

"I suppose that's true."

"Have you ever thought about how a scene like this with the snow everywhere, that we tire of for the inconvenience, would seem like a miracle to an Islander or a Kallanbori?" she said but didn't wait for an answer. "It makes me wonder what else is in the world. Is there something that some girl five hundred leagues away finds a nuisance that I would find amazing?"

He was a year younger than his sister but still felt protective of her. They were both born in Jarl, yet were viewed as foreigners and treated, at best, with cold indifference by "trueborn" Jarlites. The two siblings had few friends other than each other, and, perhaps on account of this, had each adopted a reserved demeanor. Yet at times, Mei-Fa—when she was happy, when she felt comfortable with someone—could talk and talk and talk, and Pa-Zhe wondered how different she might have been had they grown up back in the homeland rather than in this inhospitable place.

"Maybe you will get to find out one day," he offered. They often talked about how much they wanted to travel, to see the world. During these conversations, his sister came alive and her eyes brimmed with passion.

"Don't be silly," she said.

"Why is it silly?"

"Maybe, if I marry into sufficient wealth, I will one day travel to Turmandheim and see the Southland. But so much of the world will forever be closed to me. Never will I see the Phaidonian castles that line the avenues of Alder or feel the breeze of the Inner Sea upon my face or walk amongst the ancient trees of the Westwood where Mandrakhar still live as they did in the old days. And our homeland will be no different to me than the stories we read about—something that doesn't exist except in our mind's eye."

"What's wrong?" he said.

She took both her hands and wiped something from her face. "Mother... She told me that as soon as I finish school she will begin looking for a suitable husband for me." They both had known this day would come but had avoided talking about it.

Downstairs there was a crash of pans and Lo Tu could be heard shouting "*Queen of whores!*"

Mei-Fa winced. "I swear to you brother. If I ever have such a marriage . . ."

"It could be worse," he said, which was true. At least they loved each other, albeit strangely.

The house servant, Shen, entered the room bearing a large tray of food.

"I thought, if it pleases, that you both would digest your evening meal here above the ground floor," he said.

After that first evening Pa-Zhe thought little of Benedictus. The man had made a strong impression, yet as far as the boy knew, he'd never see him again. Besides, Pa-Zhe had more immediate concerns, like his sister's impending matching, to preoccupy him. What if her husband was cruel? Or lived far from the city? Pa-Zhe couldn't imagine not having his sister around.

It wasn't until early spring that Pa-Zhe again saw the mysterious gambler. That year a warm streak melted the snows early and fast, leading to some of the worst flooding Jarl had seen in years. In the lowlands, the docks and the ground floors of all of the buildings along the Riffel were submerged and residents could be seen navigating that part of the city in canoes and fishing boats. The city's sewage overflowed into the streets, which along with the suddenly elevated temperatures, gave Jarl, even so far away from the river as the hills of the Lantern District, the smell of rotten excrement.

As soon as the snow melted, Lo Tu had departed for the woodlands to the north to survey some of the parcels that would soon be up for auction. Up north was hilly country so flooding wouldn't be a problem there.

For a week, due to the deluge, Pa-Zhe and his sister were forced to take a roundabout route to their schools on the east side of the city. One morning, the siblings were just a few minutes from their destinations when a group of neighborhood boys approached. These were not the well-to-do boys who attended Pa-Zhe's school but were the sons of porters and laborers and soldiers and dressed in dirty clothes, tattered from being worn every day.

"Look!" the biggest of them shouted, a boy named Lars, who Pa-Zhe recognized as the son of one of the workers at the fish market. "The two rich darkies!"

This wasn't the first time Pa-Zhe and his sister had been harassed on the streets, and by now they were accustomed to this type of remark. When traveling to rough areas of the city, Pa-Zhe's father would often bring protection in the form of some retired knight who'd fallen on hard times and needed extra income. As part of the Empire, Jarl was ostensibly more "open" to foreigners than ever. Yet neither annexation, nor any of the Imperial laws that came with it, could change the city's inhabitants' intense distrust of outsiders. The fact that three thousand Jarlite men had been conscripted in recent years to support the fighting west of Zabiz, beyond the Inner Sea, had only caused the locals to further push back against Imperial control and all the values that came along with it.

"Keep walking," Pa-Zhe whispered to his sister.

"Darky! You injure us! Why don't you speak? Do you not understand our language?" Lars said. "*Dza dzang doe ya*," he said, making nonsense sounds to simulate their native tongue.

One of the boys threw a medium-sized stone, which struck Pa-Zhe hard in the shoulder. He screamed, a single shrill cry. The boys laughed. Pa-Zhe walked faster now, pulling his sister by the arm, but a few of the boys ran across the street to cut them off.

"Where ya going, darky?" another of their group said, a harsh-looking boy with a harelip. Although still larger than Pa-Zhe, he was the smallest of the group and this made Pa-Zhe uneasy. It was always the smallest and ugliest who were meanest; they themselves, having endured a lifetime of torment, would be devoid of kindness—a stick sharpened into a spear by the grinding wheel of the cruel world.

"Let us pass," Mei-Fa said.

"Look, the darky needs a darky girl to speak for him," one said.

"The darky sluts have fiery tongues."

"She can use that fiery tongue on my cock," another added

"I wouldn't. Unless you want her to bite it off."

"I don't know. I bet she'd like it once she had a taste. Besides, once you get past her color and her tiny eyes, she's actually kind of pretty."

Pa-Zhe whipped his head left and right to survey the surroundings. Across the street an old woman swept dirt in front of a house. Further down, two of the city guard looked at the gathering with passing interest and no desire to help. Pa-Zhe recognized one of the men, the clean-shaven one who wore his gray-streaked red hair down in two thin braids. His name was Ogeth. He'd gambled with Pa-Zhe's father numerous times at The Calf. Pa-Zhe gave him a pleading look, but he just averted his gaze and walked on.

The harelipped boy reached out to touch Mei-Fa's cheek. Oddly, there appeared to be no malice in his caress but instead a kind of curiosity, even tenderness. Yet when Mei-Fa drew away from him and slapped his hand down, Pa-Zhe could see the boy's face harden.

"Foreign bitch," he said and wrapped one arm roughly around Mei-Fa to subdue her and then with his free hand mockingly stroked her cheek.

"Stop," Pa-Zhe said, but no one listened. Mei-Fa closed her eyes and began to tremble.

Most of the other boys crossed over to his side of the street and now they all stood around and laughed. When Lars's gaze crossed Pa-Zhe's, he gave him a wicked smile and flicked his tongue at him. The boy with the harelip still held Mei-Fa's with his right arm, but now his other glided over every part of her body—pinching through her woolen dress at her still-developing breasts, exploring the space between her legs.

The boy with the harelip was not expecting it, so when Mei-Fa, instead of pushing the boy's hand away, swung at his face with her closed fist, he attempted neither to dodge nor block the oncoming blow. Mei-Fa's punch landed cleanly on its target's cheek, and the harelipped boy went momentarily limp, releasing his grasp on her and plummeting to the ground. His face landed with a loud, wet smack against a low stone wall lining the street.

The boys were silent. It was Pa-Zhe who broke the quiet when he shouted at his sister in their native language. *"Run! Flee from here with haste!"*

Mei-Fa took off in as much of a sprint as her dress allowed just as her tormenter rose from the ground. Tears ran from his eyes, his harelipped mouth was covered in blood, and he held two or three teeth in his hand.

"Get the…the fucking…darky." he said in between sniffles. The seven or eight boys didn't pursue Mei-Fa and instead encircled Pa-Zhe, slowly closing in. Pa-Zhe dove towards the nearest one, hoping to land a punch to rival his sister's before being overtaken, yet before he could reach his target, Lars gripped his arms from behind.

The boys took turns punching Pa-Zhe in the stomach and chest while Lars held him back. When it was the injured boy's turn, he repeatedly kicked Pa-Zhe in his genitals. With each kick a shot of pain jolted through his body. He felt something break and could feel blood dripping down his leg. He wasn't sure how much time passed. He was on the edge of consciousness when he heard a voice, the deepest he'd ever heard, from somewhere in the distance.

"You will all leave. Now," the voice said. Pa-Zhe saw that it was the man from The Calf: Benedictus, cloaked in his dark green. Pa-Zhe could hardly think straight, yet he swore that the man seemed taller than when he'd seen him before. He loomed over the boys like a giant shadow.

Lars released him and he fell to the ground. All of the boys scattered save for the harelipped boy.

"Fuck you, foreigner!" he said, the blood from his mouth spattering out towards Benedictus as he spoke. "I'm not afraid of you!"

"That's a shame," Benedictus said and placed his hand on the boy's shoulder. Almost immediately, blood and puss started to pour from the harelipped boy's eyes and ears and he ran off screaming. Those screams were the last thing Pa-Zhe heard before he rolled over, unconscious, onto the cobblestone street.

When Pa-Zhe regained consciousness, he was lying in his bed. Outside the mountain wren sang its rapid call. The window shades were drawn and a fire burned in the hearth. Judging from the bird song and the little light that slipped in through the blinds, he knew it was morning—although, which morning? A vague, diluted pain emanated from all over his body. He had the faintest recollection of drinking a bitter tea.

He wasn't alone in the room. Across from his bed a dark figure sat beside the fire. This revelation startled him, but he then realized it was just his sister. She hadn't noticed he was awake and was staring at the shuttered window.

"Mei-Fa," he tried to say, but his throat was out of use and what came was more a groan. She stood up and approached him. "Mei-Fa." This time the words came out.

"Shh," she said. "Rest now, brother. Your injuries were very bad." His restless hands, still beneath the blankets, found the bandages around his groin. He remembered the boys, the foreboding silhouette of his savior.

"He was there. Benedictus." He had mentioned the story about The Calf once in passing to his sister.

"He brought you back to the house and tended to you here. He's been stopping in every morning."

His sister went downstairs to fetch water; shortly thereafter his mother and Shen came up to check on him. Lo Tu wasn't expected back home for a few more weeks. When his mother saw him awake, she began kissing him on his forehead.

"*I will make the tea arrive.*" Shen said and walked back out.

"*My son…my son,*" his mother repeated.

"*Is he present? Outside-country man? Benedictus?*" Pa-Zhe said.

"*Yes, yes. He is below this floor. I believe it is true he will arrive with Shen in little time.*"

He grabbed her arm. "*I don't want him to arrive.*"

"*Don't want him to arrive? Without him you are murdered pigeon, or is that false?*"

"*Yes, but…*" It was undeniable that Benedictus had saved him. Yet what he'd done…

"*My son…*" She used her palm to flatten the hair on his head.

Benedictus strode into the room dressed in gray wool pants and a white tunic. Shen followed close behind with the tea.

"You drink," the servant said, now in the Common Dialect.

Pa-Zhe looked at Benedictus.

"It dulls the pain. Amongst other things," Benedictus said. His face showed no evidence of being capable of violence.

"What else?"

"*A filial son of a good family listens much and speaks little,*" Shen said.

Mei-Fa came with water and then she, their mother and Shen went downstairs to finish meal preparations. Benedictus sat down in the chair Mei-Fa had occupied earlier that morning and started to wash and re-dress Pa-Zhe's wounds.

"Are you a doctor?" Pa-Zhe said.

He rose from the chair and opened the blinds to let sunlight into the room. "Is *that* the question you want to ask?"

"No...I don't know."

"I am not a doctor by trade, although I know a little about the healing arts."

"And where did you learn that?" he said and hesitated before squeezing the next word out. "Ilyeth?"

The tall man laughed. "Ilyeth? 'The place of legend!' Secret home to the Cree—to sorcerers!" he said mockingly. "I would have thought you were too old to believe in such things! Perhaps your father was right about you reading too many books." He sat back in his chair and proceeded to finish re-dressing the wounds.

"I saw what you did to that boy."

"I supposed you had," he said. "A nasty thing, wasn't it? You'd have to agree that he deserved it though, no? *That* I certainly didn't learn in Ilyeth. They hardly teach anything useful. All the useful things, I've had to learn on my own."

"You admit you've been there? That it exists?"

"What is all this obsession with that place?"

"But you are one of them. A Cree," the boy said.

"Fine. Guilty. Are you happy?"

How many stories, terrible and marvelous, the boy had read about the Cree: *the Childless Ones,* blessed and cursed by the Forefathers with the ability to work miracles! And now here one was: the stories of his childhood incarnated in the flesh.

"Don't look so shocked, boy. You are one too."

"What?"

"Oh, never mind." He removed a small bundle of fabric from his satchel and presented it to Pa-Zhe. "Here. A present." Inside the cloth was a silver dagger sheathed in leather, its handle inlaid with several large jewels.

"This must be worth a lot."

"It is. But not because of the jewels."

"Where'd you get it?"

"Neither of us have time for that story."

"Why are you giving it to me?"

"To smite your enemies," he said grandly, but when Pa-Zhe didn't laugh, he corrected himself. "For protection. I believe you may have need of this dagger one day."

"And why do you care about protecting me."

"Is this how your parents taught you to say 'thank you?'"

"Thank you."

"That's better." He took the blade back, wrapped it in the fabric and placed it in the chest at the foot of the bed. "This shouldn't be out in the open—in case your mother doesn't approve. I'm confident you will know the right time to take it out."

They could hear Shen humming as he walked up the stairs, ostensibly carrying food up. "We can talk more later," Benedictus said.

Benedictus continued visiting Pa-Zhe regularly—applying salves, re-dressing the boy's wounds, and giving him more of the bitter tea. When they were alone, Pa-Zhe would pepper him with questions about Ilyeth and being a sorcerer and anything else he thought a Cree might have insight into. Benedictus was usually evasive, but on occasion he'd give a straight answer. From what Pa-Zhe gathered, Ilyeth was indeed a place (on an island in the southwest corner of the Inner Sea, just as Mandel Longfellow had claimed!) and Benedictus had studied there "long ago." Pa-Zhe also gleaned that Benedictus had had a "falling out" with the powers that be in Ilyeth and since then he'd pretty much been a loner.

Many of these visits passed, and Pa-Zhe never asked the one question burning on his mind. *You are one too*, he had said. Had Pa-Zhe misheard? Certainly, if he'd meant what the boy thought he did, he would bring it up again. Yet, Benedictus was quiet on the subject and the question remained. Finally, two weeks after his injury, the boy couldn't contain himself any longer. By now he was walking again, albeit gingerly and would soon return to school. Benedictus and Pa-Zhe sat talking in the study when the boy came out with it. "That first day. When I woke up . . ." he said, hesitating, "I think you said . . . I mean . . . Did you mean to say that I was like you? Which is to say . . . a Cree?"

Benedictus grinned as if this had been a joke he'd been keeping to himself. "I was wondering how long it would take you to get to this."

"And?"

"You are."

"I am?"

He nodded.

"Are you sure?"

"Quite."

"How?"

"I knew when I saw you in The Calf. It's one of the first things they teach in Ilyeth—to recognize another of our kind. I stayed long enough for that lesson at least."

"I have no powers, can perform no miracles."

"None *yet*. Or none you recognize. That will change. You and I are of a kind. You will bear no children—and it's nothing to do with how those boys kicked you between your legs. Still, you will live longer than your grandchildren would have and, I believe, you will change the world."

"When?"

"When you're better. When you come with me."

Pa-Zhe imagined it. He wanted nothing more than to leave this city, to see the world. And yet . . . He thought of Mei-Fa. "I could never leave my family," he said.

"I felt the same way many years ago. But sometimes there is no escaping destiny."

Soon Pa-Zhe was well enough to return to school. His broken rib hadn't fully healed and his groin ached when he walked, but he was confident that in time, he'd make a full recovery. Shen arranged for him and his sister to be escorted to school by a bodyguard. In addition, Pa-Zhe surreptitiously carried the dagger beneath his clothing. He liked the feeling of it next to his hip. Its weight, the knowledge of what it would be capable of if those boys ever approached him again, comforted him. Sometimes, out behind the stables alone, he'd imagine one of the bales of hay were Lars or one of the other boys. He'd play at stabbing it, twisting it for maximum pain and injury—seeing in his mind's eye the boy's entrails falling to the floor.

Neither bodyguard nor dagger were needed. The few times Pa-Zhe had been out on the streets alone and saw any of his former attackers, the boys would cross over to the other side of the street immediately. The harelipped boy was never amongst them. Pa-Zhe was no longer quite so upset by what had happened to him. Benedictus was right: he'd deserved it.

A few days after starting school again, Pa-Zhe was paid a visit by Benedictus, who told the boy he'd be gone for a while on business, but that he would return for him in time. Pa-Zhe still insisted that he couldn't possibly leave.

"We can discuss that when I see you again," Benedictus said.

Weeks passed. The floods subsided and Lo Tu returned from his surveying expedition. By now, Pa-Zhe was almost completely recovered and showed few outward signs of his attack. His father, having heard of the incident, but now seeing little evidence of injury on his son, assumed everyone had been blowing things out of proportion. "Maybe a little beating will teach him to be more careful," he said.

Lo won several of the largest land auctions—more than in any previous year—and so, not two weeks after his return home, he again prepared to depart the city for the summer tree harvesting. Na-Wei complained about her husband being away so much, but Lo dismissed his wife's pleas. *"You savor the taste of flesh but disdain the slaying of cattle,"* he said, an idiom from the homeland.

Lo returned north. Spring changed to summer. Most nights before going to sleep, Pa-Zhe would stay up in his bed thinking about what Benedictus had revealed to him. He'd told Mei-Fa, but she'd seemed unimpressed.

Since none of Jarl's schools for girls accepted students over fourteen, that summer Mei-Fa finished her studies and Pa-Zhe began traveling to school alone. There hadn't been open talk from their parents of marriage plans for Mei-Fa, but it was assumed that something was in the works for her to be married off to some Lanzhenese immigrant who lived in this part of the Empire. As for Pa-Zhe, he had another three years of schooling, after which time he would either continue his education in the north or begin working in the family business.

Normally during the two siblings' summer holiday, their father set them on tasks around the house or with the business. Since this summer Lo had departed early and wasn't around to monitor his children's duties, Mei-Fa and Pa-Zhe instead spent those three weeks idling away their time in the Royal Park or along the river reading and talking. Their mother was tasked with keeping the two busy with house chores, but Na-Wei knew this might be the last summer her children would be together and so allowed them to spend their time as they wished.

"Shen told me mother has been speaking to potential husbands," Mei-Fa said one sunny afternoon in the park as the two sat with their feet dangling over the recently re-named *Imperial* Canal. "He says there is a spice merchant recently moved to Jarl from the West that she plans to match me with." A gathering of birds approached her and she threw them crumbs from the rind of bread she'd been eating.

"A spice merchant?"

"Or silk. I don't remember. He is old though. Near forty."

"Why would mother and father consent to such a match?"

"He's very rich." It sounded like something that would be their father's idea. She went on: "You must promise me never to leave Jarl. Never go to the North for university or follow that sorcerer. Even if you are a Cree," she said and laughed. "Stay here with me. I couldn't bear it if I was stuck with my old husband and you were gone."

He hugged her and kissed her on the forehead. "Of course, I promise. You're my sister. My one true friend."

A few days later, Pa-Zhe was in the study reading when he heard a loud knocking on the servant's door that led to the alleyway behind the house. Though it was mid-morning, the sky was dark with storm clouds that pounded the city with rain and thunder. Shen was away buying provisions and the boy's mother and sister were at the dressmaker getting measurements for a dress Mei-Fa would wear at her introduction to the spice merchant.

He opened the door and found a cloaked figure standing just outside, the cloak soaked through by the driving rain, which rushed diagonally through the door and into the house. The man pulled his soaked hood back. Benedictus's face was badly swollen, his eyes mere slits. There was a large gash on the side of his head and the collar of his shirt was soaked in blood. He stumbled through the doorway, falling to one knee.

"Hurry up," the sorcerer groaned, gathering himself off the ground. "Shut the door."

Pa-Zhe warmed some fish soup from the cauldron that Shen had made earlier and left Benedictus in the kitchen to eat while he went upstairs to fetch the man a dry cloak. His father was much smaller than Benedictus, so the garment looked silly on the sorcerer.

"What happened?"

"Suffice it to say there are those associated with the Empire and with Ilyeth who are not friendly towards me."

"Why?"

"Why," he repeated to himself. "Because they would have me and everyone from here to the Islands bow down to the Alderians like the rest of my brethren, and I refuse them. Because they wish to expand until the entire Continent, and any land they might sail to, flies one flag. They have been searching for me for some time."

It was one thing to be the enemy of neighborhood boys, quite another to have Redcloaks and sorcerers after you. "What…what will you do?" Pa-Zhe said.

"I must leave the city. But not yet. There are Ilyan Brothers who watch the city gates and the docks with a close eye and the aid of sorcery. So, for now, I wait." He abandoned his spoon, picked up the bowl and slurped the rest of the soup down. "Will you come with me when I leave?"

The more he had thought about it, the more tempting the offer was. What could he hope for here in Jarl but the endless berating of his father and harassment on the streets? With Benedictus he could make something of himself, see the world.

Yet, there was Mei-Fa.

"I can't. I've told you already."

"Your family," the sorcerer said, as if considering the phrase. "There are things more important than blood. Your father despises you; your mother treats you as a child. I on the other hand understand your potential. I understand what you were *meant* to do."

"I know. It's just—"

"And the ones who come for me will come for you eventually. They will say they are *training* you, when really they wish only to turn you to their backwards way of thinking."

"I can't leave."

He bit his lower lip, restraining himself. He closed his eyes, either out of exhaustion or frustration. "I cannot force you," he said then. "I can only lead you down a path of wisdom. One day you will see."

There was a knocking on the front door now and Benedictus grabbed the boy by the arm. "It's them. Answer, but say nothing of me."

Pa-Zhe took deep breaths as he walked through the front foyer and opened the door. Three men stood on the doorstep underneath the overhang and out of the rain—two men of the city guard, one bearded, the other clean-shaven, and another in a gray hood. Pa-Zhe recognized the clean-shaven guard, Ogeth, who had stood by as he was beaten nearly to death. The bearded guard, who appeared to be the older and higher ranking, spoke first: "Boy, is your father here?"

"No, he's away north. My mother is gone also. To the dressmaker."

"We are looking for someone. A foreigner."

From a young age his parents had instilled in him a healthy respect for authority. These were city guards at the door—even if one of them was Ogeth. And yet…

"We are all foreigners who live here," Pa-Zhe said.

"Aye, to be sure. But the man we look for is not of your kind. He is lighter with brown, not black, hair and green eyes. He was spotted recently in this area of the city."

"I've seen no one of that description, sir."

"Very well. If you do, please come find someone in the city guard. This man is very dangerous."

"Of course. I will tell my mother as well."

The two city guards turned around and the three men were about to leave when the third, the hooded man, interjected. "Just a minute," he said.

The man who had been speaking to Pa-Zhe seemed surprised. "You sensing anything?" he said to the hooded man and laughed.

The hooded man said nothing. He stepped in front of the two guards and pulled down his hood. He had olive skin and a dark beard. He looked upon Pa-Zhe with his brown eyes, much like Benedictus had that first time in The Calf. "What is your name?"

A chill went through Pa-Zhe. He couldn't describe what was happening—perhaps nothing. He told the man his name. The man introduced himself as Aron.

"You are sure you haven't seen anyone fitting the description of the man we seek?" Aron said. "You have nothing to fear from us."

"I'm sorry. I haven't."

"Very well. Good health to you."

Pa-Zhe closed the door.

He felt as if something momentous had occurred—that he'd made a decision from which there was no turning back.

He half expected Benedictus to be gone when he returned to the kitchen, but the sorcerer was exactly where he'd left him and had refilled his bowl of soup from the cauldron.

"You're still here."

"Of course. I trust you."

"One of the men at the door…He was dressed all in gray and said his name was—"

"Aron, yes. One of the Ilyan Brothers. They all wear that gray. It suits their drab sensibilities. Now, if you don't mind," he said gesturing to the bowl before him. "We'll speak more later."

Benedictus finished his soup and walked back to the servants' door. He seemed to have regained a little of his strength. The weather outside had not improved and a loud burst of thunder shook the house.

"I'm not sure when I will see you again, but I will try to visit when I'm able," he said and disappeared into the rain.

Mei-Fa and her mother were formally introduced to the spice merchant the next week. The thought originally was to wait for Lo to return from the forest, but Na-Wei decided this was an unnecessary delay. Pa-Zhe wasn't invited to the introduction, which took place at the spice merchant's estate on the western side of the city; however, he tried to comfort his sister as best he could when she returned home in tears.

"Was he cruel?" he asked, when they were safely in the confines of her bedroom. She shook her head, no. "Ugly?" Again, no. "Then what is it?"

"His smell."

"Smell?"

"Like…rotten vegetables," she said and started bawling again.

Pa-Zhe only saw Benedictus one more time over this period. One evening when he was retiring for the night, he found the sorcerer sitting in the chair next to his bed.

"How did you get here?" the boy said, feigning anger at the intrusion.

The man rolled his eyes. "Of all the things you have witnessed or heard me tell you of, you are amazed at how I can break into your bedroom?" He gestured to the open window.

"Has something happened?"

"I'm leaving the city."

The sorcerer explained that many of the Ilyan Brothers who'd been looking for him had left Jarl, assuming he was no longer in the city either. The gates weren't being watched as closely, and so, within the next few days, he would make his escape.

"You haven't changed your mind about coming with me?" he said.

"No. I can't leave."

"Very well," Benedictus said. "I wish you all the best. We will meet again someday. Remember: my former Ilyan Brothers are not to be trusted." Those were his last words, and he stepped quietly through the window and onto the roof.

Pa-Zhe was returning home from school two days later when he saw the fire. He walked alone that day since he, Shen, and his mother had jointly decided that he no longer required an escort so long as his route to and from school remained in the more civilized parts of the city. Pa-Zhe had seen the smoke billowing skywards from far away, yet thought nothing of it. It was the beginning of the Summer Festival and it wasn't uncommon for some of the more religiously zealous Jarlites to burn huge straw effigies of The Demon in the streets to place their piousness on display.

Once he turned the corner onto his street, he realized that not even the largest effigy could be responsible for the smoke that filled the air. He ran through the haze to discover where the smoke originated. His panic mounted as he approached the source.

Plumes of smoke poured from every window and crevice of his house and more than half the building was engulfed in flames, some so hot that they burned a bluish green. Even from a distance, Pa-Zhe felt the heat radiating off the house.

A crowd had gathered around to witness the blaze. Pa-Zhe looked for Mei-Fa or his mother or Shen. All three would have likely been home now. A few of the neighbors used buckets of water in an attempt to prevent the fire from spreading, yet everyone seemed resigned to giving up on the Tu house.

There was a crash as part of the house's second level collapsed onto the lower floor. There was a scream: his sister.

"Please! Someone! My sister is inside!" Pa-Zhe shouted. A few of the onlookers turned to him, but no one made any move to help.

The front door was completely blocked by debris, so the boy searched for some other way into the house. He ran to the side of the structure near the garden where the house had not yet caught fire and entered the side door. Even here, the smoke was so thick he could hardly see.

"Mei-Fa! Mei-Fa!" he said. He made his way through the kitchen and dining room, shielding his eyes and mouth as best he could from the smoke. In the study, a wall of flames impeded his path forward. The heat was singeing his skin; he had to leave. Just as he turned around though, there was another popping sound and the entrance back to the dining room collapsed in an impassable heap of burning wood and hot stone.

Small as he was, the windows were too narrow for him to fit through. He tried to force his way back through the doorway he had come in through, hurling his body against the debris, but it wouldn't budge and his tunic caught fire.

He removed his burning clothes and threw them into the fire. He could barely breathe from all the smoke. He sat on the ground in the middle of the room. "Help!" he said. "Help!" He could feel the heat creeping closer.

In another life, perhaps he would have developed whatever abilities Benedictus claimed he had. In another life, he'd be able to escape this fire and save his sister. More as a joke than an actual attempt, he focused on the debris blocking the exit. *Ha!* As if he could simply wave his hand and unblock the way, like some great sorcerer in the stories. He wasn't in a story.

But then, just like in the stories, the debris exploded into a thousand, thousand splinters of wood and shards of rock. He looked down at his hands as if to ask them *how did you do that,* but the answer came a second later when a shirtless Benedictus entered the room, his thin, yet muscled torso gleaming with perspiration. He scooped the boy up off the ground and prepared to escape the burning house, but then, seeing the fires everywhere in the dining room, placed Pa-Zhe back on his feet and got down into a crouch.

Pa-Zhe wasn't sure what Benedictus was doing, but it appeared he was concentrating on something. Benedictus muttered some unintelligible words, placed his two hands together and out of them produced a shiny black orb. The orb flickered as it fluctuated in size between the sorcerer's palms. There was the feeling of a great wind, sucking into the orb. Pa-Zhe felt as if the breath was taken from his lungs. And then the wind was gone and the fire and smoke with it.

When it was over, Benedictus lay on the ground in exhaustion. Not waiting for the sorcerer, Pa-Zhe ran through the charred and collapsing house searching for his sister.

He found the bodies of Shen and his mother first—both of them in the pantry, one of the rooms that never caught fire. Still, their bodies were just as lifeless, their lungs choked from the smoke.

His sister's body was in the great room. Her clothes as well as much of her skin were burned off, and she was covered in seared blood that had turned a strange, foul green. He tried to hold her charred body close, but the very attempt burned his arms. He screamed—pain and grief wrapped into one.

"Come," Benedictus said when he finally entered the room, "there's nothing further for you here."

He went with the sorcerer, in a daze, out of the house, through the back alleys of the Lantern District, and down to the lowlands by the river where some buildings still hadn't been reclaimed after the floods of earlier in the year. Along the way, Pa-Zhe often had to lend a supporting arm to the sorcerer to prevent him from falling over. When they came to one particularly dilapidated wooden building that looked to be half falling over from the damage it had sustained in the floods, Benedictus bid Pa-Zhe enter. They walked up a stairway to the building's second level where it appeared Benedictus had taken up residence. Benedictus sat down in the room's only chair. Pa-Zhe couldn't help but recall the image of his sister's blackened corpse.

"I am sorry," Benedictus said. There were tears in his eyes. "I saw the fire, but not in time."

For the next week Pa-Zhe stayed at an inn not far from where his house had been. The boy didn't have any coin, but the innkeeper knew of Lo Tu's wealth and that he'd be able to pay his son's debts when the time came. Pa-Zhe stopped going to school—he didn't see the point—and instead spent those sunny days sitting on the canal in the Royal Park just as he and Mei-Fa had a few weeks earlier.

When his father returned for the funeral, Pa-Zhe briefly moved into the house that his father had leased in the Mercantile Quarter of the city. Other than a few brief words at mealtime, Lo pretended his son didn't exist and would spend most of his day shut in his room with a bottle of wine. Often, Pa-Zhe could hear his father wailing through the walls. The one time he knocked on his father's door, Lo answered with bloodshot eyes and told the boy to go away.

Shen's body was cremated and Na-Wei and Mei-Fa were buried in a family plot in a burial ground outside the city. The Jarlites were a superstitious bunch and refused to allow any burial grounds within the city's walls lest the ghosts return to haunt the citizenry. Pa-Zhe would have welcomed his mother or sister's ghosts. Haunting, in his estimation, was better than nothing.

Benedictus and Pa-Zhe made preparations to leave Jarl. Benedictus's informants had confirmed that most of the Ilyan Brothers who were looking for him had moved their search elsewhere—convinced their fugitive had already fled the city.

It was decided Pa-Zhe would drive a wagon out of the city and that Benedictus would hide in back. If anyone asked, the boy was running supplies back to the lumber camp for his father. By the time anyone would have time to verify with Lo, the two of them would have abandoned the wagon, ridden off with the horses, and be long gone.

On the morning they were to leave, Pa-Zhe left a note for his father stating that he had decided to go away to the North. He couldn't risk telling him the truth should those hunting Benedictus somehow get ahold of the letter.

Their departure from the city was uneventful. It was a clear day but a breeze blew in from the west. When the cart passed through the north-gate, flanked on either side by forty-foot-tall stone guard towers, Pa-Zhe waved to the soldiers in the windows. He imagined what he'd do if they ordered him to stop. They didn't; they waved him through.

Beyond the gate, several miles of grasslands expanded out before them as the Riffel curled off to the northwest. According to Benedictus, the grasslands would eventually turn to rolling hills and woodlands. It was there amongst the trees they planned on abandoning the wagon and taking the horses. They would not travel along the highway that, were one to follow, would go more than a thousand miles north all the way to the capital. Instead, they would travel off-road along the foothills of the mountains before heading southeast, where Benedictus had friends that would give them shelter.

"We've made it. We're out of the city," Pa-Zhe said to the sorcerer once they were beyond earshot of the walls.

"Stay silent," Benedictus said in a whisper from the back of the wagon. "No one else is around."

"Just listen. We're still close to the city."

They traveled much of the morning in silence and Pa-Zhe watched the grasslands, an occasional farm or homestead, pass slowly by. The beginning of the woodlands was within view, perhaps just a half-mile's distance, when a group of riders approached from the south—back in the direction of the city. The riders didn't appear to be riding them down, but even at a canter, the group moved much faster than the wagon.

"Who's coming?" Benedictus said from the back of the wagon.

"I'm not sure." The riders bore no banner and were not clothed in the deep red of Imperial soldiers.

Soon it was apparent that three of the riders were gray-cloaked Ilyan Brothers, with the other three looking to be bodyguards of some sort. One of the three gray-cloaked men was Aron, who had come by his house that day looking for Benedictus. The riders slowed as they got close and Aron rode up to the cart with one of the bodyguards. There was no point trying to outrun riders with a wagon; Pa-Zhe brought his horses to a halt.

"Greetings," Aron said, clearly recognizing the boy. "You are . . . *Pah-duh*, correct?"

"*Zhuh*," he corrected, but Aron gave him a quizzical look. "*Juh* is close enough."

Aron smiled. "One doesn't see a boy your age on the road alone too often."

"I'm older than I look," he said and then, just as he'd rehearsed, he told the man he was off running an errand for his father—bringing supplies to one of the lumber camps. A tragedy had struck his family, he explained, and his father had not been able to get out of bed due to a grief-stricken heart.

"A fine son you are," Aron said.

"Thank you, sir."

One of the bodyguards, a tall Jarlite with a rapier hanging from his belt, dismounted his horse and took a drink from his water skin.

"And I did hear about the tragedy that struck your family. A terrible thing," Aron said. Out of the corner of his eye Pa-Zhe saw the bodyguard casually come around to the rear of the wagon.

"Yes, thank you for—"

A bang and a loud tearing sound came from behind. The man who had wandered around to the back of the wagon gripped his own throat, blood spurting from a bright red wound. The four other riders who had stopped some distance away hastened towards them now. There was a flash of light and all four of the approaching horses, as well as the horse Aron sat upon, crashed down beneath their riders, sending each of the mounted men tumbling to the ground.

Benedictus emerged from the back of the wagon, his cloak billowing in a wind that gathered unnaturally around him. All in one motion the sorcerer unharnessed one of the horses and mounted it without a saddle.

"Come boy!" He stretched a hand out towards Pa-Zhe.

Pa-Zhe stared at the hand. He wanted to grab it, but his body was frozen in fright.

Aron, the only of the six riders who'd already returned to his feet, ran towards them. Benedictus slapped his horse and rode hard towards the tree line. For a time Aron kept pace with the horse but Benedictus eventually gained an insurmountable lead. Some two hundred paces away, Aron gave up his chase.

Pa-Zhe attempted to saddle the remaining of the two horses that had been pulling the wagon, but before he could get away, one of the four other men had gotten up off the ground and grabbed the boy roughly by the wrist. The man unsheathed his sword and held it to Pa-Zhe's neck.

In the distance, Benedictus's horse disappeared into the forest.

He was brought back to Jarl and placed in a cramped cell in the city jail that smelled of stagnant water. No one spoke to him and for supper he was given a piece of stale bread and a foul-tasting stew. That night he slept, cold and afraid, on the cell's dirty straw mattress. He dreamed of Mei-Fa and his mother, and when he woke he started crying when he remembered both of them were dead.

Aron visited the next day. Pa-Zhe's heart was beating fast when the Ilyan Brother was let into the cell. He'd seen what Benedictus had done to the harelipped boy. This man might do the same, or worse, to him. He tried in vain not to show any signs of fear.

"Calm," Aron said. "I won't hurt you. You've gone through enough."

"What do you know?" Pa-Zhe said, defiant and frightened all at once.

"I know your mother and sister died. I know you lived in a house that burned down—by mage fire. I know that not many of us in Ilyeth can wield such a thing. The man you call Benedictus can."

Pa-Zhe couldn't believe what the man was implying. "You lie. He saved me. He's my friend!" the boy shouted.

"My guess is that he was untruthful on many accounts. You have nothing to be ashamed of, though. He has pulled greater deceptions on lords and sorcerers. I have been hunting him for some time. He goes by Benedictus now, but he once went by a different name and was my friend." Pa-Zhe looked up into Aron's calm, honest-looking eyes.

"There, there," Aron said and put an arm around the boy's shaking shoulders.

"What happens to me now?" Pa-Zhe said once he'd regained himself.

"It's up to you," Aron said. "The man you called Benedictus was truthful about one thing: you are one of us. If you wish, we could make a place for you in Ilyeth."

Pa-Zhe remembered Benedictus's warnings. He wasn't sure what to believe. However, what better option did he have than to take a chance on Aron now?

After Pa-Zhe was released, Aron asked if he wished that anyone contact his father to explain what had become of him. The boy shook his head no.

They arranged for Pa-Zhe's travel—by land to the eastern coast of the Inner Sea and then sea passage to Ilyeth. It was a long journey that took nearly a month, but time no longer mattered to Pa-Zhe; all those who had loved him were dead and gone. His time was entirely his own. Pa-Zhe's first life had ended in that fire; he was eager to see what his second one would bring.

Over the next fifteen years, he seldom left the island unless it was required for his studies, and he became one of the fastest ever to be promoted to master. Only the legendary Azkhar Aramayo, who'd sailed with Mandel Longfellow across the Great Northern Ocean, had achieved the distinction faster. In time, Pa-Zhe was regarded as one of the greatest sorcerers in the entire known world and the most talented healer anyone in Ilyeth could remember. Indeed, his accomplishments during his self-imposed exile from the Continent could make for an entire book unto itself.

As the years passed, Pa-Zhe came to believe what Aron told him that day in Jarl—about Benedictus and about who had started the fire that killed his sister and mother. Nonetheless, he always kept the warnings he'd been given regarding the Ilyan Brotherhood in the back of his mind. And so, throughout his time on the island, he was vigilant against someone trying to indoctrinate him or turn him to some secret agenda. As far as Pa-Zhe could tell, it never happened.

Once a master, he did not settle in Ilyeth, nor did he return to live in Jarl. There was nothing for him there. Shortly after the death of his mother and sister, his father married a young bride and started a new family and had made no attempts to find his first son.

Instead of settling anywhere, Pa-Zhe, who was now called "Padgett" for simplicity, returned to the mainland and travelled from place to place throughout the Empire and beyond with few possessions save the clothes on his back and his silver dagger. For a time he lived in a small hamlet on the sea outside of Vicus Remorum, and at night he would stay up in bed listening to the crashing of waves. Another year he sailed beyond the Inner Sea—to Zabiz, the city of a thousand spices, and eventually to Tel Moran and Kotchalia and his homeland of Lanzhao, where for the first time in his life he could blend in with a crowd of people. Eventually, he drifted back eastward.

He imagined that his sister, were she still alive, would have envied this nomadic life. Given his talents, it was never hard for him to find food and shelter. Every village could make use of his skills as a healer, if nothing else.

Throughout all this time, he would not always travel by himself. Often he would travel with merchants or pilgrims when their routes coincided. He enjoyed the company. Mostly though, he was alone in the world.

Padgett often thought about Benedictus. He dreamed of him, those bright green eyes. A few years after leaving Ilyeth, he found himself in the capital, where he curried favor with intelligence officers and anyone who might have knowledge of the man he had known as Benedictus. Word of him—associated with some mischief or another—sprang up from time to time. He was outside Brigantium living as a sheep farmer; no, he was in the Westwood living amongst the Mandrakhar; no, he was across the sea.

Padgett would follow these rumors, traveling thousands of leagues to track down the man who, in Padgett's mind at least, had become his adversary. A few times he'd been close to catching him, but the fugitive sorcerer was always a few steps ahead. Padgett had faith he would find his man though. He had premonitioned it, and the premonitions of a Cree have a tendency of coming true.

During the Uprising in the North, there was news that Benedictus had played a part in the fighting and that he was in Kallanboro on the sea. At that time, the war was raging and it was impossible for Padgett to reach the city and seek his enemy out. Instead he rode with the Redcloaks to the front lines, serving as healer and waiting for his opportunity. He had no particular love for the Empire, yet the Empire brought stability and stability brought peace and there was a kind of virtue in that.

Finally, almost a decade after the war had ended and not long after the last Lunaris emperor had died and his cousin, Lord Galsworth had ascended the throne, Padgett had his chance. Benedictus, who was wanted on a large number of crimes around the Empire, had been tracked by a group of Brothers to the hill country west of the capital. Luck would have it that, when Padgett caught word of this, he himself was in the capital, working as a healer in one of the poorest parts of the city. He left the city within the hour and rode west.

By this time, Padgett's father had been dead for fifteen years and he thought how his mother too would likely have succumbed by now had she not died prematurely. Mei-Fa might have grandchildren. Even Padgett's baby half-brother, who Padgett had only seen once through a window when he was traveling through the South, was in middle age now.

It had been so long and the hate he carried for Benedictus had become a part of him.

By the time Padgett caught up to those hunting the sorcerer, they had already tracked him to an abandoned inn on the banks of the Black River and had the building surrounded. A half dozen Ilyan Brothers weaved their sorcery around the barren-looking building to prevent Benedictus from using any sorcery of his own. Padgett was held in such high esteem amongst the Brothers that when he asked if he might go inside the inn first, the gray-cloaks conceded.

"He's dangerous. Even without sorcery," Master Tarmichel, one of his Sisters, said, "but you know that."

Padgett dismounted his palfrey and walked to the inn door.

Just inside, Benedictus sat at a bench, in a tattered black tunic and torn pants. A cloak of Imperial red, darkened from the blood soaked into it, sat in a heap on the floor. When Benedictus beheld Padgett, a smile, without malice, grew on his face. He looked much the same as he had all those years before except now wore two weeks' worth of a beard. It wasn't until Benedictus turned to speak that Padgett could see a broken piece of an arrow shaft jutting out from where his shoulder met his neck.

"I hoped we would get to speak again."

"Why?" Padgett said.

"I am proud of you. Of everything you've accomplished. I had hoped that your accomplishments would be by my side, but I see that was not to be. I am proud of you nonetheless."

"Don't talk to me as if we are friends, Benedictus...Or whatever you go by."

"Call me whatever you wish."

"Murderer."

"Sadly, the name fits. There are many things I regret."

"Like killing my mother...Mei-Fa...Shen . . ."

A grave expression crossed his face. "So I am responsible for that now too?"

"You deny it?"

"What evidence have you? The word of my enemies?" He winced once from the wound in his neck. "But you've made up your mind...I see you've kept my dagger in good condition."

"So you deny it?"

Benedictus cleared his throat. "I've killed many people. I take no pride in this, but it is a fact. You could argue thousands of lives were lost during the war on account of my actions. Perhaps then it doesn't matter if three more are wrongly added to the count. Anyway, there's nothing I could say to change your mind."

Padgett wanted to believe him, but the man called Benedictus spoke lies. He'd lied about his own name. Padgett's hand gripped the dagger hanging from his belt. He stood just an arm's length from him now. "You know you will not escape again—neither by sorcery nor trickery."

To this Benedictus started laughing. "Yes. It took me a long time to see that—to see the truth—but now it's unmistakable." He coughed once and spat blood on the ground. "I would have liked to learn how this all worked out, but that will be up to you now. To finish my work, to put the pieces together."

"Your work?"

"My premonition. Amongst other things."

"What premonition?"

"You probably don't have the patience to hear about all of it now. When the time is right you can read about all of it in my journal in that satchel." He gestured to a worn leather bag sitting on the floor next to an overturned table. "There is another thing in there for you as well. A jewel. I would have wanted to have the scepter by now, but—"

"I have no interest in your work nor your premonitions nor anything else you might offer."

"Maybe, but take the jewel…and read the journal. Will you promise me that?"

"Why would I promise you anything?"

"A dying man's last wish."

Padgett thought about this and then nodded once.

"Very well," Benedictus said and stood slowly. "Shall we get on with it?"

Padgett unsheathed the dagger, which he'd never used save to stab a bale of hay, to cut some cheese or an apple.

He seldom thought of his father anymore, but he thought of him now—a walk through the city they had once long ago. That day, his father had talked to him about the family business. *One day this will all be yours.*

His hand trembled, but he steadied himself. Before he raised the dagger, he flipped his hold on the thing so he could thrust it with maximum force. The man called Benedictus looked down in resignation. Padgett eyed the spot on the chest where he estimated the heart was and thrust down.

Once the blow was struck, Benedictus had a look on his face as if he were surprised by the sensation. Then the faintest of smiles appeared on his lips. He fell first to his knees, then to the ground.

Padgett studied the crumpled form at his feet and thought about everything that had transpired the last forty years. He wondered what his sister would have been like as an old woman. He wiped his eyes with his sleeve, making sure not to get any of Benedictus's blood on his face.

He picked up Benedictus's bag now and searched its contents. Sure enough, there was a large red jewel inside as well as a journal with the name *Benedictus* inscribed in a seal on the book's cover. Padgett closed the bag and took it with him when he went back outside to greet the men surrounding the inn. He left the dagger behind.

Henry & Sarah's Wedding Website

Our Story

Once upon a time, Sarah spent two weeks at an artist's retreat in an old house in Western Massachusetts, finishing a set of watercolor paintings for a children's book she was working on. As many of you know, illustration was a long-time passion of Sarah's and, as a result, she was very much looking forward to her time at the retreat.

It was December, and the freshly fallen snow made the grounds of the old house incredibly beautiful.

On one particularly snowy day, as Sarah was working on her paintings, in walked a handsome man with tortoiseshell glasses and a funny accent named Henry. Henry was a writer who had come to the retreat to finish a book he was working on.

Sarah and Henry hit it off pretty quickly. After a few more days in the house together, a lovely and fun hike through forested hills, and several late nights talking around the fireplace, they decided that they liked each other a lot—although there's still some debate as to who made the first move.

Since they lived in different cities, they knew that starting a relationship wouldn't be easy; however, the two were smitten, so they decided they'd try to make things work. Seeing as Henry had a lovely daughter, Maggie, to take care of (whereas Sarah only had her goldfish, Maxfield), Sarah agreed she would try to come to New York at least once a week, and Henry would come down to Philadelphia whenever time allowed.

So commenced several months of early-morning/late-night trains for both of them, during which time Sarah grew to love Maggie like her own daughter, and Henry discovered that pretty much any food was superior to the stuff they served on Amtrak. While certainly not an easy way to date, Henry and Sarah made it work and soon could recite all the train stops on their stretch of the Northeast corridor.

After some time, the goodbyes got harder, and Sarah decided to move to New York. In March of this year, Sarah traded cheesesteaks and angry sports fans for pizza and hipsters, and left Philly for Brooklyn. Sarah subletted for a few months but soon joined Henry and Maggie in their apartment in Greenpoint. Several more months passed—these full of living room dance parties, late-night burrito runs to Calexico, and storytelling competitions between Sarah and Henry (with Maggie as judge). The three of them were having a blast.

In the fall of that year, Henry, Sarah, and Maggie were going on a road trip to Kentucky to attend a wedding for Henry's friend, Marceau. Along the way, the three almost got in a car accident in Pittsburg and visited Sarah's old stomping grounds of Cincinnati, Ohio. On the return trip they made (what Sarah thought was) an impromptu stop at the New River Gorge Bridge in West Virginia and signed up for a tour that followed a narrow footpath underneath the bridge. A fog, with a magical quality, Sarah thought, floated up out of the gorge that day. Henry was prepared for the right moment. He dropped to one knee, and there, on the misty bridge, pulled out a ring. Maggie cheered…Sarah cried…and then she said yes!

NINE

AN UNEXPECTED CHAIN OF EVENTS
2018-2020

It was a second marriage for them both, but since neither Jack nor Neha had had children the first go around, and since they were both still in their thirties (not an uncommon time to have a first child in this modern age), they decided to try and conceive.

There had been a time when Jack and his first wife had tried to have a child, but by then the cracks in their marriage had already begun to reveal themselves, and the couple had taken a what-will-be-will-be approach, jointly agreeing that if they couldn't conceive naturally that they wouldn't push the matter. After all, his first wife had said after one of their many arguments—this one about the fact she never checked the prices of items at the grocery store before purchasing them (*fifteen dollars on grapes?*)—maybe it was a sign from the universe that they shouldn't have children together, that they weren't *meant* to have children together. Jack hated this line of thinking; he didn't believe in destiny or *everything happens for a reason*. Still, he had his own doubts about the two of them bringing a child into the world. "Maybe you're right," he said to her.

When Jack married Neha, ten months after serendipitously reconnecting with her on a trip he'd taken to Ireland, the couple decided to move to the Midwest, where Neha had grown up and where her parents still lived. Jack got a job running marketing for the business school at the local university to supplement his writing income; Neha opened up a holistic medicine practice above a Middle Eastern restaurant in their small city's downtown. They rented an apartment for two months but quickly fell in love with, and purchased, a gutted and remodeled four-bedroom house on one of the many quaint streets in town. Neha regularly described their new home as her "dream house," and they both agreed that the newly purchased piece of real estate was far bigger and nicer than what they could have afforded had they stayed on the East Coast.

Not long after closing on the new house, as they surveyed the upstairs bedrooms and decided what furniture needed buying, Neha suggested they hold off furnishing one of the extra bedrooms. If they furnished the room now, maybe they would eventually have to replace some of the newly purchased items with a bassinet, a cute dresser painted light blue or pink.

They had talked about children before the wedding but only in a vague way, as if too much discussion on the topic were bad luck. "Are you not-so-subtly suggesting something?" Jack said as they sat on the hardwood floors in the echoey upstairs room.

"I've been thinking about it a lot and...wouldn't it be cool to, you know, create something out of this?" she said, gesturing to the space between them.

It was strange how only now—after his wife concretely put this idea into the world—did Jack realize that this was what he wanted too.

He scooted close to her, placed his arm around her shoulder and blew a loud zerbert on her neck. She screamed and punched him on the shoulder.

The first few months of trying to conceive were one of the most joyful and carefree periods of their marriage. Implicit in their decision to have a child was a kind of re-commitment to each other, a doubling down of the high stakes they already had on the relationship. Now Jack would often find himself thinking fondly of his wife while he sat at his desk writing (or more likely, writing memos or marketing plans to the dean of the business school), whereas before he seldom experienced such episodes of romantic fancy. It almost felt like a second courtship, except without the accompanying worry of a just-beginning relationship.

It also helped that this was a period of great fucking.

Neha, who, after a lucrative, if soul-numbing, career in human resources consulting had returned to school to pursue a second career as a practitioner of naturopathic and oriental medicine, held the stance that, although western pharmaceuticals had their place, they should generally be avoided unless absolutely necessary. To Jack's chagrin, the birth control pill was one of these less-than-absolutely-necessary pharmaceuticals, and in the time before getting married, the two would use a combination of condoms and fertility tracking that had both of them eagerly waiting the coming of Neha's period each month.

"There's stupid, and then there's *this*," Jack had said of Neha's rather complex system of temperature taking and ovulation tracking, all of which was carefully graphed onto charts that reminded him of something he might see on a CNBC program discussing commodities prices. "We're using Chinese birth control practices. *Chinese* birth control. Do you see the irony here? There are like 1.4 billion Chinese people."

After deciding to have a child, all this changed. They could make love without barriers of latex or lambskin separating their flesh, without worry of what would or wouldn't happen on day twenty-eight. And he could finish inside her, something he'd never done, without risk or worry. In fact, it was his duty to deposit as much semen inside her as possible—albeit, she reminded him, on or around her ovulation.

"Let's just hit as many days as possible to cover our bases," he said.

The increased lovemaking seemed to have the effect of increasing her libido even further, of awakening something inside her, and she began to not only go along with, but to actively suggest, ways to further spice up their sex life. She went online and purchased costumes: the rather clichéd school girl and French maid and naughty nurse, of course, but also a high-heeled ninja assassin/geisha combo, a scantily clad *luchador*, a steam-punk adventurer woman, an extra slutty Princess Leia outfit that Jack, although he wasn't much of a *Star Wars* fan, had to admit she looked fabulous in. They bought swings and straps and shoes and other paraphernalia. They'd set up complex scenarios and role-plays, meet in public places pretending not to know one another. They'd fuck in every room of their house—in the kitchen, in the unfinished basement, in the empty bedrooms upstairs, on top of the running washing machine during the spin cycle, in the backyard, on the lawns of neighbors, in public parks, in public restrooms, in department store changing rooms (she'd bring a large shopping bag, he'd step inside to conceal the second pair of feet), in the back of a rented Avis van, in the back of a Hertz subcompact, in the back of movie theaters during an unpopular movie's final run on the big screen, and anywhere else they could devise where it wasn't too likely they'd be caught.

During this time whenever the couple would be out with friends (though they'd only been in town a short while, Neha was a social person and made friends fast) or Jack's colleagues, the newlyweds might steal a glance at one another across a dinner table or a crowded bar, a knowing smile on each of their lips, and their mutual knowledge of their sex lives would pass, unspoken, between their eyes. It was as if they were superheroes, Jack thought, with only each other knowing their hidden identities—only instead of fighting crime or saving the world, their secret was wild, unapologetic fucking.

When the first two months passed without Neha getting pregnant, they were almost glad. They wanted a child but didn't mind delaying things a little so they could continue to enjoy one another in this newly discovered way. It was August, and if they conceived in September or October, their child would have a summer birthday just like they both did. Jack imagined enormous, combined summer birthday parties, grilling outside in the Kansas heat, water balloon fights and maybe even a Slip 'N Slide. Life was very good.

Fall came and the fields of enormous sunflowers bloomed and died. Halloween brought a record number of trick-or-treaters to their house and *damn weren't some of these kids just the cutest?* Another day twenty-eight passed without incident. And another. She still wasn't pregnant. By Thanksgiving, when they drove to her parents' house in Overland Park, there was a kind of unspoken inflection point, and during the forty-five-minute drive that morning, she suggested that perhaps they were having *too much* fun. Maybe he should save his semen for the window of time where her temperature rose and her cervical fluid was in evidence. He reluctantly agreed, and after the four-day weekend, they continued to try under this more puritanical regime. Though Jack didn't say anything, his thoughts began drifting back to the conception troubles he'd had with his first wife and the idea that these problems had somehow been his fault began to take root in his mind.

In fact, it was during this time that Jack started to think a lot, generally, about his ex-wife again—not just how they hadn't been able to have a baby, but also how the very fact of their separation was evidence to the ephemeralness, the precariousness, of even the most seemingly stable parts of our lives. He realized how troubled he was by how little he knew about her now. A person who he'd once talked to every day, touched, laughed with, fought, considered having a child with, was now a mystery. Since he'd moved to the Midwest, he no longer ran into her. He tried to glean what he could from social media and googling, but she was mostly a private person in this regard and so his internet searches yielded relatively little: old archived newspaper articles about her high school basketball career, the wedding website from her second marriage, a few mentions on others' social media profiles. None of it satisfied him and he was left to fill in the gaps himself. What was her life like now? Did she still eat rye toast with olive oil and salt for breakfast? Did she make the same sound, that kind of guttural chirping, when she made love with another man? What had it been like when she met her new husband—who himself was a writer, a fact that Jack found simultaneously flattering and troubling. The answers to all these questions were unobtainable; all he could do was imagine. And so he did, going so far as to write a few stories about her life, which he went back to whenever he reached some sort of impasse with the writing he was supposed to be working on.

When the doctor came back and told them there was a problem with his sperm, Jack wasn't completely surprised. The doctor, his name was Steiner, looked to be younger than Jack, probably just out of residency, and Jack found this fact both humiliating and offensive. This man—this child is going to tell me about my sperm? This man, whose own balls are probably producing millions of healthy sperm just waiting to attack a vulnerable egg. The fucking nerve. Jack was so worked up that he only vaguely heard the doctor's explanation regarding motility and morphology and some other words that he didn't really understand but suspected were bad. Neha, at least, seemed to be paying attention.

One thing the doctor had said that Jack gathered was that the quality of his sperm was such that, while it was unlikely they'd conceive naturally, it wasn't technically impossible. And so, at his wife's insistence, he embarked on a variety of strategies she'd gathered from her network of holistic medical practitioners. He switched to a diet high in antioxidants. He took herbs and supplements in both tea and pill form and then granular. He refrained from riding his bike to work. Six more months passed—each one an anti-climactic tease as they waited, with increasing pessimism, hoping for the exact opposite of what they'd hoped for before they were married— that the period wouldn't come. Each month it came.

During this time, Jack was supposed to be finishing the manuscript for the fourth in the series of mildly successful romance novels he wrote to pay the bills, each of which followed the exploits of an independent woman living in 1880s New York named Virgie Chapman. In this most recent book, Virgie falls for a dashing gray-haired police inspector and Civil War veteran named Solomon Mack. Despite Solomon Mack being in his forties, Jack had no doubt as to the man's virility. In fact, it was quite a surprise that good ol' Virgie never got knocked up. Simultaneous to this novel project, Jack was also trying to finish a collection of literary fantasy stories that he'd been writing on-again, off-again for the better part of two decades. Instead of working on either of these projects though, he found himself writing more and more about his ex-wife: stories about how she met her new husband, stories about her teenage years, stories about how she'd be in old age. Words had never come so easily to Jack.

At the end of the next June, Neha's period didn't come on day twenty-eight, despite usually being exceedingly regular. Day twenty-nine passed without a period and Neha and Jack both studied the Excel spreadsheet she now maintained that tracked her daily temperature, her daily mood, and each instance of intercourse. What did it mean that during ovulation her temperature had risen but not as much as in previous months? Day thirty came and went and thirty-one as well. "Do you think I should buy a pregnancy test?" she said. The expression on her face as she asked was an expression of someone who had become afraid of hoping. He suggested they wait until she was a week late.

One day before the week cutoff, on day thirty-four, Jack was at home writing in his office when he received a text from Neha:

Got period today ☹

IVF was the next thing the doctor suggested. The three rounds of expected treatment would cost around thirty thousand dollars, but Jack and Neha decided this was something worth dipping into their savings for, and Neha's parents had kindly offered to pay for half of the treatments so the financial burden wouldn't be quite so great.

During this time, they nearly stopped making love completely. Part of it was on account of their doctor, as she (Dr. Steiner had been replaced by Dr. White at the Kansas City Reproductive Clinic) suggested they give a period of "pelvic rest" for about ten days following the embryo transfer. However, even outside these windows, their lovemaking was infrequent and, when it did happen, felt chore-like since Dr. White had beseeched them to "maintain intimacy" during the treatment for infertility.

And so, they went on dates, had other couples over for dinner, and fucked when they were up for it.

"You want to put in some work tonight?" Jack said one night as Neha was reading in bed.

"Not if you're going to call it *work*," she said looking up from her book. "It's not *work*."

He dropped his boxers and swiveled his hips from side to side so that his flaccid penis flapped back and forth, slapping against his hips. "How about now?" he said.

"You really know how to turn a girl on."

Still, despite her feigned disgust, they made a go of it.

After several rounds of failed IVF they broached the topic of sperm donation. It was, after all, quite likely that his sperm was the root of the problem.

If, some years prior, one were to have asked Jack—hypothetically—how he felt about sperm donation, he would have given a completely different response to what he felt now. Actually, that wasn't precisely accurate. He was still wholeheartedly in support of sperm donation—*for other people*. Sperm donation for *his* child, if he dare call this hypothetical child *his* child at all, was another matter. It would mean admitting failure, inadequacy. One could argue that the single thing he'd been "born to do" (it seemed increasingly clear to him that it wasn't writing) was for him to extend his genetic line, to pass his DNA on so that it could then be passed on further and the whole meaningless cycle could keep on keeping on. Accepting a sperm donation meant admitting he was unequivocally fucking this up. Millions of years of evolution and direct lines of descent back to the time of the Australopithecus were leading to this dead end: himself.

One Saturday afternoon, as they drove back to Lawrence from a Trader Joe's run in Kansas City, Neha was quick to point out that Jack's way of thinking was self-pitying and illogical. If they could have a child with his sperm, then that was the preference, but so far that had proven not to be the case, and that was the reason they were looking into other options. "So you're a genetic dead-end either way. The only question is whether I'll be," she said.

"Thanks for being supportive," he said as the monotonous farmland outside of Eudora flew by outside. Objectively, he had to acknowledge his wife was making perfect sense; yet why then did he resist her argument? "Maybe we just need to keep trying. It hasn't been *that* long."

"Yeah, sure," she said. She was driving and her anger caused her to bear down on the gas pedal. "Let's just wait until I'm forty, right? What's the rush? I can always get a sperm donor then. Celebrities and actresses do it that way all the time, right?" She whipped the car into the left lane and accelerated past another car at what must have been ninety miles per hour.

"Hey, calm down, Dale Earnhardt."

"I work with women on infertility pretty regularly—women who are *several years younger* than me. I don't have that much time, Jack."

He first uttered the word adoption one night when they'd driven out to the Kansas countryside to look at stars. For her birthday the previous year he'd bought her a high-end telescope with the idea being they'd go out on clear nights and park in an abandoned field, that they'd look up at the stars and together, taking turns, would marvel at the wonders of the universe. If the weather was right, maybe they'd set out a blanket and make love outdoors. This had been back when they still hoped to have a child naturally. In this scenario Jack imagined that they'd name their child something celestial. "Luna or Stella, if it's a girl," he'd offered after Neha had unwrapped the box and he'd relayed the little fantasy to her.

She'd kissed him on both cheeks. "And what if it's a boy?" she said.

He wracked his brain. "Pluto?" he said and they laughed.

The reality of the telescope was that it had been a huge pain to assemble and then required understanding complex instructions to learn to use. And then they were busy with work, or else the Kansas weather didn't cooperate, and it was always too hot or too cold or overcast. And then there was the increasingly frustrating business of trying to get pregnant, such that they were never in the mood for such a romantic, idealistic outing anyway. It was more than a year later, one of their "date nights" as suggested by Dr. White, when they finally dragged themselves and the telescope, which Jack noted had been a brand-new model at the time of purchase but now was selling at a considerable discount on Amazon, into the car and out to the countryside south of town.

Looking at the stars, it turned out, was really fun for the first five minutes but quickly leveled off after that. And though the temperature might have been right for outdoor lovemaking, Jack had failed in his fantasy to consider the formidable bugs that swirled around them in the Kansas night: mosquitoes and chiggers and oak mites, all of which would have made a feast of them, turning their naked flesh into a sea of itchy, red wounds.

It was there, in their boredom and disappointment, which combined with their child-related disappointment into a kind of general, all-encompassing disappointment, that he blurted out, "We could always adopt."

She took her eye away from the telescope's view piece and gave him a look. "I thought you wanted to keep trying."

"Yeah, I mean...If that doesn't work."

"Why would we do that before trying a sperm donor?"

A large truck rumbled down the two-lane highway they had pulled off of and he paused to let the truck pass. "It would be a kind of solidarity, you know?"

"Like, if you can't have a biological kid, then I shouldn't either?"

"I don't know. Maybe."

"Don't you think that's really fucking selfish?"

It was, but he couldn't help wanting what he wanted. "It was just a thought, an idea. I didn't really think it through."

Neha suggested they pack up the telescope and head home.

The next Saturday when Jack was supposed to be working on the Virgie Chapman manuscript, but was instead surfing the web, he discovered through social media that his ex-wife had officially adopted the ten-year-old daughter of the man she'd married. It wasn't through her own profile that he'd learned this (her privacy settings were all on lockdown) but instead through the profile of her new husband. His name was Henry, and Jack didn't fail to take note of how handsome he was or what a good dresser he was. *The Boston Globe* had called Henry's latest book "A triumph" and the *New York Review of Books* had said that his sentences were both "spare and exquisite." Jack, whose own books had never been reviewed by either of those publications, comforted himself by thinking about how, if it ever came down to it, he could probably kick Henry's ass.

Jack wondered if Henry and his ex-wife would ever have their own child together. She was probably capable.

He saved the document he'd been working on and opened up a new file. He started writing another story about his ex-wife, only this time it was about her relationship with the adopted daughter, whose name was Maggie, and was set in a kind of post-apocalyptic future. Post-apocalyptic stories were all the rage now, weren't they?

In August, Neha's father suffered a mild heart attack when he was running on the treadmill at the Freestate Sports Club. Fortunately, it wasn't too bad as far as heart attacks go and after a few days of rest he was pretty much back to his old jovial self. Still, Neha took the event as a sign that they needed to have a child as soon as possible, and in the ensuing days she would mention sperm donation every chance she got.

"Come here. Just look at this website," she'd say to Jack. "They even list the donor's celebrity lookalike. Maybe we could find someone who kind of looks like you."

"Why do you keep bringing this up? I've said already that I didn't want to go this route. Can't you respect that?"

When the following week, Neha's parents came to stay by them while her father was recovering, they added to their daughter's pleas that he consider the sperm donor option.

"Maybe just go for consultation?" Mr. Joshi said. "What harm is consultation? Just check out. After consultation you're not interested, you don't do."

During the Joshi's weeklong visit, Jack spent extra time at the university, going to the library—rather than back to the house—to write when his workday was over. His home had started feeling like hostile territory and he wanted to be there as little as possible.

In the evenings, he'd return home, the house smelling like Indian spices from Mrs. Joshi cooking all day, and they'd sit around the table eating food that was too spicy for his palate, talking about their days. Every morning Mrs. Joshi went to the newly renovated public pool to swim laps and she'd give them all the play-by-play of how many laps she swam and which strokes she used. Mr. Joshi, who hadn't yet been cleared for strenuous exercise, would go to the pool in his argyle cargo shorts and collared short-sleeve shirt and sit in one of the lounge chairs reading the latest books by his favorite conservative news anchors on his e-reader, his face shielded from the Kansas sun by a sombrero he'd bought last year when he went on a cruise to Cabo.

"Why would people get job?" he'd say during one of his monologues inspired by the day's reading. "They sit at home and check comes. They get job, no check. They are just being logical based on government rules, so we have to change rules."

At some point, the Joshi's would inevitably ask Jack how his writing was going and whether he "got some good work done." To this question, Jack, simultaneously trying to mop up the spice-induced sweat that poured down his face, would give some vague answer about how he was "relatively productive" but how one "never gets as much done as one hopes." Neha would try to get him to tell her parents about the fantasy book, but Jack would always decline, at which point she would just assure her parents that it was "really good" and that she was "sure the book would sell" when he eventually finished.

The truth was that Jack was making virtually no progress on the fantasy book. The deadline for the Virgie manuscript was pushing him to do a little there, but other than that, virtually all of his writing time was going towards the stories about his ex-wife, all of which would probably sit in his drawer, never seeing a single reader aside from himself. Of course, he couldn't tell them this. He was in the business of finding the right words for things, but he couldn't find any words to describe what he was feeling that didn't sound offensive, illogical, ridiculous. What could he say? That he was writing stories about his ex-wife because he couldn't stop thinking about the mistakes he'd made, but that if somehow he could sire a real flesh and blood child that everything would be better? That didn't make sense. None of it did. What did a bullshit story he made up about his ex-wife having an affair with her high school basketball coach have to do with how shitty a husband Jack had been during his first marriage? How was the way she'd met her second husband connected to Jack's hang ups on using a sperm donor?

A month later, Jack was at the university's recreation center playing basketball when he received the message. Though he'd played football in college, his first love had always been hoops. In high school, he'd played on the varsity squad all four years, but by the time his senior year rolled around no one was really interested in recruiting him. His first wife had been a pretty good basketball player herself, and early on in their relationship, the two of them used to go to the Pottruck Recreation Center at Penn to shoot around. As the years passed, Jack played less and less and nowadays he couldn't play two games without being sore the next day. When the call came, he was on the court, so he didn't hear the buzzing of his phone on the bleachers beneath his gym towel. The team Jack was on won and he was getting ready to play again when, after wiping his face with his towel, he saw the missed call.

"It's me," Neha said on the message, and he knew something was wrong. "I was...maybe I shouldn't have, but I was looking through your computer at home trying to find one of your stories to show my parents, because my mom was asking. And...I found something else. I wasn't trying to read them, but I just saw the name, and so I read a little more and then...I mean...these stories...I'm not sure what I should think about this. I'm *not* going to think about it. I'm…you know it's just really disappointing…I think I'm going to drive over to my parents' place tonight."

Something in him dropped at the thought of what had just happened. He told his teammates he had to leave and that they should pick up another player. Outside, the heat was stifling, so Jack stood in the gym lobby while he called her back. After the fourth ring, he thought she wasn't going to pick up, but then the ringing ceased and her breath was on the other end.

"I don't want to talk right now," she said.

"Let me admit it probably seems a little weird, but—"

"A *little weird*? You're writing hundreds of pages about your *ex*-wife…Is any of this stuff true? I mean it can't all be true…like how would you know this stuff? Are you still in contact with her?"

"No. Not since we moved."

"I don't know if that's more or less fucked up. I mean, here we are trying to start a family, and you're obsessed with another woman."

Maybe there was an obsession *of sorts*, but not in the way she was suggesting. Nonetheless, the distinction between the two was too fine to make here on the phone. He imagined this must be what it was like to be caught in infidelity. He had never cheated on Neha in any common definition of the word—although from the outside he could see how one might view these stories as a kind of betrayal. He had however, been unfaithful to his ex-wife—in every sense—and now perhaps he was going to pay too much whereas before he'd paid too little.

"Just come home and we can talk about it," he said.

"I don't want to come home," she said through little sobs. "I don't want to talk about it."

Just then he had one of those rare out-of-body experiences where he was able to look at his life from ten thousand feet rather than from the ground, and the thought crossed his mind: *so this is how it ends*. Not immediately. Maybe it would take some time, but this was the beginning of the cancer that would spread and consume the body of their marriage. What a stupid way this would be.

"So what are you going to do?" he said.

"I don't know."

"I'm sorry you found those stories. That's a shitty thing. A shitty, shitty thing."

"I gotta go," she said and hung up.

❧

By the time Jack went home, showered, changed, and got back in his car to drive the forty-five minutes to the Joshi's house, the sky had turned a thick, foreboding gray. What started as a light but steady downpour soon turned into torrential sheets of rain; the windshield wipers, even at their fastest, struggled to keep up. Despite the treacherous weather, Jack didn't slow down much. He needed to see her as soon as possible—to try and explain things, if she would hear him out.

The farmland flew by and the rain kept coming down, and Jack thought about what it would be like if his wife never came back home. In a literal sense, this was improbable. Even if she took the extreme position of leaving him, the logistics of a separation would undoubtedly require her to come back to the house at some point. Still, he thought about the literal idea of her never coming back to better grasp the metaphoric possibility. He would see her again, but maybe things would never be the same. He'd never been in this particular situation before, yet it felt like he was repeating a mistake he'd made time and again with his first wife. Wasn't he bored of this yet? Or was there something in his blood that made this all inescapable? Maybe it was good he wouldn't be passing on his DNA.

Perhaps it was that he was lost in his thoughts, or perhaps it was just that the visibility was terrible, but whatever the reason, Jack didn't notice the half-broken wooden chair sitting in the middle of his lane until he was dangerously close. In retrospect, Jack would have been better off just running over it. He might have sustained a little damage—a scuffed bumper, a flat tire—but instead his instincts took over. He swerved the car to the right lane, which fortunately was unoccupied at the time. Still, the rapid change in direction caused the car to hydroplane towards the side of the road. He felt his body lurch over towards where the parking brake separated his seat from the passenger side. He pumped the brakes but couldn't stop the car from sliding off the road—first into the shallow ditch beside the road and then, after rolling violently over once, into a large cottonwood tree.

When it was over, Jack was dizzy but still conscious. The sound of the car rolling over and crashing had been so loud that, now, the fact that it was so deathly quiet other than the rain, felt wrong. His face hurt all over and blood covered his hands. He had an intense desire to look at himself to assess the damage, but the rearview mirror along with most of the front windshield had been lost in the crash. Very slowly, he unbuckled his seatbelt and stumbled out of the car. He didn't get far before the need to lay down overtook him. "Help," he yelled, but already he could see that several cars had pulled over near where his car had gone off the road.

He lay down in the mud and waited.

Four surgeries and five days later, Jack lay in his hospital bed at the University of Kansas Medical Center, his right leg in a cast, his face heavily bandaged. He'd suffered a broken tibia and fibula in his right leg, multiple orbital and skull fractures on the right side of his head, and severe injuries to his right eye. Neha sat at his bedside reading a magazine. She'd visited him every day since the accident, but all those times he had been too hopped up on painkillers to have a coherent conversation.

"Hey," he said and she put the magazine down to stand over him.

"You're awake." she whispered.

She bent over him and kissed him on one of the few patches of facial real estate that wasn't covered in bandages.

"I'm sorry you found those stories." He'd said this on the phone before he'd gotten in the car those days before, but he needed to say it again. It didn't matter what his intentions had been in writing them. He'd hurt the person who mattered most.

"We can talk about this later. For now, you should just worry about getting—"

"And I want you to know there's no one else in the world that I want to be with." It hurt when he moved his mouth too much so he had to force the sounds out of his unmoving lips like a ventriloquist. "I know it might seem…otherwise…from the fact I've been writing those stories, but it's the truth. And it's not the drugs talking, and it's not the accident and—"

"When I read those, it just made me so sad," she said and her voice started cracking.

"I know. I know," he said. The quaver in his voice matched hers.

"But let's just focus on getting you better."

He couldn't really move his head so instead he took her hand in his own and guided it to his mouth for a kiss. "I'm going to make this work," he said.

"Okay."

Later, they talked for a while about a number of logistical details—who Neha had notified of the accident and who she had yet to notify and how long he had to stay in the hospital. Afterwards, she kissed him on the cheek and told him to get some rest.

When Neha left the room, Jack closed his one good eye and tried to take a nap. It was a long time before he fell asleep. He kept thinking how grateful he was that maybe, just maybe they'd averted disaster. But he knew he couldn't take her for granted. If only he could do something—a grand gesture.

There was, of course, something.

Two months passed. Jack was still on crutches—though his cast had been replaced by a removable boot that allowed him to shower—when he and Neha visited the reproductive center in Kansas City. Over where his right eye would have been he sported a patch now, which he opted for over a glass eye. Neha liked to encourage him by telling him he looked like a "sexy pirate" now; Jack had his doubts.

When they returned home that evening from the clinic, with a tote full of literature in hand, they went online to the website of the partner sperm bank, located in California. On the site, you could filter the donor by every conceivable trait: hair color, weight, height, ethnicity, field of study, blood type, complexion, occupation, and on and on. Unlike the website they'd previously visited, the profiles didn't describe the donor in terms of their celebrity look-a-like; however, by becoming a subscriber to the site (and since they had become serious about this sperm donor business, a $250 subscription fee seemed like a small thing), they could view the childhood photos of the donors.

"Look, these kids are so cute," Neha said. The remark was made in innocence, but Jack still found it slightly discomfiting. True, the photos were of children, but they were children who had turned into adults whose semen they were considering placing inside his wife. Jack though had committed to the process and wasn't going to quibble over details.

It had been two days after Jack came home from the hospital that he told her about his decision to go ahead with the sperm donation idea.

"I don't want you to do it because you feel guilty about the stories," she said.

"It's not guilt," he said. "It's that I realized how important you are to me and so why shouldn't you have this thing that you want so much, if we can do it?"

She still had a slightly suspicious look on her face and suggested that he think about it for a month; however, when the month was up his mind remained unchanged and they made the next available appointment at the clinic.

❖

They settled on a handsome boy, who looked about six in the photo, and whose eye color, complexion, hair color, and adult height all roughly matched Jack. The boy didn't much look like Jack had as a kid, and Neha asked if he wanted to keep looking, but Jack thought there was a strange hubris in insisting on finding his childhood doppelganger.

"No. This one is fine."

"Just fine?"

"Good," he said. "As long as they're healthy, all this other stuff doesn't matter."

A few weeks later they went in to have the insemination. The crutches were gone by then, though Jack's leg was still weak from how much its muscles had atrophied.

They were prepared for the possibility that it would take several attempts before Neha got pregnant, but after a few weeks and only one try, the pregnancy test clearly showed two lines instead of one. Neha asked Jack to double-check the package instructions just to make sure she wasn't misreading things.

When the doctor confirmed the pregnancy, Neha vowed not to get too excited, and for the next several weeks her mantra was "a lot can happen" and she fixated on various statistics, which pointed out that miscarriages were more common than people think, especially in the early stages. Jack, for his part, was less conservative in his emotions and started spending the little free time he had that wasn't occupied by his writing projects or physical therapy browsing the internet for baby names and baby furniture and tips on raising healthy babies. It was as if the moment he learned his wife was pregnant, all of his reservations about using another man's sperm fell away—as if this child, still just cells clumped together, only needed to come into existence to relieve him of his doubts.

Once the first trimester passed Neha began feeling sufficiently secure in her pregnancy to join in with her husband's enthusiasm, and it was only at this point that she started telling anyone other than her immediate family.

"We're really going to do this, aren't we?" she'd say to Jack as the two of them lay next to each other at night. They had switched to occupying different sides of the bed than had been customary before the accident so Jack's good eye wasn't against the mattress and he could see Neha more easily.

"It sure looks like it," he'd say and she'd smile and he'd kiss her growing stomach.

Despite Jack's uneasiness at the idea, Neha insisted on doing a home birth with a midwife. That said, Jack was reasonably assured by how professional and experienced the midwife seemed in their initial meetings and eventually went along with the idea.

The baby arrived exactly on time in late September, little more than a year after the accident. The whole birthing process, between the first contractions and the baby arriving, took a day and a half, and in the final hours before the birth, Neha, who had been adamant about not using any pain medication, shouted colorful obscenities at Jack at the top of her lungs. Mostly, he accepted the verbal abuse without comment; given everything, it was the least he could do.

They'd wanted to be surprised by the baby's sex but had prepared names for both male and female possibilities. "Rhys" if it were a boy and either "Serafina" or "Corinne" if it were a girl. However, when the baby girl came, it felt like the names they'd prepared no longer fit, and they decided to take a day or two before making a final decision.

When Neha was sleeping, Jack took the baby out of the room and brought her to the adjacent, and currently empty, bedroom. There in that room, which would soon be furnished and become the little girl's own, Jack held his daughter for only the second or third time; however, he was still so hopped up on adrenaline that he didn't really have any cogent thoughts, just a general feeling of dizziness and protectiveness and overwhelming joy—all on account of this fragile, nameless creature engulfed by his arms.

It wasn't until the next day, while holding her again, the baby raising her impossibly small hand towards his patched eye, that Jack had a thought that he would have countless times in the years to come: *the stories somehow led to this.* Without them, he might have never gotten out of his own way; without them, none of this might have happened. And he wasn't prepared to say that it was all destiny or that everything happened for a reason, but there still was a kind of wonder to how things worked out, how a chain of events could lead to such unexpected outcomes that one becomes, in a way, humbled as to their ability to predict or plan anything. And when, at last, Neha suggested they look at Irish names, since that was the country where their relationship was rekindled, and then a day later asked him what he thought about the name "Moira," he couldn't help but find a kind of irony when he looked up the meaning of the name and found it to be "fate."

From *Premonitions of the Cree*
By Master Szilvia of Ilyeth

One of the mysteries that have long confounded members of our order has been the ability, for a select number of us, to prophesize future events through, what we Cree have labeled, *premonitions*. Contributing to the mystery is the fact that there seems to be great variability in the quality of these visions, their "literalness," and the manner in which they are delivered.

As opposed to conventional dreams, premonitions need not occur when the *receiver* (the one having the premonition) is sleeping, although it is possible for it to occur during sleep. A trained receiver is able to distinguish between conventional dreams and premonitions by examining the flow of the meridian channels during the premonition; as one might guess, this still makes distinguishing one's own premonitions that occur during sleep difficult, given that during sleep the receiver is, by definition, unconscious.

Probably the most controversial topic around the study of premonitions has been the assertion by some that premonitions are always "true." While it is beyond refute that many premonitions have come to pass, other documented premonitions have been found to only be "metaphorically" true. This lack of literal truth seems to be particularly characteristic of premonitions that have been either i) far into the future or ii) involving events not directly tied to the receiver. When considering premonitions, the problem with accepting metaphorical truth is that determining whether or not something is metaphorically true is highly subjective. Or, in other words, once we allow for "metaphorical truth," are there substantial grounds to call it truth anymore?

A rather famous example of the concept of metaphorical truth that I am describing is the oft-cited premonition of one of the most talented receivers of his era, Master Wei-Lu (234–403 YAF), nearly two centuries ago. Wei was particular noted as a receiver because of his propensity to have what he labeled *macro-premonitions*. Whereas the vast majority of premonitions are personal to the receiver and usually involve him or her directly. Macro-premonitions, of the variety that Wei was famous for, often involved events on a much larger scale. For those unfamiliar, let us examine Wei's own description of his famous "Kallanboro Question" premonition:

A group of wild horses are running on an open plain. A rush of clouds come in from the south, and the sky turns dark. From amidst the clouds a great silver falcon, the size of the dragons of old, swoops down from the sky with a high-pitched scream. The horses scatter, but they cannot escape. One by one the falcon picks off each horse. Some are impaled with the falcon's giant talons; others are lifted off the ground and then dropped to their death. At last the falcon stands alone on the plain. All the horses are dead.

At the time, this premonition was interpreted as predicting a great war between the Alderians, whose banner was a *red* falcon on a background of gray (or silver) and the Kallanbori, whose sigil was the horse. It was only later, after Kallanboro was annexed through political arrangement and *not* war, that Wei's disciples (the master had by this time succumbed) changed the interpretation to fit what happened historically. While even the most literal-minded can see how Wei's premonition might have been metaphorically accurate, one can also find reasonable an interpretation where the opposite was the case. So, are premonitions always true? The only reasonable answer, which may not be a very useful one, is that it depends on your perspective.

The question of premonitions and metaphoric truth far pre-dates Wei. In fact, the Ilyan philosopher, Yosephy wrote on this very issue as early as twenty years after the Founding. Yosephy's theory, which admittedly is difficult to understand, is that there is a plane of being where all time exists simultaneously. To humans, this plane is inaccessible, and so it feels as if there is a kind of "forward progress" through time, when in fact this is an illusion. The receiver, through his access to the meridians, is sometimes able to access this other plane of "simultaneous time." Nonetheless, it is the human mind, that is undoubtedly metaphoric, that needs to interpret the information coming from the meridians. And so, while the premonitions are always "true," the translations through the mind of the receiver may be mired in metaphor, misinterpreted, misremembered, or even outright false.

While this theory is certainly not without its critics, and is a long way from being outright proven, it certainly seems to make sense given the anecdotal experience of both myself as well as many other receivers to whom I have conversed at length on these matters.

TEN

AFTER THE EVENING BELLS
555-560 Years After *The Fall*

As was her habit every month on Feast Day, that evening—after the meal was done and the dishes were washed and put away, after her prayers to the Forefathers were recited before the altar in the front room of her family's small yet immaculate house—Kellah put on her blue celebration dress and departed for Amin's. Megah accompanied her on the excursion and, during the fifteen-minute walk up the road and through the town gates, the two best friends gossiped about who they thought might be in attendance that night. In truth, there was only one person Kellah was eager to see, and he, as was the plan, would *not* be inside the music hall.

When the girls arrived at the one-level sandstone building, they sat at their usual table in back. In the middle of the room a harpist and two fiddlers played a song the girls knew well.

Several of the long stone-slab tables near the musicians were occupied by a contingent of Redcloaks—each dressed in his matching gray uniform. In the nine months since the fighting had stopped it wasn't unusual to see Imperial soldiers at Amin's.

Many of the locals of Bajiran, including Kellah's father and elder brother, hated having foreign soldiers stationed in town so long after war's end. Their country, they'd say, was not part of the Empire, and being occupied by foreign soldiers was an affront to their nation's sovereignty. The counter to this was that there was no "occupation," and that these very soldiers were still around to *prevent* someone from occupying. Kellah didn't much care either way. She didn't love the idea of the Redcloaks as a permanent fixture in town, but they weren't *that* bad, and she'd never known them to be anything but polite.

The two girls hadn't yet been served tea, when a local boy Kellah knew from the market approached their table and asked her to dance. Since the boys of Bajiran had returned from the war, they seemed to have become bolder in the way they'd approach her. Just the other day when she was in town buying soap, one of Megah's cousins stopped her in the street to proposition marriage to her. When she asked him, unable to contain her laughter, if he was serious, he assured her that, on his life, he was.

She told the boy from the market she didn't want to dance, and he turned to Megah. Megah was pretty in her own right, and the daughter of a family that had grown well-to-do during the war; Kellah wondered if her friend resented her for being most boys' first choice while she was relegated to consolation prize. Then again, it wasn't her fault she was beautiful, was it? If Megah was annoyed this evening, she showed no sign of it, and she smiled at the boy before taking his hand and walking to the faintly lit center of the room where a dozen or so pairs danced to the music.

Just like the last three months, after another half hour or so of sitting at her table—making sure to be seen by anyone who might know her brother or father—she would, at the sounding of the evening bells, steal away outside, behind the slaughterhouse shed where Haman would be waiting.

She blushed at the memory of what had happened two months ago and again last month: how they had gone out of the town via the side gates, which were no longer manned now that the fighting had ended, and walked through the dry grass under the guidance of the full moon until they were far enough away that the torches on the town walls were flickering sparks in the distance. And she remembered how he'd helped her take off her dress, fold it, and set it aside so that it didn't get wrinkled or soiled, and how when this was done, he'd removed his own clothes and laid down on the blanket he'd unfurled upon the grass. It wasn't the usual thing for the woman to be above the man, he'd told her, but he made an exception since he didn't want his lady getting dirty. She hadn't found it exactly pleasurable that first time, nor really the second either, but there was a kind of loveliness in the act, and she liked the feeling of him moving beneath her, her hands gliding along the smooth skin of his chest.

On both occasions, she'd been nervous about accidentally becoming with child, but Haman had assured her that so long as she moved off him when he told her, and he left his seed in the grass beside them, she had nothing to fear.

She tried to conjure up his image in her mind: his angular, handsome face, long dark hair, his earliest beginnings of a beard, which suggested the man he was to become even though he was still just sixteen, the same as her. How lucky was she to have, at such a young age, found a beloved that gave her such joy! She must remember to thank the Forefathers again at tomorrow's prayers.

Kellah was so lost in thoughts of her beloved that she didn't notice the soldier approaching her table until he was right in front of her.

"Excuse me," he said. When she didn't respond, he spoke up over the music and waved his hand in front of her face. "Excuse me!"

When she finally noticed him, inches away from her, she flinched from the shock of it and sat upright.

"What's your name?" he said. He was young, maybe the age of her older brother, and was dressed in the same uniform as all the others except he had a special insignia, a gold bird of some sort, pinned to his chest.

"What's yours?" she said, having regained her composure. He might be older than her and a soldier, yet it didn't escape her that *he* had gotten out of his seat and walked over to talk to *her*.

"Joram, at your service." He bowed. He wasn't particularly handsome. His nose was too flat and too wide and his small ears stuck out from his head.

"I need no service. We already have a waiter bringing our tea."

He laughed. "I like you."

"Because of my wit?"

He coughed. "Perhaps you will allow me to serve you in some way other than fetching your tea. I could dance with you, for instance. You appear to be good dancers in these parts, and I am not. But I would like to give it a try, if you dare." He extended a cordial hand towards her.

"I don't," she said, her arms bolted to her sides. "I just come to listen."

A disconcerted look flashed across his face. "Very well," he said before bowing again and backing away. "Next time." He turned to rejoin his compatriots a few tables down before swiveling back around. "I almost forgot. I didn't get your name."

"What's that?" she said. "Oh, Megah."

"A pleasure to meet you, *Omega*. A beautiful name." She laughed now. He went back to his table. She could hear all the soldiers ribbing him when he returned, and, although she'd never admit it, this made her happy.

Fifteen minutes after the ringing of the temple bells, Haman was still nowhere to be found. Kellah pulled her shawl tight around herself to ward off the chill as she waited under the shed's overhang. She was just about to return to Amin's when an unseen hand grabbed her from behind. She would have screamed had another hand not reached around and covered her mouth. No sooner did she start to struggle against the attacker than she was spun around and there, in the light of the full moon, she saw it was her beloved, smiling like a mischievous child.

"What were you thinking?" she said and punched him in the chest. He feigned injury but then puckered his lips. "No. Someone could see." She pushed him away. It wasn't until his second attempt at a kiss that she relented.

She had never thought of herself as a loose girl, but with Haman the unacceptable felt acceptable. To start, he was the most beautiful boy she had ever laid eyes on. Whenever she saw him in town, there was nothing she enjoyed more than witnessing how other girls would steal admiring glances his way when he walked past. *He is mine*, she would think, and these thoughts would give her great joy. Also, their fathers were best friends, so the two had known each other for as long as either could remember. And soon they were to be married. All of which was how she figured her actions were, in fact, not wrong at all. How could it be a sin to do today that which would be the mandate of the Forefathers in six months' time? True, they hadn't yet set a date for the wedding nor had their families officially agreed to the marriage arrangement, but these were technicalities. From a very young age everyone seemed to agree that Haman and Kellah should eventually be wed. The logistics would be figured out soon enough.

They walked hand in hand to the same place they had been to the last two months and, just like on those occasions, he helped her with her dress and laid it down on a patch of thick grass. He unrolled the small blanket he was carrying and laid down.

She wanted to believe she was experiencing pleasure as he moved in and out of her, as he sat up to kiss her neck and collarbones and breasts. At the very least, it wasn't as painful as before. Megah had relayed to Kellah how her own married sister once told her that men loved it most when they thought their woman was enjoying this act. Kellah, remembering this, tried to imagine feelings of euphoria coursing through her and sighed and breathed accordingly in an attempt to make him believe the lie.

Afterwards they sat together on the blanket. He'd put his trousers back on, but kept his shirt off and, as they talked, she traced the contours of his thin torso.

"Sing me that song again," she said. He had a lovely voice and had he wanted, he could have easily been hired as a performer at Amin's or anywhere else for that matter. They'd both first heard this particular song at Amin's some months ago and Kellah had insisted Haman learn it. Although the song initially sounded happy, if one paid close attention to the words they'd realize it was a sad song—a song about a soldier's life-long journey to return home after a great and terrible war.

As Haman sang, Kellah wrapped her arms around her future husband and inhaled the smell of his hair. During the song's refrain, she would mouth the words and it was as if his voice flowed through her lips.

"At the teahouse they said that the Elders in Zabiz have come to an agreement with the Redcloaks," Farek said to their father.

Kellah was in the kitchen brewing the morning *qahveh*, but she could hear the conversation between her father and older brother in the adjacent room. Not that she cared about politics. She was more concerned about when she'd spend time with Haman again. Another month felt a lifetime away.

"There are all sorts of rumor mongers who buzz around the place like flies on a rotting pastry," her father said.

Technically, she *saw* Haman every few days when she was in town running errands, yet they had never dared to make those encounters more than those of two acquaintances running into each other in the streets.

"But they say it's true this time," her brother said. "In six months, half of the Redcloaks will sail back east, with the remaining three thousand staying for three more years in an 'advisory capacity.'"

She would have to think of some excuse to go into town today. Perhaps her father needed her to bring some of his candles to market or maybe their household was in need of items from the store.

"Bah! Three more years…Why would the Elders agree to that?"

"I don't know, but more than a few of the men at the teahouse spoke of armed insurrection."

The drink was ready, so she loaded the pot and cups onto a tray and brought all of it to the other room.

"I don't like these soldiers any more than the next man," her father said, "but this talk of insurrection is—"

She placed a cup in front of her father and poured. He was a small man—both in height and frame—although in recent years he'd grown a hard belly in spite of the long walks he took early every morning. He was much older than the fathers of most girls Kellah's age and had been twenty years older than Kellah's mother.

"Good morning, daughter."

"Good morning, father."

Sometimes she wondered if the age difference was what had prompted her mother to leave all those years ago. Her father seldom spoke of their mother and Kellah herself could only just vaguely remember what the woman looked like—and this was mostly due to the aid of a miniature painting of her mother placed in a small locket Kellah had found years ago in one of the storage crates behind the house. From that day forward, she brought the locket wherever she went, usually hiding it in a pocket or satchel.

"Did you enjoy yourself with Megah last night?"

"It was nice," she said and poured her brother's cup.

"I don't know why you let her go to these music halls," her brother said. "Who knows what kind of mischief she could get into? You know the Redcloaks go to these establishments, right?"

"Who knows what kind of mischief you get into when you ride around the country with those idiot friends of yours," Kellah said.

"I am five years older than you, a veteran of the war, and most importantly, a man."

Kellah rolled her eyes at her brother. *Veteran.* He'd taken care of the Redcloak horses.

"Were there Redcloaks at Amin's last night?" her father said.

"A few…but I didn't talk to them. They were on the other side of the room."

"You see?" he said to Farek. "Your sister is a smart girl—and virtuous. She would never do anything to dishonor her family."

While in town, Kellah would try to run into Haman as frequently as possible. Mostly he worked in his father's store on the eastern end of the town, but given that one could walk Bajiran's entire walled perimeter in less than a quarter hour, Kellah never had to go far out of her way. She would make it a point to have whatever household errands she was running bring her nearby, and, if the house required some item they sold at the store, she would make sure to buy it there—even if it might be found elsewhere for less.

Any time she walked inside the store, she'd make a point to carry herself very properly. She loved to go in and pretend she hardly knew Haman save through her father. And when she spoke to him, requesting a bag of grain, or bottle of oil, or bolt of cloth, she would speak formally and it would be as if she were speaking in a secret language where every word had another, hidden meaning that only the two of them understood.

When she had no actual occasion to visit the store, she might take a circuitous route that happened to go nearby. There was always the chance she might see him outside, sweeping or bringing in goods from a wagon. Otherwise, she could just glimpse in through the window and see him fetching items for customers or climbing up and down the ladder to stock goods.

The day before the new moon, Kellah walked by the store, a basket of her father's candles strapped to her back to deliver to market, hoping to briefly see her beloved. Unfortunately, he wasn't outside and she had no reason to actually go in; from across the road she peered through the window.

He was wearing a cream-colored tunic—the same one he'd worn the last time she'd seen him—and his hair was tied back with a small piece of yarn. He was talking to a customer although Kellah couldn't see whom. She kept walking slowly past.

A wave of disorientation passed over her. From this new angle, she could see the person Haman was speaking to: Melandrah.

Kellah wasn't prone to jealousy. She *liked* when other girls admired her beloved. Melandrah was the exception. She was from one of the wealthy families in town—her grandfather was one of the Elders in Zabiz—and one could tell just by how she strutted in her fine dresses that she looked down on those of humbler means. Kellah didn't have anything against the rich; Megah's family (whom she loved) had themselves grown wealthy during the war. Arrogance was Melandrah's problem, not wealth.

More than for any other reason though, Kellah hated Melandrah because she was beautiful. Melandrah's figure was perfectly proportioned, and she had enormous hazel eyes and perfectly straight black hair that you could tell had been well cared for. Kellah still remembered that time she had been talking with Megah by the chestnut tree near their houses and she'd asked her who she thought the prettiest girl in town was.

"I don't know," Megah had said. And then, nonchalantly, "Melandrah is very beautiful, no?" Kellah couldn't contain the disappointment on her face. "Oh, of course you are very beautiful too," Megah added.

So when Kellah saw Melandrah in the store, she couldn't help but feel a constriction in her chest. She pretended to be reading one of the signs posted on the gate across the street from the store, despite the fact that she couldn't read. Every so often, she would glance back through the store window. Melandrah had moved to a part of the store where Kellah could no longer see her face, but she could still see Haman, who suddenly burst out in visible laughter—laughter! Five, then ten seconds passed and he was still laughing. She tried to remember whether he'd ever laughed so heartily in her own presence and the only conclusion she could come to was that no, he had not.

She stormed off, walking briskly to the market where she needed to drop off her father's candles. When the market stand owner, a portly man a few years older than her father, greeted her and asked her how she was, Kellah replied, "Well," in a monotone that suggested she was anything but.

She was on her way home, near the town gates when she heard shouting coming from behind her. At first she was unsure what the voice was saying, but as it approached she began to make out the word. "Omega! Omega!" She turned and saw it was the soldier, Joram, from Amin's, jogging towards her with his plate armor clanging with each step.

"Wait," he said, now only a few steps behind. "Can I speak with you a moment?"

Usually she might allow herself to be entertained with what the Redcloak had to say, but today she wasn't in the mood. "I need to get home to prepare our evening meal. My father is waiting for me," she said, without looking at him.

"Very well. May I walk with you?"

"I'd prefer if you didn't, but do as you like."

"Did I wrong you?"

"My father tells me not to talk to you," she said. Not that this had ever stopped her from something in the past.

"Me specifically?"

"Your kind."

"Polite, strapping war heroes?" He paused for a response. She rolled her eyes. "A bad joke."

"Invaders. Occupiers," she said. She didn't care that he was a Redcloak. If he touched her she'd scream, bite him, tear his eyes out.

"Liberators? Protectors?" he countered.

"Delusional people."

"You don't believe all that. You know we're not that bad."

"You are an authority on what I believe?"

Just then there was another voice calling in their direction: "Captain!" It was another Redcloak running towards them. When he was closer he saluted Joram in the usual way, his right palm up. Kellah's anger subsided a little and, out of curiosity, she stayed to watch.

"What is it, soldier? I'm off duty," Joram said.

"There's been an incident, sir. At the garrison."

"Why are you telling me?"

"The Commander is away. Mouflon hunting west of town."

"So it's urgent?"

"Somewhat, sir."

"Okay, return to the camp. I'll be there soon," he said.

"You seem young to command," Kellah said once the other man had left.

"You didn't run off," he said and smiled.

Kellah didn't say anything.

"I am. Youngest captain west of the Inner Sea."

"Are you some great warrior, then?" she said, half mockingly.

He shook his head. "Stupid is more like it. And lucky. It's a long story. I'll tell it to you sometime."

"If you must." To this he bowed and went off in the direction the other soldier had gone. "Oh," she said as he was leaving, "my name isn't Omega. It's Kellah."

That afternoon, while she tidied the house and prepared fish stew for the evening, Kellah's emotions vacillated between heartbreak and rage. Maybe she would tell Haman she hated him and never wanted to see him again. Or else maybe she would just kill herself. That would show him—although unfortunately, she realized, her death would preclude her from enjoying this particular form of revenge. Even her best plans were flawed.

It wasn't until that evening—overhearing the conversation of Farek and her father—that she learned what had happened in town. Two Redcloaks had been kidnapped from an alehouse the night before and were subsequently tortured and killed, their throats slit roughly, before being hung by their capes within sight of the makeshift Imperial Administration Office. The words "RED CLOAKS GO HOME" had been written in blood behind where the two men hung.

Both Kellah's father and brother agreed the violence was not something to be condoned, and yet, what did the Redcloaks expect? This was their home, their country, and it was being treated as if it were one of the provinces. When Kellah suggested it seemed a little ungrateful how the Redcloaks were being treated, seeing as they fought and died to keep *their* enemies at bay in the West, Farek commented to her father that it was clear why they ought not to let women participate in politics.

Three days later—after the three supposed perpetrators of the attack on the Redcloaks, as well as their two dozen "co-conspirators," had all been rounded up and hung—word came that, in light of the killings, the Redcloaks would be removing all soldiers from Bajiran and that they would instead only keep a contingent in Zabiz on the sea; if the Bajirani hated their Redcloak protectors so much then they might as well see what it was like without them. The night the news came there was celebrating and music and dancing in the streets—although Kellah only heard about this second-hand from Megah, since her own father forbid her from joining the festivities for fear that violence would break out.

The full moon came and the next month's Feast Day came with it. Kellah and Megah returned to Amin's. That night there were again soldiers present, but their numbers were fewer than the month before and their attitudes less mirthful. Kellah didn't fail to notice that, as opposed to in previous months, all the men kept a dagger, maybe two, strapped to his side.

Still, when Joram saw the girls arrive he grabbed one of the men with him at his table, a younger boy by the look of him, and approached the two girls. The men bowed formally.

"Captain," Kellah said and nodded.

"Please. Use my given name." And then, clearing his throat, he gestured to his fellow soldier. "This is Mr. Bisby Belasmus, and he very much wanted to ask your friend to dance. I told him I would help him with an introduction."

"Is that so?" Kellah said and introduced Megah to the two men. Megah shrugged her shoulders and stood up to dance with Bisby.

"May I sit down?" Joram said.

"Well, you see…I don't have much time…when the bells ring . . ."

"You are meeting someone," he said as if it were the most obvious thing in the world. "But until then?"

She nodded and he sat down. "He is very lucky," Joram said.

"Who?" she said, although she knew.

"The man you go to meet."

"How do you know it's a man?"

"Is it not a man?"

She hesitated. "We are to be married."

"Then why the secrecy?"

"It would be improper for us to meet alone before the betrothal. Often people do not meet before their wedding days."

"And yet your friend dances openly with men, and that doesn't seem to be a problem."

"It is different," she said.

"I guess I don't understand your customs."

"There's much you men from the East don't understand, and that's why you don't belong here," she said. It came out harsher than she'd intended.

He looked at her as if trying to measure her.

No, he was not handsome at all.

"You were going to tell me," she said, "about the stupid thing you did to be made captain."

"Mmm... Yes." He looked down into his opened palms. "I saved a man."

"You *saved a man*. Many a man is lost or saved in war, no?"

"Yes, well, the circumstances were special. I don't think it was an ordinary man." She looked at him strangely. "It was at Tel Moran."

Even Kellah, who had followed news of the war as little as anyone, had heard of that great battle a little more than a year ago where, if the stories were to be believed, the tide of the fighting had turned in their favor.

"A portion of our men had, a week prior, attacked some of the enemy camps to the north along the river in an attempt to draw the Bridgelander forces out of the city. The plan worked and within three days, most of the enemy soldiers inside the city had mobilized and were heading north leaving Tel Moran less well defended. I was amongst the five thousand soldiers hiding in the hills to the east who now were to take the city. I was, however, not amongst the general attack force. Myself and twenty-three others made up a group tasked with escorting a *special operative* into the city during the attack."

"Special operative?"

"We weren't given any more information than that. Only that he was important and that he needed to get into the city alive and that this couldn't wait until after the city had fallen."

"Who was he? A general? A prince?"

"He was no general, and if he was a prince, he didn't look it. An ordinary man by appearances: no armor, no sword—just a gray cloak with the hood always pulled up. He told us his name was Aron, but that's all he would say."

"Then what was special about him?"

"We never knew. Men talk and rumors went around. Some claimed he was part of the Imperial family or that he was an Ilyan Brother, although I'm not sure I believe in that sort of thing."

"What brother?" she said.

"A sorcerer."

She laughed.

His face flushed. "I didn't say that's what *I* thought, just that that's what some of the others said. Anyhow, the fighting was going very well as the enemy positions were only lightly defended. Our climbers had breached the city walls and it was only a matter of time before they'd open the gates for us and we'd charge in. But then—I remember it so well—a single shrill sound of a horn. And from the south they came." He paused, reliving the memory. "Have you ever seen one of the half-horses?"

"The Haroumi? Only once, long ago. My family was traveling to the village west of here to visit our cousins. On the second day of our travels, out there across the plain, we saw two or three—at least we thought we did."

"I have never heard a sound like that of two thousand plate-wearing half-horses thundering down the hills. It is said the half-horses are great archers—perhaps even rivaling the Kallanbori—but what I also learned is that up close they do not shoot arrows. Instead they wield a terrible scythe, longer than a man's body. Within a few minutes they had reached our lines and they cut through our ranks like a knife through fresh cheese. Men panicked. I panicked. In all the fighting, the man we were escorting was separated from us. Then, just as I dodged the swing of a half-horse's scythe, I saw him, the man we were protecting, lying on the ground with an arrow through his thigh. I called to some of my comrades and a dozen of us ran back, trying our best to dodge arrows and the huge forms of the half-horses galloping on either side. By the time we reached a ditch a hundred yards to the side of the fighting, only Rory, the one who helped me carry Aron off the battlefield, and myself were still standing. An hour later, in that ditch, Rory died from a wound in his side. I asked him how he was doing and he told me 'I'll be fine.' Then he closed his eyes."

"And did the other man—Aron—live?"

"I think so. Some hours later reinforcements came from the north and we were able to beat back the enemy and take the city. The doctors told me Aron was badly hurt but that they thought he'd live."

"And that is why you are captain now?"

"That is why I am captain. Because I was stupid enough to try and save a man, and lucky enough to survive the attempt."

Over the music, one could hear the ringing of the bells in the distance. Kellah hadn't even taken a sip of her tea yet.

"You need to go," Joram said.

"Yes. I do."

The moment she saw Haman standing by the shed, the captain's story vanished from her mind. All the anger she'd held for her beloved melted away. She ran to him and kissed him. "I've missed you so much," she said.

They walked out to the field outside of town. When they arrived at their spot and Kellah started taking off her dress, Haman held her wrist.

"What's wrong?" she said.

"Maybe not today," he said. "Maybe we can just talk."

"We can talk too." She started to pull her dress over her head again.

"No." He grew angry. "Is that the only thing we can do anymore?"

She was confused; she thought they did this for him. "Do you not find me beautiful?" she said. Megah's sister had warned that once a man gets in between your legs he would lose interest. Could that have happened already? She thought of Melandrah.

"Of course, I find you beautiful...It's just—"

"Then please."

Some strong emotion filled his eyes, although she was unsure if it was anger or sadness or something else. He roughly pulled her dress over her head and threw it in the grass. Instead of lying down, he got on top of her, held her down hard by her wrists. The grass was scratchy, uncomfortable, against her back.

"What are you doing? Why are you being like this?"

"Isn't this what you wanted?"

She didn't respond. It was and it wasn't. She felt hurt, upset—but also strangely aroused, more than on the previous occasions.

After a time, she felt a rising sensation, and she held in her mind the image of a bucket filling up in a heavy downpour; eventually it had to overflow. The feeling wasn't completely unlike the one she could elicit in herself when she was alone at home or off sitting in the fields on one of the walks she went on. But it was different. Stronger. And for those few moments she forgot about her sadness and her confusion and Melandrah and Joram and even Haman.

She hardly realized how much noise she was making until she felt him place his hand over her mouth. "Shh," he said with anger in his voice. "Someone will hear."

As they dressed, Haman averted his gaze. Perhaps he was upset about the noises she'd made, but she was too embarrassed to ask him about it.

"I meant to ask you this on the way home the other night from Amin's, but do you think that Haman might be smitten with Melandrah?" This was some days later as Kellah and Megah chatted beneath a Zabissian cedar on a bench in town.

"Why would you think that?"

"I don't know. I saw her in the store a few weeks ago."

"You were spying on him?"

"Not *spying*. Watching."

"And?"

"They were talking."

"That's it?"

"No. He was laughing a lot."

To this, Megah herself started laughing. "You worry too much. Are you smitten with every boy who tells you a joke?"

"Well...no."

"Plus, I think Melandrah is already promised to some boy or another from town."

The girls parted to run their respective errands. Her chat with Megah had raised her spirits. Megah was right. Nothing was amiss; she was just being sensitive.

She had just exited the town gate when she saw Joram walk up beside her in freshly shined armor with his blood-red cape hanging behind him, its hem dragging in the dusty street. He took the bags she was carrying and continued walking beside her.

Given her good mood, Kellah didn't try to dissuade the captain from accompanying her. Besides, her arms were tired from holding her bags. Better to let him hold them. They exchanged routine pleasantries and Joram told her about the preparations to sail back east. But then the tone of his voice shifted to the serious. "May I ask you a bold question," he said.

"If you wish."

"I was curious...I mean, I was thinking about...Well . . .You are absolutely sure of your desire to marry this man you go to see?"

"Captain, are you propositioning me?"

"Would it mean anything to you if I was?"

"And how do you suppose this would work? Do you intend to stay here or to take me back to the East?"

"I cannot stay, but back home I've been promised a good position in the military administration now that the war is over. You would have a comfortable life."

"*A comfortable life*," she repeated. "Tempting. And flattering...But, yes, I do intend to marry him."

"I thought as much. I just had to ask. I hope you did not take offense. I would never be able to live with myself if I didn't at least inquire."

He walked with her the remaining distance home and returned her bags to her. Kellah looked around to make sure her brother or father weren't around to see her walking with a Redcloak.

Her blood did not come on the usual day that month, although she hardly noticed at first. It wasn't until later, when she saw Megah, that she remembered. Megah and Kellah's blood would usually come near the same time and when Megah, on her way to the bath, complained about the pains in her abdomen, it crossed Kellah's mind that her own blood had not yet come.

She mentioned this in passing to Megah and the girl looked at her as if trying to read something in her friend's face. "You said you and Haman were only kissing in the field, yes?"

Her cheeks grew warm. She looked away.

Megah put her face in her hands. "Your father...He will be furious."

"You don't understand," Kellah said. "I can't be with child. He . . ." She lowered her voice to a whisper. "He never put his seed inside me."

"How can you be sure?"

"I...he...said . . ." She started weeping.

Megah placed her arm around her friend's shoulder. "Maybe I'm wrong. Maybe the blood will come. We just need to wait."

But the blood did not come. Not that day nor the next nor all that week.

At night, Kellah could hardly sleep as she imagined what Haman would say. He wouldn't be happy about this, but at the same time, they had on occasion discussed the children they'd one day have, and so maybe a part of him would be excited at the prospect of "one day" coming sooner than they'd anticipated.

It did not evade Kellah's father how tired his daughter suddenly seemed, and several times, when taking a break from his candle making, he caught her sleeping in the front room when she was supposed to be accomplishing chores around the house.

"My dear," he would say as he gently woke her up. "What is the matter?"

"Nothing," she'd say. "I just didn't sleep well."

She thought to tell him. He was a kind and loving father. And yet he was also a man of tradition—a man who took his honor and the honor of his family seriously. She couldn't tell him.

Over the next two weeks, she saw Haman several times in passing, yet never had sufficient opportunity to speak to him alone. She would just have to wait until the full moon.

In the meantime, everywhere around town, it became obvious the Redcloaks were leaving. The watchtowers that had been erected at the four corners of their camp had begun to be disassembled and anytime one walked by the old temple that had been transformed into the Redcloak administrative office, they could see a host of wagons being loaded with supplies, weapons, and other goods the Redcloaks had brought.

The whole way to Amin's that next month, the girls discussed how Kellah would break the news to Haman. Perhaps if Haman insisted to his father, he and Kellah could be betrothed and married quickly before Kellah was even known to be with child. When the baby came early people might suspect something, but by then she and Haman would be man and wife so no one would make a big deal of things.

When they reached Amin's, Megah stayed at the table with Kellah rather than going to dance. Shortly after the girls' arrival, Joram approached, but Kellah told him, as politely as she could, that she didn't feel like talking.

"Just for a minute," the captain said.

"She said she doesn't want to talk, Redcloak." Kellah had never seen Megah speak so fiercely. It was good to know she had such a loyal friend.

"It's okay," Kellah said. "Just for a little while."

Joram looked for Megah to leave, but seeing that he wasn't going to get the privacy he desired, he started talking. "I wanted to say goodbye. In two days I will leave here."

"And where will you go?" she said. She was trying her best to seem interested. He had been kind to her.

"East, of course. First to my village to see my mother. It's been more than three years since I've seen her. And then eventually on to the capital, to Alder."

"Are you and your mother close?"

"You could say that. My father died at a young age and I had no brothers or sisters." Kellah thought about her own mother and whether she might have had some sage advice for her if she were still around. Whenever she imagined her mother, she always assumed they would have been the dearest of friends.

"I see. Well, safe travels, Captain," Kellah said. Megah gestured for him to leave.

"Best of luck to you," he said and squeezed her hand.

She was fond of him, in a way, and perhaps would have been sad to see him go if not for everything else on her mind.

She sat at her table for what seemed an eternity, quietly going over her plan with Megah. Eventually the bells rang to mark the evening.

"I have something I have to tell you," she said to him when they were outside the town walls.

He looked her over. His eyes were bloodshot and his mouth seemed to be bent into the slightest of frowns. "I have something to tell you too."

"Please. You first," she said. She wanted to delay her telling as long as she could. Little did she know that, as a result, she would never tell him.

There would be three times in her life that Kellah would receive what she considered "terrible news." The first of these was when, as a child, her father told her and Farek that their mother had left and was never returning. This night was the second of the three. The third and final instance would be some years later when her midwife would inform her that her daughter, her second child, was stillborn. Of the three occasions, this second with Haman was the only of the three where Kellah did not cry. One might take this as evidence that it was the least of the three, but in fact, it was the opposite. She was shocked *beyond* tears, hurt *beyond* her body's ability to respond. She had been too young to truly understand what her mother's departure meant; her dead daughter had been inside her a mere seven months when she passed. Haman, she had wanted all her life.

It was his father who'd arranged it, he said. He didn't want this. Yet the marriage pact had been made and now he was promised to another.

She told him she didn't understand. What was he talking about? Their fathers were best friends, and had always informally agreed they'd be married.

"Your father is the one who encouraged my father."

"You're lying," she said. "He would never…why?" Her hands were shaking.

"The soldiers are leaving. Business will be slower. My family will be able to make use of a large dowry."

Dowry. That's when she knew it was true. This was something her father, ever the pragmatist, would encourage.

And then something dawned on her. "Is it…is it…Melandrah?" She tried to be brave, told herself that she would be able to bear this terrible news—despite the predicament she now found herself in, despite the baby growing in her womb—so long as it wasn't Melandrah.

"No. It isn't," he said.

She was relieved. And yet the look on his face suggested that she shouldn't be.

"Then who?" she said.

"I'm sorry," he said. "I didn't want this."

Afterwards, he just held her for a while, shifting his weight back and forth between his feet to create a kind of rocking sensation. Maybe because he had no other words to say, he sang to her softly: that same sad song she loved so much.

"We'll run away. We'll go far, far away and no one will ever find us," she said. His only response was the song's refrain.

An hour later Kellah was walking silently with Megah back towards their homes. Megah inquired how he'd taken the news, but Kellah just said she didn't want to talk about it.

The thought crossed Kellah's mind: what if she just killed her? Waited until they were in some unlit corner and strangled her or bashed her on the head with a rock? Could she come up with an explanation that anyone would believe?

Of course, she would never be able to bring herself to do any of these things to her best friend. It wasn't her fault. From what Haman had said, Megah still didn't even know.

The next day she was supposed to be carrying a large basket of candles to town for her father; instead, she deposited the candles in a cloth bag behind the house and filled the basket with the few belongings she'd take with her: her favorite articles of clothing, a childhood blanket, the locket with the picture of her mother.

Most of the Redcloaks, including many officers, were housed in a camp that encircled the sandstone temple that served as the makeshift Imperial

Administration Office. Kellah approached the guard at the camp's entrance. When he asked what her business was, she told him she needed to speak to Captain Joram.

"And what do you need to speak to Captain Joram about?"

"That is between him and me," she said, putting on a mask of confidence.

"Well, you are a pretty one, but we can't just let anybody walk in who says they want to chat with an officer. I'm sure you heard about those two men who—"

"Let her in," a man's voice said. It was the soldier who had danced with Megah a month before. Bisby, if she remembered correctly. "The captain will be glad to see her."

"I'm sure he would, Sergeant Belasmus, but—"

"I'll be responsible for her. I'll take her to him."

"Fine. It's on your head if she ends up slitting anyone's throat," he said and then as she walked past him she heard him muttering something about how *they always like the heroic types.*

They hardly talked as they weaved through the labyrinth of identical brown tents. "How is your friend," Bisby said at one point. "The one I danced with...Megah."

"She's well," Kellah said. Bisby looked for her to elaborate, but she kept her mouth shut.

Joram was sitting at a small desk reading a scroll when Bisby pulled back the tent's entrance flap and presented Kellah. A look of surprise formed on the Captain's face, but he was pleased also. She stepped into the tent; Bisby set her basket down inside and went away.

"I didn't think I'd ever see you again," he said.

"You read?" she said, nodding to the scroll.

"Oh, this? Yes."

"Where did you learn?"

"My mother."

"I haven't met many women who know to read."

"It is not so rare in the East for a woman to read," he said. They stared at each other. "But you didn't come here to talk about how I learned my letters, did you?"

"You leave tomorrow, yes?"

He nodded. "Gone forever to the East to bother you no more."

"Will you take me with you?"

His face flashed a bitter look. "I don't find your jokes amusing or very becoming of—"

"No joke."

"No?"

She shook her head.

"What about the man...the man you meet...after the evening bells?"

"He's gone."

"How do you mean?"

"It doesn't matter."

"I disagree."

"It doesn't matter," she repeated. "Just answer. Will you take me with you? As your woman...your wife?"

He looked at the ground. She thought he was about to send her away, but then he looked back in her direction. He shook his head and smiled. "I can't think of any good reason why I shouldn't."

"So . . ."

"So...Yes," he said.

She walked up close to him. He was still sitting, so when she wrapped her arms tight around his head, his face pressed up against her small breasts—breasts that, one day soon would be full of baby's milk. She kissed him on the forehead. "Do you have anywhere to be right now?"

"Now?" he said. "No, not right now."

She started to take off her clothes.

"I can wait, if you wish."

She helped him up off his chair and nudged him to lie down on the bedroll beside the table. He lay down.

In her mind, she wasn't with Joram, yet neither was she with Haman. She was alone, an empty bucket, waiting on a cloudless day for rain that would never come.

They were married by one of the military officials that evening. It wasn't completely uncommon for soldiers to bring home wives from overseas, and their wedding, in the Imperial Administration Office, was joined by two other couples—both soldiers with local girls. She knew one of the girls, the blacksmith's daughter, and the two exchanged awkward looks of recognition but no words.

That evening they ate a simple meal of rice and spicy lamb sausage, and afterwards, between lovemaking, she helped him pack the things he would bring back east. All of her own belongings were in the single wicker basket she'd brought to the camp.

"Are you sure you won't tell me what happened?" he said. "Why you're leaving?"

"Because I love you," she said.

He laughed. "One day you will tell me." He was wrong about this.

By now her father and brother must have found the note and would probably be looking for her. *Farewell,* she'd written—the one word she'd managed to spell by asking the scribe's apprentice, a boy who had had a crush on Kellah since childhood, that morning when she'd ran across him in the market.

She'd thought about leaving no note at all but concluded doing so would be cruel, too reminiscent of what her mother had done. At least they'd know she was alive. They'd never think to look for her in the Redcloaks' camp. They'd inevitably start with Megah who would lead them to Haman who would be a dead end—although perhaps they could then suspect her reasons for leaving.

The night passed without incident, even though Kellah didn't sleep much, and early the next morning a huge Imperial caravan began its day's long journey across the umber plains to Zabiz, where they would board ships east.

Despite living all her life relatively close to the sea, she had never been aboard a boat or ship and when, a day later, she finally stood aboard *The Neza* and looked out eastward across the endless blue expanse before her, a great fright took hold of her.

They had good weather for the ten-day journey and the ship's navigator commented that he'd never in all his years experienced such smooth sailing. Still, by the journey's second day Kellah was frequently seasick and could often be seen expelling the contents of her stomach over the ship's railing.

"You don't much like the sea, do you?" Joram said after one such incident.

"My stomach doesn't."

They had already arrived in Joram's childhood village and were staying with his mother when Kellah told him she was with child. They were walking through a meadow along a small stream, just a few minutes' walk from the house, when she told him.

"Are you angry?" she said.

He shook his head and put his arm around her.

"Do you hope it is a son?"

"Most men wish for their first to be a son, yes? But I think also that a daughter would be just as well."

"Whatever is the Forefathers' will," she said.

Since Kellah was pregnant, they decided to stay in the village and delay their eventual journey to the capital. Joram's decorations in war were such that pretty much anything he requested was granted and they ended up staying for another ten months in the village.

The months passed and Kellah was largely happy. So long as she could still move around well, she spent her days helping Joram's mother in the house while Joram spent his days helping other men of the village with odd jobs and handiwork. Since he saved up much of his soldier's wages from the war, he didn't need to earn much to get by. In the evenings, Joram and his mother started teaching Kellah how to read, and in no time, she was able to write passably well—although her handwriting remained very poor.

Kellah didn't think much about Haman, but the few times she did— usually triggered by a dream she'd have about him—she would be melancholy for days afterwards. She had barely known him, she realized, yet she could not talk herself out of loving him still; she could not talk herself out of missing him. With thoughts of Haman also came thoughts of her family and of Megah. For all she knew, Megah might be married and pregnant by now. On more than one occasion she thought to write her family a letter to tell them what had become of her, yet every time she started writing, the proper words eluded her.

The baby boy, who they named Thom after Joram's father, came a month earlier than expected, but Joram, his mother, and the midwife were all relieved at how robust and healthy the baby was for one born early. Everyone agreed that in terms of complexion the boy took after his mother much more—although Joram's mother noted, the baby had his father's mouth. Yes, Kellah said. I see what you mean.

When Kellah was well enough to travel, they parted from Joram's mother and went to the capital. There in that great city, Joram was somewhat of a celebrity as news of his heroics in the war had spread over the past year and a half. He was quickly promoted to an administrative position in the Imperial government. The known world was at peace, he explained to Kellah, and the Empire was in much greater need of bureaucrats than soldiers.

Two more years passed before Joram, who had quickly risen the ranks in his office, was offered the opportunity to be groomed for a governorship in the North. The current governor was quite advanced in age, and the emperor wanted to have a replacement ready if and when this governor finally died or was otherwise unable to fulfill his duties.

Joram explained how this governorship would not be in a great city like the capital but instead would be located in a kind of desert backwater. Still, a governorship was a governorship, and should everything go right, they would eventually live in a castle.

Kellah didn't care much about castles, but she loved the idea of getting out of the capital. She hated the smell of the place and longed to bring her son, who by now could talk and walk and recognize several letters of the alphabet, to less crowded environs.

"Yes," she told him. "We will go."

The town, called Wahan, was a backwater indeed. It had once been along a major trade route that went south from the northern coast up through the capital, but continued drought had made traveling through that country increasingly difficult until eventually traders just avoided that land entirely, opting instead for a less direct, but more pleasant, journey around the desert.

They were given a well-kept house directly adjacent to the castle, and while Joram was off performing his duties, Kellah spent most of the day alone in her house with Thom. Just as her husband had promised her, it was by and large a comfortable life. Lonely in a way, but comfortable.

There in the desert the days would often be hot and the nights often cold, but there was a small time in the early morning, before her son woke from his sleep, that Kellah would go on long walks outside the gates of the town into the desert. She would climb up the highest dune and watch the sunrise in the distance.

One morning, little Thom woke from his sleep early and, not finding his mother in the house, screamed and cried until Garen, the new steward, heard the screaming, entered the house and pacified the boy. When Kellah returned the boy again burst out in hysterical crying.

"Mama, where were you? Why'd you leave me?"

She held little Thom and, right then, became particularly aware of the locket hanging from her neck. She imagined it burning its oval shape into her chest.

"I will never leave you again," she said.

After that, whenever she went on her walks, she would bring her son along and carry him in a harness, which she strapped to her back. And when they reached the top of the dune, she would lay out an old blanket, one of the few things she'd brought with her from home, and the two of them would sit, mostly silently, eating figs and waiting for day to break. And she'd sing into the small boy's ear a song that reminded her of her home and of her past and of a hurt she kept hidden from everyone, especially her husband.

The boy was starting—more and more, she noticed—to look like his father.

A Selection of Henry Fitzroy's Twitter Feed

Henry Fitzroy
@henryfitzroy

Following

@newhavenVW got me back on the road in no time.
#serviceisntdead #brooklynhereicome

Henry Fitzroy
@henryfitzroy

Following

Wonderful time at Berkshire Bookfest . . . except car
just broke down on way home :(

Henry Fitzroy
@henryfitzroy

Following

Great panel today on "Is The Great American Novel
Dead" w/ @juliemandelbaum

Henry Fitzroy
@henryfitzroy

Following

Perfect night to see @MetOpera with my two girls.

ELEVEN

FIRE
2025

In the dream, she and Maggie were trapped in a room with windows but no door. A fire, surrounding them now in a perfect ring, burned ever closer. It reached Maggie first, and Sarah watched as it crept up her daughter's arms and legs and torso and face. There was nothing she could do.

When Sarah woke around four, she coaxed her body out of bed and padded quietly to the kitchen. She and Maggie had been up until past one listening to the radio. Three hours of sleep would have to be enough.

She needed to get herself and Maggie—especially Maggie—out of the city. According to the news, there were still "credible threats" of additional attacks, although the nature of these remained vague. That said, the MTA was completely shut down, and for now the roads in or out of the five boroughs were still being blockaded by the military; however, there had been reports they would open at least a few of the highways *out* of the city around noon.

She poured herself a cup of yesterday's coffee and, for several hours, sat in the bay window of her third-floor apartment, pondering the brightening city skyline in the distance. There wasn't much new on the radio now—just the same terrible stuff over and over.

The estimates ranged from a few hundred thousand to three million dead in eighteen, nearly simultaneous, bombings from San Francisco and Las Vegas to DC and Philly and, yes, Boston too. She recalled, as if in a kind of preparation, what she'd felt at the loss of a single loved one (her older sister those many years ago, her father more recently) and tried to mentally multiply that times these unthinkable numbers. Too much to comprehend. It was still unclear which of the bombs had been conventionally nuclear and which were "dirty bombs," although it seemed to have been reported that at least the bombs in Philly and Washington were low-yield nuclear devices. Sarah tried not to think about all the people that she knew who lived in those cities.

By the time the sun had fully risen she could have almost fooled herself into believing it any other day—save for the constant ebb and flow of emergency sirens in the distance, save for the fighter jets roaring overhead every half hour. Last night had been different, what with power out across the eastern seaboard and the entire city a black expanse—reminding everyone of how, though New York had been inexplicably spared from the worst of it, they weren't completely unaffected.

She wished Henry were here. He'd been in Western Massachusetts, far enough away from any of the attack sites, but she'd still heard nothing from him. Between the power outage and the destruction to infrastructure, her cellphone had become a useless brick of glass and metal and plastic.

The president, from an undisclosed location, came on the radio and reported that, as of yet, no one had taken responsibility. But then, with a deep kind of resolve in her voice, told them they were doing everything in their power to find out who had perpetrated this heinous crime.

"What is she talking about?" Maggie said. There was still sleep in the girl's voice and eyes. She wore her little cotton shorts and a tank top. She wasn't yet fifteen but seemed to have skipped over the awkward stage and jumped straight from being a beautiful little girl to a beautiful young woman.

"Nothing new," Sarah said, over the president's voice.

"Oh," Maggie said. "Power still out?"

Sarah got up from her seat and wrapped her arms around her stepdaughter. Sarah was still quite a bit taller than Maggie and she pulled the girl close against her chest.

"Power's still out?" Maggie said again.

"I think so."

"The battery on my phone is totally dead."

"It probably wouldn't work anyway."

"I know, but at least I could listen to music or something."

Sarah sighed. Here all those people incinerated or screaming in agony from radiation and this girl was concerned about not being able to access her Spotify.

They had been the best of friends when she first married Henry. She had been the fun stepmom who would fill the void left when her mother died, teach her how to be a woman, how to braid her hair and do her makeup and use a tampon. But then, just as Maggie had entered adolescence, something changed and the girl began treating Sarah like an intruder. She no longer wanted to go on long walks and get tea in Greenpoint or picnic in McCarren Park. "I'm busy," had become the girl's favorite refrain.

All that felt trivial now

"You should eat some breakfast," Sarah said.

"Have you heard from my dad?"

"No, not yet. But I'm sure he's fine," she said. He was in the Berkshires— he wouldn't have gone to Boston, would he? You often hear about people who just miss death: the plane crash they would have been on if they hadn't gotten caught in the security line or given their loved one that last kiss. But what about people who, through coincidence, just happen to be in the wrong place at the wrong time? She imagined Henry deciding at the last minute to go into Boston to buy her or Maggie a special gift. He was always doing things like that: surprising them, spoiling them.

"I'm going to try to find a way for us to get out to Connecticut to my mom's house," Sarah said as Maggie poured herself a bowl of cereal.

"How are we going to get out there? Dad has the car...Are the trains running?"

"No. But I'll figure something out." She tried to say this confidently. Cabs and car services were mostly unavailable. Some of her friends or co-workers might help, but with no phone or internet, they were completely unreachable. It was only around an hour's drive, but how long would it take them to walk?

The water was still working so Sarah lit a few candles and took a room-temperature shower. She continued to wrack her brain to no avail. It was only afterwards, when Maggie had gone in the shower and Sarah was sitting in her dark bedroom with her towel around her waist that an idea came to her.

Casey had been a friend of Sarah's in high school—not her best friend, but amongst them. They'd lost touch sometime in college but re-connected years later when Sarah moved in with Henry and discovered Casey lived right down the street with her own new husband. There was a spell of months then when Sarah hung out frequently with Casey, who took great pleasure in showing her all of her favorite spots in the neighborhood: fancy restaurants that were impossible to get a reservation for, "hidden" speakeasies that required a password or secret handshake to gain entrance.

After some time, their friendship waned. They both were busy and it dawned on Sarah that, as a mom now (or at least *stepmom*), she had little in common with her old friend. Eventually, the two would only see each other at large gatherings or around the neighborhood: at the grocery store or park. It had been nearly six months since they'd last bumped into one another.

One thing Sarah *did* remember was that Casey and her husband had a car. When Maggie got out of the shower, Sarah went to her room and told her to get dressed and that they were leaving. If some of the roads re-opened at noon, maybe they could be first in line.

"Where are we going?"

"To Casey's. Do you remember—"

"Yeah. I know who she is," Maggie said, unenthused.

"I want to see if they might be able to give us a ride out of the city."

Maggie checked her phone again but put it down when it still wouldn't power on.

"Hey, Mags, are you listening?"

"We're not going to *literally* leave the city right now, right? Can't you just go by yourself, see what the deal is and then come back?"

"I am not *asking* you. You need to get dressed and come with me." It had usually been Henry who was the disciplinarian. But Henry wasn't here.

"Don't you think you're overreacting? It's not like terrorists are going to specifically target our apartment in the ten minutes it takes you to go over there."

"Maggie. Get dressed."

Casey and her husband Prasanth's apartment was a two-minute walk down Kent Street in one of the luxury high rises that dominated the Brooklyn waterfront. Whereas Henry and Sarah's apartment was a relatively modest two bedrooms, Casey and her husband had one of their building's palatial penthouses, whose second level contained an unheard-of fourth bedroom and an enormous private deck, which looked out at unimpeded panoramic views of Manhattan and Williamsburg and Long Island City.

When Sarah and Maggie arrived at the lobby, the doorman let them right through despite the fact he couldn't call up to Casey's apartment. Sarah supposed she and Maggie didn't look particularly threatening. "I'm pretty sure they're home, but since the powers out, you're going to have to take the stairs," the doorman said.

Eighteen surprisingly difficult flights of stairs later, they rang Casey's bell. When she opened the door, Sarah settled on a kind of reserved half smile.

They hugged and Casey invited them in. She wore a tight t-shirt and yoga pants that showed off her almost-too-toned figure.

The two old friends exchanged awkward pleasantries, made all the more awkward by the circumstances. After a moment, Prasanth joined them from one of the bedrooms and the four of them all stood around regarding one another. Prasanth ran IT at a large bank, and although he was very tall (somewhere between six-six and six-seven, Casey bragged), his slouched posture, developed perhaps through sitting at a screen for an ungodly number of hours, made him come off much shorter than he actually was.

"Hello, Sarah," Prasanth said in a monotone. He was never the warmest guy and it seemed the end of the world hadn't changed anything.

Sarah could feel Maggie's gaze boring a hole in her back now but tried to ignore her.

"So," she said, "on one hand I just wanted to check in on you guys. Buuut... I also wanted to see if, with some of the roads opening back up, you were planning on leaving the city... maybe going out to your folks' place . . ."

To this, Prasanth made a self-satisfied grunt, as if he'd predicted Sarah's motives were self-interested.

"... And if you were, maybe we could, Maggie and I, get a ride out to—"

Prasanth cleared nothing out of his throat. Casey spoke up. "Prasanth and I talked about leaving. We *are* in New York, right? But we also got to thinking: not all the attacks were just in big cities. There was a bomb in—"

"Nashua, New Hampshire," Casey's husband interrupted. "Another attack in... in... fucking Podunk, Virginia... Nowhere is safe. At least we're comfortable here."

"I see," Sarah said, though this logic was insanity. True, some smaller places had been hit, but if one played the odds, it was clear New York fucking City wasn't a good place to be.

She remembered her dream: the sight of Maggie burning.

Was there anyone else who could give them a ride?

There was no one else.

"I wouldn't normally ask except that Henry has the car and I can't get a hold of him or anyone else, and the Metro North is shut down, you know?"

Casey looked to Prasanth. He nodded and she turned back to Sarah. "Yeah, I'm really sorry, but we've thought a lot about this and we don't think we want to leave."

"We would give you a ride and come back," Prasanth said. "But the radio is saying there is total gridlock traffic leaving the city, not to mention gas is going to be impossible to get for a while. We would hate to leave and then not be able to get back."

"I'm sorry," Casey said again.

Maggie tugged on Sarah's arm. "Let's go," she said under her breath.

Sarah turned to her stepdaughter and glanced briefly but intensely at the girl's beautiful, young face. Almost immediately an unfamiliar feeling came over her—a clarity of purpose she couldn't ever recall having. Despite their rocky relationship these last few years, she loved Maggie so much—*so much*. And with Henry gone it was *her* responsibility to protect the girl; she was the mother, by law if not blood.

We all have the capacity to, given the circumstances, be terrible people, and if this was Sarah's circumstance, she could live with that.

She gave Maggie a look that she hoped the girl understood: *be quiet, let me handle this, and don't contradict what I'm about to say.*

Sarah had always had an unnatural ability to pretend-cry. As a child, she'd use this ability to get things and/or get out of things with her dad. As an adult, she began employing her talent to humorous ends to play a joke on a boyfriend, or later, a husband. Henry hated her fake crying.

"I didn't... I didn't really want to bring this up," she said to Casey and Prasanth now. She needed to make sure not to overdo it. "It's just that... I mean, you know my mom, right, Casey?"

"Yeah. What is it?" She placed her hand on Sarah's shoulder.

"Well, the last year she's been... really sick." She waited for a second before she said the next word. "Cancer."

"Oh, God. I'm so sorry to hear that." Sarah tried to see Prasanth's reaction but couldn't turn her head far enough without being obvious.

"And... right before the cell towers went out, I was on the phone with my mom. And she really wasn't feeling well... And now I have no way to reach her and I'm so worried. I don't know if her helper is with her, and God knows what could happen to her, and I just need to get to her. I... I... understand that you guys don't want to leave, but I just really need to get to her." Sarah grabbed her friend in a hug and allowed herself a few little sobs.

Sarah had counted on Casey convincing her husband they should give them a ride, but it was Prasanth who spoke up first.

"Okay," he said. "I didn't understand the situation. I'll take you. My car's parked up in Long Island City, at the office, but it shouldn't take too long for us to walk up that way. If you can just give me a couple minutes . . ."

"We'll . . . we'll . . . go back and grab a few things," Sarah said. "Should we meet you downstairs?"

"Sure," Prasanth said.

"You guys aren't leaving without me," Casey said then.

"You sure, Case?" Prasanth said. "I'll go and come back—"

"I'm going."

"Okay, we'll all go together."

"Thank you so much," Sarah said to Prasanth and gave him a hug, which he reluctantly accepted. "We'll see you downstairs in a bit."

"I can't believe you just blatantly lied like that," Maggie said as they walked the two blocks back to their apartment. "Like, I know you want to get out of the city, but—"

"I'm doing what I have to. For you." She didn't feel *good* about the lie but still felt absolutely confident in it being the right decision.

"What if they want to go in and see your mom when we get to Connecticut? Last I recall, your mom looks pretty good for a woman—"

"If it happens, we'll figure out something."

"I don't know. It just seems like a pretty shitty thing to do to your so-called friend."

"First off, watch your language."

"*Watch your language?* Really?"

"Second," she said and stopped to grab Maggie by the shoulders and look straight at her. "You need to know that I am going to do whatever necessary to get you out of harm's way. I will lie to *anyone*. I will steal a car from a sweet little old lady. I will swim with you on my back across the Long Island Sound. And I hope—really, I do—that Casey and Prasanth stay out of the city too. I'm going to try and convince them. But either way, we're getting out of here. Do you understand?"

Maggie didn't say anything after that.

Back at their apartment, Sarah told Maggie to just pack a change of clothes or two—that, with luck, things would calm down in a couple of days and they could come back. She herself couldn't help looking around the apartment as if she might never return. Should she take the photo albums with her? Some of Henry's notebooks? In the end, she packed only a small duffle bag with clothes and a few toiletries, as if her act of faith that everything would be all right would make such an outcome more probable. Maggie brought her backpack. Right before leaving, Sarah scrawled a short note to Henry:

H,

Maggie and I are fine. They're opening up the roads and we're catching a ride up to my mom's house with Casey and her husband Prasanth. I don't think it's safe to stay in the city for now. I'll keep calling, but the phones might stay down for a while. If you get this, please come up to Connecticut. Will see you soon. Stay safe. I love you.

Me

She took the single sheet of lined paper and taped it to the floor right beyond the welcome mat at the front door.

The four of them walked up Kent along the waterfront—Prasanth leading, Sarah walking beside Casey, and Maggie bringing up the rear a few paces behind.

Casey was in a chatty mood so long as they weren't talking about the situation at hand. Somehow the conversation topic shifted to travel and she went on at length about her and Prasanth's recent vacation to South America and the trip to Israel they were planning ("but who knows how all this is going to affect the trip"). Sarah nodded to give the illusion she was paying attention even though she was far too amped up—like how she might imagine a soldier walking through a war zone would feel—to fully engage in conversation.

"You know, some people, friends from Prasanth's work," Casey said, taking a swig from the Fiji bottle she'd brought for the walk, "It's all just like the Hamptons this and the Hamptons that and you'd think it's the only place in the world to visit in the summer. But me, I'd rather see the world, you know? Get a little culture. I don't need all this luxury. Don't get me wrong, it's not like we're just staying in the Holiday Inn or something when we go on these trips, but still, it's good to rough it a little. To see how real people live." Sarah turned to make sure Maggie was keeping pace behind them and saw that her stepdaughter was rolling her eyes.

On the fence that separated the waterfront park from the street, someone had hung a large sign that read: "LOVE THY NEIGHBOR. GOD BLESS AMERICA." Beyond the fence, the park was bustling with people. Several groups of twenty-something's had started bonfires in pits dug right out of the grass and were grilling burgers or skewers on makeshift barbecues. Around the nearest fire, two skinny guys with unkempt beards and long hair played the guitar and sang while their carefree and attractive group of friends passed a paper bag, taking swigs of whatever was inside.

"I heard on the radio that a lot of gas stations have sold out, and the ones that aren't are like this," Prasanth said when they past a Citgo station not far beyond the park that had a backup of at least seventy cars. "The government is trying to prevent people from being opportunistic, and so they made an announcement that any price gouging would be met with *swift punishment* or something like that."

"Like execution by firing squad?" Maggie offered, but no one minded her.

They turned eastward to catch McGuiness going north to the Pulaski Bridge. Sitting on the stoops of one of the old row houses a young man with a bandana over his head consoled a chubby, tan-skinned girl who was crying. After they were out of earshot from the couple, Maggie asked no one in particular: "Do you think she lost someone in the bombings?"

"Probably," Casey said, although Sarah thought that it was just as likely she was crying from the general tragedy of it all.

It was another fifteen minutes before they made it across the Pulaski to the garage in which Prasanth's BMW was parked, next to the massive blue-green glass building where he worked.

The nearest highway entrance was closed, so they drove on city streets through Woodside to where they could get on 278. They passed several more gas stations on the way and Sarah noticed that, just as Prasanth had warned, each of these was closed; several posted large "SOLD OUT" or "CLOSED" notices from signs or else on the marquees where the prices usually were.

Once on the highway, it seemed like everyone with a car was trying to leave the city. Whereas the lanes going into the city were still blocked off by tanks and military vehicles and were otherwise empty, the outbound lanes were jammed with thousands upon thousands of vehicles. The number of cars combined with random lane closures and military checkpoints made traffic move at no more than a power walker's pace, and after an hour they'd only gone a few miles. Just past the Whitestone Bridge traffic slowed further and eventually they were at a complete standstill.

Fifteen minutes went by without any movement, then a half hour. Prasanth turned off the ignition.

"Fuck." he said and smashed his hands and then his forehead into the steering wheel. "This is what I was worried about."

"Calm down, honey," Casey said. "There's nothing we can do to make traffic go any faster."

Sarah didn't say anything, worried her words might only make the situation tenser. Beside her in the backseat, Maggie looked at her with accusing eyes. *This is your fault.*

Let the girl give her dirty looks. She could take it.

When they heard an explosion somewhere to the west everyone in the car looked at each other.

"Shit, what was that?" Casey said. They looked in the direction of the noise, but there was nothing to see: no smoke, no fire, no mushroom cloud. They couldn't worry about it now. Prasanth briefly turned on the radio, but no one seemed to be talking about an explosion in New York, and he was worried that listening too long would drain the battery.

After another half hour of not moving, people in some of the adjacent cars started getting out of their vehicles to stretch or to see what was going on.

"Someone want to come with me to see what's up?" Prasanth said.

"I'll stay with the car," Casey said.

Sarah didn't want to leave her stepdaughter, but they needed to figure out whether they were going to be able to start moving again. Maggie would be as safe or safer in the car than she would be anywhere else. "I'll go," she said.

Sarah and Prasanth walked for several minutes amongst the river of frozen cars. When they passed by a group of men in their late twenties playing poker on the dashboard of an SUV, Sarah asked if they had any idea what the holdup was. The men shrugged their shoulders. "World's ending," one of them offered.

They continued on for a bit until a bearded man, who looked like the platonic ideal of a trucker, stopped them.

"The military stopped the traffic. But apparently they're going to open things up again in a few minutes. Better go back to your cars," he said. Sarah was surprised by the man's English accent and she was reminded of Henry. His voice was deeper than Henry's, but the accent was enough, and all of a sudden the worry she had tried to suppress returned full force.

They walked back to the car. A blast of panic struck Sarah when she didn't see Maggie or Casey sitting inside the vehicle. She scanned the area, her eyes darting in every direction. "Where'd they go?" she said to Prasanth. Before he could answer, Sarah saw the two of them walking back from the grass on the side of the highway.

"What's the dealio?" Maggie said. Both Casey and her stepdaughter smelled like cigarettes.

"Where'd you guys go?" Sarah demanded.

"Just for a little walk," Maggie said. Sarah looked to Casey, but her friend avoided her gaze.

"The military told people traffic should start moving again soon," Prasanth said. They got back in the car.

No sooner had they all put on their seat belts than a woman came and knocked on the drivers' side window. She was beautiful, with perfect dark skin and long dreadlocks that nearly went to her waist. Sarah thought she might be an actress or model.

"My car is just a couple back," the woman said, gesturing in the direction from which they'd come, "and I thought you should know that some guy was siphoning off your gas."

"What?" Prasanth said. "Of this car?"

"Oh my god," said Casey.

Prasanth turned to his wife. "How long of a walk did you take?"

"Not far," she said.

He turned the ignition. The meter was close to "E" and the "low fuel" light clicked on with a heart-wrenching, two-note chime.

"Motherfucker," Maggie said.

"Watch your language," Sarah said.

"Oh man. That sucks. I'm really sorry," the lady with the dreadlocks said before excusing herself back towards her car.

Traffic started moving again, albeit slowly. Prasanth guessed they had thirty or forty miles left in the tank, but that was assuming they wouldn't be stuck in traffic for hours on end. "Either way," he said, "we don't have enough to get all the way to Connecticut and back."

They took the next exit to see if they could find gas now that they were a little bit outside the city; however, here too, every station they passed was closed.

It turned out they had even less gas than Prasanth estimated, and the engine sputtered into quietness just as the car passed Pelham Bay Park. They finally rolled to a stop on a serene stretch of road in a wooded suburban area.

All four of them sat silent in the unmoving car.

"Crap. I'm really sorry guys," Sarah said.

"Fuck, fuck, fuck." Prasanth said. "I *knew* something was going to happen. I *knew* we should have stayed in New York."

"You were the one who said we should—"

"Shut up, Casey. Just don't say anything. If you would have stayed with the car, none of this would have happened."

They split up to see if they could find a gas station nearby that was open. Back the way they'd come was just the park; however, up ahead, the road branched out into a T-junction and Sarah and Maggie went left, away from the shoreline, while Casey and Prasanth kept down the road they'd been traveling.

Maggie was quiet as they walked. "If you're upset about something, you can talk to me about it," Sarah said.

"What would I be upset about? World War Three has started, my dad's missing and you got us stranded."

"I didn't know this was going to happen." Sarah tried to put her hand on Maggie's shoulder, but the girl brushed her off. The truth was, even if she did know they were going to get stranded, she probably still would have done what she had. At least they were out of the city now.

"Let's just find gas," Maggie said.

There were few cars on the street and Sarah was reminded of those apocalyptically snowy days when everyone stayed inside. The only difference was that it was a beautifully sunny, early fall day.

If a nuclear bomb hit Manhattan, would they feel the blast all the way out here? She saw the fire—the one from her dreams—consuming Maggie again.

They found a Getty station, but this too, had a large, handmade sign out front that said "SOLD OUT—Go home, hug your children, and tell your family you love them." Despite the sign, there was a man at the register in the attached convenience store.

They walked towards the store and, upon closer inspection, the man at the register wasn't a man at all but a sturdy woman of middle age donning a pixie cut. Her eyes were bloodshot and it looked like she hadn't slept. When they walked in, she was taking puffs from one of the Swisher Sweets they sold at the register and a thick cloud of smoke hung in the air.

Entire rows of the store's shelves were empty where once there had ostensibly been snacks, drinks, household supplies. "We're in luck. They still have Funyuns," Maggie said, pointing to the rotating rack next to the magazines.

Sarah approached the counter. "Excuse me," she said, "but is there any chance at all that you might even have a gallon of gas hidden somewhere in the back? Our car got stranded down the road a little ways and—"

The woman didn't say anything; she just took another puff of the cigar and tapped hard on the glass counter where a sign was posted: *NO GAS. NO TIMETABLE FOR NEXT DELIVERY*

"Or maybe you know of somewhere else around here where we might—"

"Sorry," she said, exhaling some more smoke into the air. "You wanna buy anything?"

"Will that change whether there's gas?"

"Nope."

They left with a bag of Funyuns and a bottle of Gatorade and kept walking down the street.

They walked ten more minutes but didn't see anything remotely promising in terms of a place where they might get gasoline and ended up just turning around and going back to the car.

From a distance, they could see Prasanth and Casey had already returned and were waiting for them. Casey sat on the hood and Prasanth stood next to the driver side door. Though Sarah was out of earshot, it was clear the two were arguing about something. Casey and Prasanth both stopped talking as soon as they saw Sarah and Maggie coming from a block away.

"Any luck?" Casey shouted to them when they were still a good distance.

"No. There was a gas station, but they were sold out," said Sarah.

"I have some good news and bad news," Prasanth said then. "We found a guy up this way who has gas in his car and he's willing to give us a ride."

Sarah could almost scream from elation.

"But," Casey said, a warning

"*But,*" Prasanth echoed, "he's headed to New Jersey, so he's only willing to go south. Even as it is, he can't go into the city, so we'll have to find our way from the Cross Bronx Expressway. I figure it should only take us two hours or so to walk from there."

Sarah's heart sank. "It's not safe in New York. I really don't think you guys should go back," she said.

"This is our ride. We're going," Prasanth said, and Casey nodded.

"Okay. That's your decision, but *we're* not going back," Sarah said. "Maggie and I will just have to figure something else out."

"Come on, Sarah," Maggie said. "We should just go back with them."

"I'm sorry," she said, "but this is *not* a democracy. Hopefully we can find a ride, but if we have to, we'll walk." To this, Maggie's whole body sighed in melodramatic exasperation.

"I wish we could have gotten you up to Connecticut. I really hope everything is okay up there," Casey said.

"Thanks so much to both of you. And I'm sorry your car got stranded here. I really appreciate you helping me, especially given the situation."

"Are you fucking kidding me?" Maggie said.

From Maggie's tone, Sarah knew what her stepdaughter was about to do. She tried to pacify the girl with pleading eyes, but it was too late.

"No, don't give me that look," Maggie said. "I get wanting to leave the city, I guess, but you can't just go around lying to people's face. I mean, isn't she your friend? And who knows where's safe? Maybe they're going to blow up Connecticut next to get rid of all the waspy assholes who live up there."

Casey turned to Sarah. "What is she talking about?"

Sarah shrugged her shoulders. She'd done the right thing but couldn't help still feeling terrible.

"Stop fucking lying!" Maggie said.

"What? Is your mom not really sick?" Casey said. She had genuine hurt on her face.

"It's not safe in New York. You guys should not go back," Sarah said.

"Are you fucking kidding? Am I hearing what I think I'm hearing?" Prasanth said. "All this? We spend hours waiting in traffic? We get our gas stolen? We get stranded, and we're going to have to walk from the Bronx, and your mom isn't even sick? This is bullshit, Sarah."

"I'm sorry."

Casey put her face in her hands and walked back to her husband.

"Well, good luck," Prasanth said and gestured in such a way with his hand to show that he was done with his two former passengers. He turned to Casey. "Let's get our stuff and get the fuck out of here."

"I'm sorry, Case."

"That fucking sucked, Sarah," Prasanth said.

Casey and her husband opened up the car and placed Sarah and Maggie's bags on the sidewalk. They took a few of their own belongings from the car, locked up, and headed off in the direction they'd walked to earlier where their ride back to the city was waiting.

There were virtually no cars on the road here in the suburbs, and the two times they managed to get someone to pull over for them, the driver regretfully told them they weren't headed north. Eventually they stopped trying altogether and resigned themselves to walking the thirty-some miles remaining to Fairfield.

"What do you think happened to my dad?" Maggie said as they walked down a nondescript stretch of suburban road near New Rochelle. She seemed to have calmed down a little since they parted from Prasanth and Casey.

"He probably just had car trouble or ran out of gas. Maybe he's walking somewhere, just like us." She hoped this was the case. Then years later, when they and the rest of the world were through mourning all the dead, they could joke about the irony of their similar situations.

"But what if he's hurt? Or lying in a ditch somewhere?" Maggie picked up a pinecone sitting in the middle of the sidewalk and hurled it at a STOP sign at the corner.

"He's going to be all right," Sarah said and rubbed the girl's upper back. "And so are we."

That evening they stopped in a park situated on the water in what they thought was Mamaroneck. They might have found a motel somewhere on Route 1, but they'd have to walk out of the way to look, and there was no guarantee they'd find anything. Further, the weather was pleasant—cool but not overly— so staying in the park might actually be enjoyable. Just the thing to get their minds off everything.

Sarah checked her cell phone. Still no signal.

"We'll just get a few hours of rest. It can't be more than twenty more miles to Fairfield, which we can knock off tomorrow morning if we start early."

She laid the large sweater she'd packed on the grass as a makeshift blanket for Maggie. She had only packed a couple energy bars in the morning, but there would be plenty of food at her mom's house when they got there; a day with little to eat wouldn't kill them. She gave one of the bars to Maggie and afterwards the two found a nearby water fountain where they drank their fill and replenished the water bottle they shared.

The temperature stayed nice even after sunset, though Sarah hadn't counted on it being quite so buggy out. Oh well. They'd make due. Once the sky had fully darkened, they lay down for a while and looked up at the stars. With all the power still out, there was virtually no light pollution and the stars were brighter than Sarah could ever remember seeing them.

"You see that?" she said. "Those stars?"

"Which?"

Sarah took Maggie's hand and guided it in an upward line across the sky and then out from the line in two diverging arcs. "Those."

"Okay."

"That's *The Memory Tree*."

"What's that?"

"A tree—although I'm not sure of the exact story behind it. I think it's from some myth or folktale. But do you see how the stars cut out from that first row? Those are the branches, see?"

"I guess."

"It takes a bit of imagination," Sarah said. But that's what humans did. They looked for meaning and when they looked hard enough, they found it. Already, she was sure there were some crazies probably saying this attack was due to America's sins, gay marriage, gene therapy, etcetera. In reality, this wasn't so different from the men who used to look up in the sky and see magic trees and dragons and beings that were half-horse and half-man. Faced with the chaos of the world, they looked for things to help make sense of it all.

They heard something coming up the path behind them. So far they hadn't seen a single other person in the park and Sarah instinctively reached for the pocketknife connected to her keychain. When she turned around she saw it was a man straddling a bicycle. She stood up.

"Hey," the bicyclist said. He wasn't a man but a teenage boy. She still wasn't putting her knife away.

"Hi," Sarah said.

"What are you guys doing out here?" He was tall and skinny and wore jeans and a Legend of Zelda t-shirt. He looked to be about fifteen or sixteen.

"Just hanging out," Sarah said.

"Oh," he said and started to get back on his bike, but after a single pedal, he pushed the brakes and turned back towards them. "Why?"

"What's it to you?" Sarah said.

"Don't be rude," Maggie said from behind her.

"Maggie, let me handle this."

"We're trying to get up to Connecticut and we kind of got stranded," Maggie said.

"Do you guys need any help?" he said.

"You don't happen to have a car with gas in it, do you? Or a working phone?" Sarah said.

"No," he said. "My parents are away with one of the cars and their other one is in the shop. I saved up money and was going to buy my own car, except I failed the driver's test. They said I didn't check my mirrors enough."

"Well, then," Sarah said. "Looks like there's not much for you to do in the way of helping. Thanks though."

"Okay." He looked to start on his way again, but stopped himself once more. "But I do live nearby. And we have plenty of room—especially with my parents gone."

"We like it here," Sarah said, thinking about the mosquitoes swirling all around.

"Do you have food?" Maggie asked.

"Yeah, totally. My parents are like big-time Costco fans so they buy everything in bulk, you know?"

Sarah considered this. If she were honest, it would probably be a better idea following this teenage boy to his house than it would be to sleep in an empty park. She gripped her pocketknife. If he tried anything though . . .

"How far did you say it was?" she asked.

"Just a five-minute walk from here," he said and then stuck out his hand. "I'm Andrew, by the way."

She took it. "I'm Sarah. And this is Maggie."

"Hi," Maggie said and Sarah thought she noticed Andrew open his eyes a little wider when he caught a better look at her stepdaughter.

He walked his bike alongside Maggie; Sarah followed close behind. "Wow, it makes you think about how reliant we are on cars," Andrew said after Maggie told him about their ordeal that day. "I don't think of New York as far away, but if you have to walk it's like an eternity."

They turned onto a tree-lined street and then onto another where the houses were a little larger and more spread apart. All the streetlights were out, so the only illumination came from Andrew's bike light and the moon and stars overhead. Through the window of a large yellow and white house, Sarah spied a man and a woman eating a meal by candlelight, and she thought again about Henry and how she regretted how they had parted. It wasn't like they'd gotten in a fight or anything, but that morning she had been late to a client meeting and so she rushed out of the house without even giving him an embrace. "See you in a few days," she'd shouted and ran out to the elevator.

The house was a handsome two-story structure with a Spanish-tiled roof. Andrew ran his bike along the side of the house to the backyard and opened the front door for them to come inside.

Sarah realized she'd been holding her bladder all this time and made a beeline for the bathroom.

"It's just on the left," Andrew said, gesturing down a short hall.

"Come with me, Maggie," Sarah said.

"What? Why?"

"Because."

"No, I'm not coming with you to the bathroom."

Sarah had to go urgently, so she decided to let it go; however, she made sure to leave the door slightly open so she could hear if Maggie needed help.

When Sarah came out, a few candles were lit around the dining room and there was a spread of junk food on the table in front of Maggie: Ruffles and Handi-Snacks and chocolate covered whatever and a two-liter bottle of Pepsi.

"What would you like?" Andrew said as he turned on his emergency radio and started lighting more candles around the kitchen.

"What are my options?"

"PB&J sandwich? I'd offer something better, but the stove isn't working. It's gas, but it's still not turning on for some reason."

"It's probably the pilot light," Sarah said. "You can probably light it by hand if you want."

"Oh, really? You're free to give it a try."

"No, that's okay. PB&J is fine. Maybe I can show you tomorrow morning if you'd like."

On the radio they were talking about how there had been relatively little damage to San Francisco although "the terrorists" (this is what they were calling them because they still had no idea who the perpetrators were) had managed to take the Golden Gate Bridge down. The coast guard was still sweeping through the bay searching for survivors. Maggie sat silently, popping chocolate-covered almonds into her mouth.

Sarah plopped down on a chair. Andrew fetched the ingredients and began constructing the sandwich. "You said your parents were out of town?" she asked, but Andrew didn't seem to hear the question; he was focused on the radio and on spreading the peanut butter evenly over the bread. "Andrew?"

He looked up at her. "Yeah," he said and swallowed.

Maggie stopped eating now and joined in on the conversation. "Where were they going?" she said.

Andrew had had his face turned towards them, but now he turned away as if he were looking for something that had gone down the drain of the kitchen sink. "D.C.," he said.

"I'm sorry," Sarah said.

"Me too," said Maggie.

Andrew finished making the sandwich. When he placed it in front of

Sarah, she could see that he'd cut it diagonally and placed one of those tropical-colored umbrella toothpicks in each half. "I don't know when else we'd use these stupid things," he said, which made her smile a little.

"Do you mind if I try and find something else?" Maggie said, gesturing to the radio that was still talking about San Francisco.

"Sure," Andrew said. "I've kind of heard all of this stuff already anyway."

"Yeah, what we really need is some good music." Maggie went one by one through all the stations, but other than the soft rock and Spanish-music station, all she found were different voices saying the same things. "I'm just going to turn this off for a little bit." she said.

Andrew looked like he wanted to say something but was wondering whether he should. "I play a little guitar," he said. "I mean, I'm not that good, but—"

"Yeah, yeah, do it!" Maggie said.

"You sure?" Andrew said, looking for more encouragement.

"Yes!" Maggie said and Sarah nodded in agreement.

When Andrew ran up the stairs to get his guitar, Sarah turned to her stepdaughter. "He's cute, right?"

Maggie sighed. "Can't I be nice to someone without you bringing everything there?" she said.

"I'm not bringing anything anywhere," she said.

"He might have just lost his parents for god's sake."

"I know," Sarah said, and she wanted to add that that was the very reason that she was saying what she was, that it was in moments like this that it was especially important to *bring things there*.

Andrew came down with an acoustic and sat on the couch in the living room. Maggie and Sarah followed him in and sat on the carpet. Over the mantel were two large framed photos; the first showed a man in glasses and a tuxedo, who might just as well be a young Bill Gates, standing beside a friendly looking, big-haired woman in a wedding gown. The second photo showed the same two people, older, beside a six or seven-year-old Andrew. They sat on an idyllic looking rock overlooking what Sarah assumed to be the Long Island Sound.

"So I'm an okay singer, but I'm a pretty amateurish guitarist," Andrew said as he tuned the strings.

"No downplaying," Maggie said.

"I'm sure you're great," Sarah added.

Andrew played a song by the Beatles that Sarah recognized but couldn't name and followed it up with *Tangled Up in Blue* and a couple Pearl Jam songs. There was nothing wrong with Andrew's guitar playing as far as she could hear, but his voice—his voice—was so much deeper and stronger than one would have expected from a spindly teenager like him. And he sang as himself rather than trying to imitate the voice of the person who'd originally sang the song. After the Pearl Jam, Andrew sang a song Sarah had never heard before. Although the song initially sounded happy, when Sarah paid close attention to the words, she realized it was a sad song—a song about a soldier's life-long journey to return home after a great and terrible war.

Following every song, they clapped and cheered with increasing fervor and when Sarah looked over at Maggie she thought, why would someone try to destroy a world this lovely?

Andrew finished by playing REMs "It's the End of the World as We Know It," and they all laughed.

After Andrew put his guitar away, they played Monopoly until Sarah's eyes were involuntarily shutting between each turn. "I don't know if I've ever finished a game of Monopoly my entire life," Sarah said with a yawn.

Andrew set up the bed in the guest room for them and Sarah said her goodnights and went to bed.

That night, she vaguely had the sense of Maggie getting into the bed beside her, but she wasn't sure what time it was.

Sarah woke to the smell of bacon and her first thought was that she was a child back in Ohio in that big house she'd loved so much, and that her mom and dad and brother and sister were all below getting ready for breakfast. Sarah kept her eyes closed and snuggled into the warm blankets, comforted by the thought of what awaited her downstairs.

But her sister had been dead more than thirty years; her father had died a few years ago. They hadn't lived in Ohio in decades, and when they had, her brother hadn't even been born yet.

She opened her eyes and sat upright. She looked at the unfamiliar furniture, the unfamiliar curtains. Then it came to her. She remembered the previous night's events and remembered where she was in time, in space.

The smell of bacon hadn't been a dream. Where was Maggie? Was the power back on? A clock radio on the nightstand stared, numberless, at her. She checked her phone, whose battery was down to one bar: nothing.

At the bottom of the stairs the smell of bacon mixed with the smell of other breakfast-related aromas. "Is that waffles?" Sarah said.

"Pancakes," Andrew said. "Good morning."

Maggie was sitting on a high-backed chair at the island in the center of the kitchen fiddling with Andrew's guitar. She wore the t-shirt and shorts that were her usual sleeping outfit.

"The power's not on, is it?" Sarah said, turning now to Andrew who was simultaneously managing a pancake skillet, a bacon skillet, and an egg skillet.

"No, but I figured out that pilot light thingy you were talking about."

"Andrew's teaching me to play guitar," Maggie said. "He's already taught me a C chord and a . . ."

"G chord," he said and she strummed the two chords. Not perfect, but they sounded like something.

"Okay, what's next?" Maggie said.

"The D chord I showed you earlier," he said while pouring out another pancake. Sarah sat in a chair facing a window, looking out at the sunny autumn day. She briefly fantasized of what it would be like if this was her new life: she in this house with Maggie and Andrew, a son and daughter, neither of which were her blood. They would fall in love and move to the house across the street and they'd have beautiful children of their own that she and Henry would babysit when they wanted to go out for Saturday night dinner.

Maggie played what were clearly the wrong strings. "No, the third finger should be on the bottom string, *second* fret," Andrew said.

Maggie looked up at him with an expression of exaggerated frustration. The final pancakes were just about done and he flipped them onto the growing stack he had piled on a plate next to the stove. He came up to her and pointed to the place where he wanted her to put her fingers. When she still looked confused, he swiveled her stool so that her back was to him and placed his arms around her, showing her the chord, as if his hands were hers. He strummed the chord once and then gently took her hands, shaping her fingers like little pieces of clay and molding them into the proper position. He told her to strum and she did and the chord came out, crisp and right.

They packed their things after breakfast and got ready to walk the last twenty-or-so miles up to Fairfield. Sarah thanked Andrew for his hospitality and was giving him a hug, when Maggie blurted out, "Why don't you come with us?"

Of course he should come with.

Sarah was ashamed at not having thought of this herself.

"Oh, yeah. You should come. You *have to* come," she said, hoping her insistence would make up for her not having thought of this earlier.

"But...I was just thinking that maybe I should stay here. You know. Where...*someone* might think to look for me."

"Well, you'll have your cell phone and I'm sure they'll get service back soon." This was a lie. She had no idea when service would be restored. Still, if this little lie would get him to come, then it was worth it. "And," she added, "you can leave a note. In case," she almost said *your parents come home* but then caught the words in her mouth. ". . . In case anyone comes looking for you."

Andrew relented and they waited while he gathered a few things, including his guitar, which he placed in a soft, canvas case that, along with his backpack of clothes, he slung over his shoulders. When they were just about to leave, Andrew announced that he hadn't thought about it earlier but his parents' bikes were just sitting in the garage and twenty miles by bike would be a heck of a lot faster than on foot. It seemed like their fortunes were getting better and better.

On bikes, the miles flew by, and Sarah wondered how they ever would have walked all this distance otherwise. They passed the Connecticut border and then Greenwich and Stamford and Norwalk and Westport before finally making it to Fairfield. When they reached the house and pedaled down the hundred-yard-long tree-lined driveway, Andrew marveled at how big the house was. "Nice place," he said and Maggie responded by making it clear that it was the house of her stepmom's mom and therefore the opulence should not reflect on her. They left the bikes in front of the garage and walked the narrow brick path to the front of the house. Sarah hesitated before knocking. After a few seconds of standing in front of the door, Maggie sidestepped her and rang the doorbell.

Henry's own car, they later learned, had run out of gas more than thirty miles away and was now sitting in the parking lot of the New Haven IKEA. However, he'd gotten a ride and, given the lack of cell service and the fact that he couldn't get into New York City anyway due to the road blocks, thought the best place to go would be Sarah's mother's house.

When the door opened, it was Mrs. D'Albero—not Henry, who was in the bathroom—that answered the door, but from the glint in her mother's eye, Sarah sensed something was up. "Is Henry here?" she asked even before she gave her mother a hug. The older woman, in remarkably good shape given her age (certainly no signs of cancer), just smiled. Sarah called out into the empty foyer: "Henry?" she said and then finally wrapped her arms around her mother and began to cry.

Sarah and her mother embraced for a long time and blocked the door so that all four of them were still standing awkwardly at the entryway when Henry came into view, dressed in a plain blue t-shirt and khakis. When Sarah saw him, she didn't let her mother go, as if she could somehow hug her husband vicariously through the woman in her arms. Maggie darted passed the two women and lunged towards her dad.

After Sarah hugged and kissed Henry and Sarah's mother gave Maggie a grandmotherly hug and pat on the back, they introduced Andrew and explained the previous night's events.

"Thanks for taking care of my girls," Henry said in his English accent and embraced the boy tight.

That evening they emptied the refrigerator of meats and vegetables and had an enormous grill-out in the well-manicured back yard. Henry was in particularly good spirits; he seemed to take especial pleasure in cooking this way under the stars and pretending he was living in some bygone era. And then, suddenly and without notice, the power came back on.

Sarah's mother had recently had a party at the house for all of the volunteers at the County Playhouse, and for the event, she'd had strings and strings of white lights draped across much of the back patio. Now that the electricity had returned, all the lights, which had been on a timer, came on, creating a canopy of illumination over their heads.

"Beautiful!" Maggie said and then, either as a spontaneous display of joy or, more likely, something she'd been waiting the opportunity for, she took hold of Andrew and kissed him on the cheek. Sarah smiled and was happy and sought out her husband so she too could have someone to kiss.

It was only later as Sarah was bringing in the dishes, swollen with the food she'd eaten and the joy she felt in her heart, that she noticed the television was on in the family room. It must have somehow automatically turned back on when the power came back. It wasn't a news station, but like with the radio, all that was on these days was the news.

As soon as she glanced at the screen, she fell to her knees—struck by an invisible blow to the chest. She wanted to scream out to Henry but couldn't find the strength. She had to take deep breaths just to keep her food down.

Perhaps a different person might have read the news headline that scrolled along the bottom of the screen and felt vindicated, or at least lucky that they'd managed, with their only daughter, to escape the disaster—but not Sarah. Instead, all she could think of were the thousands and thousands of other parents and other children and lovers and lonely people and Casey and Prasanth who had likely blinked out of existence when the bombs—the fire she had feared so much—finally reached the city she called home.

For Immediate Distribution to All Brothers Living in the Vicinity of the Southlands
The 2nd Day After the First New Moon of Autumn, 559 Years After *The Fall*

The Council of the Arch-Masters has received reports that one formerly of the Order has been acting in the assistance of rebel elements in Jarl in and around the Southland provinces. We believe the man in question is a former apprentice named Rhys, who may now go by an assumed name and who studied in Ilyeth from the 525th year to the 532nd. Accounts of Rhys describe him as above average height, medium build, and of olive complexion with brown hair and green eyes. In recent months, his activities in the South have been manifold, and we believe he is responsible for significant loss of property and life in attacks against the Alderians. While it is our policy not to become embroiled in the politics of the Continent, when one (formerly) of our own, through the use of abilities gained (at least in part) under our supervision, uses said abilities in an irresponsible and/ or criminal manner, it is our sacred duty to put a stop to the misuse.

You are hereby put on notice that if you happen upon, or otherwise have information regarding the whereabouts of Rhys, please do not attempt to apprehend or otherwise approach him. His abilities are formidable, and we hold him to be exceedingly dangerous. We have, as of yesterday, dispatched a team under the leadership of Master Aron Vairn, who has been redeployed after his successful mission in the West, to track down and detain the fugitive by use of any means necessary. By the time you receive this notification, this team should have either already arrived in Jarl or be scheduled to arrive imminently. As such, please forward any and all information you have regarding this matter in care of Master Aron to the Jarl IAO.

Regards,
Arch-Master Githault

TWELVE

A DREAM COME TRUE
499-603 Years After *The Fall*

I

As soon as he exits the pass through the cliff side, Kam—who, for many years now, has mostly been known by another name—can smell the saltiness of the sea and knows he's home. It's been so long since he's returned to The Finger, where once stood the village of his birth: the place he passed his youth in what he only much later realized was happiness, the place where one of the two people he loved most is buried beneath the rocky soil.

The Finger is a small stretch of coastal land surrounded on three sides by rocky shoreline and rough waters. The fourth side is a set of jagged cliffs ("the knuckle," some called it). It had once been a thriving fishing village belonging to the kingdom of Vilben, but all that is left are a few abandoned stone buildings, their thatch roofs long ago lifted away by the sea storms. Traders and other rare outsiders reached town via a canyon that was difficult to traverse on horseback and impossible by wagon; most locals traveled to the village on boats. Kam, his own boat having sunk three days ago, passes through the treacherous canyon—just like an outsider.

This will probably be his last time here and tomorrow he will return the way he came. The premonitions are seldom wrong, although are often shrouded in riddles; yet after so many wrong turns, missteps, false interpretations, he is sure now of two things: that the thing he seeks is here and that the endgame of all this can't be far away now.

One of the ironies is that, though The Finger had seen war and pirates and terrible, cataclysmic storms and annexation and a series of other, lesser misfortunes, the undoing of the place was mostly the plain, economic realities of fish prices. For several years the rivers on the interior of the Empire yielded bountiful fish harvests and it no longer made sense to ship dried fish inland from the southern coasts. No exports meant no imports and the village struggled to survive. Years passed. The villagers moved inland or to Hammer Bay. The old-timers who refused to relocate died off. This was all many years after Kam left.

The house he lived in with his wife is completely gone and it is only through tracing the steps from the half-ruined stone granary that he finds the precise spot. He sits down where he believes his high-backed wooden chair would have been. And if here the chair—he gets up and starts to draw the imagined layout in the mud with a walking stick he picked up in the canyon—then there the hearth, and there their bed, and there . . . the other bed.

His son. Only not.

He looks down at the lines he's drawn in the mud.

He should get on with it. He has never been bothered by the sight of bodies, the sight of death. This, of course, will be different.

He finds the tree still standing, behind where the house once was, and starts digging.

II

The house Kam Rhys lived in with Olwyn was not the house of his childhood. That house was down the hill some ways, closer to the shore. Kam's father had been a fisherman and his mother used to say that the house had been built with its sole window facing the docks so that she could easily see when his father's boat returned from its journeys out to the icy seas to the south.

The Rhyses had two daughters, each considerably older than Kam—Marlyn and the eldest, Lauralyn. Both of the girls married and moved away by the time Kam was seven so later he would remember little of his time with them, save for a solitary, clear memory of how they used to make him braid their chestnut hair.

Young Kam passed most of his hours with his mother, helping where he could with the household chores. He had been sick as a boy and didn't walk well; any time he tried to play with the other children he would be teased or abused, so that his mother soon forbade him from leaving her side. It wasn't until he was nearly a man that he could walk and run without a limp.

When he was fifteen his mother died suddenly from the sweating sickness. Afterwards, his father tried to comfort him in his own way but as a fisherman, he was frequently out to sea, and even when he was present, the elder Rhys could never quite find the proper words to console his son. Kam withdrew and became a sullen young man whose mind was oft filled with dark thoughts. He'd frequently go on walks, out to where the shore broke up, so that, to keep going out to sea, he needed to hop from stone to slippery stone. As he would make his way further and further out, the rocks grew scarcer until he would stand upon the furthest stone a person could reach without first wading through the frigid water below. Out in front of him the water would stretch on and on. In those days, the more superstitious of his village believed that out there, beyond the sea, was where their dead went after they passed from their mortal bodies. Kam was not one to believe in these stories but, as he stood on that furthest rock looking out, his mother never far from his thoughts, he still wished, fervently, that they were true.

It was a few months after his mother had died that Kam first had *the dream*, which only later he would discover was not a dream at all, and that would go on to become the silent, yet powerful, force behind so much of his life. The dream would recur frequently in these early years and each time it would be slightly altered, though the basic structure was usually the same. In what looks to be an old tavern or inn two men stand opposite one another. One is tall, cloaked in dark red with his hood pulled low so his face is shrouded in darkness. The sight of this man gives Kam an ominous feeling. The other also wears a cloak; however, the hood is not pulled down, and Kam can see that he is dark skinned with a mostly bald head. This man is slight in stature and more than a head shorter than his counterpart. The two men talk, although Kam cannot hear their words. Towards the end, the dark-skinned man pulls out a silver blade and stabs it into the heart of the bigger man. For some reason, this act does not alarm Kam but rather gives him a great sense of relief, happiness even. In some versions of the dream, this is the end. In others, the dark-skinned man stands over his victim for a time before searching through the dead man's bag; inside he finds a leather-bound book and a white scepter molded out of some ancient wood. When the dark-skinned man wraps his fingers around the scepter, the stone at its end begins changing colors, cycling through a million hues before settling on a blindingly bright white. That was as far as it ever went.

He was eighteen when he first saw Olwyn. She was twenty-two then, had already been widowed, and came to The Finger to live with her aunt and uncle—the only family she had left. Kam was hauling an enormous gathering of rope back from the docks and Olwyn was out behind her uncle's house tending to the pigs. Her skin was a shade lighter than the olive complexion that was common among the people of The Finger and her brown hair had the slightest hint of red in it. She was pretty but not remarkably so. What stood out was how every one of her movements seemed purposeful—how she carried herself with a complete lack of self-consciousness or regard for what the world thought of her. When she worked around her uncle's house she could often be seen wearing breeches rather than a dress. And rather than cover her head with bonnet or scarf, she wore her shoulder-length hair down for all the world to see.

Kam didn't speak to her. He was terrified of even the meekest of girls. He could never muster up the courage to talk to this confident creature. Instead, he watched and observed her whenever he could—outside her uncle's house, at the fish market near the docks, walking here or there on some errand. Even when she wasn't wearing breeches, by all accounts she dressed very modestly: drab and loose and thick garments. Yet even these bleak rags sat on her in a way that suggested to Kam a kind of eroticism that made him anxious with excitement. He would frequently be alone now for weeks at a time when his father was on voyages, and often at night he would imagine her next to him in bed as he touched himself in a way that no woman ever had.

Kam wasn't the only one to notice Olwyn. Most of the more brazen men of the village had propositioned her in one manner or another (often lewdly), but she laughed them all off. And when Kam saw this, always from a distance, he knew that such a woman could never be his.

A few months later, Kam's father was lost at sea. When the ship his father had sailed upon returned, Kam was given the normal small payment and asked if he would be his father's replacement. Work as a fisherman paid better than Kam's job as a laborer. Besides he had nothing keeping him in the village. He agreed. His father had died at sea, but Kam figured his own life wasn't so great, so risking it was no great wager.

He made a poor fisherman. When he started working as a laborer, his body had begun filling out and, he had thought, growing into a man's strength. Yet the strength required for sailing was a different kind—not just the strength of brute force, of moving large crates, but also the strength of hand for tying trustworthy knots or pulling the nets over the bow and a hardiness of body to withstand the icy winds of the southern seas. On his first voyage he nearly died repeatedly, or so it seemed, and spent more time overboard than he ever thought possible. Still, he'd later hold a kind of nostalgia for this time of his life. He would remember the thrill he felt as they sailed amongst those icy islands, a few miles from the inhospitable shores of the Wastes, where even in the height of summer, the landscape was spotted with the white of ice and snow.

It was when he was back in the village from his third or fourth fishing voyage that he met Olwyn. That day he spent much of the afternoon sitting alone in the village's only tavern, drinking ale to pass the time. Some months before he had trysted with a local girl and thought he might even wed her, but upon arriving back in the village, he learned she'd been sent off to another village to marry. This girl was not the sole source of Kam's melancholy but rather the latest catalyst to trigger a kind of non-specific yet all-encompassing sadness that seemed to hang over his life ever since his mother died—a dark storm cloud on a windless day.

By now, Kam was no longer so deathly shy towards the fairer sex. Nonetheless, had he not been drinking heavily, he never would have had the courage to approach Olwyn when she entered the tavern and sat down a few tables away.

"You're Olwyn," he said, all he could think to say.

Later they'd joke about this; often in greeting she'd say, "You're Kam."

"Are all you fishermen so smart?" she said. Kam wasn't sure how to respond, but, because he couldn't bear the silence anymore and because his pocket was weighed down with the coin he'd made on the last voyage, he offered to buy her some wine.

"Ale instead," she said.

They began spending time together—taking walks through the snow, sitting and talking before the tavern fire. Some months passed. Then one day before that very fire, she leaned over towards him. The fire was warm, but the heat from her body was warmer, and she pulled his face towards his own and kissed him. He thought she was somehow teasing him. Yet the look on her face said otherwise. "Would you like to be my husband?" she said and he nodded, yes.

In the years ahead, he'd ask her why she'd chosen him—for that is how he felt: *chosen*. He wasn't the handsomest or smartest or strongest or richest of her potential suitors. But any time he'd ask her this, she'd just brush it off with a vague non-answer: she liked his green eyes, or she saw something "special" in him.

"Special? Like what?" he'd ask.

"Does Kam need a compliment today?"

His next voyage was his last. It was the height of summer and the fish were further south, necessitating them to sail further than they ever had to fill their nets. The weather was calm and the sailing smooth. Many times they were within sight of the coasts of the Wastes, and once Kam even spied what he thought were dragons flying far off on the horizon. Upon their return voyage, they docked for a night at a tiny hamlet at the southern edge of the kingdom, which, though nameless, was unofficially called Last Village by the sailors. Kam knew this would be his final time at sea and wanted to get a present for Olwyn to celebrate the occasion. That evening, after the men went ashore, Kam went looking amongst the village's shopkeepers to find something suitable. He had no success. All the wares looked cheap and totally unworthy.

He resigned himself to not finding anything when he went into the inn to warm up and have a drink. Inside the dank-smelling building a few of his fellow sailors were conversing with local men. Kam wasn't great friends with the other sailors and he drank his ale alone at the far end of the room.

He'd nearly emptied his cup and was preparing to leave when a voice called from behind. "Sir," the high voice said, and Kam turned. Sitting at a table behind him was a boy of nine or so dressed in rags. He had tan skin like most other Vilbenians, yet his eyes were of the lightest blue. "Could you come here please?"

Kam was usually fond of children, but something about this boy made him wary. Still, he sat down.

"Are you in love," the boy said, more statement than question. An odd way to open a conversation.

Kam grinned, but the expression evaporated when the boy didn't reciprocate. "Why do you ask?"

"Your eyes," the boy said. "The way you move. She is very beautiful, is she not?"

"You're here in the tavern alone? Where are your parents?"

The boy said nothing.

"She is very beautiful to me," Kam said then.

"A beautiful woman requires a beautiful gift, no?" At that the boy pulled out a necklace from the inside of his filthy tunic. At the end of the chain hung a large red stone.

"A ruby?" Kam said.

"More precious."

"How'd you come upon it then?" Most likely it was stolen.

"It's been with us a long time," the boy said.

"A family heirloom then?" The boy smiled for the first time, but the smile seemed unnatural. "And you wish to sell it?"

"How much silver have you?"

"Wouldn't your mother be angry if you sold your family heirloom?"

"Mother's been dead a long time."

"In any case, if the thing's more valuable than a ruby, I don't have nearly enough coin."

"Try me, sir. I want you to have it. It belongs with you and your love."

Kam took out as much silver as he thought he could spare—nearly half his purse, but still far less than a ruby necklace would be worth—and dropped it on the table. "Very well," the boy said. "A fine gift this will make."

When Kam returned to The Finger, he and Olwyn were married, the necklace serving as the wedding gift for his bride. He spent the little he had left, along with the money he received from selling his parents' house, for a flock of sheep and a small tract of land up the hill from the village. For the remainder of the summer and into early autumn, Kam and Olwyn slept in a tent and built, with their own hands, a house for themselves and a small barn for the animals. Kam would have liked to claim he took the lead with the building; in truth, he served as little more than a beast of burden. Olwyn proved the far more competent carpenter.

Those next three years were the happiest of his life. Coin was never in great supply, but they had enough. Kam sold wool to the weaver and lamb meat to the butcher, and in the warm months, Olwyn brought vegetables into the village to sell at market. Most evenings they would eat a simple meal and then wile away the remaining hours with lovemaking. Olwyn's appetites were seemingly insatiable and many a night Kam would turn her away from a third go-round so that they might get some sleep. He would have thought that after a half year of this she would surely be with child, yet her belly remained as flat as the sea on the calmest morning. This was not a problem for Kam, more an observation. He wanted a child but was in no rush.

Then the war came.

❖

III

It takes him longer than expected to find the body. Perhaps over the years the ground had shifted gradually, moving the remains a few paces to the left or to the right. It is nearly dusk when his shovel strikes the wooden coffin he'd buried her in. When he is done unearthing it, he casts a simple spell—feeling that familiar tingling down his arm—to lift it out of its hole.

Now that the coffin is here beside him, he finds other things to occupy himself. He gives water to the horse. He chews on a bit of the stale bread and cured meat he's brought in his sack. He walks down to the shore.

When he returns it's dark. He'll make camp for the evening and wait until morning to do it. He's not leaving until the next day anyway.

It's cold that night, and sitting by the fire with her coffin across from him, he can imagine she's alive again.

"You know I've missed you," he says aloud to the damp wooden box. He remembers building the thing. He'd insisted he build it and for this reason it is slightly crooked, the top not closing properly.

"Yes," he goes on, "things weren't good at the end. After Ben left, you were never the same. But do we have to judge everything by how they were at the end? All things end badly, when it comes down to it."

The coffin doesn't say anything.

"Here we are. How many years now? A lot, I know. Me: with all this blood on my hands." He throws a twig into the fire. "You wouldn't approve of what I've been up to. But at least I've done what I thought right."

He smothers the fire with dirt, goes inside his tent and lies down. He can't sleep. His mind is filled with memories: of her and of that insufferable premonition, the only thing he has left. Some hours pass. He thinks he falls asleep, but when he wakes, it is still dark. He will just get on with it.

He casts a lantern spell to illuminate his campsite. The wood of the coffin has partially rotted, so he can pry open the top simply by placing his sword in the space between it and the base of the coffin and pulling downward.

He lays the top of the coffin on the ground and prepares himself for the unsightly remains that undoubtedly await. When he sees her, he recoils but out of surprise, not disgust. In the last six decades she hasn't decomposed a day; she looks exactly as she did when he buried her: pale skin, puffy cheeks, a few strands of reddish brown amongst a sea of gray.

The stone at the end of her necklace, the necklace he had given her, the necklace he has come for, glows red against the darkness.

IV

The men of The Finger traveled by boat four days north to Hammer Bay. A war had begun with the Alderians, and they would all, they were told, be fighting for the freedom of their country.

They were only in the city for a single night before moving outside the walls to a vast field of tents used to house the soldiers. Kam, having never yet left The Finger except on fishing voyages into the wilderness, marveled at how massive Hammer Bay was with its three and four-story buildings.

The Vilbenian navy was small but able. It was said that the balingers docked in Hammer Bay could, when the oars were fully manned, travel twice the speed of the fastest Imperial vessels. Further, each was outfitted with two metal hoses that spouted *Hammer Fire*, which could efficiently destroy any Imperial ships that came within range. The strength of the navy, combined with the fact that the seas were stormier than usual that spring, made it likely that the Redcloaks would approach over land.

Kam's skills as a sailor were meager compared to many of his countrymen, and he was rejected almost immediately from the naval defense forces. Instead he was made a pike man with the other untrained fighters. He remained in the tent city for eight months, practicing formations and movements with his pike regiment for hours each day. He missed Olwyn terribly: the slightly musky smell of her body, her high-pitched laugh, which he'd once thought grating, the feeling that someone knew him. Messengers were still running between Hammer Bay and the Finger, but Kam could neither read nor write and he was only able to communicate with his wife a few times when he managed to scrounge together the necessary funds to employ a scribe.

It was in her second letter (unlike Kam, Olwyn had learned to read and write), two months after he'd left, that she told him she was with child. The night after hearing this, he sat in his cot brooding. This was ill timing. In addition to the war, there were always the normal dangers of childbirth, and he felt these were heightened without him by her side. The months passed.

The road leading into Hammer Bay was completely flat until it climbed up a single hill, upon which the tent city was situated and beyond which lay the city gates. When the Redcloaks finally came, the Vilbenians could see them from a great distance—column after column of crimson far on the horizon. As the Alderians approached, their horns blaring militaristic calls, a dust cloud floated overhead from the endless, synchronized marching.

The Redcloaks halted a quarter mile from the Vilbenian lines and all the drumming and horns and pomp and circumstance abruptly ceased. Kam, standing in the front row of his regiment, pike in hand, had an unimpeded view of the large Imperial host: the infantry, a mass of cavalry, the tall standards waving gently in the breeze. He only just then became aware of the man to his left's pike, which shook, ever so slightly, back and forth, back and forth. A silence descended on the space between the two armies. After a few minutes, the Redcloaks brought their archers forwards in an orderly, methodical march, as if participating in an exercise or ceremony. The archers, having closed in part of the distance between the main Redcloak host and the Vilbenians, stood in perfectly spaced rows. There was a shout as the archers, all in unison, pulled their bows tight and angled their aim upward. After another shout they let loose the first of several volleys of arrows towards Kam and his countrymen.

The Vilbenians had been expecting archers so they each raised their wooden shields in defense. Kam cowered beneath his shield, which, he realized now, was woefully small to protect a man of any reasonable size. On the first volley, and then again on the third, an arrow struck his shield with a hard thud.

When all the arrows had been shot and their lines, save a few unlucky men, still mostly stood, the rows of archers receded and the Imperial cavalry began their charge up the slow incline of the hill. Kam yanked the two arrows out of his shield and dropped them and the shield in the grass. The sound of the horses grew louder. The one thing that had been impressed upon Kam and his fellow pike men, above all, was the necessity to hold formations. *If the formation is broken, all is lost,* was the mantra the commanders had them repeat over and over in training; however, so long as the formation held, they could dispel any cavalry or infantry that attacked. Kam gripped the wooden handle of his pike and waited for the onslaught.

The first wave of cavalry crashed against their lines right near where Kam stood. Four or more pikes—including his own—pierced through the light mail and flesh of one of the charging horses. The dying beast made a final, ear-piercing sound and torrents of warm blood spattered the men in the face. The jolt of Kam's pike going through the flesh of the horse jerked his spear upward, nearly lifting him from the ground. He managed to control the pike at the last instant, but not before feeling something break in his side from the force. The cavalryman riding the slain beast toppled to the ground head first in an awkward heap, almost certainly dead from the fall. Still, Kam's countrymen didn't take any chances and the poor Redcloak was skewered by half a dozen pikes in his armpits, above his throat guard and in all of his other unarmored places.

The Redcloaks who managed to fend off the pikes thrusting at them and stay on their horses road back to their lines. The Vilbenians cheered. Down the line to Kam's left, one of the more enthusiastic men used the blade end of his pike to saw through the neck of one of the dead cavalrymen before placing the bloodied head on the end of his spear and lifting it up with an animalistic howl. The cheers intensified. Kam raised his own pike in solidarity with his countrymen but kept his mouth firmly closed.

The Redcloaks gathered for another charge. The Vilbenians' success deflecting the first attack had bolstered their confidence, and as the riders approached, Kam could hear his fellow pike men shouting taunts to the oncoming cavalry. Yet, just thirty paces away, the horses stopped in unison. All at once, each of the riders drew, from beneath their horses' packs, a small bow, half the size of the archers' long bows.

Someone shouted "Kallanbori!" but it was too late. The Vilbenian lines were so tightly packed together that it was difficult to shoot an arrow in their direction and *not* hit someone. Some of the men tried picking up their shields, but many did so in vain and fell as the steel-tipped arrows of the cavalry archers pierced their throats, their chests, their stomachs. Instinctively, Kam threw down his spear and ran as fast as his feet would take him away from the lines and the arrows and death.

Shouting and the sounds of battle were everywhere and the pain in his side made each step excruciating. Men were dying now, all around. A mounted Redcloak, this one with sword not bow, closed from Kam's flank. Having abandoned his spear, the only weapon Kam had was a short knife he kept sheathed at his side—little use against a mounted, armored rider wielding a long sword. Upon the rider's first pass, Kam dove upon the grass out of the way of his attacker's horse and sword. The rider spun his mount around and began a second charge. Kam rose to his feet and readied himself to die. But then, just a horse's length from Kam, both rider and mount toppled to the side as if swept away by a giant wave.

Of course, there was no wave, the sea being more than a mile away.

Kam didn't have time to second-guess his luck; he ran towards the tree line. Even later, after learning about the meridians and the mystical arts and sorcery, he could only guess as to precisely what had happened that day.

By nightfall the Vilbenian casualties numbered over three thousand dead or wounded, the city had fallen, and Kam, despite his attempted escape into the forests surrounding the city, found himself prisoner along with five thousand of his fellow soldiers. Kam was, more than anything, relieved.

The Alderian Empire was known to be ruthless (tyrannical, many would say), and Kam hated it. But they did not have a history of mass executions. There was a good chance he was going to survive.

V

He peers down at his beloved lying in the coffin and touches her cheek with the back of his hand. It is not warm; she is not alive. But the skin feels soft and supple, the flesh of someone who has just passed from this world.

All the years she wore the necklace, he'd never seen the stone glow. He examines it, lifts it from where it rests above her breasts. It is cold, light without heat. In his hand the stone turns clear and the light it emits shifts from red to white. He returns it to her chest and it is red again. He has seen all manner of sorcery and talismans, and read about many more during his years on the island, but he has no idea as to the nature of this stone.

When he unclasps the necklace from around her fleshy throat, her body begins to change. Within the span of a minute her skin dries and shrivels and cracks; he panics and tries to return the necklace to her, but it's too late. Her skin and muscles and organs dissolve into air until all that is left is dust and bones and her auburn-streaked, gray hair inside her suddenly ragged clothes.

He pockets the necklace and does his best to re-close the coffin before casting a spell and returning it to the hole from which it came. He begins the reburying. As shovel after shovel of earth fall upon the coffin, he remembers the first time he did this. By the time he's finished, it's mid-morning. He looks out to the sea one more time—knowing intuitively it is the final time he shall ever see this stretch of coastline—and heads back to The Knuckle.

VI

The Redcloaks spent the next three days rooting out the final pockets of resistance around Hammer Bay, and the Vilbenian tent city was seamlessly transformed into a prison camp. Alderian guards stood sentry in every direction and the prisoners were ordered, under penalty of death, to stay within their tents, except during mealtime. For his part, Kam found captivity a relative improvement to life as a soldier. There was less work, more food and the specter of death seemed to diminish by the day. During all this idle time, his thoughts again went back to Olwyn and his child, who must be nearing birth by now.

When the city was fully secured, the Redcloaks gathered all the prisoners for "processing." From the rumors Kam had heard, each of them would be briefly interviewed by some Imperial bureaucrat to determine if he was dangerous or could be placed in a work group. Once it was decided a prisoner could be assigned to a work group, they were herded into a further line for interviews where yet more bureaucrats decided whether they were placed in a manual labor or skilled labor group, which had further benefits like improved meals and housing.

When Kam reached the front of the line for his first interview, he was led into a white tent and sat down across from a pudgy, middle-aged man who read from a scroll without looking up.

Would you consider yourself a "die-hard" Vilbenian patriot?

What are your thoughts on the Alderian Empire?

Did you kill anyone during the war?

Before the war? If so, how many, and what were the circumstances of these killings?

If there was a sharp instrument within arm's reach, would you try and use it to stab me, slit my throat or otherwise do me harm?

Would any close friends or relatives characterize you as an angry person?

Ten minutes of questioning later, the bureaucrat placed a seal on a document and looked up at Kam for the first time. "Work group," he said, in the most perfunctory voice imaginable. A guard materialized and escorted Kam to the next line.

Back outside, Kam watched two Redcloaks sort through stacks of decomposing bodies. The men seemed to be interested in the cause of death of each and so, with every corpse, they'd roll it over, examining it until they found what they were looking for. When one of the men came upon a decapitated body of what looked to be a boy of no more than fourteen, he tapped the other man on the shoulder. "What do you think?" he said, using his scabbarded sword to gesture to the severed spine, which jutted out from the flesh of the corpse's neck.

"I don't know. Plague maybe?" the other said.

"Really? Plague you think? I was thinking that maybe he died of old age or something." Both men laughed.

A similar-looking bureaucrat conducted Kam's second interview in a tent identical to the first. Could he read? No. Could he write? No. Could he weave? No.

Five minutes in Kam heard someone enter the tent behind him. He made a quick turn and saw an old woman and a man of about his age. Each was dressed in a gray cloak. The old woman's skin was dark and, though her face was heavily wrinkled, there was a ferocity and alertness in her gaze that suggested someone in their prime. The young man was of lighter complexion and wore a beard the color of umber, which—seeing as the Alderian soldiers were all clean-shaven—confirmed he wasn't a Redcloak. The old woman whispered into the bureaucrat's ear. He nodded, rose from his chair and exited the tent. The young man brought an extra chair around to face Kam and the two newcomers sat down.

"Hello, Mr. Rhys," the old woman said and that fierceness he'd just seen melted into grandmotherly warmth. "My name is Szilvia, and this is Aron." The young man nodded.

The old woman went on. "We are not part of the Imperial administration, although from time to time we have worked with the Alderians on issues of mutual importance. Have you heard of Ilyeth?"

Kam couldn't contain his smirk. Every child who'd ever listened to old tales around a fire had heard of Ilyeth, mythical home to sorcerers.

The old woman's face transformed into a stern mask. "I will be direct in this matter. We are here because we want you to return to Ilyeth with us. To study."

"Me?" Kam said. "You must have the wrong man. I can't even read."

"An impediment to study, no doubt, but you can learn," she said.

"Why?"

"If you've heard of Ilyeth, then you have some idea of our business," the old woman said.

Now Kam *knew* they had the wrong man. "What? You're saying I'm a sorcerer?"

"Not yet," the younger man—this "Aron"—said, "but with time."

Kam wasn't buying any of this but played along. "What about my service to the Empire?"

"It can be arranged to have you released," Szilvia said.

"Arranged?"

She nodded.

"So what? The Empire has sold me to you?"

"Oh no," she said. "Nothing like that. You are free to come with us or not. If you stay, you will be left to the circumstances in which we found you."

"And if I come, how long must I remain with you?"

"I wouldn't look at it like that. Most who study do so for at least a few years, although many stay for longer. I have lived in Ilyeth for a long, long time. At the very least you would stay on the island for the first two years until you are promoted to apprentice. We wish for all of our students to gain a minimal competency with their…talents…before they are *let out into the wild.*"

"So you're telling me I'm a *sorcerer,* and if I go with you to *Ilyeth* to study, I will get out of my service to the Alderians?"

"You *will be* a sorcerer, but otherwise an excellent summary," Szilvia said. "We will make a fine student of you yet."

Certainly they had the wrong man, but maybe—just maybe—he would be able to use their mistake to his advantage. "And may I bring my wife with me? She is with child and I worry for her."

The two sitting across from Kam looked at one another. The young man seemed about to speak, but Szilvia cut him off. "Not for the first two years. However, I would note that our students all receive a healthy stipend. You could remit part of that sum to your wife, if you so choose."

Not ideal but an enticing proposition nonetheless. "And how long do I have to decide?"

They were departing in the morning, they said; he had until dawn.

That night he didn't sleep. He still didn't believe he was a sorcerer (or had the potential to be one), but it was clear there was a decision to be made. He didn't want to go so far away from Olwyn and his unborn child. Yet so long as he was stuck in an Imperial work camp, what difference did it make if he was a few days away or a thousand miles? And the extra money would undoubtedly help.

When he woke the next morning he told his jailer he needed to see Szilvia.

He'd decided to go.

VII

The house is mostly as he remembers: a narrow wooden building and three stories tall with a single large window on each floor. The house's security, on the other hand, has been significantly augmented. Surrounding the house is a ten-foot stone wall with a locked oak gate, itself encircled by a trench thirty feet across and ten-feet deep. Inside the trench are a few hundred tightly packed spears, lances and other sharp objects. The only way across is a retractable ladder-bridge that right now is pointing straight up to the sky. On the outside of the trench, nearest Kam, is a low wooden fence on which the words "Visitors Most Certainly Not Welcome" are written in pitch.

The last time he saw Old Rumalti must have been at least thirty years before, and even then, he had already been *Old* Rumalti for many years. Still, if he's alive, he might be able to tell him something about the stone.

Rumalti was never much of a sorcerer himself but has long been one of the foremost authorities on talismans, charms, and other objects with *sorcerous* properties. Rumalti left the Brotherhood sometime after being promoted to master and took up a solitary existence almost completely dedicated to the study, collecting, and cataloging of ancient artifacts. As far as Kam knows, Rumalti didn't have any specific problem with the Brotherhood; he just didn't like people in general.

He doesn't sense Rumalti inside; however, the old hermit was known to make a habit of concealing his presence with spells for the specific purpose of not being sensed. There's no bell or way to communicate with the house, so Kam just shouts.

"Rumalti! You in there?"

Nothing. He shouts a few more times and is getting ready to leave when the old man shouts back.

"I'm not here!"

"I need to talk to you."

"What part of 'not here' you not comprehend?"

"It's urgent. I have something I need to show you."

Across the trench, a small view hole opens in the gate and Kam can see the old man's squinting eyes. "Do I know you?"

"You know you know me."

"I don't *know* anything. I can barely see the difference between my dog and my foot anymore." The view hole is slammed shut. There is a brief pause and then the gate swings open. Rumalti, wearing a tattered sleeping gown and looking as decrepit as ever, comes out hobbling on a staff. He steps out beyond the wall and, with a key tied around his neck, unlocks a small metal wheel, which he turns, lowering the iron bridge to Kam's side of the trench.

The inside of the house doesn't seem to have changed much in recent decades, nor does it seem to have been cleaned in that time. A thick layer of dust covers most of the surfaces of the furniture, the floor.

From behind an old bookshelf, a mangy black dog with a half-missing ear pokes its head out and starts barking. "Don't mind that little yapper. That's just Ko-jeck," he says.

"What did you call him?"

"Ko-jeck."

"What kind of name is that?"

"I don't know. I've been dreaming a lot about a man named Ko-jeck, so when I found this little asshole, that's what I called him. You know, I've been having all kinds of odd dreams with this guy these last few years. I'd hope that if I was going to have a recurring dream that it would be something to do with me visiting a whorehouse or the like, but no. Instead, I have all of these boring dreams about some boring man named Ko-jek."

"Are they premonitions of some kind?"

"You think I don't know the difference between a dream and a premonition? You think they're just passing out those master sashes in Ilyeth for nothing? From what I remember, you never even got yours despite all that *greatest-Cree-in-generations* nonsense they were spewing back then. Look how all that turned out . . ."

"I didn't mean to offend," Kam says. Rumalti huffs.

They walk up one flight of stairs to Rumalti's office. The walls are lined with shelves, a few of which house leather-bound volumes, the others spilling over with ancient-looking items of every variety. One shelf seems to be reserved for weaponry: daggers, sabers, a halberd, two spears, the head of a battle axe, a broken broadsword, a mace; another shelf contains only armor: a green helmet made of a glass-like substance, a gauntlet with several bright jewels inlaid into it, an old cracked cuirass with a faded painting of a dragon on the chest; still another shelf contains jewelry: amulets and rings and bracelets of every size and shape, a crown of silver and jade leaves. Finally, a long table has a number of uncategorizable curios on it: a tiny brain in a jar floating in milky liquid, a large piece of scaled black hide that shimmers when the light hits it, a jar of beans, a golden egg, a copper-colored lamp, a golden horn, nine flat, golden triangles that fit together to form another, larger triangle.

The two men sit down in the only two chairs that don't have manuscripts or other items stacked on top of them. "Now what is it that you have to show me?" Rumalti says.

"A necklace. Or a jewel, rather—the necklace isn't important, I think. The jewel though . . . it seems central to a premonition I've been having, although I can't exactly figure out why."

"You talked to me some years ago about some premonition, right?"

"Yeah, same one."

"Speaking of which . . . You still got that silver dagger? *That* was a nice piece . . ."

"No . . . No, I don't."

"A shame," he says. "So what have you got?"

Kam pulls the necklace from his trousers' pocket and hands it to Rumalti.

Rumalti removes a monocle from a drawer and looks at it. "Well, the necklace is shit," he says. He rips the amulet off the necklace and throws the chain on the ground, "but this stone is something."

Kam bends over to scoop up the chain. "I think it belongs in a scepter," he says.

"Right-o, it does. This is quite an item. *Quite* an item. Now tell me: where'd you find such a thing?"

VIII

Kam and the two sorcerers boarded an Islander trade vessel, whose name translated to The Coral Snake, and which flew enormous, pitch-black sails. They embarked from the harbor in Hammer Bay and set out to sea for a day before turning back inland along the Wyr to begin, what seemed then to Kam, the impossibly long journey.

The voyage was pleasant enough. Meals were regular and Kam wasn't expected to do much work. The first mate assigned him a small cot in the crew's quarters, which, while cramped, was reasonably comfortable when he situated his body upon it in the right way. The crew themselves emanated a slightly sour smell, but months in the tent city had accustomed him to worse.

Most of the crew only spoke their guttural-sounding Islander tongue so Kam mostly kept to himself. Szilvia and Aron were onboard yet seldom left their cabins.

He had been away from his wife for the better part of a year, but now that the war was over and he had time on his hands, he missed her more than ever and spent most of those days' idleness second-guessing his choice to go with Szilvia and Aron. By now, the baby would have surely been born, but it would be a long time before Kam would see it. This way, at least, he'd be able to send coin home. That was something, wasn't it? He had told her as much in the letter he'd had the scribe write just before they set sail. As Szilvia had instructed, he hadn't mentioned Ilyeth or the Cree and instead just vaguely explained that he'd been selected to work at a school in Port Marlton, a city on the southeast coast of the Inner Sea.

During the final days of this first leg of their voyage, Kam began seeing more of Aron aboard the ship—outside the galley during meals, standing on the deck on one of the many pleasant evenings. By now Kam was starved for conversation, and for the last three days of the river voyage the two men spent whatever free time they had sitting on the deck chatting and watching the lush, green landscapes of Nyrribia move slowly past.

During one of their first lengthy conversations, Aron explained he was from a town called Xanthas, a few day's ride from *the capital* (which Kam discovered was what people within the Empire called Alder). Aron mentioned the town was "only slightly bigger than Hammer Bay," a fact that astonished Kam; he could hardly imagine *anything* bigger, much less calling such a place merely a "town." They spoke of their earlier lives and Aron took great interest in Kam's time as a fisherman and his voyages to the distant south. Kam couldn't help noticing that anytime the conversation went to Olwyn, a look of discomfort crossed Aron's face.

"Are *you* married?" Kam asked once.

"No. Few of us are."

"Why's that?"

"I can't say for sure," Aron said. "Perhaps we realize how different we are from other people and so…those differences make things…difficult."

"In my opinion," Kam said, "marriage and family are the greatest blessing. Nothing makes me happier than the thought of my child. I pray the baby and my wife are both healthy and prospering."

To this, Aron only nodded, halfheartedly, in agreement.

They disembarked at a village located on the banks of a lake at the river's source. The village's structures were all flat-roofed, rectangular buildings made of identical stone blocks. Most of the crew remained with the ship. After a night in the house of a seamstress that served as the village inn, they hired horses and a wagon and embarked on the balance of their journey west. According to Aron, it was another five weeks overland to the coastline of the Inner Sea, after which time it would be a two-day voyage to Ilyeth.

After they crossed the Riffel, which, hundreds of miles to the north, eventually bisected the Imperial capital, the landscape changed. This country was far dryer: Calembere's Desert, Aron called it. It was not the sandy deserts of stories; instead, it was a vast, dry grassland that stretched on and on, endlessly into the quiet distance.

In the evenings now, Szilvia would wander off for a few hours away from the wagon and their camp, and it was during this time that Kam and Aron continued their conversations.

"What is it that she does every night?" Kam asked once.

"*Meditate*, might be the best word," he said. "Szilvia is very talented with what we call *premonitions*, but even for someone like her, they require a great deal of focus and quiet."

"Premonitions? Like fortune telling?"

"Yes and no. It's more like having a vision. It's complicated. They will teach you about it when you arrive at the Sanctum."

"Could she possibly tell me anything about Olwyn? Would she know if my child is alive and healthy?"

"She might . . .," Aron said.

"What is it? Do *you* know something?"

Aron frowned to himself. "I am not sure how to say this," he began, "but no Cree has ever sired a child. Ever. Such a thing is impossible. In all our history there has never been a documented case. You have heard the tales, no doubt? *The Childless Ones* they call us."

"Yes, but . . . I didn't think . . . Maybe I'm not really a Cree," he said. He thought then of all the times he had lain with his wife and all the lovemaking and planting his seed in her womb and how she never became with child. "I knew from the start that you were mistaken about that. It's ridiculous, really. *Me*, a sorcerer? I only wish we could have figured this out before we'd traveled so—"

"There's no mistake," Aron said. There was a kind of resignation in the upward curl of his mouth. "When I look at you, I sense the meridians flowing through you in the way that can only mean you are a Cree. And powerful too. A *natural.*"

Kam wanted to protest further but knew Aron told the truth.

What saddened him most was the loss of the child—*his* child, his impossible child.

He spent the night mentally filing through the various letters he could dictate and send Olwyn when he arrived in Ilyeth: angry, cold, pretend ignorance, pretend understanding, vengeful, forgiving. They were all insufficient, dishonest. The only way he might communicate what he felt in his heart would be to send them all.

Four days later they reached Port Marlton, a town on the coast of the Inner Sea where most of the traffic to and from Ilyeth passed through. This was also the place where any unofficial correspondences to Ilyeth were sent. Aron explained that, while the existence of the Ilyan Brotherhood was known amongst high-ranking Alderian officials, for the most part, having some kind of front allowed the Brotherhood to continue as a secret to the masses, which in turn allowed them to go about their affairs more freely.

They entered the town, whose colorful houses and immaculate streets gave the place an air of affluence, and Szilvia had the wagon driven to the messenger's office. Kam and Aron waited outside the impressive gray-stoned building, with its large windows of colored glass, as Szilvia went inside. When the old women came out, she carried a stack of envelopes, scrolls, and other documents.

"Anything for me?" Aron said. Szilvia extricated a cream-colored envelope from the stack.

"No," she said, and handed the envelope to Kam.

He examined the battered letter like it was some strange artifact whose use he couldn't discern. He couldn't read the words written on it, but recognized the script as Olwyn's hand.

"How did this arrive here ahead of us?" Kam said.

"Of all the things we can do," Szilvia said, "speeding up the mail is perhaps the least impressive."

At the inn that evening, after they had supped on a luxurious meal of roasted chicken, potatoes and sweet pie, Kam took the letter to Aron's room. He found the sorcerer reading by the light of a single candle.

"Are you sure you want me to read it?" he said. "You could hire a scribe in town. If you haven't the coin, I can lend it to you. It may be easier to have someone you don't know—"

"No," Kam said. "You."

He nodded and opened the sealed envelope with a small blade he kept in his suitcase.

He unfolded the letter. "My dear husband," he started, his eyes darting over the page, ahead of where he was reading. He paused, cleared his throat and started again.

"'My dear husband. I hope this letter finds you in good health and that you had a safe journey west. It's not my wish for you to start your new work with such ill news, but I can't allow you to go on working and sending coin home under false pretenses. There is no delicate way of saying this, so I will come out with it. While you have been away I have been unfaithful to you and lain with another man.

"'Were it that this act took place after you were away for many months, maybe I could find it within myself to seek forgiveness. That is not what occurred. My sins took place after little time had passed, before any of the fighting had started, and for this I am especially ashamed.

"'I love you still, not that the word means anything from the likes of me, and could I hide my mistakes from you, maybe I would try. Yet two weeks ago the baby was born and, from the first time I beheld it, it was obvious to me, as it would be obvious to you, that it is not your child.

"'Please do not send money home. It would deepen my shame to accept anything from you now. I shall find a way to get by.

"'Goodbye, my love. Maybe we will do better in another life. Yours, Olwyn.'"

The two men sat wordless for a time. "There is a postscript," Aron said.

Kam looked up from where his gaze had been fixed upon his shoes. "All right."

"Here it is. 'Postscript. If it seems odd I have given you no details about the child, know that I have done this to protect you. I know you wanted a child very much and I thought that knowing about this baby that is not yours might cause further hurt.'"

"Is that it?"

Aron nodded and held the letter out to him.

"No," Kam said. "Burn it."

IX

Rumalti listens to the story for some hours. When it's over, the old master gets up with a groan to make tea; he tells Kam he's never seen a stone like this or the scepter that it belongs to, but he's read about them. "They're old," he says. "Do you take honey?"

"No honey...Older than you even?" Kam says.

Rumalti grabs his crotch and shifts his hips in Kam's direction. "Not quite that old. More like back to the time when I fucked your mother and sired you, you little shit. Like near a thousand years old. To the time of the Forefathers."

"You believe in them?" Kam says. Downstairs that mangy dog is barking its head off.

"If you're asking me whether I believe that long ago there were beings that created some powerful shit we still don't understand, then yes. If you want to call them the Forefathers, fine. If you want to call them the Fuckhead Brigade—"

"So what does it do?"

"Nothing much without one of those scepters you're dreaming about. Maybe that little trick you talked about with preserving a dead body, but it seems pretty clear that no scepter equals no real nothing."

"What about with one?"

"It's probably some kind of weapon. Everything always ends up being a weapon," Rumalti says.

"But how then does it fit into the premonition? I've already given the dagger to Pa-Zhe—"

"Pa what?"

"The dark-skinned man in the premonition. He studied in Ilyeth after you'd left already. In any event, it was the other man—the man in red—who had the stone and scepter."

"Shit all if I know. Interpreting premonitions isn't my thing. You should ask Szilvia...Oh that's right, she'd probably have you executed."

Kam ignored this. "What if I wanted to get my hands on one of these scepters?"

"Go back in time five hundred years or so."

"Your helpfulness amazes."

"If you could easily get your hands on one of these things, I'd already have one. I've been to nearly every set of Forefather-era ruins on the Continent."

"Nearly?"

"There are a few that are underwater now, which...luck to you if you want to figure that out. Other than that, the only one I know about that I've never visited is in the catacombs beneath the capital."

"There must be a good reason you've never been there."

"Reason? Yes. But not a good one. Those Imperial jackasses blocked all the entrances a hundred years ago because they felt it was a *security risk* allowing anyone into tunnels that connect to the palace. Idiots. You know what was a security risk? Colonizing and pissing on the whole Continent until someone got fed up with their crap, fought back, and burned half the world. But why am I telling *you*? You know more about all that than I do."

X

He decided to try and forget her.

He had a new life on this wondrous island and was determined to make the most of it. He was assigned a room in the lowest level of the Sanctum and his studies began immediately. There were a few other students who'd recently arrived with whom Kam was placed into a cohort. Mostly these others were children between ten and sixteen who spent their free time playing games in the Sanctum's courtyard or plotting tricks on one another; Kam kept to himself.

Now that they were back in Ilyeth, Aron was busy with his own duties but occasionally, the two men descended the hill into the white city below to enjoy ale together. Aron took quite an interest in Kam's studies and Kam, for his part, liked hearing Aron reminisce about when he first came to the island. It was Arch-Master Githault herself, Aron told him, who had discovered him.

"But that's all ancient history now," Aron said.

"How old were you?" Kam asked.

"Older than most. Eighteen or so."

"Couldn't have been *that* long ago then."

"Nearly forty years now," Aron said.

Cree aged differently than other men, but Kam had still always assumed he and Aron were roughly the same age; if what Aron said was true, then he was older than Kam's own father would have been.

Other than conversing with Aron from time to time, the only thing Kam did for leisure was occasionally watch the ensembles that played in the Hall of Music in town. On The Finger his exposure to music was limited to the occasional traveling lute player or else the songs he and his fellow sailors sung, inexpertly, on the deck of their fishing boat. To use the same word, *music*, for what these marvelous players in Ilyeth did felt an injustice. Sometimes there would be as many as twenty of them, with their fiddles and harps and horns, the sounds mixing together to create something otherworldly.

In general, it was a regimented life —although nothing more difficult than being a laborer or sailor on The Finger. The early morning hours were dedicated to the practice of sorcery, and these sessions took place exclusively with Kam's cohort of newcomers. The rest of the day was reserved for the more traditional studies of history, arithmetic and literature. Though Kam was the oldest of his cohort and nearly the oldest of all of the students he saw, he was far behind in terms of academic learning and would often be placed with the youngest children or a private tutor for reading or numbers. That said, Kam's former life had taught him how to work tirelessly. He quickly gained mastery over the *meridians,* the name the Brothers gave for the invisible channels of energy from which a Cree's powers were derived, and he excelled at the various combinations and spells. After only a few months, he was reading also, and he began spending his evenings poring through history and philosophy texts in the library. It was during this time that Kam first learned in earnest about premonitions; he began to wonder whether his own recurring dream was one of these.

Now, even in his waking hours, he would play out the scene in his mind: the small, dark-skinned man stabbing the man in red with his silver dagger...the feeling of elation...the small man going through the belongings of his slain adversary...the scepter...the light.

A year after arriving in Ilyeth, Kam approached Szilvia about his dream. That morning he woke early and climbed the winding stone stairs to her chamber. He wasn't technically forbidden from going to these levels, but he'd never been so high in the Sanctum. Before he could knock on her door, the old woman called out.

"Enter."

Szilvia was amongst the highest-ranking *Brothers* (an antiquated term, some claimed, that they used even for the women) and could have had whatever luxuries she desired. She lived a simple existence though, and her chamber contained no furniture save a single wardrobe and a plain wooden desk and chair. There wasn't even a bed, as Szilvia preferred sleeping on a thin straw mat lain in the corner of the room.

"What can I help you with?" she said once she rose from her position seated on the large rug situated in the center of the room.

Kam explained his dream to Szilvia and the woman nodded. When he was through, she admitted it might very well be a premonition of some sort, but that he ought to forget about interpreting it for now. Interpreting premonitions was the sole province of the masters. "You'll be there soon enough," she said. This was a less than satisfying answer for Kam, but there was nothing else to be done.

During his time in Ilyeth, another sort of dream plagued him as well—dreams of Olwyn. These, he was quite sure, were *not* premonitions; they lacked that indefinable quality the other dream had. One of these that recurred often was of Olwyn forcing him to watch her make love to other men—men from their village, men he had known at Hammer Bay, Aron even. The location of this dream was always different: in their old house, on a boat, in the Sanctum. Sometimes the baby would be present, other times not. Despite the distress these dreams caused him, Kam simultaneously found them arousing, such that he would sometimes force himself to recall them when he was in his room alone at night.

By the time his first two years in Ilyeth had passed, Kam was a transformed man. He was promoted to apprentice, awarded his gray cloak, and given a ring of amethyst to mark him as the most distinguished member of his cohort. He was a learned man now; he could recite the emperors going back several hundred years and knew the histories of all the nations of the Continent. He was passable in Eyasu, the Islander tongue, and Lanzhenese, and had even gained a rudimentary proficiency in Old Alderian, which had a reputation of being the most difficult language on the Continent. Further, he was lauded in his efforts assisting one of the masters with compiling and cataloging much of the mostly-forgotten lore involving the Mandrakhar.

Overshadowing all of Kam's academic accomplishments were his abilities with sorcery. Whereas many of the newly anointed apprentices struggled to use the meridians to throw stones further than they could with their own hands, Kam could, with the flick of his wrist, hurl medium-sized boulders across a field fifty paces long. The area, however, where he showed truly exceptional talent was with mage fire. Mage fire wasn't really fire at all but energy, light and heat, blue intertwined with green, that could cause even the least flammable objects to burn. Many of the masters, even, could not summon up much more than a flicker of the stuff, whereas Kam could manipulate it as if it were an extension of his body. On festival nights, the younger students would all petition him to go out to the beaches and put on one of his magnificent displays, where the mage fire, far from anything it might burn, would dance into a million shapes before the awestruck children. It was tiring work, but the looks on the students' faces made the endeavor worth it.

Kam's progress had given him a new confidence. He wasn't exactly happy, but he had gained a kind of relief through his studies. And so, when his two years were up, the decision to stay on was easy. Due to his fast progress, the rank of master might be attainable in another few years. Some even thought he'd break the legendary Brother Azkhar Aramayo's record for speed of promotion to master.

He moved to a room in one of the higher floors of the Sanctum: supposedly an honor but to Kam an inconvenience; he was one more floor removed from the library. The only other member of the Brotherhood whose studiousness came anywhere close to Kam's was an ancient (and most would say *crotchety*) master named Rumalti, who seldom spoke and would scowl at anyone who made noise.

Time passed swiftly, and it was in his seventh year in Ilyeth that something took place that once again changed the course of Kam's life. At the time, he had still not been promoted to master, although it was clear to most that he met the necessary criteria and that it was only the arch-masters' desire not to set new precedent that delayed him. Aron was up for promotion soon as well, and it was a running joke between the two friends that Aron might reach the milestone first, given his four-decade head start.

According to its official credo, the Brotherhood was not to get embroiled in the political affairs of nations. At the same time, political stability was to be sought for the greatest overall good; so Ilyan Brothers would often advise leaders across the Continent. Political discussions were common amongst the apprentices. It was during one such discussion with Aron and a few of the older apprentices, drinking the hot brown drink that had become Kam's favorite (*Dirt-Tea* or just *Dirty*), that Kam learned of what had transpired on The Finger.

"Yes," Romen, one of the apprentices who always seemed to be wearing a blue tunic, said, "that whole area has been overrun by pirates: fields burned, men killed, women raped. The leader of the group calls himself the Bandit King or something—as if he couldn't come up with a more creative name. They say the Alderians have tried to re-take the place, but they've been beaten back and slaughtered at every turn."

"That's probably going to do hell to fish prices," Quentyen, another of the apprentices said. "By the way, aren't you from those parts, Kam?"

XI

The incessant rain makes the journey north a slow, muddy affair, and it takes him two weeks of cold, wet travel to reach the capital from Rumalti's house outside of Brigantium.

When he arrives, he takes a room in a Draycott boarding house. The neighborhood is unsavory, its population made up in large part of prostitutes, Islanders in the ameghemite trade, and other criminal elements. Amongst such a crowd it is less likely he will accidentally run into one of the Brothers or anyone else who might be aware of the price on his head.

Over the following week, he keeps a low profile, traveling around mostly early in the early morning and at night, discreetly contacting his sources to see if any of them know of a way into the catacombs beneath the palace. After several days of little progress, Kam learns that a petty criminal and smuggler named Sylas Nottle might know of a route.

Sylas's house is a long walk from the boarding house but is situated in a similarly shoddy neighborhood north of the river called Brogan's Alley. Kam is let in the house by a pale, underfed man who must be Sylas's house servant. The house has a strong odor: a combination of burning ameghemite and perspiration. The servant leads Kam downstairs to a dimly lit room and excuses himself. When Kam sees Sylas—his eyes purple from the powder, his mouth full of rotten shards of teeth—he has half a mind to put him out of his misery after he gets his information. In the end, he decides it wouldn't be worth the risk of calling attention to himself.

After negotiating an exorbitant price, Sylas produces an old map of

Broadhaven, which he unfurls upon the large, circular table in the middle of the room. If the map is accurate, then one of the old canals in that area leads to an ancient sewer system beneath Center City. If he then follows the sewer to its end, there is eventually a tunnel on the left that leads to the catacombs.

"Goodbye, I hope we never cross paths again," Kam says as he departs Sylas's den.

"The feeling's mutual," the other hisses.

That night, Kam steals one of the flat-bottomed water taxis parked in the river docks and rows himself to the canal. Following the map by moonlight, he rows down a waterway and enters a tunnel that burrows into a cliff overlooking the river. Even during the day, these tunnels would be dark, but at night, when no sunlight filters through the sewer grates above, the tunnels are thick, syrupy, blackness. He casts a lantern spell.

When he finds the turn-off, he gets out of the boat and proceeds on foot. At this point the map no longer details the way, and Kam walks for some time back and forth through the tunnels. It is nearly daybreak, he guesses, by the time he arrives at what he seeks: a huge archway made of blue-gray stone. The words are written in Old Alderian, but he knows enough to translate:

For the glory of those who come from above!

XII

It took little effort for him to get past the Alderian lines at the entrance to the canyon. The Redcloaks were concerned with protecting against the pirates launching an assault from The Finger, not with preventing a lone man from entering the occupied peninsula. The pirates themselves had posted guards a few miles into the canyon, but these Kam also passed with a simple concealment spell. He could have slit the guards' throats with little effort, but in those days, he wasn't yet so quick to kill.

The night was dark and starless, but all along the beaches great fires burned, giving a hellish, red haze to all the land from the shore up the hill to where the canyon opened up upon The Finger. In the firelight, Kam saw his home was greatly changed. Many of the largest trees had been felled for kindling. The animal pens were empty and on Farmer Gilen's pasture, there wasn't a cow or sheep to be found. The fields where crops should grow were untended, and many were overrun with wild grass and weeds.

When he got to the house he removed his key, which he'd kept all these years, from inside his cloak. There was no need; the lock on the door had been broken and where the door handle had been was now just a hole. He nudged the door open and stepped inside. By habit, he turned left to the room that had been theirs.

Olwyn sat quietly, propped up in bed. It was dark and she didn't stir when he took a step towards her, so he wasn't sure she'd seen him. He stood still now, not wanting to startle her.

"Am I dead?" she said, startling *him* instead.

"Not unless I am too."

"Then it's really you?" He nodded. "You've changed."

"Yes," he said. Now he cast a spell to light the candle beside her bed.

"How'd you do that?" she said. Up close, he barely recognized her. She was frail, her clothes like loose rags hanging from a skeleton. Her reddish-brown hair had been cut off roughly, as if by a sword. On her arms he could see at least a half-dozen places where she'd been burned. As he took inventory of her, a fury welled up inside him—not a wild, uncontrollable thing: instead, a force focused into a kind of resolve. He stepped towards her and stooped down to kiss her on the temple.

"Is the child here?" he said.

"Boy."

He'd always imagined it'd been a boy. "Boy then."

"In the other room."

"Stay here with him until I return," he said.

"They killed him, you know."

"Who?"

"The boy's father."

He thought about this. "Just do as I say. Stay here."

"These are *terrible* men. They'll kill you."

"Stay here," he said.

Her face made the contortions of crying, but no tears or sounds accompanied the expression. "I'm sorry," she said.

He turned to leave, but then turned back to her. "I forgive you." He had not been planning to say the words, but there they were, out in the world. He left the house in search of those responsible for all this.

The Bandit King was a massive man with a large barrel chest and a belly to match. His muscled arms were covered in crudely drawn tattoos of naked women and sea monsters. He wore a long beard that went down to the middle of his chest and his mane was a tangled, gray-black mess. For a time,

Kam watched, by the dull light of the candle he'd lit when he came in, over the slumbering man lying in bed. This house had been that of the village doctor. He'd had a talkative wife and seven daughters, the oldest of which had been around Kam's age. There was no sign of any of them now.

Kam removed his cloak, unbuckled the blade at his waist, and set them on the dresser.

"Wake up," he said. The sleeping man groaned. "Wake up," he said again, louder, and this time the Bandit King shot up in bed. There was alarm and confusion in his face, but he didn't shout, nor did he reach for the dagger lying on the floor beside him. His eyes were bloodshot, and Kam suspected he'd fallen asleep drunk.

"How'd you get past the guards?" He spoke in a surprisingly sophisticated accent.

"Does it matter?"

"Who are you? Alderian assassin?"

"No. Just a man."

"A dead man, then," the Bandit King said. "Why don't you tell me your business before I introduce your throat to my blade."

"First *your* name," Kam said. For all the confidence he'd gained in Ilyeth, his voice quavered a little.

"They call me the Bandit—"

"I know what they call you. What's your real name?" He'd gathered himself, and now his voice spoke with the power and effect he was going for.

"Jimner. Or Jim if you will."

"Jim. Do you know Olwyn? Red-headed woman, lives up the hill?"

Jim gave a confused look, but then something clicked and he smiled.

"She's my wife," Kam said.

Jim burst out into laughter.

"What's funny?"

"You're upset with *me*? When we arrived here the whole town offered her up as the village whore. She was fucking a lot of folks prior to *us* landing ashore."

"Call your guards in here," Kam said.

Jim looked at Kam as if trying to figure out what he was up to. "Raz...Egen," he shouted then. Two men came into the house; as soon as they saw Kam, they drew their knives.

"Who the fuck's this?" one of them said.

"Angry husband come to air his grievances," Jim said.

"What should we do?" the other guard said and Jim, still in bed, gave a questioning look to Kam.

"You fancy yourself a fighter, I hear," Kam said. "Surely, *Bandit King*, you can dispatch a simple unarmed fisherman."

Jim pointed at Kam. "I like you. You're an idiot...who is about to be a *dead* idiot, but I like you. Let's go outside. No need to dirty the rugs."

Kam, the Bandit King, and the guards left the house and walked to a small clearing. The village was quiet, though the fires on the beaches still burned bright. The Bandit King put on a mail shirt and unsheathed a silver dagger with runes written along the blade. Kam immediately recognized the weapon. One of the guards handed Kam a blade of his own, but as soon as he took it, he threw it back on the ground.

"You are crazy," Jim said.

"Where did you get *your* dagger?"

"From inside your wife's pussy," he said and spat on the ground. The guards laughed. "You ready? I want to get a little more sleep before daybreak."

He nodded.

The Bandit King charged, but before he could take two steps, Kam cast a spell, the energy surging through his fingertips, gripping the fine chains of his assailant's mail shirt and stopping him mid-stride.

Jim looked down, perplexed, and then he shouted in animal panic. Kam chanted the words to help himself concentrate, and the mail shirt contracted into a ball. Jim screamed and collapsed onto the ground in a pile of blood and bones and gore.

The two guards stared at Kam for an instant. One of them charged. The pirate burst into green mage fire and fell screaming onto the ground. The remaining man looked upon Kam with horror. "Tell the others," Kam said. "Those who are still here at dawn will get the same. If any harm is done to anyone else in this village, I will kill the lot of you."

The frightened man nodded and ran off. Kam knelt down for a moment to regain himself. A moment later, he walked over to the Bandit King's mangled remains and removed the scabbard strapped to what had been his ribs. His blade had been dropped, and Kam picked it up. There was no doubt that this was the same blade from the dream. He sheathed it in its scabbard and walked up the hill away from the fires that still burned on the beaches.

⚓

Dawn had just broken when the pirates' longboats cast off from the docks. Kam watched from the hill overlooking the village. He had thought some of the pirates would try and stay behind, yet this was not the case; to a man they fled. One might surmise Kam would feel a kind of relief at seeing them all go; his wife was safe; his home was free—insofar as an Alderian province could be free. But there was no relief. Two lives were insufficient to repay what had happened here, and so, when two of the longboats seemed to stall against the waves not far from the docks, Kam resolved that a more equitable justice be meted out.

Many of the villagers had awakened as the bandits departed, and they watched as the longboats of their tormenters sailed off against the tide. Had the Empire finally delivered them from this terror? It wasn't until they saw a great winged beast—a dragon come out of the Far Wastes, some surmised, made of green and blue fire, lighting up the dawn sky (not unlike a creature that was known to grace the skies over Ilyeth on festival evenings, although they didn't know this)—that they concluded that their salvation was the work of the gods. And when the dragon plunged towards the surface of the water and struck the two nearest longboats, exploding them into a million shards of burnt wood and scorched flesh, the villagers all said that the wrath of the gods was fair and just.

When he returned to the house, nauseous and near collapse from exertion, Kam found Olwyn sleeping in the bedroom. Let her sleep, he thought, and walked into the front room to lie down on the wooden floor. He shouldn't feel any guilt. What he had done had been righteous; they deserved worse. And yet...He reached to his side to feel the dagger, unsheathed it, and held it up above his reclined body to examine the blade. It was destiny that he should have this thing, he thought.

With the blade still held aloft, Kam became aware of the boy watching him from the other room. He had her nose, but the eyes and the hair and the cheekbones must be of the father. He re-sheathed the blade.

"Your mother didn't tell me your name earlier," he said.

The boy was silent at first, but after a half minute opened his mouth, a single word. "Benedictus."

"A foreign name, is it? Imperial?"

"Yes, my father said that it is a good name now that we are part of the Empire. Everyone calls me Ben."

"Ben. I like the sound of that better." He got up and stood facing the boy. "Do you miss your father?"

Ben shrugged his shoulders.

"Did he used to stay with you and your mother? At night?"

"He visited sometimes."

"Was he a kind man? To you and your mother?"

"Sometimes he was kind, and sometimes he was unkind. But it doesn't matter. The bad men took him away and he won't ever return."

Kam nodded.

"Kam," said his wife from the other direction, the bedroom door now open. There was heaviness in her face. "What have you done?' she said.

He was unsure what he was talking about but then looked down and realized his cloak was covered in the Bandit King's insides. He was too exhausted to do anything about it though. He fell asleep there on the wood floor.

When he woke he found himself naked except for his small clothes, a few strides from where he'd originally fallen asleep, with a blanket over him. It was evening again—he'd slept the entire day.

"I cleaned you up a bit," Olwyn said. She was standing over by the stove. The boy, Ben, was sitting at the table looking at him as if he were some rare and dangerous species of bird.

"Thank you."

"I would have brought you to the bed, but you were too heavy."

He got up and stumbled over to the bedroom. His body ached all over and he was still a little dizzy; he'd never before done so much sorcery in one day. His old clothes were still folded neatly in the bedroom chest. When he'd dressed, he returned to the front room to eat. Olwyn had cooked up the few remaining potatoes and carrots she'd been hiding into a stew.

"Things will be better now," Kam said to the two of them as they ate. Olwyn nodded; the boy was silent.

That night after Ben went to bed, the re-united husband and wife sat before the fire for many hours and he told her everything that had happened since he left those years before. What had taken place at Hammer Bay, how after the war he had not been given a job in Port Marlton, but instead had gone to Ilyeth. He told of his studies, of his return, and of what he had done to the Bandit King and the pirates.

This last bit she did not want to believe; yet all of the evidence was there. The cheering and celebrating in the village that had continued all day and into the evening could be heard even this far up the hill.

The next day, the Redcloaks marched back into The Finger. No one knew precisely what had happened; although, once the Bandit King's mutilated corpse was found, rumors of all sorts started to float about. Some claimed a sorcerer had come and slain the Bandit King. Others said he had been betrayed by one of his own. Yet others claimed they had seen a dragon fly into the village and crush him with its giant claws. Kam himself only heard of these rumors second-hand through Olwyn. He was remaining inside the house, as he didn't want to raise any suspicions by reappearing just as the pirates were mysteriously chased off. After two days, Kam made his first appearance, armed with a story: he had been waiting behind the Redcloak lines and only after order had been restored did he dare return.

It had been his plan to remain only for a short time—perhaps a week to help get things back to normal—before making the long trek back to Ilyeth. Yet as the days passed, Olwyn kept coming up with reasons for him to stay: the house needed repairs, wouldn't he help her fix the sheep fence, she felt safer with him in the house.

At first, Ben would acknowledge Kam's presence only when he spoke directly to him, but days turned to weeks and then Kam had been back a month and Ben started warming up to this strange man. They began taking walks down to the village and to the docks when Olwyn was cooking their evening meal. On one such occasion, they went down to the shore, to the series of large stones, which stretched out into the water.

"Follow me," he told the boy.

After the first few stones, Ben's legs were too short for him to leap from one stone to the next. Kam would jump first and then catch the boy after each jump, pulling him into the safety of his arms. When the two reached the farthest stone, they sat for a while with their backs to the coastline.

"Before I left The Finger I used to be a fisherman."

"Oh."

"Have you been on a boat?"

"Once. With my father."

"And what did you think?"

He shrugged.

"You should know your way around a boat. I'm only passably good, but perhaps I can find a boat and we can sail together. Would you like that?"

Ben hesitated and then said, "Yes."

Two months after he'd arrived in the town, Kam moved from sleeping on the floor to sharing Olwyn's bed again. With the exception of those few times that she wept and he put his arm around her, they never touched. He wondered what she wept for—her dead lover, what had happened to her, or what she'd done to him. Once, when the crying didn't stop in the usual time, he whispered for her to close her eyes. She scooted herself towards him in the bed, her back against his beating heart, her legs in the cradle of his own. He placed his hand on her left temple and mouthed the words of a spell. He concentrated, brought the memory out, a treasure buried beneath the sea, and gave it to her.

They were in the Hall of Music in Ilyeth. The music started with just a harp and a fiddle, but eventually they were joined by one horn and then another and then another and then the massive drumbeat in the background. Thwoom, thwoom, thwoom. At last, there was a voice, a woman's voice, rising out from amidst all the instruments like a star in the night.

"Isn't it wonderful?" he said.

"Yes," she said.

The seasons changed. Kam never committed to staying, but it became assumed he would. Were he willing to use his sorcery, he would have easily been able to earn a healthy living, but he was hesitant. He didn't want to stand out.

He had no interest in going back to fishing. He had been gone from Olwyn and didn't want to leave her or, to tell the truth, the boy, alone. He went back to being a laborer, moving supplies and helping make routine boat repairs. The work was hard, and the years in Ilyeth had made him unaccustomed to physical labor. Every day when he returned to the house his body ached, yet he was happy. There was something invigorating about being tired from an honest day's work.

Occasionally, he would still use the things he'd learned in Ilyeth in subtle ways. He might cast a spell into the ground to encourage the plants in the garden to grow or else help lift some of the especially large beams when they decided to add a room to the house, but these were the exceptions rather than the rule. Mostly he was just a normal man again—and he took a kind of pleasure in this. Part of him knew that all this wouldn't last forever; there was, after all, still the matter of the dream, that dagger he'd found on the Bandit King. Eventually destiny would come calling; he hoped though that it would take its time.

XIII

The vastness of the catacombs cannot be overstated. Tunnel intersects with tunnel intersects with tunnel, at the end of which is a tightly spiraling staircase leading down to another equally vast, equally dark network of tunnels on the level below. In places, the passageways open up into cavernous rooms whose walls and ceilings are lined with what once must have been ornate stonework but has deteriorated into a mere suggestion of a long-faded magnificence. The rooms occasionally contain the remains of furniture—a table, a chair, a divan—or else some device of gears and tiny metal capillaries whose use Kam cannot guess.

The only chance he has of effectively searching these catacombs is to keep track of which tunnels and rooms he has searched. Within one of the smaller rooms, he finds a few sheets of ancient, crackling parchment and a quill but cannot locate anything that might work as ink. He tries using the filthy water that pools in places on the tunnel floor, but this dries unevenly and, at times, invisibly. He can only think of one other thing to use.

He does not fear the pain yet is squeamish about inflicting it himself. He looks away as he runs his knife along the top of his left forearm. He lets the blood gather, a small puddle of viscous drops, on the stone floor before dabbing the quill in it and beginning to write.

On the second day, he finds what he will call the *map room*. Two levels below the entrance to the catacombs, he enters a small enclosure with floor and walls and ceiling all made from some variety of metal. Along the walls, everywhere except the two doorways on opposite sides of the room, are panels covered with levers and switches. Above the levers and switches, at odd intervals, are black rectangles, like portrait frames made of darkened glass. In the exact center of the room is a large circular table.

One by one, he tries each of the levers and switches. Nothing ever happens. He tries some of the many possible combinations. Still nothing. He is wasting his time, but he continues anyway. Finally, after one particular permutation, a low humming sound emanates from the wall. He thinks he feels a breeze on his forehead. Leaving the switches on, he tries each of the other levers again. He is just about complete with this task when the circular table in the middle of the room comes alive with light.

Floating above the table is an unidentifiable illuminated sculpture. Kam reaches out to touch it, but his hand passes through as if it were a ghost, the spirit of a sculpture. Eventually, he realizes it isn't a sculpture at all, but a map of the Continent. The reason he didn't initially recognize it is that east was facing up, rather than right. He tilts his head ninety degrees; it's obvious now. His eyes scan to where the capital should be and he sees a bright blue spark. There are other, duller, blue specks as well. He runs his knife against his forearm and spends the next several hours detailing this map as best he can.

Five days later, Kam finishes exploring what he believes to be the final tunnel in the catacombs. He feels as though his eyes have never seen any but the unnatural illumination of his lantern spells. His forearms show a score of slices, although all but the most recent of the wounds have scabbed over.

He has filled two large burlap sacks with items and artifacts he gathered: a large, nearly completely circular metal helmet, what looks to be an ancient crossbow, a set of copper lenses that he thinks one is supposed to wear and which extend out from the face when you turn a crank at the wearer's temple, books. No scepter.

The most important thing he will bring out of the tunnels though is the map of his own making. Of this, he is already sure.

XIV

The inhabitants of The Finger rebuilt. The fishing boats once again set off on their voyages south, the farmers replanted their crops, and the Redcloaks reconstructed the Imperial garrison by the docks. Kam kept his job as a laborer and by summer, Olwyn had sufficiently regained her own health to take on work at the dry-goods store.

Kam began schooling the boy—first just to count sums and to read, and eventually in the histories of the lands and the politics of the Empire. The boy was smart, like his mother, and by autumn he was reading entire books on his own. He particularly loved writing and any time he could get his hands on a sheet of parchment he'd cover both sides with his thoughts or with stories he'd imagined up from nothing. Months went by and Kam forgot his life in Ilyeth. Sometimes it felt that he had never left The Finger— that he had always lived here with his wife and son.

It was on a snowy day that next winter, nearly a year after Kam had returned, that he was reminded of his days in Ilyeth.

That day, Kam was off from work, and so he and Ben stayed home all morning and into the afternoon, reading *Jerome's History of the Continent,* which they'd picked up from a merchant sailing up to Hammer Bay a month before. Kam had just finished building up the fire in the hearth when he sensed something—no, *someone*, a Cree. No one passed through The Finger by accident, he knew. Whoever it was had almost certainly come to see him.

"I need to go outside. Stay here," he said to the boy.

"Is something wrong, father?" Ben said, putting the heavy book down flat on the table.

"No, nothing's wrong," he said but then corrected himself. "I don't know. Lock the door and only open it for me or your mother."

The boy nodded and Kam threw on his fur-lined cloak. Outside the snow came down in clumps half the size of a fist and Kam could only just barely make out the approaching rider, cloaked in Ilyan gray.

The horse slowed and Kam shouted out. "Greetings, Brother. What's your business?"

The horse stopped and its rider dismounted. Kam readied to defend himself should the need arise.

The rider pulled back his hood. "What kind of greeting is that for an old friend who has traveled so far, in such foul weather, to see you?" Aron said.

He invited Aron inside the house and introduced him to Ben, who had been waiting just inside the front door.

"Your son?" Aron said, repeating Kam's words when Ben had gone into the other room to fetch blankets. There was no irony or ridicule in Aron's voice, so Kam wasn't sure how to take the question.

"Yes," he said.

After Ben brought blankets, Kam sent him back to the bedroom so the two men could talk in private. They caught up on the past year, and Kam was pleasantly reminded of the conversations they used to have in the white-walled cafés of the island city that had been their home. Aron had been promoted to master, and showed Kam the gold chain around his wrist and the sash proving it.

"You beat me to it," Kam said.

Aron smiled. "But I'll still never be as great a sorcerer as you might be…if you were to return."

"You've grown modest," Kam said.

"Honesty and modesty are different."

"Be that as it may, you won't have to worry about any competition from me. I've decided to stay here. With my family."

Aron looked at Kam, turned away to look at the fire, and then looked back at him again. "I thought something like this might happen when you left."

"What?"

"This," Aron said and gestured to the house that surrounded them.

"I'm happy."

"Are you?"

"Yes."

"The world needs you. A man with a good heart and all your potential. The Continent is at a crossroads. There's unrest in the north. War with the Haroumi and the Bridgelanders ever brews and there have already been border skirmishes between the Alderians and Southlanders not ten day's ride from here in the Varsun Wood—"

"And what does any of this have to do with me?"

"We may not be able to stop wars, but we can help make them as short as possible. We can bring a calming hand to the hot tempers of men with our counsel. We can bring knowledge and art and beauty into the world with our studies. Don't you see? That's why the Brotherhood was founded in the first place."

Kam got up from his chair to look out the window at the falling snow outside. "Is this then what you've come for? To bring me back?"

"I've only come to talk."

"Tell me, are you here of your own accord or is this official business of the Brotherhood?"

"Both, I guess," Aron said. "They wanted someone to speak with you. I volunteered."

"Well, I am sorry to have made you come all this way for nothing. Like I said, I'm happy here."

"You know, self-deception is the most insidious deception of all. I remember you telling me so many times, as we sat and drank dirt tea that you wanted…that you were *determined* to be great. Is *this* greatness? You: living with a woman who betrayed you the first opportunity she got. Raising a son who isn't yours."

The things that were true stung the most.

Kam stood up. "It was good to see you, Aron."

"I have seen what you're capable of. Don't waste it. After what you did to that pirate—"

Kam stopped.

"We knew," Aron said. "And there were some in Ilyeth who wanted you in chains because of it. Make you stand before the arch-masters. I talked them out of it. You have the ability to change the world."

"By serving the Empire that invaded my homeland and sets up a garrison in my village?"

"We serve nothing but the greater good."

Kam shook his head. Aron went on. "The Empire has its faults, but it has mostly brought peace and prosperity everywhere it has gone."

"Tell that to the Vilbenian dead, the Kallanbori dead, the Lakelander dead, the *Alderian* dead. Aron, I am glad you are doing well and it was nice to see you. But it's time for you to leave."

Aron rose from the chair he was sitting in and looked at Kam directly. "I hope you reconsider. I believe there is an inn down in the village, no?"

"The Bright Candle."

"I will be there for a few nights. I have ridden long and hard, and I need to rest."

"I'm not going to change my mind."

"I will be at The Bright Candle." And at that, he stepped towards the door. Just as he was about to grab the latch, the door swung open and Olwyn stepped through with a sack full of turnips in her arms. Seeing Aron, she jumped with surprise, the turnips falling back out the door to the snow-covered ground outside.

"Oh! I'm sorry. I didn't know we were expecting visitors."

"I was just leaving," Aron said.

"He is a friend…Aron…from my time in the West," Kam added.

"I'm Olwyn. What brings you to The Finger?"

"I was just passing through," Aron said. "Your husband has told me much about you."

Olwyn smiled politely, picked up the turnips and went into the other room to check on Ben. Shortly after Aron's horse stamped off down the hill, she returned to the main room. "He's one of them, isn't he? A Cree. One of them Ilyan Brothers."

Kam nodded.

"Are you in trouble?"

"No. I don't think so."

"You aren't leaving us, are you?"

He walked up to her and put his arms around her. "This is my home."

Kam meant this, and yet there was part of what Aron had said that was alluring. Staying here in The Finger, what chance did he have of ever amounting to anything? He thought about the praise his research on the Mandrakhar had received from the masters in the early days of his time with the Brotherhood; he thought about those festival nights when, on the shores of Ilyeth, all the children would cheer for him as he bent the mage fire to his will. And when he'd received that praise, when he'd heard those children, he'd felt a kind of joy that he'd never felt before, even with his family.

He returned to his job. Sometimes his work brought him within sight of the inn, and he imagined going to Aron's room and telling him he was ready to leave. The long journey back to Ilyeth wouldn't be unlike that first journey they'd taken those years before—except perhaps colder due to the season. When he returned to Ilyeth, he would dive back into his studies and be promoted to master. In time, he might even become one of the arch-masters.

A week later the snow stopped and the road through the canyon was passable again. Aron came by the house. Olwyn and Ben were gone, but it was Kam's day off again and he had been busying himself reading one of the old Lanzhenese epics. He sensed a Cree, obviously Aron, coming up the hill from the village. Soon he heard the *clop, clop* of his friend's horse against the recently shoveled path. He put his book down and closed the curtains. When there came a knocking on the door, Kam sat silently, holding his breath. He knew Aron could sense him inside, but he didn't answer. Eventually he heard Aron get back on his horse and trot further up the hill towards the canyon entrance.

That was the last he saw or heard of Aron for a long time.

Years went by; Ben grew with alarming swiftness. It seemed that every few months the boy required longer pants, larger tunics. Olwyn, too, showed signs of age: at first just a few solitary gray hairs, a wrinkling of the skin at the corners of her mouth when she smiled. In time, the solitary grays joined with others to form whole bands; the wrinkles remained even when her face was impassive. Kam's appearance never aged much, though it would be a long time before his lack of aging stood out in any noticeable way.

Kam remained cautious about using his abilities but would occasionally use sorcery to help around the village when a strong need arose. When Ben was fifteen, Kam inherited a small fishing boat from an old man he had helped as a healer.

Kam thought that this would be a good opportunity to teach Ben how to handle a boat. He also hoped to help get the boy out of the malaise he'd fallen into. Along with the changes in the boy's body came changes in his countenance. As he inched closer to manhood he grew withdrawn and quiet and, if Kam or his mother pushed him to talk, he quickly turned recalcitrant. He even seemed to be losing attention with his studies and would cause mischief with other boys from around the village.

Now, whenever Kam and Ben had free time, they spent a day out on the water. They would go to some of the shelters and caves south of The Finger or else sail to one of the other villages on the way to Hammer Bay. Ben was resistant at first but over time grew to love the sea and became more proficient at sailing than Kam himself.

All through these years, the Empire continued its inexorable expansion. Zubayah and several other principalities along the eastern coast of the Inner Sea had been brought into the Empire when Ben was twelve; three years later, Odleheim, with its vast mines of gold and silver. Many said it was only a matter of time before Jarl or even Zabiz and the lands on the other side of the Inner Sea were pulled in. Kam would remember his own experience with war. It was easy to forget that even what were characterized as "small skirmishes" meant real men dying violently, never again to see their wives and children, mothers and fathers. In all of this, there was little to no news of Ilyan involvement, yet Kam knew that wherever the Empire grew, an Ilyan "advisor" couldn't be far behind.

Ben, fully indoctrinated with patriotic fervor at his Alderian-ran school, viewed all of these developments as positive, and soon this became a major point of contention between him and his stepfather. Olwyn stayed out of the political debates. On Ben's seventeenth birthday, he announced he was joining the Imperial navy. The pay was good, and he'd be able to sail and see the world. The Alderians recruited many sailors from the lands that used to make up Vilben, but never had Kam imagined Ben would be one of them.

Olwyn cried every day for the two weeks leading up to Ben's departure. Nonetheless, she brought herself to join Kam and watch Ben board a naval vessel bound first for Hammer Bay and then the great Imperial port city of Vicus Remorum.

After Ben left, Olwyn underwent a great change. When the pirates had departed nine years before, Olwyn had never regained her appetite for physical intimacy, but now she shied away from even the chastest of her husband's caresses. The situation worsened when, seven months later, news reached The Finger that war had broken out between the Islanders and the Empire and that the Alderians were bringing the full weight of their navy to bear.

For the next year, Olwyn was interested in nothing but news of the war in the distant north; whenever she wasn't working, she would loiter around the village docks and the alehouse where she might ask any arriving boatman or traveling merchant for word on the war's progress.

The following spring, news reached The Finger of the Alderians' victory against the Islanders, and there was a great celebration in the village. Though the Islands were little more than an abstract concept to the villagers, many of The Finger's young men had gone off to fight in the Imperial navy; Alderian victory meant there was a chance they might come home.

A trickle of local boys started returning over the next months. Each time news reached Olwyn of one of these returnees, she would pay the boy's family a visit and try to get any word of Ben. None of the returning boys knew anything.

On what would have been Ben's twentieth birthday, Olwyn, without asking Kam, went out and had a large volume of empty pages bound with their son's full name inscribed on the cover. A birthday present, Olwyn said, for when Ben returned from the war. He'd always so loved writing. She then insisted on baking a large tart.

"Who's to eat it?" Kam said.

"We will," Olwyn said. "Or else we'll give it to the children in the village."

Kam felt this was a bad idea, yet after much insistence by his wife, he relented. As cruel chance would have it, it was only the next night—the tart sitting untouched beside the oven—that there was a knocking at the door, and Kam saw in his wife's eyes: *finally my son returns to me.*

He wanted to warn her because right then he sensed that the man at the door was not her son at all and that neither of them would ever see Ben again.

And yet Kam, shocked from the blow that his wife was about to receive, stayed seated in his chair, unable to prevent Olwyn from answering the door. Their visitor's voice was that of a young man—around Ben's age. *Are you Benedictus's mother? He would have wanted you to know... Ship sunk to the bottom of Drodom Bay... Set afire by the Islanders... A great battle that they will sing songs about . . .*

XV

It's morning when he returns to the boarding house in Draycott. He's dirty and unshaven; orderly rows of scabs and scars mar his forearms.

"We didn't think you'd be back," the owner says when Kam walks through the boarding house doors. "My wife tells me to throw all your things out, but I tell her: 'he's paid through the month, we don't touch his things 'til the months out.'"

Kam isn't much in the mood for chatting. He nods, walks past the owner and ascends the stairs, entering his room and locking the door behind him. He swings his bags to the floor and begins taking stock of the items he's brought back: the trinkets and jewelry and books, the map he's drawn in his own blood.

He spends five days poring through the books from the catacombs (translating from Old Alderian is slow business) and studying the map he's made. He hardly leaves the room except to wash himself and have an occasional meal downstairs. When he finally does leave the boarding house, it's only to pawn a few of the items he deems unnecessary so he can continue paying rent. He never sells more than one or two things at a time. None of the shop keeps ask any questions. He is just a drifter who lucked upon a valuable antique or two in his travels.

On one of his excursions away from the boarding house, he makes a detour to the Imperial Library. Though he keeps his hood down (what's more suspicious than a man with his hood up?), he's careful not to let anyone see his face, lest one of his old colleagues from Ilyeth, traveling to the capital for research, recognize him. When he finds what he's looking for, a common enough volume entitled *The Pre-Phaidonian Continent,* he conceals the book beneath his cloak and walks out the front door.

Back in his room, reading through the tome, it becomes clear that the blue lights on the floating map—dark *red* dots on his blood-ink facsimile—mark important historical sites, not just contemporary cities and towns. One of the dots, in the location of the capital, represents the catacombs he visited. Others are ruins near Vicus Remorum, outside Kallanboro, and on and on. If these sites were widely known to the author of a book available in most of the major libraries of the Continent, then they must also have been widely known to Rumalti, meaning they have already been picked through and are unlikely to have the scepter he seeks. One by one, he cross-references the points on his map with the ruin sites mentioned in the book. There is, however, one point on his map *not* referenced in the book: a spot out to the west—not far from the Mandrakhi settlement where he lived for a time many years ago. He looks again at his messily drawn map; could he have mistakenly marked this point? He doesn't think so; in which case, westward it is.

That night before going to sleep, he spends an hour transcribing the map he drew in the catacombs into the book originally bound for his son. He's started writing in tiny, almost indecipherably small, script as he's approached the book's final empty pages. Still, an eventual end is inevitable.

XVI

They lived together in that increasingly haunted house for twelve more years. With Ben's passing, so too went Olwyn's capacity for joy. Kam would wake in the middle of the night and find her missing, inexorably in Ben's old room lying on the floor or draped over the straw mattress that had been his.

She became fixated on the idea that if only they could have retrieved Ben's body, she would be able to move past her grief. "If I could see him one more time, it wouldn't be so bad," she'd said. "It's the not knowing for sure. Maybe he jumped overboard before it sunk…Maybe he escaped and swam to shore…It's so far away; it isn't impossible he could have survived and not gotten word to us."

Kam was initially sympathetic. Their son had died and he grieved as well, and wasn't a mother's grief the strongest there was? Yet the months came and went and then the years, and Olwyn showed no signs of recovery. A resentment aimed at her weakness solidified in his chest. Sometimes his temper would get away from him. "He's gone. Dead. He likely died a terrible death—burned alive or gasping for air with the salty water filling his lungs. You will *never* see him again. The sooner you can accept that the sooner you will be able to make something of the remainder of your days."

She slapped him hard in the face. "How dare you speak to me that way about *my* son? He isn't even yours."

Olwyn started sleeping in Ben's old room. Kam himself started only sleeping two or three hours a night. He wasn't sure if the insomnia had to do with being a Cree or something else, but he started filling the extra hours with books. He refreshed his knowledge of the histories and began reading Zoran, the pseudonym for a writer from Turmandheim who'd decried the evils of the Alderians and had subsequently been executed in the capital. Zoran's arguments made a lot of sense to Kam. Most of the tragedies of his life—and of so many other lives—could be traced back to the Empire.

It was the year following the Jarl Annexation that Kam's eldest sister, Lauralyn, visited The Finger. She was old by now, and her husband had died the previous year. Her own health was failing, and she'd asked her grandson, Coll, a young man now, to bring her to The Finger for one last visit with her brother. Kam and Olwyn made Ben's room up for the two visitors and for the first time in years, Olwyn and Kam shared the same bed.

Kam had started powdering his beard and hair a whitish-grayish tint to make himself look older. No one much paid attention to his looks so it was easy to get away with this, poorest of disguises. Still, when his grandnephew arrived, he looked at Kam with unbelieving eyes.

"Uncle, you are only eight years younger than grandmother?"

"I can't remember the exact difference anymore," Kam said.

In as much as it was possible in a small house, Olwyn stayed away from the visitors, usually going into town on the pretense that she was busy with such and such errand. Mostly, Kam and his sister spent those days talking and catching up on what the years had brought. The boy did what he could to help out around the house.

On the third night of the visit, Kam was awoken by a scream from the other room. His sister. He reached for Olwyn. Gone. He hurried to the other room. It was still dark so he lit a candle with a spell for expediency. The dim light revealed Olwyn standing over the bed his sister shared with his grandnephew, stroking the boy's shoulder and mumbling under her breath, "I've missed you so much my boy…I've missed you so much…"

Coll lay frozen, unsure what to do. Lauralyn sat up, fear and confusion in her eyes. "I'm sorry I screamed," she said to her brother.

"I've missed you so much my boy…I've missed you so much…" Olwyn's words were laced with sobs now. "I *knew* you'd come back. I knew it!"

Kam went over to his wife and nudged her back towards their room. "Come now."

"Don't take me away from my son!"

"I'm not your son," Coll said, the first words he'd spoken.

Olwyn let loose a high-pitched howl and didn't stop even after she was back in bed.

"Shh…rest now," Kam said into her ear even as she screamed and flailed. Eventually, unsure what else to do, he cast a sleeping spell over her.

That next day, while Olwyn slept, Kam asked if Lauralyn and the boy wanted to take a walk to the village to get out of the house. His sister agreed this was a good idea but mentioned that her joints were giving her trouble that morning. Over breakfast Kam gave his sister a bitter concoction he made out of lavender and pickleberry juice under pretense that it had medicinal properties. He had never been great at the betterment spells, but while she ate porridge with Coll, he walked about the front room, pretending to straighten the furniture while subtly doing what spell work he could to improve her vision and remove some of the pain from her knees.

"What are you saying, Kam," Lauralyn asked.

"Nothing much. Just talking to myself."

A few minutes later, shortly after she'd finished breakfast, Lauralyn noted how good she felt. "Brother, I think there is really something in that potion you gave me!"

Kam and his two visitors walked to the village. The whole way his sister continued commenting on her improved condition. "And my vision is better too. I say, it's a miracle!"

They walked by the house that Kam and Lauralyn had grown up in. They went down to the shore and chatted on the beach while Coll examined the ships in the docks. Even when they later stopped in The Bright Candle, Lauralyn insisted on telling anyone who would listen about the potion.

"Where'd you say you got this stuff?" Fyr, the owner of the inn asked.

"Traveling salesmen came by some time last month," Kam said.

"I don't remember him."

"He was only here for a short time. I think he was going up to Hammer Bay."

"Seems like every time something good comes through town, I always miss out on it," the innkeeper said.

On the way home, Kam got to thinking how welcome his sister's visit was. He had an image in his mind of how he would greet Olwyn, his spirit lifted, when he returned home and how maybe this happiness would rub off on her now that she'd had time to rest.

Then he saw it.

The tree to the side of the house had neither another tree nor hedge nor building anywhere close by; once the tree was in sight, there was nothing to obscure the view of the body—a woman's body—dangling from one of the strong branches. Her face was directed away from him, but he knew who it must be. "Stay here," he said to Lauralyn and Coll, and ran on.

Later, he would be surprised by how coolly he handled the situation. As if this were a thing he had been expecting for a long time. After he checked the body to confirm there was no hope of reviving her, he walked into the house to get a stepladder. When he cut the rope, the body landed on the ground with a hard thud.

His sister and nephew stayed for another two days after Olwyn was laid to rest.

On the third day, he walked Lauralyn and Coll to the entrance of the canyon and bid farewell to them. A few days later he sold the old fishing boat and most any of his other belongings that might fetch some coin from the villagers (save for the book Olwyn had bound for Ben and, of course, the dagger). The economy of The Finger was already on the decline, and there were many abandoned houses. No one would buy his. He left it. He bought two horses and departed the next morning before the sun rose.

XVII

He spends two days preparing for his journey, purchasing food and supplies, and spending the coin to upgrade his horse to the strongest and fastest he can afford. The most reputable horse traders are far outside Kam's price range, but just beyond the noisy, fragrant, bustle of the Grand Market he stumbles upon an unsavory looking man with a lazy eye who tells him he has a Zabissian stallion for sale at a price he can potentially afford. Kam tells the man he's interested, and Lazy Eye calls over to his Mandrakhi errand boy to bring the beast around. The horse's color is a gray that borders almost on silver and his mane is a pure white.

"He's a bit wild, but if you know how to treat him, you won't find a faster ride."

"What's his name?"

"The savages who sold him to me call him Qhata. But I've renamed him Silver Arrow."

The horse snorts at this.

"Doesn't sound like he likes that name very much," Kam says. "Isn't that right, Qhata?" He places his hand on the stallion, who nickers deeply in reply.

"You call him whatever you wish, if you pay for him."

The next morning as he rode out of the city, Kam had the feeling—like when he'd left The Finger—that he was seeing this place for the final time: the massive black and white domes of the Capital Building and the Imperial Palace, the twin bridges spanning the Riffel, the western gates still beneath the long, morning shadow of Farwatch Tower.

Before Ben left with the navy, he used to talk about wanting to see this place. As far as Kam could tell, he died before he ever had the opportunity. How much would he have enjoyed it if his son were still alive—had survived into old age—and today they could walk and talk—two old men, although one appearing young—around this great and terrible city.

XVIII

He rode west from The Finger for a week before hitting the Imperial highway. He had no particular destination in mind and took the road north for no other reason than that it was a long one. For some days then he rode through the rolling hills of the Varsun Wood, before crossing the Wyr on an unseasonably cold morning and beginning his travels across the flat, grassy expanses of Kilrabhi. In his mind he carried only a vague sense of the passing miles.

During this time, whenever he was travel weary, he'd stop at the next village and earn his keep—sometimes doing a laborer's work, other times performing magic shows in the village square. If he grew tired of a place, or if people started asking too many hard-to-answer questions about who he was or "how exactly did he do that magic trick so good," he'd pack his things on his horse and continue north in the still-dark hours of the early morning.

Eventually, he reached the sandy banks of the River Riffel, which, to the north, he knew, would pass through the heart of the capital city of Alder before continuing on and emptying into that vast sea that was also now Ben's watery grave.

That night, he set up camp beside the river and bathed in its waters, hoping to somehow feel more connected to his dead son. He didn't. Instead, he just felt cold.

✤

After several months of wandering steadily northwestward, on a whim, he left the road and traveled to the Mandrakhar settlement in the Westwood. He'd studied the Mandrakhar during his time in Ilyeth and was curious, if nothing else, to see them for himself. They were a fascinating race—not so unlike men, save they matured and died much faster. Unlike their kin in the capital and elsewhere, the Mandrakhar of the Westwood preserved and passed down their memories through the roots of a special Tree, the last of its kind: Saloryn Bai, they called it. Long ago, there were dozens of Mandrakhar settlements all across the Continent, each with its own Tree. Today there were still Mandrakhar in other parts of the Continent, but these, without a Memory Tree, lived and died like the rest of us—alone with their own thoughts, their own memories.

During his time in the settlement, Kam lived in a small bungalow built high up in the branches of a massive fir. He spent his days reading, conversing with the settlement's inhabitants, and writing his thoughts and observations down in the volume that had originally been intended for his son's words, not his. The Mandrakhar were not known to be trusting or hospitable to foreigners (an attitude not entirely unjustified, since many humans hated them and claimed they were spawn of the Demon); however, Kam was—through his studies in Ilyeth—knowledgeable of their customs and culture, and in this way, earned their respect and tolerance.

He hadn't intended to stay long, but there was something about being in a place so old and so foreign that brought him a peace he hadn't felt in a long time. The days fluttered by, nearly unnoticed.

A year passed. He still thought about Ben and Olwyn nearly every day, but the sting of these remembrances had faded. Occasionally, his memories were even happy. If it weren't for the dream, the premonition, coming back to him with a vivid vengeance one night, as if to shake him out of his complacency, he might have spent the rest of his days in the Westwood.

As it was, Kam realized there were things left for him to do. He packed up his belongings once more, strapped the silver dagger to his side, and set his sights eastward now—on the capital.

Like most who first visit Alder, Kam was astonished by the city's sheer scale; even more though, he was astonished with the city's extremes. He had never seen such opulence or such poverty, such beautiful temples and castles or such dilapidated shantytowns, wives of aristocrats wearing unthinkable quantities of jewels in their hair, emaciated children on their knees begging in filthy, vermin-infested alleys.

He found a boarding house in an inexpensive part of the city and, on his second day in the capital, walked to the much-heralded Phaidonian District. He spent much of the afternoon walking down the avenues of that neighborhood, lined with topiaries twice the height of men and life-sized statues of the great rulers and heroes from the Empire's long history. Overlooking the streets were huge manor after huge manor, each constructed of blue or gray stone, each with its own massive fountain out front, its own manicured gardens whose flowers bloomed a thousand colors.

So this was what all the human misery of the Empire has purchased.

At last, he came to the very center of the city: the twin monstrosities of the obsidian Capital Building and the white-walled palace. And he thought to himself that, were it the case that he had sufficient power in him, he would burn these two buildings—with a fire so hot even stone would succumb—to the ground.

Alas, great as he was as a sorcerer, this feat was beyond him.

His boarding house was located some distance from all this in the immigrant neighborhood of Draycott. There, he'd frequently observe shirtless children, many with gaunt, malnourished faces, asking any passerby for donations of copper or bread. This spectacle of poverty, when juxtaposed with the splendor he had seen that same day, filled him with righteous indignation.

He had little to occupy himself so, when he wasn't scribbling his thoughts down into the journal, he spent much of these first weeks in a tavern near where he was staying. All the talk was of the violence that had erupted in Jarl. It had been annexed two years prior, but now an organized resistance had formed. Many Alderian merchant ships had been torched in the river docks. This, combined with the continued fighting in the far west, on the borders of Zabiz, made much of the citizenry anxious. Even the Alderian coffers were not endless. The Imperial taxmen would squeeze what they could out of the provinces, but there was only so much that could be taken.

From time to time Kam would go on walks through the many districts of the city: to Borun and Bluefield and Broadhaven, to the Grand Market and Grayfield and the Mandrakhi Quarter; he would walk along the banks of the Riffel, past the Demonwharf and the Gardens at Erith Bay and all the estates along the riverfront. On one such excursion, he was walking through one of the many parks that dotted the city when, sitting on a stone bench, he saw an old man he recognized. The man's white, wispy hair was disheveled, and he looked like he'd forgotten to shave the last week. His face was buried in an oversized book with a concentration that suggested he didn't want to be interrupted. Kam went ahead anyway.

"Excuse me, Master Rumalti?"

The old man looked up with wrath in his eyes.

"I studied in Ilyeth for a time, I'm—"

"I know who you are, Kam Rhys. What do you want?"

"I don't think I've ever seen you outside a library."

"I'm here now, aren't I?"

"I'll be on my way. I only wished to say hello."

"Hello," the old man said, "and goodbye."

Kam was turning away when Rumalti stopped him. "Wait."

Kam swiveled back around.

"That blade you got there," Rumalti said, pointing to the silver dagger strapped to his hip.

"Where'd you get this?"

"I found it."

"Found it?" Rumalti said, doubtful.

"A pirate dropped it."

"Well, you ought to take better care of it than he did. It's valuable. And old: Pre-Phaidonian."

"That would make it, what, five hundred years old?"

"Older. If you're thinking about selling it—"

"I'm not," Kam said.

"Still, if you do." He ripped a small square of blank paper from the book he was holding. "Those assholes at the Imperial Library will never know," he said. He wrote something on each side of the paper using a quill and ink he had in his bag. "My address in the city on one side. And on the other, my home, in case I've left the capital."

"Farewell, Master Rumalti."

"Some of those Pre-Phaidonian artifacts have powers. Not saying this one has, but take care of it all the same, will you?"

One evening not long after, as Kam took his meal of stew at the boarding house, he looked through the window and saw a boy with no legs sliding his body along the cobblestone street. Seeing maimed or crippled children wasn't particularly unusual, yet there was something about this boy that was particularly pitiable. When someone would walk passed, the boy would raise his arm, palm open as if grasping for some invisible object. But the passersby would just avert their gaze and move on. What else could a person do but look away?

After a time, Kam went outside. "What's your name?" he said, but the boy didn't turn. Kam tapped him on the shoulder to get his attention. "What's your name?"

The boy looked at Kam and moaned unintelligibly.

"Hmm...That won't do," he said and stroked the boy on his cheek. "I'll have to call you something then. I had a friend named Aron once. Perhaps I can call you that?" He pointed to the boy. "Aron?" he said, moving his lips overdramatically.

He moaned in what seemed like approval.

Kam picked up the boy, who was now "Aron," and carried him, as if he were his bride. Aron howled in terror but eventually seemed to understand that Kam meant no harm.

"What are you doing?" the attendant at the boardinghouse desk said when Kam re-entered. "If you bring one of 'em in here, they're going to think they're all welcome."

Kam silenced the man with a look. "I'll have another bowl of stew for my friend," he said. Kam brought Aron into the dining area and placed him upright in the chair across from his own.

The stew was brought, but Aron was so weak he could hardly lift the spoon. Kam took it and started feeding him.

When the meal was done, he brought Aron to the bath. A layer of filth covered his skin and his legs were riddled with festering sores. Kam worked some healing spells on the boy to make him more comfortable. That night, much to the consternation of the owner of the boardinghouse, Kam brought the boy into his room and laid him down on the bed; Kam slept on the wooden floor.

All that night, despite the room being warm, despite all of the blankets, despite even Kam's spells, the boy coughed and shivered uncontrollably. When Kam left to fetch the boy water downstairs, he returned to find blood in and around the boy's mouth. He was far beyond the skill of Kam's own sorcery. Maybe he could find a more skilled healer in the city, but even if he did, what then? Kam couldn't care for him.

The boy uttered the woeful sounds of a dying animal. Kam stood over him until he couldn't watch any longer. And so, in his grief for this child, which mixed in his heart with a renewed grief for Olwyn and for Ben and for all the other things he'd lost, he cast one more spell, and the boy went into a painless, everlasting sleep.

Kam sat for a long while in his chair and stared at the child's body— his stumps of legs that were cut off right below the knee, the sores which covered his chest and neck. It was all too much. He stomped his feet upon the floor. He pounded his fist against the wall. He smashed a chair against the ground.

Someone in the room below pounded on their roof with what sounded like a broomstick. "Shut the fuck up!" a man's voice shouted.

Kam stomped on the floor again in reply.

The wave of anger passed and tiredness overcame him. He lied back down on the floor and stared up at the ceiling.

It was then that the premonition materialized in his mind's eye again.

The dark-skinned man stabbing the red-cloaked figure with Kam's dagger.

And it struck him. He was a fool for not grasping its meaning earlier. The dark red cloak…the great feeling of relief when it was done…it was his destiny—his duty—to bring change to the world, to do something about this empire that brought misery to those within and without.

A noble endeavor if there ever was one.

But first he needed to find this dark-skinned man.

The next day, Kam brought the boy's body to the public cemetery and buried him with the proceeds from selling some of his belongings. Again, the only items he refused to sell were his dagger and the journal. He commissioned a small stone to commemorate the boy's place. Kam wouldn't be around to see it, but he wrote down what he wanted the stone to say:

Though he was neglected during his life, he will not be forgotten in death.

After all of this was arranged, Kam returned to his room. He had no idea where he'd find the dark-skinned man, but in the Southland, in Jarl, men were fighting against the Alderians. That was a start. His time in the capital was over.

XIX

He eats a small meal of bread and cheese while studying his map, this one purchased in the capital, not written in the book or in his own blood. It's a blustery spring day and the corner of the map opposite the one he's holding down with his forearm is flapping in the wind. If he's reading the map right, he should be able to reach the ruins in another week, maybe ten days. The road west will take him right through the Westwood and the Mandrakhar settlement.

Funny how things had a tendency of going in cycles, of repeating . . .

He puts the map away and pulls out the journal, its pages yellow and rigid with age. He flips through a few excerpts. He turns to a passage he wrote early on, when he wasn't yet writing all the way to the edge of each page, and reads for a short while. Everyone he knew at the Mandrakhar settlement would be dead now. He doesn't have the time anyway. If the catacombs beneath the palace are any indication, searching these ruins may take quite a while. He puts the book away and gets back on Qhata.

That night, while sitting and meditating at his campfire, he has the premonition again.

He's had it so many times and it is so familiar that whenever it comes, he greets it, is glad to see it—like an enemy for whom he has, through endless struggle and stalemate, forged a hard-won respect.

For half his life, he wanted to know what it meant; for another half, he thought—wrongly—that he knew. Now he has entered a new stage. He accepts its mystery but marches forwards nonetheless.

He smothers the fire with dirt and begins readying himself for sleep when he senses something. Like a tickle at the back of his throat first, but the minutes pass, and then the source of the sensation is clear.

Another Cree.

No, several.

They're coming.

He stands up and packs his single pot, his bedroll, and loads them upon Qhata.

"You thought you were going to get to rest, didn't you, my friend?" he says to the horse. "But it looks like you have some miles yet to go tonight."

By the time he is riding off, he can hear the drumbeat of hooves in the distance. Just before he brings his horse off the road to lose his pursuers in the trees, he turns back and sees a small orb of white light launch skyward, up and up and up.

Some spell work intended to ensnare him, no doubt. He spurs Qhata on. Faster. Faster.

When the ball of light reaches its apex at the tops of the trees, it explodes into a gigantic dome of light that encloses a half-mile-wide circle of the wilderness.

Kam and his horse are just beyond the borders of the dome though and escape into the night.

XX

"Ben," he said, and it was too late to take back the word.

The leader of the Jarlite Resistance was a surprisingly un-formidable-looking man named Jevig with a patchy brown beard and a lisp. Kam, not trusting anyone with his identity, had decided to use the pseudonym Horton. Still, when asked for his name, *Ben* somehow escaped his lips.

"Ben?" the man whose name was Jevig said, repeating the name.

There was no going back on the lie now, so he decided to fully embrace the name. "Yes. Short for Benedictus."

"A good Alderian name, eh?"

"The better to hide amongst their ranks," Kam said.

In the subsequent months, working with the Jarlite Resistance—attacking Imperial settlements, burning supply ships that came into the river docks, and otherwise making life difficult for the Redcloaks—Kam's co-conspirators, perhaps as a sign of respect for the sorcerer's formidable abilities, insisted on calling him the full name. In this way, Benedictus became known all around the Southlands as one of the most fearsome enemies of the Empire and a man to be reckoned with.

The first time he saw the boy was in the Lantern District of Jarl on a snowy and bitterly cold afternoon.

Kam, who was Benedictus now, who, once a week, wrote his thoughts using a tight, compact script into a book with the name *Benedictus* inscribed on its cover, walked with Jevig through the knee-high snow, discussing some of the upcoming raids on the Imperial gold stores. If successful, the raids would deal a hard blow to the Imperial coffers while simultaneously helping the Resistance fund activity outside the city and hire more mercenaries for the fighting still going on around Turmandheim.

When Kam saw the boy, he stopped mid-sentence, forgetting the word already halfway out his mouth. The boy was only ten or so by the looks of him—far from the man he'd eventually become. But he *was* the one he'd seen in the premonition. Of this there could be no doubt.

The boy walked down the street with a similar-looking, dark-skinned girl, and the two disappeared around a corner.

"Benedictus, what's wrong with you?" Jevig followed Kam's gaze, but all he saw were a few foreign children trudging through the snow.

"Nothing, I'm sorry," he said. "Something has come up and I must leave."

"*Something has come up*? How is that possible? We were just talking and nothing happened . . ."

"It's urgent."

"Fucking sorcerers!" Jevig said, but Kam was already walking briskly in the direction the boy had gone. He followed him home to a large, well-appointed house—surely owned by a prosperous family.

For several days afterwards, Kam shadowed the boy from afar, following him and the members of his household: his father, a wealthy timber merchant with a penchant for gambling; his mother; his sister, who had been the girl he was walking with on that first day. The boy's name, he learned, was Pa-Zhe Tu, and his parents had emigrated from Lanzhao to seek their fortune some fifteen years earlier.

Much of what happened afterwards has already been well chronicled:

1. Kam, who was called Benedictus, arranged for a "chance" meeting with Pa-Zhe during a card game with the boy's father. Upon seeing the boy up close, Kam's suspicions were confirmed: he was a Cree.

2. Several weeks later, Kam rescued Pa-Zhe from a group of neighborhood bullies who were, at the time, mercilessly beating the boy. Afterwards, Kam helped Pa-Zhe recover from his injuries.

3. The two started conversing regularly. Kam told Pa-Zhe that both of them were Cree. He gave him the silver dagger. He didn't tell him about the premonition.

4. During all this time, Kam was exerting considerable effort evading the Redcloaks, the Jarlite authorities, and the Ilyan Brotherhood, who'd sent several Brothers, including his old friend, Aron, to bring him in. On several occasions, they nearly captured or killed him.

5. Kam, realizing he had to leave Jarl, attempted to persuade Pa-Zhe to leave with him. They were, after all, connected through the premonition. The boy, on account of his family, refused.

6. After a tragic fire, which killed several members of Pa-Zhe's family, the young Cree had a change of heart.

7. On the day that Kam and Pa-Zhe left the city, the two were intercepted by Aron and a group of Ilyan Brothers. Kam managed to escape into the wilderness, but the boy fell into the hands of the Brotherhood.

XXI

He rides hard through the wooded countryside. At times, he returns to the road to cover distance more quickly. Other times, he leaves the highway or doubles back on his own trail in hopes of losing his pursuers. This strategy is partially successful. A few times when his path takes him up one of the hills that dot the country around here, he sees his would-be captors or assassins in the distance. On each occasion, the group of riders following him has been whittled down further. Likely they had to break into smaller parties when they weren't sure which direction he'd gone.

When he reaches the top of the next rise, he can see a yet-smaller group a mile or so down the hill: seven riders.

"We need to go, Qhata," he says to his mount, and the horse breaks into a canter again.

Despite Kam's spells, which artificially invigorate the beast, as well as the horse's great natural endurance, Qhata tires and begins to slow. Kam feels Qhata's sides heaving and sees the froth gathering around the saddle. It won't be so long before they catch up to him.

He has been running for so long—so many years—that a part of him assumes there must be some way out again. He could run on foot, but that would only slightly prolong the inevitable. The horse is struggling now. His mind races.

He finds a place where the road, traveling again steadily uphill, takes a sharp turn such that travelers cannot see what is beyond the turn from afar. He dismounts Qhata and walks the horse to a clearing before returning to the road. Above him is a small cliff capped by a boulder. This will be as good a place as any.

A spell, to prevent the Brothers from sensing him ahead of time, still circulates around him. He stands where they won't see him until the last instant. It should only be a few minutes now.

When he hears the horses coming up the hill, his hands start to shake. His mind drifts back to that first time he was ever in battle, nearly a century ago.

How little he knew then. If he could return to that time, when his son who was not his son was still growing inside Olwyn's belly... He'd do much differently. There was no sense in regrets now though.

The moment the first two Redcloaks come around the corner—the sun catching on their breast plates, their dark red capes, pinned with brooches below their throats—Kam casts a spell to dislodge the boulder and bring it toppling off its ledge. A loud crash reverberates through the air as the rock smashes down into the road. The first of the riders is crushed, the breaking of his body audible even amongst the other chaotic noise of shouting and hooves that swirl around; the second Redcloak, still alive, is knocked from his horse with his leg caught beneath the boulder. A third rider, following the first two close behind, pulls hard at his reins, and the horse, rearing, topples them both. Two more Redcloaks turn the corner now, bows raised and arrows at the string. One of the Brothers is with them. The two Redcloaks look to be Kallanbori, Kam thinks, and he again remembers back to that battle long ago outside of Hammer Bay. He is a little better equipped to deal with cavalry archers this time.

The two men with the bows shout something and each fire multiple arrows in quick succession. Kam redirects three of the flying arrows with a wave of his wrist, striking the Brother—who has not yet cast a single spell—and the bowmen, all in the throat. Still, two arrows have escaped Kam's spells, and one glances off his thigh; the other hits him squarely in the right shoulder. His collarbone snaps with a whip-crack.

"Ah! Shit!" Kam shouts and grits his teeth.

The final gray-cloaked Brother, who'd brought up the rear of the party, turns the corner now. Kam senses the spell—meridians of energy being bent around him to constrict him, crush him; he casts a spell to counter and the two sorcerers face each other, their spells at a stalemate.

Kam recognizes the face of his assailant now.

He supposes it had to be this way. If not today, then eventually. Sadness wells up in him; one of them will die today.

The two men remain at a distance, perhaps fifty paces from one another. If someone were present to witness the confrontation, assuming they were not also a sorcerer, they would see only two men—one slumped over from his injuries, another on his horse—staring at each other, concentration in each of their eyes, avalanches of sweat cascading down their brows, unintelligible utterances flowing from their mouths as if each were possessed by malevolent spirits. To a sorcerer though, what takes place is a magnificent display of attacking and defending and countering as the meridians of energy, invisible to the untrained eye, dance back and forth, controlled by incredibly skilled minds. The two men stand like this for only a few minutes, yet to each of them it feels much longer.

Eventually a time comes when the horsed man, more experienced but less naturally gifted, perhaps on account of the mounting fatigue of continuous sorcery, makes the tiniest of mistakes, leaves the slightest of invisible cracks. Kam exploits this, knocks his opponent down, sucks the air from his lungs, lands his fatal blow.

Kam himself is exhausted and he has half a mind to just collapse down upon the road. Somehow though he musters the strength to drag himself over to where his fallen enemy—his fallen friend—lays.

The dying sorcerer gasps for breath, blood coming from his nose and mouth. He is trying to say something. "I always knew you were better...the better sorcerer," Aron says as more blood spills from his mouth onto his brown-gray beard.

"Why did you come?" Kam says. "You could have refused. We were friends."

Aron smiles a smile that turns to a grimace. "I'd hate to see what you do to people who *weren't* your friends." He closes his eyes for a moment then opens them again. "You know...the boy...he's not a boy anymore. Padgett. He'll come for you."

"I've been waiting for him for longer than I can remember—since before I knew you, even. I'm not afraid of him."

"You should be. He thinks you killed his sister...his mother."

"Where would he have gotten that idea?" Kam says.

Aron doesn't answer.

Instead, he dies.

It'd been some years since Kam had cried, but now tears flow freely down his face. He's unsure whether he cries for his dead friend or himself or something else entirely.

He removes his bloodied cloak, pulls aside the collar of his tunic and casts a fire spell to cauterize his wounds as best he can, though a piece of arrow and shaft are still lodged in his shoulder. When this is done he checks the fallen men to see what he might salvage off them. He takes the cleanest of the dead men's cloaks and puts it on. One of the soldiers, he notices now, the one whose leg is pinned by the boulder, is still alive.

He walks over to him and can hear the man's groans. He lifts the boulder and casts it aside. The soldier's leg is crushed, and Kam can see the bone jutting out from the flesh. At best, he will lose the leg. Kam lifts up the half-conscious man and sets him on a horse, sending the horse back down the road they had come. When this is done, he walks over to where he's left Qhata. Hopefully his horse has had enough time to rest.

XXII

For months after Kam's escape outside Jarl, a dozen Ilyan Brothers and all the Redcloaks that could be spared searched through the Southland for their fugitive.

Kam hid in dank caves, in a ditch away from the road, inside a barrel (briefly), within the burned-out remains of a Southland farmhouse and, for two weeks, in a stone barn belonging to a sheep farmer who was sympathetic to the cause. All the while, he kept watch and would move on—ever farther southeast into the wilderness—if any signs pointed to his enemies being near.

Though he was ever under threat of capture or death, those were also boring days when much time was spent waiting in idleness. And so he had much time to think—an activity that seemed to only draw him deeper into feelings of hopelessness. Word had reached him that much of the Jarlite Resistance had been captured in his absence; they would soon face trial and, no doubt, execution. Pa-Zhe was in the hands of the Brotherhood and out of his reach. He could return to Jarl and fight, but such was unlikely to lead to anything but the gallows.

He would continue running, he decided, and wait for the boy to become a man. There would be a time for action, but for now patience was required.

Years passed. He joined no other opposition group, no militia, no rebellion, but instead did his best to bring what justice he could where the Empire or the world at large had done injustice: the farmer who'd had his land taken away, the shopkeeper who'd been taxed into poverty, the grieving widow. He seldom stayed in any location long but instead became like a restless ghost, wreaking havoc amongst the Redcloaks from Kallanboro to Nyrribia, from Vicus Remorum to the Old Country.

He tried to keep tabs on the boy, who soon grew out of boyhood. News from Ilyeth was scarce and hard to come by, but from what Kam could glean, it sounded as if Pa-Zhe was indeed showing great promise.

❀

It was in the five hundredth and eighty-eighth year After the Fall, during a stretch of time when Kam, who still went by Benedictus, had joined an Islander pirate captain to raid and destroy Alderian supply ships, that he first heard the phrase "Northern Alliance."

The blue-and-yellow-painted ship Kam sailed with was stopped for a night in Ithakaldo to unload the bounty they'd taken on their last raid. The city had been, since the time Ben had died in the waters not five miles away, an Imperial possession; however, anti-Imperial sentiment abounded, making it easy to find someone willing to buy goods stolen from the Redcloaks—especially at a discounted price.

That night, in one of the bustling music halls that Kam frequented, he was approached by a pair of middle-aged Islanders, who, other than their facial hair (one had a bushy beard, the other was clean shaven) were identical.

"We hear you've no love for the Empire," the bearded one said, in Eyasu, a language Kam understood only passably well.

"Does anyone around here?"

"Good point," the clean-shaven one said. "But not everyone around here is a sorcerer."

Kam had tried to keep his abilities a secret, but given that he'd often cast spells in front of the other men on the ship, he knew it would only be a matter of time before word got around. "What do you want," he said.

"Come with us," the bearded one, who introduced himself as Mosho said then. "We can't talk here."

Kam did not trust them but was intrigued and knew that if either made a false move, he could boil their blood with a thought.

The three men left the music hall and walked down the muddy road to a nondescript structure with no windows made of large boards of pine. Inside was a plain room—completely empty. The two identical men sat down on the floor. Kam stood.

The clean-shaven one was Tholo, and the two of them were the sons of one of the great Islander chieftains—a man whose brothers had been put to the sword after the last war with the Alderians, a man who wanted revenge.

"I'm listening," Kam said.

More than a dozen of the chieftains were planning, in secret, an attack on the Alderians—an attack that, if it were successful, would end Imperial rule in the Islands forever and perhaps would topple the Empire once and for all. They had brokered a treaty with the men from beyond the ocean—

the Domani, who had the pale skin of a Southlander and hair as black as night—and together, with the element of surprise, they would crush the Alderians.

"If it is such a good plan," Kam said, "what do you need me for?"

"You know the Ilyan Brotherhood are the Alderians' lackeys," Mosho said. "We cannot hope for victory without sorcerers of our own."

"I am but one man. The Ilyan Brotherhood numbers in the thousands."

"You misunderstand, friend," said Tholo. "We have gathered many of those with the gift and the curse, but the sorcerers of the Islands and of the lands beyond are mere medicine men, witches. We seek someone to train them. You, we are told, might be such a person."

The next day Kam retired from pirating and boarded a small sailing vessel with Mosho and Tholo heading further north. When they arrived two days later, the island looked to be deserted, but once they came ashore and walked over a small rise, Kam could see a large gathering of what looked to be hundreds of huts.

"This is where we have brought them," Mosho said.

"Who?" Kam said, although he already knew. Only in Ilyeth had he ever felt such a gathering together as this.

They were of a wide range of experience—some were already proficient in casting simple healing or weather spells, others had never cast a spell in their lives. For the next year, Kam remained in that small, isolated place and began training them. Real training in sorcery would have taken many years, but Kam condensed the curriculum and skipped much of the foundational education, instead favoring the teaching of practical skills: how to lift large objects, how to deflect an arrow traveling towards you at great speed, mage fire.

If one were to judge Kam on the results of his training based on how his pupils fared in combat, they would have to give him quite high praise. For when the year was out and the newly trained sorcerers set sail with three hundred Islander vessels and another hundred filled with the pale-skinned Domani, they set the Continent on fire.

Rather than trying to liberate the Islands directly, the Northern Alliance made landfall at Kallanboro and steadily burned and murdered and pillaged their way southward. On the Continent, they called this The Great Uprising, but amongst the Northerners they called it The Liberation.

Once it began, Kam, witnessing first-hand the ever-growing crescent of carnage that bloomed steadily southward, wondered whether this thing he had helped create was even worse than the Alderians. Of course, it didn't matter. Once these sorcerers, raised to hate the Empire, were loosed upon the world, there was no turning back.

Three years of war followed, and hundreds of thousands perished. Much heroism was displayed by those on both sides of the conflict. And much deceit. And much kindness. And much cruelty. But those are other stories for other times.

In the end, despite the death and destruction, the Northerners were not victorious. Rather than seeing the other provinces join in rebellion, the Northern Alliance found the Empire unified against a common enemy. After three years of bloody war, the walls around Alder still stood and the Islands were still not free; Kam had much blood on his hands but little else to pay him back for his efforts.

The boy, now a man, had not come; the premonition had not been fulfilled.

When the final treaty had been signed and all the Islander chieftains had been beheaded before the obsidian walls of the Capital Building, Kam—somehow still alive, still free—rode off into the east, to live the life of a hermit and ponder where things had gone wrong.

Kam was living in a small village on the Brahlan coast when, some years later, he learned of the Emperor Kaleb's death by way of a traveling circus come from the capital.

And so ended the Lunaris dynasty.

Emperor Kilborne, first of the Galsworths, had assumed the throne and was promising reforms and an end to Imperial expansion. Kam knew he should feel happy, but he didn't. Everything had been for nothing. So many had struggled and died, and now a mere chance circumstance—that the emperor's eldest son had been ill—had achieved everything that all those years of toil could not. His whole life had been one big mistake—a joke too terrible to laugh at. He was no hero. He was just a man who had made too many wrong turns, brought pain and death to the world, and accomplished nothing.

It took him a long time to sleep that night. When he finally did, he fell, almost immediately, into that old, familiar dream. The damn, treacherous thing.

But then, something happened.

How could he have not seen it? Sitting at the end of the scepter was a familiar stone. It had been right there under his nose all those years and then he'd buried the thing with his dead wife.

There was no redemption for the things he had done, but there might still be some good he might do. He didn't know what it was precisely, but he knew he had to try.

XXIII

It isn't long before some of the others are on his trail again.

Whenever he lets Qhata rest, he tries to work the spells that should, at least temporarily, knit the flesh of his leg and shoulder back together. But healing has never been his most proficient skill; he's always been more adept at taking apart, tearing down, burning up. These wounds aren't particularly grave and, could he lie in bed, remove the arrow shard from his shoulder, and properly dress his wounds while assisting the healing with his spell work, he might be good as new in a matter of days. He doesn't have a matter of days; the moment he gets back on the horse, the motion from the riding jolts his just-beginning-to-close wounds back open. Already he has lost much blood, though one can't properly see it beneath the dark red cloak he wears now.

He has lived a long life. Not quite so long as many Cree but far longer than most men. He doesn't fear death. What he fears is that he's wasted his life; only by staying alive might he somehow change that. He tries to remember the feeling in the dream—that all-encompassing relief that courses through his body in the end. He can't die yet. Not before the premonition is fulfilled. Not before the dream comes to pass, whatever that means now. It's true that some premonitions take place after their receivers have died—yet then, what was that feeling he had? It was like he was both in the premonition and not in the premonition all at once.

It's raining when Qhata finally stops, refusing to go further despite how much Kam tugs at the reins or spurs the horse forward, and it is only through sorcery that he gets the horse to go another mile before it collapses in the mud, throwing him from the saddle to strike his head on a low hanging tree branch.

Some moments pass before he gets up. He can feel blood dripping down his face and his head spins. He turns and sees Qhata lying dead. "I'm sorry," he says to his last friend in the world and places one hand on the horse's still flank. He picks up his muddy bag of belongings—inside which are the book and the stone, his water skin, a little food—and starts walking up the wooded hill.

The ground flattens, goes steeply downhill for a time, and then levels again. Somewhere ahead he hears running water—not just the rain—and he walks towards it. Just maybe this is where he can lose his pursuers.

He falls to his knees within view of the riverbank, unable to walk anymore. He lies down, and the hard rain pelts him on his upturned cheek; he closes his eyes but makes sure not to fall asleep. When he pulls himself back up, he sees that only a few hundred paces away, right on the river, is an old, abandoned-looking building of stone and wood. Out front a dilapidated sign reads *Shepherd's Roost Inn*. He will take shelter but just for a little while.

Inside, cobwebs impede every step; still, it's better than being out in the rain. He lays down on one of the dusty benches and takes a long swig from his water skin. Despite his current state, one might still think he would recognize the building; yet even after he hears the horses outside, he fails to identify this as the place that has haunted him for so many years. He peeks through the partially boarded window and can see a half-dozen Brothers charging towards the old inn. They are accompanied by dozens of Redcloaks. He can't fathom how they arrived so quickly.

Then something in him drops.

He looks around and realizes (finally!) that he knows this place. He looks at his red cloak, soaked through with rain and sweat and blood, and he throws it off as if this can somehow change what he knows now will happen.

He looks back outside. The riders have formed a perimeter around the place; the Brothers outside are casting a spell he's only seen once before, coming down like an invisible dome. He senses the meridians around him fall out of reach. He seats himself on the floor and waits for his eventual killer.

He clutches his bag against his chest like it is the rope and he is overboard in the rough southern seas just outside the Wastes. This is all he has now. There is no escaping destiny. His dream is coming true.

Come to me, boy. My son who is not my son.

XXIV

As soon as he exited the pass through the cliffside, Kam—who for many years now had mostly been known by another name, the name of his son— could smell the saltiness of the sea and knew he was home.

Press Release

The Anthony and Alice D'Albero Foundation, Inc. announces 43 grants totaling $25,616,000 to 18 charitable organizations in fiscal year 2034–2035.

FAIRFIELD, CT, December 2, 2035 - Now entering its twenty-first year of grant making, The Anthony and Alice D'Albero Foundation, Inc. has reaffirmed its mission of supporting arts, education, and environmental causes around the world. The Anthony and Alice D'Albero Foundation, Inc. is pleased to announce that 43 grants totaling $25,616,000 were awarded to 18 different charitable organizations internationally in fiscal year 2034-2035. Since its inception in 2014, the foundation has awarded over 275 million dollars to charities in 14 countries.

"These grants supported a wide variety of causes," said Foundation Trustee Sarah Fitzroy (née D'Albero), "from a literacy initiative in inner-city Cincinnati to an environmental project in the Brazilian rainforest aimed at curbing deforestation and re-introducing certain rare, endangered tree species to the ecosystem. The common link between all of these initiatives is simple—they're all forward-looking in nature. Whether that's making sure future generations are educated in the arts or making sure they have clean water to drink, we want to do our part to make a better world going forwards."

We would like to welcome you to learn more about the initiatives we have supported by visiting the Grantee Update section of our website: www.dfiorefound.org. The case studies found there represent an ongoing effort to showcase the great projects of many of our grantees.

A complete list of awarded grants in fiscal year 2034-2035 follows this release.

THIRTEEN

THE LITERAL AND THE SYMBOLIC

2058

Moira watched with tears in her eyes as Cori crossed the security checkpoint. "Love you! Have fun with your dad!" she shouted, but her daughter just kept walking and then disappeared down the x-ray tunnel. Had Cori not heard, or were ten-year-olds already embarrassed of their parents?

Even after Cori was out of sight, Moira stood at the checkpoint watching other travelers go through the baggage and retinal scan lines. It was perfectly natural, what she was feeling. She'd never been away from her daughter for more than a day and now an entire four-day weekend was going to pass. Of course, if she hated it, it was her own fault. Well, mostly. She was the one who'd decided to move back to Kansas.

When she got back in her car she almost hit the Home button but then remembered Home still meant Los Angeles Island, so she entered her new address instead, reclined her seat, and closed her eyes. It wasn't even six a.m. yet, but Moira was amped and couldn't fall back asleep.

On a whim, she changed the car's destination to Grinter's Farm. She'd been there twice this year with Cori to see the sunflowers but was curious how it would feel to be there so early in the morning before other visitors arrived. She didn't have any appointments until noon, so she'd have most of the morning to herself. And she could catch up on her sleep and paperwork over the weekend.

By the time she arrived, the sun was up on a bright, cloudless day. Other than one guy setting up holography equipment, who ostensibly was trying to capture the place with the perfect morning light, no one else was around. Moira gave the man a nod of acknowledgement and proceeded to walk deep into the fields of sunflowers, further than she'd ever been, until it was yellow in every direction, as far she could see.

It was early October and in all likelihood, this was the last time she would be here before the flowers dried up and the crop was harvested to make oil. Moira pulled one particularly large flower down to her face. She liked examining the patterns and geometric shapes she could find in the petals and disc florets at this distance—things one would completely miss from afar. She remembered the trips they used to take here when she was a child—how her mom took so many pictures, how her dad complained about his shoes getting muddy. One fall she'd brought Robert to Lawrence to meet her parents, and they'd come out here. She was so excited to show her then-fiancé these magnificent fields, as if to prove to him that there were things worth seeing here—that it wasn't just flyover country. "It has its charm, I guess," was all Robert had said.

She imagined Robert showing up, somehow, in the sunflower field and begging for her forgiveness. He'd told her the affair was over and Moira believed him, but she couldn't stand being in the same place they'd lived in when the infidelity had gone on. As a last resort, she'd given him an ultimatum. Come with her. Leave California.Start again somewhere else.

"I can't go. This is my dream job. Mars!" he'd said. "We're talking about Mars!" Robert was an aeronautics engineer and worked for JPL in Pasadena on the Mars outpost. There were plans to increase the outpost's population from ten to more than a thousand. It was true that this was a dream job for him, but what about his family? What about her? Was she being unreasonable? "You sell real estate. You could live anywhere," he'd said, and though this might be true, it felt to her like the worst kind of slight.

When Moira got back to the house, she made herself masala tea and a big breakfast of bacon and eggs and rye toast with butter. Ever since science class did a unit on food production in the Ag Colonies, Cori had insisted on going vegan, and so it was rare that Moira ate like this. It reminded her of childhood.

She was loading the dishwasher when she noticed a vid message on her com. It was her mom. Her mom knew Cori was leaving that morning, so she was probably just worried about her—especially since she and her dad weren't going to be around to keep Moira company this weekend.

She called out to open the message and the short hologram was projected in front of her field of vision.

"Hiya Moy," her mom said. From the chart of acupuncture meridians behind her mom's head, it looked like she was in her office already. "I guess you're not back yet from dropping off Cori. Anyhow, if you can give me a call when you have a chance, I actually have a favor to ask of you."

Jack attempted to hold himself in a twisting half-moon—something he'd only recently been able to accomplish for any length of time—when the sound of Luna's voice distracted him and sent him stumbling to his mat.

"Sorry for interrupting," she said, sounding genuinely apologetic. The vid screen that guided him through the poses froze. "You have a joint call from Neha and Moira. Shall I patch them through?"

"Is it an emergency?" He hated being disturbed from his workouts.

"They made no note of an emergency, nor did their tone of voice suggest such."

"I'll take the call, but can you tell them to just hold for another minute?"

He rushed through his vinyasa and popped up, balancing on his other foot this time, first into warrior three, then half-moon, twisting half-moon, and finally standing splits (in his case, more of a standing "L").

With his face pointed down to his mat, he noted the yellowish hue of his toenails. God, when did he get so old? Not just middle aged, but *old*. He came out of the position as gracefully as he could, which wasn't very, and picked up his towel to mop his face. "Okay, Luna."

"They're requesting virtual, is that okay?"

"Fine."

His daughter's and wife's translucent projections blinked into existence. "Hiya, dad," Moira said. "Luna told me you were doing yoga."

"Well," he said, and jumped into royal dancer but lost his balance a second later and stumbled out of the pose.

"Impressive," she said.

"Yeah, it only took him thirty-five years to start listening to me," Neha said.

"I'd rather play basketball or go for a run. The only problem is I'm too damn old to do any of that nowadays."

"Ninety-seven, dad," Moira said. "Ninety-seven."

"What's that?" his wife said.

"I just read it in the *Beijing Bulletin*. It's the average life expectancy of someone who makes it to seventy," Moira said, "I've been telling dad every time he plays his woe-is-me, I'm-so-old bit."

Ninety-seven. Despite whatever Moira said, he doubted this statistic—thought there must be some kind of fine print behind it. *Of someone who makes it to seventy...* And even if he does make it to ninety-seven, that means he has just twenty years left.

"So to what do I owe this joint call by my second and third favorite women?"

"Second and third favorite?" his wife said.

"Cori is my new number one. Sorry, guys."

"Who's second and who's third?" Moira said.

"Don't stir up trouble," Neha said. "Anyhow, the *raison d'etre* for this call is that unfortunately one of my maternity patients started going into labor early and she needs me. It's her first, so I doubt she'll be done by this afternoon."

"And what does this mean for our three o'clock tickets?" Jack said. While the main purpose of the trip out east was the readings and events for his book launch, he had been looking at the trip not just as a work obligation but also as a celebration, a mini-vacation.

"It means I need to get a substitute."

"To take care of your patient?"

"No. For the trip."

"Who?"

"Hi, dad!"

Moira had told her dad they could take her car to the hyperloop station in Kansas City, so that afternoon she picked him up at the house. She didn't love taking the hyperloop and always felt slightly nauseous after riding it, but with all the hassle of airport security—telling the Homeland Protection marshal no you can't retinal scan my dad's right eye, it's robotic and then proving it with the paperwork, etcetera, etcetera, it was more convenient than flying.

Her dad was waiting on the curb with his bags when she arrived. He got in the car and kissed her on the cheek. "We're late," he said.

"It's 1:35."

"That's past one thirty, isn't it?"

"We only have to be at the station fifteen minutes ahead, and the drive is only forty-five minutes—"

"Assuming no traffic."

"We'll get there."

"Your optimism vis-à-vis traffic is something I see you've inherited from your mother. What is the car saying?"

She looked down at the screen on the dash. "Forty-seven minutes."

"See."

They drove through town and were soon speeding down the highway—no sign of traffic—across the empty farmland of northeast Kansas.

After a while, she set the car on auto and swiveled her seat to face her dad. "So how do you feel about your book coming out after a million years?" she said. Over the last four decades he'd published more than twenty romance novels, a children's book, and three "how-to" guides, but this current book, a set of interconnected fantasy stories, was a project he'd been working on since before Moira was even born.

"Excited?" he said and shrugged his shoulders. "But a new book is always sort of anti-climactic. You have this expectation that the world, or at least your own life, is going to change, but in truth the most you can expect is for it to be like a pebble thrown into a big lake: a few ripples and then that's it."

"Ripples are good. Besides, this book is different than your other stuff. Who knows how it will do?" she said.

"You're right. It might *totally* bomb."

"It's not going to bomb... Hey, by the way, I saw your virtual-cast on the university station the other day ..."

"What did you think?"

"You were...good."

"I'm glad my daughter can give me such a glowing recommendation."

"No, it's not that...it's...I didn't know all that stuff about you burning the manuscript... during your...your first marriage and then how you re-wrote the whole thing from memory—"

"It wasn't from memory exactly. It changed a lot."

"Yeah, but, you know...Also, even after all this time, it's still weird for me to think of you as having divorced someone—as you having been with anyone but mom."

"That's the only reality you ever knew."

He was right. She, like many people, had, in her twenties, gone through the stage of finally seeing her parents as fallible human beings. Yet, in the realm of romantic relationships they had always seemed, if not an ideal (definitely not an ideal!), at least pretty decent examples.

"Oh, hey…One more thing…Are you going to let me read the book…*finally?*" she said.

"It came out on Tuesday! Buy a copy! Every sale counts," he said, opening his briefcase and pulling out a copy he had inside.

She took the book and examined it briefly. "*The Childless Ones,*" she said, reading the title aloud. Her dad didn't say anything. She placed the slim volume in her bag. "Hey, Dad? Back to what we were talking about…I was just thinking that you've never really told me much about your first marriage."

"You're right. The second wife generally doesn't like it when you do that."

"Well, she's not here."

"What do you want to know?"

"I dunno. Everything?"

"We probably don't have time for that," he said and pointed to an approaching road sign that told them the station was just a few miles ahead.

Jack looked through the train window and through the glass tunnel that enclosed the track, as the flat, green expanses of Missouri flew by. To his left, Moira slept with her mouth open, a slight snore just audible beneath the hum of the train. The copy of his book he'd given her lay open to page three on her lap. Just as soon as Cori had called to tell her mother she'd arrived in LAI without incident, Moira had put the book down and tilted her head back. "I'm just going to close my eyes for a second," she'd said.

There were four stops before New York (St. Louis, Indianapolis, Columbus, and Pittsburg), and the ride took just over five hours. When they got into the Atlantic Terminal, they'd take a car to the hotel in Bedford Stuyvesant. Tomorrow afternoon he was having a "launch party" his agent had set up for him that was open to the public. In the evening, he'd do a little informal reading at what his agent told him was a "sci-fi pub," where a lot of influential SF vloggers regularly went. On Sunday, it would be up to Providence for another reading and then yet another in Boston on Monday afternoon. If everything went according to plan, they'd take the late Monday afternoon hyperloop back home.

He picked up the book from Moira's lap and flipped to some of the sections he was planning on reading. He'd decided to just keep things simple and start by reading the beginning of the first story in the collection, partially because he thought it stood the best alone, but also because it introduced one of the primary themes of the book. He looked at his watch and tried to figure out how far he could get in ten minutes. Every time he re-read any of his work he always felt that it was either far better or far worse than he remembered. Right now, it was the latter.

The launch party took place in a bookstore in the DUMBO neighborhood of Brooklyn whose space, Moira thought, felt less like an actual bookstore and more like an art installation trying to say something about bookstores. The ceilings were at least thirty feet high and the walls, ceiling, and floor were all of clean, gray concrete. The tables with books were far apart and spaced randomly throughout the cavernous space. The event/reading area was a kind of indentation in the concrete, surrounded by concrete benches; Moira couldn't decide if the area looked more like part of a skate park or somewhere the Roman senate would have used for speeches. The crowd was surprisingly large, a mismatched combination of middle-aged women who were fans of her father's romance novels and early-twenties fantasy readers who had no idea who her father was but were interested by some of the advance reviews.

Her dad read for about twenty minutes—a segment of a story called, *The Memory Tree*, which, if Moira followed, was about this race of people who passed their memories on to future generations via a tree. Moira tried to guess what must have been her father's inspiration for the story; he seemed to have a whole interior life she had never been privy to.

After the formal portion of the event, Moira hovered near the snacks in the rear of the room, watching her dad schmooze with the attendees. There was a moment after he said goodbye to a few people, when a blond woman walked purposefully up to him. She looked to be of middle age, probably late forties or early fifties, although remarkably well preserved. Her figure was trim and, if not beautiful, she was at least "put together." She wore an expensive-looking blazer and high heels that were, at once, stylish without being frivolous looking.

Moira couldn't hear their conversation over the general drone of the event, but, as she took another plate of carrots and edamame purée, she tried to guess the gist of it based on body language and facial expressions. Her father sticks out his hand and greets the woman, just like everyone else. The blond woman says something. Her father is surprised. The woman keeps talking; her father is nodding solemnly.

Moira decided she had to go over and see what this was all about. When she's halfway to him, her father looked up and smiled as if unsure whether her arrival would make the situation more or less uncomfortable.

"This is my daughter, Moira," he said.

"Hi, nice to meet you," the blond woman said, all business, and shook her hand.

"Moy, this is Margaret Fitzroy."

Something about the name sounded familiar but Moira couldn't quite place it. "Have we met before?" she said.

"I don't believe so," Margaret said.

"She's Henry's…," her dad started, "…my ex-wife, Sarah's stepdaughter."

"Daughter, technically," Margaret said. "She adopted me after she married my dad."

"Oh, that's right," he said.

"Nice to meet you," Moira said, despite not being sure if the statement was true.

"Yeah. Nice to meet you, too. I was telling your dad that it was a really nice event."

"You a fan of fantasy?"

"Me? Not really. I actually…The actual reason I came down here was because…uh…my mom's really sick."

"Oh. I'm sorry to hear that," Moira said.

"Yeah, she's been dealing with Alzheimer's for some time now."

Moira's father had his right thumb resting on his chin with his index finger crossing his mouth in a pensive pose. His gaze was averted at a forty-five degree angle towards the floor, and Moira guessed this was the second time he'd heard all this.

"It's been mostly manageable with the gene therapy," Margaret said, "but recently it's taken a turn for the worse. She's confused a lot. Sometimes she doesn't really seem to recognize me."

"God, that's terrible," Moira said.

Margaret nodded. "But anyhow…The reason I came down here was that," she turned to Moira's dad for a moment now, "as I told you," she turned back to Moira, "she's been talking a lot about your father. Calling for him. Talking as if he's there. I'm not sure if she wants to see him or if she's just confused, but when I saw online that he was going to be in town. Well, not that I believe in that kind of thing, but I just thought, *fate*, you know? And I thought I'd see if he might come up to Connecticut, maybe…while he's in town…if there's time."

✣

Jack and Moira took a cab back to the hotel for a short rest before the evening reading. The way he'd left things with Margaret was that they had a pretty tight schedule, but if he could have a couple hours to figure things out, he'd let her know if they might have time tomorrow to stop in Connecticut on the way to Rhode Island. Margaret had said that would work and had sent her number to Jack's com.

It had been twenty years ago at Norman Wong's daughter's wedding in Chicago that he last saw Sarah. She certainly hadn't shown any signs of Alzheimer's then. He specifically remembered thinking that she looked to be in good health. She'd worn an age-appropriate blue dress that he'd had to admit looked elegant. *God, twenty years!* Even when things were the worst between them, he never imagined it would be possible for twenty years to go by between seeing her. But now what? He was going to see her again—all sick and not knowing what's anything and that would be his last memory of her?

And yet, there was a part of him, not just a small part, that wanted to go—*really* wanted to go—see her. Even if she was just a shell of the woman she'd been. Plus, he thought, and maybe this was selfish (it *was* selfish!), that shell might allow him to relive his own memories again, one last time. Had he never gotten over her? Neha had been the woman he'd made his life with, but was it possible that we never got over the people we really loved? Was it possible that the holes people leave in us never heal, that we just move through life collecting more and more of them until there comes a day when we're more hole than substance?

"So what are you going to do?" Moira said, just as the cab announced they were nearing the hotel.

"Maybe I should call your mother and see what she thinks."

"What do *you* want to do?"

"I'm torn."

"In what sense? Maybe it would be helpful if you weighed out the options. You know, like the pros and cons."

Pros and cons. If only it were so simple. When he imagined Sarah—likely in some huge old house—up in Connecticut, but with her mind half gone and herself so close to the end, it hurt.

We have arrived at your destination and are parked safely. Feel free to get out whenever you're ready.

"I'm sorry, dad," Moira said. "Do you want to talk about it? Only if you want to though."

One of the benefits that writing stories afforded him was the ability to gain perspective—to look at himself not as himself, but as a character in a story, the story of his own life and the story of others' lives. Stories hinged on the decisions of their characters, decisions that would come to define both the characters and the story as a whole.

Please exit the vehicle or enter a new destination. Otherwise, you will be billed for additional waiting time.

"No. Not right now. But I think I've figured out what I want to do."

Moira sat on one of the two double beds in the hotel flipping through the vid monitor's massive library of interactives from the twenties and thirties. Thinking back to her teenage years, she couldn't believe how much time she'd spent inside her favorites, playing out each episode, often as multiple characters to see how the lives of these people she loved so much would change if she'd just acted a little different here or a little different there. Man, she'd wasted a lot of time with those.

When they'd gotten back to the hotel, her dad said he was going to stay downstairs to call her mom and tell her about his plan to go to Connecticut. A few minutes later, he returned to the room. Moira looked to him to see how things had gone, but his face didn't show any signs.

"Here, Moy," he said, handing her the com. "Your mom wants to talk to you."

"Oh, okay," she said and took it from him. "Hi mom." Moira tried to have a neutral tone, unsure what kind of mood her mom would be in.

"You guys having fun?" her mom said.

"Yeah, the event was nice. We went to a nice Senegalese restaurant down in Bed-Stuy last night. How was the birth-slash-pregnancy? Everything okay?"

"Fine. Easy. I got there, put a couple of needles in, a little acupressure, and the baby came right out. No problem."

"God, I wish it had been that easy with Cori."

"When Corinne was born you were screaming at me, remember? 'Don't fucking touch me with those needles,' you said."

"I think it was 'Don't touch me with those fucking needles, *you crazy bitch.*' So what's up?"

"Well, your father told me about—"

"Yeah. I know. Are you upset?"

"Why would I be upset?"

"I don't know. Jealous?"

"Jealous of a poor woman who's half lost her mind? I'm too old for that."

"Oh, okay. Great then."

"I just want you to take care of your father. I think he might not handle all this too well."

The event that night would have been a lot of fun if Jack hadn't had Sarah so much on his mind. The venue was a dive bar called The Pan-Galactic Gargle Blaster, and a huge array of sci-fi tchotchkes and souvenirs were on display in glass cases around the room. Along one whole wall a massive mural depicted Luke Skywalker, Ellen Ripley, Dr. Who, Neo from The Matrix, and every other sci-fi hero in a pitched battle against Darth Vader, the worm from Dune, the Predator, the Borg and every other sci-fi villain. And the place was packed—although Jack got the impression much of it was for the reader who preceded him, a Moldovan guy, who was at least seven-feet tall and had written a literary re-telling of E.E. "Doc" Smith's remarkably crappy Lensman Saga.

After Jack read, the audience asked thoughtful, fun questions and at the end quite a few came up to buy his book.

Still, Sarah was always there. Tickling the back of his mind.

Prior to the start of the event, Jack had called Margaret to tell her he could come by tomorrow morning—as long as they left by around lunchtime. "Is it the same house?" he said. "The one in Fairfield?"

"Oh, no. After Mrs. D'Albero...My grandmother...passed away, Sarah sold that house. It was just too big and empty feeling." Margaret gave Jack the new address and they ended the call.

After the reading, Jack and Moira went to dinner at a little restaurant on Cornelia Street that Jack remembered going to many years before. Even though he'd lived in Philadelphia, he'd had friends in New York and visited often. He couldn't remember who he'd gone to the restaurant with (he assumed it must have been a girl), but the one thing he did remember was that there had been a plate of the most delicious-looking chocolate chip cookies in the window, even though there was no way to actually order cookies for dessert. Jack had found this curious and on the way out asked if he might take a couple cookies for the road. They agreed and Jack had taken two or three. They had been the best cookies he'd ever had. That was maybe fifty years ago. With all the restaurant turnover in New York, it was a small miracle this place was still open.

"That's so awesome, dad. That you remember that," Moira said after he'd told her the anecdote.

"Why's it awesome? When you get old, you have a lot of old memories,"

"One might hope," Moira said. Jack wasn't sure whether she'd been making a veiled reference to his ex-wife's condition. His daughter took a bite of her pasta, chewed, swallowed, looked back up at him. "So are you going to talk to me or do I have to drag any information I get out of you now?"

He took a bite of his own dinner: a little trout, with some risotto balanced on one forkful. "Says the daughter who is so open with talking about her feelings and relationships," he said after he'd swallowed.

"Fair enough," Moira said. "Let's make a deal then. You answer one of my questions, then I answer one of yours."

He took a sip of wine. It was only his second glass, but he was already starting to feel the effects. "Fine, let's shake on it," he said and stuck out his hand. She took it and shook.

God, he loved this girl... this woman. Loved, loved, loved.

"Me first. How are you feeling about the visit?" she said.

"Well... In order for me to answer one of your questions, I have to be *able* to answer it. I don't know how I feel."

"Weak! Try."

He paused, thought for a moment. "Let me tell you this way. Whenever I write a story, I usually think about the story's meaning on a literal as well as symbolic level. I think you can look at life through similar lenses. *Literally*, I guess I am excited to see a person I loved so much, but I'm also nervous that I might see her and she'll be unrecognizable—not just physically, but mentally, and that I won't feel *anything*. As for the symbolic, there is the obvious symbolism, right? *Another one bites the dust*. My friends have been dying for years, so you'd think I'd be used to it, but this is... different. Here's a woman who at one point, I promised to spend the rest of my life with."

"Promises," she said, as if commiserating.

"Yeah, I know. Didn't do such a good job with that one."

"Although, if you had, I wouldn't have been born."

"Well, technically . . ."

"Because Mom would have gotten a sperm donor that looked like you had you not been in the picture?"

"You have a point. Anyhow, it's my turn. Is there any chance you and Robert are going to get back together?"

Moira made a face to protest the question, but Jack cut her off. "My question is my question. It's not ridiculous. I see how you look when you holo-chat with him."

"He's Cori's dad." There was silence for a few seconds. "I don't know. Sometimes, I miss him, but—"

"Do you still love him?"

"Yes." She hesitated. "But love isn't everything. Trust is important."

"True. But people—men especially—have an incredible propensity to fuck things up."

"Are you speaking from experience?"

"Of course."

The waitress came a few minutes later and cleared their empty plates. "Can I get you anything for dessert?"

Moira looked away from the waitress at her father. "Did you see any cookies in the window when we walked in?"

From the highway, their car weaved down a series of streets that seemed to grow progressively more affluent. While Moira's parents' house—the house she'd grown up in—was located on a block that was, by all accounts, nice, the streets they drove upon now would best be described as perfect. Without fail, front yard after front yard had been expertly and tastefully landscaped: perfectly trimmed hedges, orderly rows of flowers or other flora, manicured lawns. This was Sarah's house they were going to, not Margaret's, but the street seemed to fit with the image she'd constructed in her mind of the younger woman the day before at the bookstore: the meticulous hair, the blazer that lacked even a suggestion of wrinkles.

They reached a T-junction with nothing in front but the Long Island Sound behind an enormous levee. She'd heard about these on her com feed a while back. The affluent homeowners hadn't wanted some ugly pile of concrete mucking up their view and instead the levee had been created out of a perfectly clear plastic that was nearly invisible unless you came right up to it. Through it they saw water, higher than the land, fish, like a giant aquarium. The car made a right.

"Someone's done well for themselves," Moira said.

"Her family had quite a bit of money," he said. That morning he'd gotten up early and put on a jacket and tie—something he hadn't done for either of the events the day before. "But Sarah had a pretty successful career herself for a lot of years."

Even before they got to the front door of the house—a blue and cream two-story building with huge bay windows facing the levee—Margaret stepped out onto the lawn. She was dressed casually today in jeans and a gingham shirt, yet she managed to even make these clothes look expensive.

She wasn't wearing a jacket, so she hugged her elbows with her hands to shelter herself from the breeze blowing in off the water.

"I'm so glad you guys could make it," she said.

Her dad got out of the car and gave Margaret a hug. "I'm glad I could come," he said.

They entered the house into a sitting room that was as well-decorated and furnished as one would expect. From another room came the sound of someone playing piano: nothing too complex, the sort of thing one might expect a precocious child to play. In this first room there were a number of large, framed photos on the wall.

"Is this your dad?" Moira said, gesturing to a photo with an older man standing next to a version of Margaret that Moira guessed was fifteen years younger.

"Yeah," Margaret said. "He died…nine years ago."

"You mentioned that. I'm sorry."

"So…my mom is in the den, if you want to follow me over there."

They walked through a sunlit dining room towards the piano music. "Recently she's started playing the piano a lot. Always the same four or five songs."

Sarah was seated at the piano, her back to them, with her long gray hair tied into a ponytail. She wore slacks and a red and white striped sweater, and Moira could see underneath the piano bench to her bare feet on the pedals. Often her fingers hesitated before pressing down on the keys, but she never missed a note. Moira had seen pictures of her father's ex-wife but had never met the woman. Seeing her now gave Moira a slightly disquieting feeling—like she was a child peeking into a door that she'd been expressly told to keep closed.

"Mom," Margaret called in the voice of one talking to a child. "Mom, I have someone here to see you."

Sarah kept playing. "Mom?" Sarah struck a false note now and then slammed her hands on the keys.

She swiveled her head. "What?" she said, exasperated, but then her face changed when she saw the two visitors. It wasn't a look of recognition, more like she was trying to remember something. She spun around on the piano bench and sat with her hands in her lap.

"Do you know who this is?" Margaret said.

"What did I tell you about tricks. I don't like tricks. No, I most certainly do not know!"

Her father turned to Margaret, as if asking for permission. She nodded and he took two steps towards her and bent down.

"Sar, it's me."

"Who's *me*?"

"Jack."

To this she started laughing. "You think I don't know what my own husband looks like?"

Jack turned to Margaret and Moira and shrugged his shoulders.

Sarah kept laughing for a while but then at last stopped, finally recognizing him. "Where have you been?" she said in a scolding tone.

"Do you mind if I sit?" he said to her, gesturing to the couch facing the piano bench.

She nodded and he sat down.

"I'm going to get everyone some coffee," Margaret said.

"I'll help," Moira said, and the two women retreated to the kitchen.

"How are you, Sar?"

"I'm fine, how are you?"

"I'm good. Margaret said you were asking for me."

"And why shouldn't I? You're my husband."

"I was. But not for a long time."

She looked at him suspiciously. "What? No! No!"

"Margaret...is your adopted daughter. She's—"

"Of course she's my daughter."

"But she's not *mine*. She was Henry's. Do you remember Henry?"

Sarah looked at her wrinkled, but still delicate, hands and started singing in what was little more than a whisper. "*There's a hole in my bucket, dear Henry, dear Henry. There's a hole in my bucket dear Henry, a hole*...You know that song?"

He did but only through her. She used to sing it when she was feeling whimsical. "A little," he said.

"Emily taught it to me. Do you know Emily?"

"No. We never met." Had she ever told him that her sister had taught her that song? He didn't think so. Even when they were together, there was a lot, he supposed, he didn't know about her.

"That's a shame."

Years ago, after their divorce, he had written some stories about her. Not things that were true per se but things he had imagined, to fill in the gaps in his knowledge now that they were no longer together. At the time these stories he'd written had felt so *right* to him—not their events but their feeling, their essence.

It'd made sense that he'd been able to write about her; they'd been married, after all. But now he knew: he'd been wrong. He'd never known her as well as he'd thought. What he knew had been a ghost—a figment of his imagination created, perhaps in her image, but not her.

"Can I ask you a question?" she said. "I'm not trying to be mean, but it's the thing that's *on the tip of my tongue*. No, that's not right. The tip of my brain."

"Okay."

"Why do you look so old?" she said.

Jack laughed. "I wonder the same thing." He took her hands in his own. "They're cold," he said and brought them to his mouth and exhaled on them to warm them up.

He was still holding onto her hands when he heard Margaret's voice. She was standing next to Moira holding a tray with a French press and a small pitcher of cream. She put the tray down on a nearby table.

"Do you take sugar?" Margaret said, but didn't wait for a response. "I forgot the sugar. Let's go get some."

Her father and Sarah weren't speaking when Moira and Margaret entered and then excused themselves.

In the hall again, Moira said, "Is it just me or does it feel like something sorta intense is going on in there?"

"Not just you," Margaret said. "Say, any interest in getting some fresh air? It's a nice day. It's beautiful to just walk along the water."

"What about the sugar?" Moira said.

"Let's forget about the sugar."

Moira agreed. Margaret retreated to another room and came back with a corduroy jacket.

They walked along a three-foot-wide patch of gravel between the shoulder of the road and the levee.

A school of fish swam up to the clear wall. Margaret pointed.

"Neat," Moira said.

"So . . . when we were making the coffee. You said you had a . . . daughter?"

"Yeah, Cori."

"Oh, that's cute."

"It's short for Corinne."

"That's a nice name. Wait. Why does that sound familiar?"

"Maybe because it was the name of the character in the story my dad read yesterday?"

"That's right! And she's back in Kansas?"

"California, actually. She's visiting her dad."

"Oh," she said and then paused. "Relationships are hard, right? Not that I presume to know any more of your life than what you shared over ten minutes in the kitchen."

"No. You're right. They're hard. Sounds like you know firsthand?" The path and levee curved now. Through the clear levee wall, maybe a hundred meters out, Moira could see what remained of an old lighthouse, partially submerged, that must have been abandoned when the waters rose and the levee was built

"Maybe. Not really. From time to time there are men."

"Plural, huh? Sounds fun."

"You'd think, but it gets old. Occasionally some last a little longer. But something always happens. He's intimidated I make more money than him. Or I work too much, blah, blah, blah."

"Still, you own a business. You love your job. That must be really fulfilling. I mean, real estate is fine and all, but sometimes I wish there was something I was... *passionate* about."

"Passion's overrated."

"Is it?"

They walked for a while longer. When Moira and Margaret came back into the house, Moira could hear her dad's voice but couldn't make out the words. They went into the kitchen and found her dad reading to Sarah at the dining table. The old woman seemed to be paying close attention and she stared down at the table as her body rocked back and forth.

"'She was known to ride with Nob from time to time,'" her dad read. "'To tell the truth, she didn't love it. But perhaps it was time for her to get over all that.'" He closed the book. "That's it, Sar."

"I've never heard that story, have I?" the old woman said.

"No, you haven't. That's a new one. The last."

A trace of a smile appeared on her mouth.

"You guys have a good time?" Margaret said. She pulled one of the dining chairs out and sat down; Moira followed suit.

"Yes, but can you read me one of the stories... The stories from the book?" Sarah said to Margaret, gesturing to the book in Moira's father's hands.

"Well, that's not my book, so—"

"Please. Keep it," her dad said. "I have lots." He slid the book over to Sarah, who snatched it and brought it close to her face. She examined it as if it were some ancient artifact whose use she couldn't fathom. "And how was the walk?"

"Good," Moira said. "A lot of girl talk."

"Glad I wasn't there," he said.

Moira saw the time on the antique wall clock. "Should we be hitting the road? I don't want you to be late for your event."

He glanced at his com. "Wow, yes."

Everyone stood up except Sarah. "Thanks so much for coming," Margaret said.

"I have to go now," Jack said to Sarah. "It was very nice seeing you again." He hugged her as if worried he might break her and kissed her on the forehead.

Jack drifted in and out of sleep much of the ride up to Providence. He had been worried about how seeing Sarah would make him feel, but now he realized his fears had been unwarranted.

He was in a brief stretch of being awake (though he didn't open his eyes), when he heard Moira on her com.

"Hi, Robert…Oh good. I'm glad you and Cori are having a good time…What's that? No. Actually…I wanted…I wanted to talk to you…I'm glad. Okay. Yeah, I know you're busy and everything. That sounds great. We'll talk next week when Cori gets back and everything…Yeah…Great…I'm looking forward to it too."

From *Padgett's Rise and Fall of the Alderian Empire*, published
613 Years After *The Fall*
"On the End of the Lunaris Dynasty"

In the 601st Year, Emperor Kaleb finally succumbed to the illnesses
brought on by his advanced age, thus ending his fifty-three-year
reign, which was characterized by great military success and Imperial
expansion but also by costly wars. Though Kaleb sired four children,
two of whom survived into adulthood, neither were able to succeed
their father. The former Crown Prince Patrin (who would have been
Emperor Patrin VII) died only months before his father, never having
sired any offspring, despite being married twice. Kaleb's second son,
Marcellus, while surviving his father, had several years earlier been
diagnosed with madness and sent to live in a sanitarium. As a result,
when Kaleb died, the throne passed, as the Alderian Council had
dictated, to Kaleb's second cousin, Kilborne, making him the first of
a new Galsworth dynasty. While many suspected that Imperial policy
would remain relatively unchanged after the dynastic succession, this
prediction was not borne out. Within the first six months on the
throne, Emperor Kilborne I—who as a soldier during the Second
Haroumi War and general during the Great Uprising, was no stranger
to the darker side of Imperial expansion—laid out what he called
the Six Pillars of Reform, which amongst other things, put an end
to aggressive Alderian expansion, assigned grand council seats to
each of the provinces, and created a path for independence, albeit a
difficult one, for those provinces who wished for it. Of course, many
Imperial officials predicted that few of the provinces would actually
opt for secession. While annexation into the Empire may have been a

violation of those former nation's sovereign rule, once in the Empire, many of the annexed territories enjoyed a number of economic and political advantages that they were not likely to want to give up.

FOURTEEN

THE SAPLING
611-612 Years After *The Fall*

All that morning Padgett dreamed of fire and death tearing through the Westwood.

The bodies of Mandrakhar—pierced by arrow, ripped asunder by sword and axe, or trampled beneath the thunder of horse hoof—littered the forest floor. The ancient trees burned in a great conflagration whose smoke blacked out the sky. At the center of the blaze, where the fire had started and where it now burned hottest, was where the oldest of the trees had been.

Padgett could see the ephemeral embodiments of the memories held within, floating off into the sky, gone forever, as the Tree shriveled, blackened and died.

But then he was somewhere else: a courtyard surrounded by a decrepit building of many faded colors. And he saw the jewel inside the scepter glow, its hue cycling through every imaginable color before settling on a pure, brilliant white that blazed brighter than the sun. Root-like structures began growing from the bottom of the scepter, which, when they reached the soil, plunged into the earth.

He opened his one good eye.

He was back in his chamber in the Sanctum of Ilyeth, staring upward at the detailed, vaulted ceilings. He sat up and exhaled a long, slow breath. The outward look of serenity on his face hid his combination of excitement and horror.

He went to his wardrobe, a fine piece of late-Phaidonian make he'd inherited when Master Szilvia finally passed, and located the items he sought, placing them on his desk: the white scepter and the small, egg-shaped red jewel that belonged inside it. So much of his life had been dedicated, in a roundabout way, to these two things. The former had been found some years ago in the tunnels beneath the old Phaidonian ruins in the Westwood. The latter had been in his possession slightly longer but had come at greater cost. Even after he possessed both of them, he'd searched for so long—five years—to understand their purpose.

Now he had it. But at what cost?

He should have guessed it would have to do with the Mandrakhar. These two items were allegedly of the Forefathers; according to legend, the Mandrakhar were the Forefather's *chosen people*.

He removed a volume from his bookshelf and flipped through the old journal that had belonged to his one-time friend and mentor. He'd read these pages so many times he almost knew all the words by heart.

Setting the book down, Padgett got dressed, packed some belongings, and readied himself to leave the island. The first ship left just after dawn and he would be on it. It would be a long journey back to the Westwood. To think, when he found the scepter, he had been right near where he'd needed to go. He just hadn't known it.

He hurried down the corkscrew staircases of the Sanctum. Few were awake yet and everywhere around the air was still and silent such that each of his footsteps felt like a kind of trespass. He was already an old man by normal standards, but this journey, he thought, would mark an end to something that began in his own adolescence, long ago. And afterwards, he would enter a new, perhaps final, stage of life.

Vorlan, seed keeper, woke to shouting, the trample of horses, and the smells of things burning that were not meant to burn. A red glow showed through the single window of his cottage. Not far away came the terrible music of steel on steel. He recalled something from long ago—war, death, so much blood—more feeling than memory, the *yulthanispel*, memories of the ancestors.

He regained himself and stepped out onto the landing, high up amongst the branches. It was nearly winter, but a hot wind greeted him. The sky was still dark, but the fire—fire everywhere—provided ample light. Two hundred paces away many of the huts at ground level, many of the trees, burned brightly. Below, against the backdrop of the flames, a woman ran towards the gates. She pulled along a child in each hand. He couldn't make out her face in the smoky red light. The horse sounds grew near. Time seemed to pass very slowly. Two riders, humans not Mandrakhar, gained on the running woman, the children, from behind. The distance between them closed. She called out, a single scream. Then the falling of the first rider's axe, the second rider's sword, and the screams stopped. The children never made a sound.

He stepped back into his cottage, closed the door, and sat on the floor, out of view from the window. He slid over to his dresser and found his hatchet. Up until now it had only been used to cut fallen tree branches.

He heard someone, slow methodical steps, walking up the stairs. He tried to grip the hatchet, but it just sat in his semi-closed hand. He was no fighter. The door opened and Vorlan prepared to meet his end.

It was only Flynn.

"*What takes place in the current world near to us?*" Vorlan said.

"*Someone attacks us currently,*" Flynn said. His voice was quiet, strained. He was one of the oldest in the settlement—nearly twenty now. He had begun to show the first signs of the wasting sickness. For months, his hair had been the white of a swan's feather, his skin a translucent cream that had begun to reveal his bluish and reddish veins beneath.

"*By which people and for what reasons?*"

"*I...I know not,*" Flynn said. "*But the unknowns transformed it to fire...the Tree.*"

Vorlan knew which tree.

"*You must...become nothing from this place,*" Flynn said. "*You own the role 'seed keeper.' Keep the seeds safe.*" He hunched over. He looked tired. But so it was with the sickness.

Vorlan shook his head. Being seed keeper was only a ceremonial role. Everyone knew this. No Trees had been planted in fifty generations. Without the methods of the ancients, methods that were beyond them, the seeds could not sprout. They would just sit inactive in the soil. Their fate would be the same as all the other Mandrakhar throughout the Continent: adrift in the world, untethered from their pasts. "*Does not such an action lack purpose? If the Tree no longer lives, we have lost ourselves.*"

"Perhaps. But the title you own mandates certain duties." He gestured to the small, gold-inlaid wooden chest on the table.

Vorlan unlatched the box to behold the smooth black acorn-shaped things inside. He closed the box again.

"My horse. Take it," Flynn said. He pointed down through the floor.

"Will not you need it?"

"My body maintains a state of tiredness prohibiting travel," he said. *"I will…sit…and rest."* Flynn sat down on the straw mattress.

"Where should I go?"

"Eventually to Ilyeth, home of sorcerers. Some generations past a sorcerer lived amongst us. People called him Kam Rhys. Perhaps he can help. But for now, that is too distant a journey. For now, go east… The capital of the empire of men."

"The capital?"

"Many Mandrakhar live there. You can blend in and find safety until you can get passage south. The empire of men does not love our kind, but neither do they allow murder within their walls. Also, there lives a woman there who you can trust. A human. She will help you."

"A human?"

"Yes. People call her Corinne."

Leaving his home. Going to the capital. Trusting a human. It was all too much for him. *"How will I find her? The stories tell that it requires a day's march simply to go from one end of the capital to the other."*

Flynn removed a small piece of parchment from underneath his shirt. *"A letter. I think she said where she worked. A house of knowledge. The letter has an age of three years, but maybe she works there still."*

"And what does she appear as?"

"How many years have you, Vorlan?"

"I approach my eighth," he said.

Flynn looked at his fingers as if counting. *"Yes, then I believe you shall recognize her when you see her."*

Corinne sat at her desk in the cramped Imperial Library office overlooking Bethsemene Square. Through the tall, narrow window she watched people walk beneath the domed crowns of the stone pines that lined the walkways. In one secluded section of the square, a man with black hair and a woman in a gray dress stood beside a hedge kissing. Perhaps they were in love. There would have been a time some years ago, when she had just come to the capital, that she might have wished to switch places with such a woman, to be again in the embrace of a lover. No longer. Corinne's days for romance were past. She accepted that. Her life was no longer one of the heart but one of the mind, and for this, this second act, she was grateful.

For the last week, she'd been working on making a copy of *Jerome's History of the Continent* that had been ordered by the library in Vicus Remorum. Despite the monotony, one of the things Corinne loved about her vocation was how much it permitted her to read—indeed, required it. The histories weren't her favorite; they often digressed into endless lists of places and dates and battles, but they were better than nothing. Her favorites were the epic poems of the Old Masters who told stories of love and heartbreak and courage and sacrifice and redemption. Sometimes she felt like it was only in stories that life could transcend into something greater than its usual, disappointing reality, and so in this way, the storyteller, the poet, were professions of the highest order.

When her pages dried and it was time to end the day, Corinne closed the two large tomes and descended the stairs to the office.

"How goes the book?" said Schumm, one of the head librarians and her supervisor. "Will it be ready by next week?"

"I think so." She pulled her cloak, a tattered thing she had brought with her when she came from the West those five years ago, tight around her.

"How are you, dear?" he said now. Schumm was a kindly man; although, since his wife had died two years ago, Corinne could see him regularly considering her in his eyes. What kind of wife would she make? Corinne wasn't interested. One marriage was enough for this life.

"I'm well," she said and tried to smile.

It was still another month before the spring equinox and the air was chill. Corinne rushed home along the cobblestone streets. The most direct route to the rooming house she lived in took about a quarter hour by foot; however, the route Corinne took was a circuitous one avoiding the Mandrakhi Quarter.

When she'd first arrived in the capital, she spent much of her free time in that part of the city. So long as she brought coin, she was reluctantly welcomed into their meal houses and their shops. The Mandrakhar here in the capital were different than the ones in the Westwood. Here, they lived their short lives without a Tree, without the inheritance of their ancestors' memories. Still, they had felt familiar, comfortable. Sometimes though, comfort was the last thing we needed. Now she avoided the place.

When she returned to the small one-room apartment she rented above a clothier's shop, she undressed and washed herself in the basin of water she had left over from the day before. She made a meal of boiled turnips and some of the dried meat she had stored away in her cupboard. For the rest of the evening, until she fell asleep, she read, by candlelight, a book borrowed from the library.

It was the next day she first learned of the violence in the Westwood. It was a wonder she heard of it at all. The capital hardly concerned itself with such backwaters. Schumm brought it up casually during lunch in the mess hall on the first floor of the library.

"A pity," he said. "A slaughter, they say. Nearly all of them killed and the entire settlement burned to the ground. I was no great fan of the Lunari, but there were fewer of these fanatic outlaws running around when they were in charge."

"And who did you say this group was, again?" Corinne said. She tried not to envision the attack. "The Order of—"

"Of Men? Of Man? I'm not sure. A bunch of illiterate crazies, no doubt. And a stupid name, to boot. They pretty much hate and mistrust everyone; they think the Mandrakhar are the offspring of the Demon, think the Kallanbori are conspiring to take over the Empire. I understand much of the Westland is no longer Alderian territory, but if you let that kind of cancer grow outside your borders, sooner or later it will be at your door." Schumm picked up his bowl of stew and slurped down the remainder of the liquid. "Now you lived in the West, Corinne. Did you ever have any dealings with these elves?"

"What's that?"

"Oh, is this stew too spicy for you? Here, let me give you my handkerchief."

The stew wasn't too spicy. She took the handkerchief and wiped her eyes. "Thank you. Now what were you saying?"

"Oh...I was asking about the elves. Did you ever have any dealings with them in the West?"

"They don't like being called 'elves,'" Corinne said but then tried to give him a reassuring smile to show she wasn't personally offended.

"Oh, is that right? See, I've seldom ever spoken to one, so how should I know? So does that mean you *did* have dealings with them?"

"Yes," she said. "From time to time."

It was long enough ago that most of the Mandrakhar she'd known would have most likely succumbed to the wasting sickness by now anyway. She felt a disabling sadness move through her nonetheless. If the Tree had been destroyed then Erlan truly was gone.

Sera and Nob had just got done with a tough job, over the course of which they'd each taken their share of physical abuse and racked up quite the bill with the local healer. The case was a complicated affair involving corrupt nobles, murder, infidelity, incest, and stolen jewels that Sera still wasn't sure she'd gotten straight in her head. The point was, they were in bad shape—and the fact that both she and Nob were getting a little older (fine, a lot older) certainly didn't help. In no particular order, Nob had been:

- stabbed in the arm by a butcher's knife
- sliced with a spear on both hands
- burned by a cattle brand
- smacked in the face by said cattle brand
- punched by a dwarf (not Sera, a he-dwarf)
- kicked by a half-horse in the chest and
- thrown off his own horse into a thicket of thorny rose bushes

Sera's list of injuries, while less extensive, still included being:

- clubbed by Redcloaks on two separate occasions
- choked and then kicked between her legs (thank the gods she was a woman) by the aforementioned dwarf
- locked in a barrel, and
- almost drowned by accident

Sera was considering retirement. At the very least, they were both in dire need of a little time off.

Alas, it was not meant to be.

Not three days after bringing this latest job to a close, Sera and Nob were returning home after an aggressive night of imbibing spirits and generally making merry (drunkenness dulled the pain of their recent injuries, Sera reasoned), when Sera opened the door to the office, and there, sitting in the dark room, was a man whose face was hidden in the shadows. Sera and Nob were both given quite the surprise, their shock undoubtedly heightened by their inebriated states.

Neither of the pair were usually the type to resort immediately to violence—Sera because she wasn't much good at violence, Nob simply because he was predisposed to politeness—but on this particular night,

Nob was, as Sera would have labeled it, "out-of-his-mind drunk." Without a word, he unsheathed his claymore and charged the shadowy trespasser, who remained unmoving in his chair.

"Slow down, Nob," Sera said, but he didn't. It was only as Sera drew closer, as Nob's blade came downward in a deadly arc, that she recognized the figure.

"Stop!" she screamed, but it was too late. Yet just before the blow landed, the blade stopped in midair, inches from its intended target's mostly bald head. Nob released his grip from the sword and it just stayed there, frozen in the air.

"What the?" Nob said, staring first at his empty hands and then at the floating blade.

An invisible force threw the sword harmlessly to the floor.

"Nob," Sera said, "this is my friend Padgett."

Nob looked confused for an instant but then remembered something buried deep in his memory. "That's right! I think you mentioned him before, Ser," he said. "Nice to meet you, and sorry about the mix-up and...you know...trying to kill you."

"Don't worry about it," Padgett said in his mix of Lanzehenese and Southland accents.

"Okay," Nob said and sat down across from the man who seconds earlier he'd tried to cut in half.

Sera stepped outside to light one of her candles on a street lamp. No sooner did she return inside and place the candle down on the desk than every candle and lantern in the room spontaneously burst to life. "He's a sorcerer or some such shit," she said by way of explanation to Nob.

"I prefer *Cree* if you must use labels," Padgett said.

"Whatever," she said.

Though it'd been almost ten years since Sera had last seen him, Padgett looked pretty much exactly how she remembered: a slight man with dark skin and his head shaven, except for a little stubble at his temples. The only major difference was that he wore a patch now over his right eye.

"It's been a long time, Sera," Padgett said.

"It has." She slapped herself once in the face. Despite the excitement, she was still fighting off the wine sleep. "What happened to your eye?"

"Oh, I won't bore you with all that. But how are *you?*"

"Is that why you broke into my office?" she said. "To see how I was doing?"

"I need your help."

"Well, you could have left a note. Or waited outside."

"It's cold outside."

It was. "Fine. What's up?"

"Maybe you should make some tea," he said then.

"A long story, then?" she said.

He nodded. Not exactly what Sera was looking forward to that night, but what could she do?

It was a very long story, Padgett thought. Depending on how one considered it, they might say it started long before his own birth, which itself was many, many years ago now. But perhaps the same could be said of every story—that they start long before our births and go on indefinitely long after we're gone. Of course, such is not a very practical way to look at things.

"You, I'm sure, know of the Mandrakhar," Padgett said, when Sera returned with the tea.

"Sure," she said, "there's a whole neighborhood of them up here on the north side of the Riffel."

"Yes. And do you know what makes them different than the rest of us?" Padgett said.

"Other than the pointy ears?" she said. Padgett nodded.

"They don't live long, right? Only fifteen or twenty years or so?" Nob said, interjecting.

"Yes," Padgett said. "But in the old days, there was another difference. In the old days, each Mandrakhi settlement had what they called *Saloryn Bai*—Memory Tree. Through this Tree, they would each pass down their memories from one generation to the next. And so, though each Mandrakhar would live but a score of years, within each lived the lives of hundreds, maybe thousands, of years of their civilization."

"How come I've never heard of this?" Sera said.

"Because most of the Memory Trees died a couple hundred years ago," Padgett said, gripping the scepter beneath his cloak.

"Why didn't they just plant new ones?" Sera said

"Each Memory Tree produces several seeds over its life, but they can only sprout when treated with a special process—"

"Sorcery," Nob said.

"One could call it that, but it is different in nature than the powers practiced by myself or my Brothers and Sisters. This process is something long since lost even to those of my order."

"Okay, so I'm guessing this has something to do with how you said *most* died hundreds of years ago," Sera said.

"Precisely. There was one surviving Tree. In the Westwood. Halfway between here and the Inner Sea."

"What happened?"

"Four months ago, a group of religious fanatics who call themselves the Order of Men attacked the Mandrakhi settlement and burned down the Tree, slaughtering most of the Mandrakhar of that settlement along the way."

"It's a terrible world," Sera said, shaking her head. "But I still don't see where we come in. Or where you come in for that matter."

"I have, through some trials and tribulations, come into possession of two artifacts that I believe together will get the seeds of the Tree to sprout."

"Trials and tribulations?" Sera said.

Padgett thought of the fateful events that had led him to come into possession of the jewel, then later, the months of searching in the dark tunnels beneath the ruins. "You really don't have enough time for *that* story."

Sera yawned a big, gaping yawn. "Okay. Well I'm glad everything worked out. Sounds like a happy ending to a tragic story," she said.

"You misunderstand," Padgett said. "When I became aware of what was going on in the Westwood, I headed there immediately—even calling upon some of my fellow Ilyan Brothers and Sisters to help gather and protect the surviving Mandrakhar. Still, by the time we arrived, the Mandrakhir who holds the last remaining seeds had already fled. I've tracked this Mandrakhir, the 'seed keeper' they call him, to the capital, but the city is vast and time is of the essence, less some of the Order find him before I do."

"So *that's* where I come in."

"You are an expert at finding people and things, are you not?"

Sera sighed, looked at Nob, who shrugged his shoulders in resignation, and then looked back at Padgett. "So it sounds like you need us to start right away?"

"More for you, honored guest?" Milaeus said.

It had been three weeks since Vorlan arrived in the capital. In that time, he'd gotten a little better at understanding his host's accented Mandrakhi, though he still had to pay extra attention when she spoke.

She offered him the basket of unleavened bread. Her son, Cairlan, had finished his own meal but was not offered more. "*I graciously decline,*" Vorlan said in Mandrakhi. "*I require no more sustenance.*" He didn't want to take more of what little they had. They had been generous to take him in.

"*Very well,*" she said.

Cairlan looked at his mother. Maybe he wondered why he'd not been offered more to eat. The boy looked around three years old—nearly full-grown. If they were in the Westwood, if the Tree hadn't been burned, it would have been only another few months before he would be brought to it to receive *yulthanispel.*

Vorlan reached to his side and fingered the cloth bag that held the box of seeds. He might be amongst the last of his kind to experience the Tree. He tried to recall one particular memory that had fluttered like a bird through his mind on many occasions. It made him very happy any time he recalled it, but he couldn't seem to access it right now. The memories of the ancestors were slippery things.

The boy went to fetch water. Milaeus began cleaning up the mat upon which they'd eaten.

"*Tell me, Vorlan,*" she said. "*Do you long for the Westwood?*"

"*I long for the place a small amount. I long for my friends the most,*" he said.

"*News of what occurred grieves me,*" she said. It was only a few days since the stories of what transpired finally reached the capital—although Vorlan pretended it was only coincidence he had left home just as tragedy befell his people.

"*Yes. It grieves me as well.*"

That night, laying on the floor in the front room of Milaeus's house, Vorlan couldn't fall asleep. After two hours of rolling around, he got up. He donned his cloak, placed his small wooden box, which he brought with himself everywhere, in a canvas shoulder bag and left the house. He went quietly so as not to wake his host.

He walked south out of the Mandrakhi Quarter, through a vast area where the humans placed their dead underneath the ground, and then towards the docks on the bank of the river. The streets and alleys near the docks were still crowded with people—though Vorlan couldn't fathom their business at this hour. Across the river, he could see the lantern towers that illuminated the Capital Building and the Imperial Palace. He had not traveled to see them up close but guessed they must be taller even than the trees of the Westwood. He sat down on one of the stone benches that lined the river.

The journey to the capital had taken him much longer than expected. He had been cautious and evaded anyone he saw up ahead on the road; any time he spied other travelers in the distance, he'd leave the road and travel through the wooded countryside for a time before eventually looping back to the highway.

After a week, while riding through treacherous terrain off the main road, Vorlan's horse stepped where leaves made the ground falsely appear flat and tumbled to the ground. Vorlan only just managed to leap off the beast before being crushed beneath its weight.

The horse's leg was broken, the bone pushing up against flesh near the left gaskin. He stood over the suffering animal for an hour before building up the courage to put her out of her misery. He took up his hatchet and, with all his strength, struck the horse on her underside where he thought her heart was. The horse screamed, and the terrible wound oozed blood. Vorlan, panicking now, struck the writhing horse repeatedly with the hatchet, but the horse refused to die. At last, he threw the hatchet to the dirt and picked up a stone nearby on the ground, bashing the horse on the head until she was still.

From then on, blood covering the only pair of clothes he had, Vorlan went on foot.

After weeks of walking, he arrived in the capital. Despite the stories and some hazy memories from the ancestors, he wasn't prepared for the vastness of the city. He asked around for directions to the "house of knowledge" mentioned in the letter: the *Imperial Library*, it was called. Many misunderstood his speaking of the Common Dialect, but eventually he found the place.

He didn't go inside. Instead, he just sat in the square opposite the library, the hood of his filthy cloak pulled over his head to cover his ears, and watched all the people going in and out of the magnificent stone edifice. How could he trust one of these humans after everything they'd done? It was possible that everyone he'd ever known was dead. Eventually, he rose from the bench and left.

He sought out the nearby Mandrakhi Quarter and spoke to one of the elders there, telling him he was from the Westwood but being vague about his reasons for coming to the capital—only saying he needed his presence to be kept secret. The elder reluctantly agreed not to press Vorlan for answers and, after a night, placed him with Milaeus, who had volunteered to take him in. All involved agreed to claim Vorlan was Milaeus's cousin who had come to visit from the settlement in Vicus Remorum.

In time, Vorlan would inquire about gaining passage to this "Ilyeth" place, but for now he would rest. He needed time to recover from his lengthy and exhausting travels.

The first of the morning bells had rung by the time Vorlan returned to the house. He hoped Milaeus hadn't risen early and worried why he wasn't there.

As Vorlan approached the small shack, he noticed the door slightly ajar.

Certainly, he had remembered to close it when he left. His body filled with dread when, upon closer inspection, he discovered the door had not merely been left open but had been forced open, the small lock cracked off and thrown to the ground.

He opened the door an inch further and there, just beyond the entryway, lay Milaeus in a gathering of her own blood, her throat slashed, her eyes open and seeing nothing. Vorlan closed the door. Had the boy been killed as well? He was too frightened to look now. Whoever had come here would be searching for him, for the seeds.

He gripped the small wooden box through his bag and started running.

On her walk to work, Corinne tried not to think about what had transpired the previous evening. After months of gentle but persistent invitations, she'd finally agreed to join Schumm for dinner at his home. Though Corinne had said she could find her own way to his house in Park West, he'd insisted on sending a carriage. His house was a modest but clean, two-story building on a narrow lane a few minutes' walk from the river.

Schumm greeted her at the door dressed in what Corinne thought must be his best outfit: a tailored coat, which fit more snuggly than it probably once had, over a white tunic with light embroidery on the front. "Hello!" he said, "please come in, come in!" He took her hand and kissed it in a way that felt much practiced.

While Schumm's house-lady finished preparing the meal in the kitchen, the two sat awkwardly regarding one another in the parlor. Corinne had never noticed how much ear hair Schumm had. She was relieved when he asked about the book she had started working on in the library—another copy of *The Travels of Mandel Longfellow,* a book she'd already copied out a dozen times.

"A fine book," Schumm said. "A classic."

They ate mostly in silence, the quiet only occasionally broken by Schumm's comments on politics or Corinne's on how delicious the stew was.

After dessert, Corinne quickly remarked as to lateness of the hour.

"Yes, yes! You are right! I will get you a coach. I should have arranged to have one waiting for you! I am a fool! I am not so used to having guests so sometimes I forget the most common courtesies. I hope you don't—"

"It's all right," she said, just wanting him to stop talking.

Out on the street Schumm removed a whistle from his pocket and blew it repeatedly until a carriage came clattering by.

"Thank you for everything," Corinne had said.

"No, thank *you* for coming. I'll see you tomorrow."

"Yes," she said, and they embraced. It was only after she started disengaging from him, started turning to climb up the carriage, that she realized he'd made an attempt to kiss her—lunging face-first like the trained seals of the traveling circus that catch rings with their snouts. She continued up the carriage and pretended to not notice his advance.

"Goodbye, Schumm," she said, only when she was safely on board.

"Goodbye," he said.

When she reached the library that morning and entered through the main doors, Corinne tried to walk quickly by him so she wouldn't have to face him or talk with him.

"Good morning, Corinne," Schumm called, but she pretended not to hear and rushed past. "This morning someone came in who—"

She went up the seven flights of stairs in a near run, panting and out of breath by the time she arrived at the top. She pushed the door open to her office and inside, sitting in the spare chair, was a man she'd never seen before...no, a Mandrakhir.

He was slight of build with black hair down to his shoulders and just the slightest bit of whisker-like hair above his lip. Few Mandrakhir had beards. He wore a brown shirt and black trousers. His eyes were purple, which was common enough for his kind, but Corinne noticed a particular intensity in his gaze. If she were honest, she would have to say he was probably more handsome than Erlan had been. He held a small wooden box close to his chest.

"May I help you?" she said, a little shaken.

He didn't say anything at first; he just looked at her as if she'd surprised *him* with her presence rather than the other way around. "Say again? I...apologize for my words," he said. Mandrakhar tended to speak fast, but this one was slowed down by his struggles with the Common Dialect. "People call me...I am...Vorlan. Forgive my intrusion, but your...leader. I believe he is *Shoom*, let me in. He told to me that he...that you were...expected shortly and that...wisdom...dictated I wait."

"And...what do you need from me?"

He told her. She had difficulty understanding at times, but mostly she could piece together his meaning. Some of it she knew already—about the nature of Mandrakhar and about the attack in the Westwood. But other parts of the tale he told were new: his journey, his hiding in the capital, the murder of his host the previous night, his desire to go to Ilyeth, a place she wasn't even sure existed.

"Flynn told me I shall...I *can* trust you—that I should come to you."

Flynn. She remembered when he was just a boy and then later how he'd helped Erlan. "Yet you didn't find me when first you came to the capital."

"No. I contained nervous...I did not want to trust human."

"And now?" she said.

She could see how old Vorlan was and knew what that meant. *Erlan...a piece of him...is swimming around in there.*

"Now I trust...not all humans...I trust you."

"Why?" she said. She wanted him to say it.

"Because...I know your face. Because...part of me, I think...loves you."

Padgett had to take care of some "Cree business" related to this magic tree thing but said he'd check in with them in a day. He'd told Sera he'd already asked around in the Mandrakhi Quarter without luck, but Sera thought hers might be better.

Sera had lived in Alder her whole life, but she'd only just barely passed through the outskirts of the Mandrakhi Quarter once or twice. There wasn't ever much reason for her to visit that particular corner of despair. It was one of the poorest parts of the city, with little more than a collection of run-down buildings and shanties, so it wouldn't be a destination for a leisurely stroll. As far as for work, Sera didn't usually work for free, and most Mandrakhar tended to be a little lacking in the money department.

There was no clear demarcation for when the Mandrakhi Quarter started; instead, one just saw the buildings get crappier and crappier until what they found hardly qualified as buildings. The cobblestone streets appeared not to have been repaired since the first Lunaris emperor and were labyrinths of missing stones and potholes.

When they arrived, Sera and Nob went door to door for a little while trying to happen into some information. Everyone they spoke to didn't know anything or refused to talk to them or couldn't speak the Common Dialect.

Down the main road a bit they passed a small structure consisting of a pitched roof, four wooden poles, and some hides hung for walls all around. From the crude sign out front depicting a steaming chicken with its head cut off, Sera guessed this place was some kind of Mandrakhar meal house; she and Nob went inside.

When they pulled one of the hides to the side and walked in, the hum of talking stopped abruptly (not that she or Nob understood a word of

Mandrakhi). They were the only humans there, and everyone turned to look at them. They walked to the counter where the guy who was ostensibly the owner sat on a stool. He had black hair down to his shoulders and a burn mark on his face where it looked like he'd lost a fight with a cattle brand.

"Hey look," Sera said to Nob and pointed to the spot on his shoulder where he'd gotten his own burn. "You guys have something in common." Nob wasn't impressed and told Sera about an uncomfortable place she could stick her own fist.

"What do the humans want?" the owner said. He had a high, heavily accented voice and, like many Mandrakhar, his words came fast.

"Food," Sera said, and the owner looked at her with skepticism. "And information."

"I have neither for you."

"There exist many places for you, little woman," one of the male patrons said. "Why do you dirty this one for us?"

"To be honest? We're looking for one of your kind."

"Then we definitely will not help," the owner said again.

Nob unbuckled his scabbard and laid it on the floor to come off less threatening. "Well, the thing is, friend, we are actually trying to help one of your folk, and if we don't find him, we're afraid some very bad men might get ahold of him first."

The owner seemed to be considering Nob's statement when one of the other Mandrakhir patrons spoke from one of the tables: "We do not trust you. The last human who came by these parts with a big sword, came back with a bunch of thugs and killed Milaeus in her own house."

Nob looked at Sera. "What are you talking about?" she said. "When did this happen?"

"Just yesterday," the patron said and took a bite of the bread sitting in front of him. "So you see why we do not trust—"

"This woman didn't by chance have anyone visiting her?" Sera said.

"I did not know her well. I cannot say."

Sera looked around at the other patrons and then at the owner of the place who had a guilty look on his face.

"My friend," Nob said to him, "you can tell us. What harm could it do now?"

"She had a cousin staying with her. From Vicus Remorum, I think."

"Where is this house?" Sera said.

He gave them directions and they were out the door.

It only took a few minutes to reach the place. A crowd of Mandrakhar had gathered around the wooden shack when Sera and Nob got there. A few kneeled and prayed next to some candles that had been laid out and lit. When the Mandrakhar noticed the pair, a few gave expressions of disgust; Sera wasn't bothered. As a little person and a woman and someone whose business was to get into other people's business, she'd received more than her share of dirty looks.

"Who's in charge here?" she called. A few looked at her, but no one said anything. "Come on. I know a bunch of you understand what I'm saying." Not a word.

She and Nob pushed through to the house.

Right in the front hallway a dead Mandrakhar woman lay in a puddle of her own thick, dark blood. She was wearing what was at one time a white tunic and brown pants, but now both were soaked through with red.

Sera had seen her share of bodies, but that didn't mean she liked it. Tell the truth, she actually thought she'd gotten more squeamish with old age. "Ah fucking shit, Nob."

"A mess, eh? So where do you think our man went—if he was indeed here?" he said.

"He was here," she said. She tried to keep her gaze away from the body. "I just hope he got out before whoever did this got ahold of him."

A voice called to them from the entrance to the house in a Mandrakhi accent. "You cannot be here." It was an old Mandrakhir in a dirty robe.

"I'm Master Serafina Nicoletto and this is my associate Nob. We're investigators and we're looking into what happened here."

"You are with the Redcloaks?"

Sera pulled up her brown cloak to look at it for a moment. "Doesn't look that way."

"Then who are you with?"

"Investigator for hire. You want to talk outside?" The metallic smell of blood was making her nauseous. He nodded and the three of them went back out the way they'd come. They walked back through the crowd to an open area in front of an adjacent house.

"What do you know about the Mandrakhir who was staying with the dead woman?"

"Nothing. They…related to each other as cousins. He hailed from Vicus Remorum."

Mandrakhar are terrible liars.

"Look, if we don't find him, then the guys who busted up that house and killed that woman are going to."

"I told you everything I know. I cannot help you." He turned to go.

"What now?" Nob said. They started walking down the street.

They had just about left the Mandrakhi Quarter when a Mandrakhir adolescent stopped them.

"You will try to help him?" he said. The tip of his nose was red and it looked like he'd been crying.

"Who?" Sera said.

"The cousin of Milaeus." Sera assumed Milaeus was the dead woman.

"Yeah, who are you? Do you know anything?"

He sniffled a little. "I…son of Milaeus. I hide when the men come."

"The one staying with you…" Sera said. "He wasn't your mother's cousin, was he?"

He shook his head "no."

"Do you have any idea where he went?"

"I think I do, yes. He showed much interest in a place…a *house of knowledge*, he called it."

In a secluded room at the far end of the library, Padgett went through books and books, but no answers were to be found.

For a long time, he'd assumed he'd be able to premonition the necessary process, but he'd meditated every evening, first on his travels from Ilyeth to the Westwood and then on the journey from there to the capital, and nothing useful had been discovered. There was a cruel irony to how, though he finally understood what the scepter and stone *could do*, he had no idea how to make the thing do it when the time came.

So now each night since arriving in the capital, Padgett would undertake a process of trial and error where he tested out every permutation of spells he could think of to get the scepter to grow roots like in the premonition— or at the very least, do *something*. The previous evening had been no different. After his evening meal, he hired a carriage to take him to Patrin's Park on the waterfront. On account of the park's reputation of being dangerous after dark, few people went there at night. Padgett could do what he needed without worry of onlooker or bystander. In truth, he was less concerned about being found out as a sorcerer than he was about accidentally setting someone on fire. Many of the spells he was trying had a propensity for collateral damage.

Yet despite the number of spells attempted, the scepter and its stone did nothing.

In the morning, after sleeping only a few hours, Padgett had gone to the Imperial Library in hope of finding some information to assist him. It had been years since he'd been to the capital, but in the old days when he lived in the city, he used to visit the library often. When Padgett arrived it was still quite early and one of the librarians was just unlocking the chains that barred the main doors of the building.

"Hello," Padgett had said to the man. "Does Kendrik still work here in the library?"

"Ah, no. Unfortunately, he died some years ago," the librarian said. He was a robust looking man of middle age, with thick red hair. Something about his face seemed a little distraught.

"Are you all right, sir?" Padgett had asked.

"Yes, yes. Only lady troubles," he said and laughed.

Padgett nodded knowingly, although he had little experience in such matters. "What's your name?"

"Schumm," the librarian said.

"Nice to meet you. I'm Padgett. I wish you good luck with your troubles."

And at that Padgett had quickly gathered up an enormous stack of books and sequestered himself in a secluded part of the library.

So intently did he read through the books that day that he failed to see a particular Mandrakhar who, not many minutes after Padgett's own arrival, entered the library to pay visit to a library employee whom Padgett also would have recognized—although he had only met her briefly and many years before.

The alehouse door swung open and a man with a beard entered, walking with purpose towards Vorlan, who readied himself to run. At the last moment, the man veered towards the counter to order a drink.

Vorlan exhaled.

He adjusted his hood back over his head to cover his ears. Every time someone walked in he wondered if this might be the same person who had slain Milaeus and was now coming for him.

How was he going to stay here several more hours?

The human woman...Corinne...had told him to wait for her here until she came to get him when she was finished working at the library across the street. She'd given him coin to get something to eat and told him not to attract any attention. He'd done as she'd asked, but when he still had several hours until Corinne's day finished, he'd gone ahead and ordered some of the ale he saw the men drinking at the counter.

He'd never imbibed the humans' drink before, although deep in the *yulthanispel* he could vaguely recall some of the ancestors trying it. As a younger man, he'd been warned to stay away from the stuff, but he was curious and bored and so he had the bartender bring him a mug. He'd watched some of these men drink five or six glasses; surely one wouldn't harm him.

Upon his first sip, Vorlan had nearly spit out the bitter liquid; but after drinking half the mug his mouth grew accustomed to the taste. He might even say he liked it. And best of all, the more he drank, the more he felt a kind of gentle haze throughout his body, his anxiety melting away.

This wasn't poison.

In fact, he would have another.

A strange thing seemed to happen by the time he drank his third mug's worth; his anxiety returned, but now it was laced with a strange paranoia and an inability to walk straight. Now every person who walked in was there to kill him.

"*How can I exist in this place for several more hours?*" he said to himself aloud now in Mandrakhi.

Not long after midday, he returned to the library. Corinne did not seem particularly happy to see him return so soon but agreed to have him sit in one of the public rooms on the lower floors until she was done with her work for the day.

He laid his head down on one of the desks and fell asleep. At some point, Corinne woke him and led him outside on the street. He followed the woman and, after what could have been five minutes or five hours, they reached the two-floor building she lived in.

Now they were in the front room of Corinne's apartment. Vorlan's mind began to clear a little, though his haziness seemed to have been replaced by a terrible headache. They sat in chairs facing each other. Corinne brought him tea and said something about what they should do next. Vorlan hardly heard any of it. It was difficult for him to pay attention with everything going on in his head mixing with the effects of the drink.

"I wish to…apologize. Could you repeat your words?" he said after she had told him something he hadn't retained.

He looked at her face.

The memories of the ancestors were often cloudy and fleeting, but now that he was in her home with her, he had a distracting sort of clarity with one of the memories.

He himself had experienced being infatuated with some of the

Mandrakhar girls in the settlement. Countless of the ancestors had been in love before. Yet never had he met one of the objects of his ancestors' affections until now. Actually, that was not precisely accurate. When he was four years old, just after he received the Tree's memories, there was an incident. One of the residents of the settlement had died young in an accident. And so, even after Vorlan received his memories, the dead Mandrakhir's widow had still been alive. She was much older than she'd appeared in the *yulthanispel*, but Vorlan remembered feeling something indescribable in his chest every time he saw her at the herb master or at the market. Like a dream come to life.

But that old Mandrakhar had looked hardly recognizable to what he saw with the *yulthanispel*. Corinne, on the other hand, looked hardly different at all.

"I said I'm not sure what we should do or how I'm going to get you to Ilyeth, but for the time being you can just stay with me. They may come looking for you eventually, but you're safer here than wandering out on the streets... Are you still drunk?"

"Yes, I believe... No, I no longer feel the drink... And yes, I believe what you suggest would be the right course of action."

He took a long sip of his tea to give him some time to think about what he was going to say next.

"Then why are you looking at me like that?" she said.

"How am I looking at you?"

She stood up from her chair and went over to the window. She wiped an arc of condensation from off the glass. Her gaze pointed outward, but Vorlan guessed she was not looking at anything.

"How much do you remember?" she said.

"How much do I remember of what?"

"What do you think?" she said.

"You."

"..."

"Some," he said. "A lot... No... More than usual... I did not remember it until I saw you."

"And what specifically do you remember?"

"It comes and goes. I have difficulty to say."

"Try."

Not much was solid. Mostly it was feelings and a sense of recognition. But there were memories.

He closed his eyes to help himself visualize it. "Walking through the woods after... your wedding, was it?" She didn't say anything. "Mating in your cottage the day...You were planting flowers in the garden...Irises. And I...*he* stooped down beside you and kissed you right . . ." He opened his eyes, stood up, and reached out to touch her on the nape of her neck with his finger. She did not draw away from his touch but neither did she seem to accept it. "Right there," he said.

"It never crossed my mind that those days would be anyone's but ours. I suppose if I thought about it, I knew they would, but... "

A feeling stirred inside him and then, more reflex than anything else, he put his lips on hers. Her lips pushed back for the briefest of instants and then drew away.

"No. You're not him," she said. This was true.

Corinne rose early the next morning. Vorlan remained fast asleep, probably still recovering from the ale the day before. His chest rose and fell in an even rhythm.

It didn't matter what memories he had. Erlan was dead.

She went down the street to send a messenger to Schumm at the library to tell him she was sick and wouldn't be able to come to work. She didn't suppose he'd believe it. Although he hadn't outright asked the previous day, he'd been curious why a Mandrakhar was visiting her at the library. He'd probably assume her absence was either to do with that (which it was) or their awkward dinner two days before (which it wasn't).

When she returned from the courier's office, Vorlan was still lying on the floor, but he appeared to be half awake now.

"How do you feel?" she said.

"I understand now why they told us not to drink human poison."

She built the fire in the stove and placed water in a pot to make tea. When the tea was ready they drank while eating bread she had from the day before.

"So what will we do today?" he said.

"Ilyeth, if the place exists, is a long way off. It may take me a few days to figure out how to find you passage there. But in the meantime, I need you not to draw any more attention to yourself."

"You say passage *for me*? Will you not come?"

"I can't," she said.

Corinne left the house again later that morning to go down to the docks and inquire about river passage south. Mostly, anytime she mentioned "Ilyeth" she was laughed at, but one sea captain told her he'd heard stories that one could get there if they first traveled to Port Marlton. Travel there would require river passage far south to Jarl and then a long overland journey west to the coast of the Inner Sea. And it wasn't going to be cheap.

Not long after Corinne returned home to have lunch with Vorlan, someone knocked on her door.

She signaled to Vorlan to be silent. "Who is it?" she said.

"It's me, Corinne." She recognized Schumm's voice. There was nowhere for Vorlan to hide, and she didn't want to go about explaining what he was doing in her apartment.

"It's very kind of you to check on me, but I don't want to get you sick," she said.

"Please," he said, "at least let me give you this tincture I picked up."

"No, I'm sorry," she said. "I look terrible."

"I'm sure you're as lovely as ever. Even if you were just slightly less lovely, you'd still be one of the loveliest women—"

"Please go," she said. "Just leave the tincture and I will pick it up once you've left." She hadn't meant for her tone to sound so harsh, but she needed him to leave.

There was a silence on the other side of the door.

"Schumm?"

"Very well," he said.

"Thank you, Schumm," she said.

"Just one more thing," he said.

"What?"

"Some people came around yesterday evening after you'd left, asking after that Mandrakhar. And others this morning. I didn't speak to them. Morris did. I think he mentioned that the Mandrakhar had been looking for you."

Shit. It probably wouldn't be long now before they discovered where she lived. "Okay."

"Are you in some kind of trouble?"

"No Schumm. I'm just sick. I'll see you tomorrow."

"All right. I hope you feel better, Corinne." The sound of his footsteps descended the stairs to the main door. She gave Vorlan a look of relief and he nodded.

A few moments passed, and then a loud voice sounded outside in front of her building. "D'ya know if there's a woman...by the name of Corinne who lives here?" the voice asked.

"What business do you have with Corinne?" It was Schumm's voice now.

Vorlan walked towards the window and snuck a glance through a crack in the blinds. "Come," he whispered to Corinne.

"Our business is our business," another voice, older sounding, said. "Just answer the question."

Corinne snuck beside Vorlan and looked through the window. Out front of the building, two men faced Schumm. Both wore light mail over their tunics and carried swords strapped to their sides. As their voices suggested, one was older, the other not much past twenty.

"Does this have to do with the Mandrakhar? Corinne has nothing to do with him," Schumm said.

"We'll decide that ourselves," the younger man said to Schumm and started towards the door.

"We must leave," Vorlan whispered. Corinne nodded and they came away from the window.

"You most certainly will not," Schumm shouted. "You have no right to harass Alderian citizens, and if you insist on doing so, I will call the guards."

A loud crack could be heard. Something inside Corinne tightened and she went back to the window for an instant, even though she knew she shouldn't. Outside Schumm lay on the ground bleeding, his skull split and his mouth open.

"You idiot," the older man's voice said. "You can't go around killing folk or the Redcloaks will be on us in no time. Drag the body to the side of the building so no one sees."

Corinne gestured to Vorlan to help push the bed against the door.

She could hear the men coming up the stairs now. They were on the landing. One knocked on the door across the hall. When no one answered, there was a loud crash.

"No one here," the voice of the younger man said.

"Check the other side."

Corinne opened up a drawer and drew out a short knife she kept for protection. She gestured to the back window, opened the shutters, and she and Vorlan, clutching at his seed box, stepped onto the ledge outside.

Just as they leapt, Corinne could hear a banging upon her door.

Corinne landed hard on the grassy ground below, tripped, and fell on her shoulder. She stood up, checking to see if anything was seriously injured. She seemed all right. She turned to Vorlan, who had somehow landed on his feet.

"Are you hurt?" she said. Vorlan shook his head "no." They were just about to start running when Corinne saw, not three paces in front of her, a large, mustached man carrying a broad sword. She braced herself.

❧

Based on the information they'd gotten from the librarian the evening before (that the woman the Mandrakhir had visited lived in Bridgeton), and then the local baker just an hour ago (that she probably lived on this very block), Sera and Nob figured they must be close. They'd sent a messenger to Padgett, telling him to meet them in this area, but so far there was no sign of the sorcerer.

Sera had Nob check up the street while she knocked on doors on the north end of the road.

She had just gotten through talking to a man in one of the houses who, although no help whatsoever, insisted on talking her ear off for five minutes about the recent spike in pork prices, when she heard Nob calling from up the street. "Ho-ho! Sera-rino!"

Nob was running in her direction with two others following close behind. In the last couple of years, Sera's long-distance vision had gone to shit, so it was only as they drew near that she saw that one of them was a woman with her hair cut short and the other was a Mandrakhir.

"These the folks we're looking for?" Sera said.

Nob gave a thumbs up. "This is Corinne and this is—"

"Vorlan," Sera said. "Great. But why are you running?"

They didn't have a chance to respond before she saw a half dozen men in mail, swords drawn, running at them from the direction Nob had come.

Sera's partner abruptly turned around and stood in the way of the armed men. He drew his own blade and held it out towards them with his right arm while his left hand twisted up each end of his gray mustache. "Come no closer, friends. No blood need be shed." he called to them. They stopped abruptly, dust rising up from where their boots skidded in the road.

"We have no qualm with you," one of the men said. He had gray stubble and an entirely humorless face. Sera guessed he was their leader. "Let us take the demon elf and what he carries in his bag, and we shall not molest the other three of you."

"You killed Schumm!" Corinne said.

"Who's Schumm?" Sera said, but no one seemed to pay her any mind. That's how it always was being a dwarf.

"An unfortunate thing. Done rashly by one of my men," gray stubble said. He turned briefly to look with disdain at the youngest of his group—a tall, baby-faced man-boy of eighteen or so. "Still, it would be best for you not to hinder us, less you share a similar fate."

"No can do," Nob said in his usual cheery voice and held his sword aloft in a fighting stance. By now Sera had drawn her own blade as well, and she noticed Corinne had done the same, holding her knife in a manner that suggested she knew what to do with it.

"Take Vorlan and get out of here," Sera said to Corinne.

"There's too many of them for you two," Corinne said.

"Get out of here," Sera repeated. Corinne looked at Nob, who smiled and gave another thumbs up. She nodded and grabbed Vorlan's arm, and the two went running off down the street.

One of the men, a fellow whose face was near completely covered in quite unattractive pimples, tried to give chase, but Nob stepped in the way. The pimpled guy swung his sword wildly, but Sera's partner easily blocked the blade and countered with a blow to the man's calf. The man screamed and fell to the ground. "No one needs to get hurt!" Nob shouted and then looked again at his fallen foe. "Well, except you. But it could be worse. You'll probably walk again...Maybe with a limp, but . . ."

"Fuck you, old man. You're dead," he said as he rolled in the dirt back towards his fellows.

Now the other five all charged. Nob immediately dispatched another of them when he cracked the man's skull with the pommel of his sword, but then the other four were upon them and Sera was suddenly more concerned with the man coming after her than with what Nob was doing.

"Come 'ere you little elf-loving dwarf bitch!" Sera's enemy, a black-haired man wearing a gold-mail vest, said as he backed her up against the wall of one of the nearby houses. His sword was a foot and a half longer than her dagger and his arm probably added another foot's advantage over Sera in terms of reach. Her only advantages were that she was a small target and that people had a tendency to underestimate her.

"Please! Don't hurt me!" she squealed, in the most feminine voice she could muster.

"It's too late for that," he said with a cruel sneer that made his admittedly not-that-bad-looking face, ugly. Too bad she was going to have to mess it up. "But if you don't move, I'll make it quick for ya."

Sera put her dagger down and played at cowering before him as her hand reached down to grab some of the sandy dirt below. He lifted his blade up over his head, making him relatively defenseless, as he prepared to land the kill strike. Right before he brought the blade down, Sera threw the dirt in his face.

He shouted and instinctively went to wipe his eyes. It was then that Sera, all in one motion, picked up her dagger and hacked at the space behind his left knee. Through her blade, she could feel the reverberations from his tendons and ligaments giving way to her chop. He screamed again and reached down with his sword hand to where Sera had cut. She swung another blow at his wrist. His sword fell to the ground. Were she stronger, she might have been able to cut the hand clean off. Instead, Sera just gave his arm a gaping wound down to the bone. With luck, the surgeon would end up finishing her work. He fell to the ground in agony, and Sera, ever the charitable one, stomped on his face rather than putting her dagger in his throat. She turned and ran in Nob's direction. He had downed the leader of the band but was still facing off against two swordsmen.

Nob had fought and won against far worse odds in his younger days, but he wasn't young anymore. Sera had closed half the distance to her partner when, still thirty paces away, Nob missed a parry and was skewered through by first one man's blade and then the other.

She didn't scream or shout. She just felt something inside her break.

The two men came after Sera now and she turned around and ran back in the direction she'd come. She'd never been the swiftest and getting old hadn't helped. It was only a matter of time before they caught up to her. She tried to look for somewhere she could go to evade them, but there was nowhere.

At least she and Nob would go out together.

Sera sensed her assailants' presence on her heels when abruptly the sound of their increasingly close footsteps ceased, replaced by screams. She ran a few more steps before swiveling around. The two men lay dying in the street, their bodies burning mounds of flesh and armor.

Padgett knew he was too late. That didn't stop him from trying every healing spell and technique he could think of. He'd long been regarded as the greatest healer in a generation of Ilyan Brothers, but there was no spell to raise the dead.

Sera crouched by his side, and Corinne and Vorlan stood back a few steps. The one surviving attacker who hadn't yet managed to scurry off, moaned in pain nearby. The Redcloaks still hadn't arrived, but by now a crowd of onlookers surrounded them. Padgett paid them no attention and kept casting yet more spells. Nob's flesh knit itself back together before their eyes. The wounds were mended, but the spirit was already gone.

"Come on, Nob!" Sera said.

He cast a resuscitation spell and Nob's head and torso churned upward in a wave before flopping back down in the dust, still and unmoving. Padgett put his face in his hands.

"Why are you stopping?" Sera said. "Try something else."

"I am...I am," he said, though he knew there was nothing else.

She grabbed him by the collar. "Why the fuck weren't you here earlier?" She struck him now on the face. He could have deflected the blow but didn't make the effort.

He was bleeding a little from his mouth. He took out his handkerchief and wiped the blood. He placed his dark hand on Sera's shoulder, intending to cast a spell to calm her a little, to help her with the grief that he sensed coursing through her.

"Don't fucking touch me," she said.

There, standing in the road, Vorlan thought of all the murder and death he'd witnessed—recently, or else in the memories of the ancestors.

"He does not own the fault," Vorlan said. "Your friend died for me...for my people."

"Don't talk to me, elf!" the small woman screamed, before walking away and beginning to weep.

Vorlan turned now to the dark-skinned man. "You belong to...you are one of the Ilyan Brothers, yes?"

He nodded, his gaze never averting from the body lying before him.

"Flynn told me to seek out your order. That you might help with *Saloryn Bai.*"

The dark man didn't look up. "Yes, I believe I can help."

"Are you called Kam Rhys?" Vorlan said.

Upon hearing this name, the sorcerer faced Vorlan. "No, I'm Padgett. Kam Rhys is dead."

Vorlan was about to ask another question, but down the road now, he saw many men dressed in red, riding towards them.

"I will talk to them," Padgett said.

Corinne couldn't hear their conversation, but whatever Padgett said to the Redcloaks seemed to be satisfactory to them. A few minutes later, two death carriages clattered up the road to take the bodies away. By now the crowd had mostly dispersed. Death carriages were a boring business.

When they loaded up Schumm's body, Corinne told the driver in charge who he was and gave him Schumm's address.

"You his wife?"

She shook her head.

"Do you know who his next of kin is?" the driver said.

She didn't but suggested they contact his house-lady.

"All right, we'll take it from here," he said and tipped his hat towards her.

Corinne went back over to where Padgett was standing with Vorlan and the dwarf, Master Nicoletto.

"Padgett says he…belongs…to the Ilyan Brothers," Vorlan said, "and he can help us grow a new Tree."

Her mind was still spinning from everything. "Is that right? Good."

She had so many questions for the sorcerer.

"Do you remember me?" she said to him.

"Yes, Corinne. I do."

Vorlan and Master Nicoletto both looked to Corinne. "You know him?" Vorlan said.

"We met. Years ago," Corinne said and turned to Padgett. "Do you remember the note you gave to me then? Did you know all this was going to happen?"

"Perhaps I should have. I saw an image is all. That is how the premonitions often work. I didn't put everything together until I saw you just now."

"Can someone tell me what the shit you guys are talking about?" Master Nicoletto said, her eyes wet and red.

Padgett started to speak, but Master Nicoletto cut him off. "Actually, never mind. I don't care."

They hired a carriage and all went together to the Mandrakhi Quarter. According to Padgett, there was a place there—a courtyard within a large house where a Memory Tree had once grown. If a Tree could grow there once, then it reasoned that the soil was such that one could grow there again.

The house, colored a faded blue and green and red and yellow, was, Corinne thought, like a magnificent corpse: broken and in disrepair but hinting at a former glory. According to Padgett, only a few of the Mandrakhar elders lived there today.

That very evening, Padgett had some of the Mandrakhar dig a large hole in the center of the courtyard.

"You should be the one to bury the seed," he said to Vorlan, who took the shiny black thing out of his wooden box and placed it in the dirt. Afterwards, they filled the hole and encircled it with a dozen large stones.

�֍

Sera spent two days going through Nob's papers and attending to his affairs.

They buried him at a family plot in a cemetery in Bluefield she found mentioned in his will. Nob had seldom talked about his family other than a few anecdotes about his father's time in the military, but there, reading the engravings of the headstones, Sera learned more about them than she had in nearly a quarter century of knowing her partner. For instance, after leaving the military, Nob's father, Arn, had been a barber and, if the headstone was to be believed, *the greatest sculptor of mustache, beard, and chops the capital has ever known.*

Imagine fucking that.

There weren't many people at the burial—just a dozen or so acquaintances from the neighborhood, Padgett, the Mandrakhar and his lady friend. Sera spoke a few short words and that was that. Afterwards, she saw Nob's cousin Sylas Nottle amongst the attendees. She hadn't seen Sylas in years, but it looked like he'd cleaned himself up a little.

Afterwards, Sera went back with Padgett and the others to the Mandrakhi Quarter to check on any progress they were having with that Tree.

"You've done more than your part," Padgett said as he and Sera sat together with Vorlan and Corinne in the carriage. "You don't need to come with us."

"No," she said, "I'll go with." Now that Nob was gone, Sera didn't want to be at the office that doubled as her apartment alone. And besides, she wanted to make sure that Nob didn't die for nothing.

When they got to the Mandrakhi Quarter, Sera could see Padgett had been busy the last couple days. In addition to a bunch of his gray-cloaked buddies, he'd called in a favor with the Redcloaks, and they were running a security perimeter around the whole neighborhood.

"Once the Tree begins to grow," Vorlan said, "Padgett's Brothers will assist in building a great wall and gate to protect the new Tree. The architects have already begun drawing up plans."

"And how's it going getting the seed to sprout?" Sera said. "That was the problem, wasn't it?"

Vorlan looked at Padgett who spoke up now. "Not so good just yet."

Padgett and the other Ilyan Brothers and Sisters were seated at a large table in the house whose courtyard the seed had been planted in.

"Is it possible you were mistaken with the premonition, Master Padgett?" said Master Quentyan. "We've tried every spell that seems reasonable for us to have attempted, no?"

They had, Padgett knew. Yet the image of the premonition had been unambiguous: the stone turning bright white, the white-wooded scepter growing claw-like roots that sunk deep into the earth before retracting, the new Tree, *Saloryn Bai*, born again. "No, I cannot be mistaken," he said.

Several more days passed. Padgett seldom slept or ate save for small naps he would take in a seated position out in the courtyard, a bite he'd have of the Mandrakhar's unleavened bread.

During this time, he'd often think again of his family and of the man he'd called Benedictus—all of them dead now. He had to see this through.

It was raining hard when Vorlan came out to the courtyard to check on Padgett. The sorcerer was seated in the mud holding the scepter. The rain pummeled his face. The other Brothers had told Vorlan not to bother, that Padgett wouldn't heed anyone's advice, but Vorlan felt he should try nonetheless.

"Padgett," he called, over the crackling of the rain.

"What do you need?" Padgett said. His back was to Vorlan and he didn't turn around.

"Are you hungry?"

"I will eat when this is done," the sorcerer said.

Vorlan walked out into the rain and stood over Padgett, placing his hand on the sorcerer's shoulder. "Please. You must eat something," Vorlan said. "You must come in to wash, to rest."

Padgett stood up and faced Vorlan. "No. I need to do this."

"Yes, but after you rest."

Padgett was silent for a moment, but then his serene exterior burst. "I need to figure this out! I need . . ." he said and threw the white scepter down on the ground. He began sobbing.

"Come, friend," Vorlan said and guided Padgett out of the rain. When they were under the roof's overhang but not yet to the door, Padgett fell to the ground in exhaustion.

Vorlan went to help him up, but Padgett waved him off. "Just give me a minute."

"Should I get one of the others?"

"No. I just need a little time."

Vorlan nodded and walked out from the overhang back into the rain to pick up the scepter, which still lay in the mud. He had never touched it before. It was lighter than he'd expected but still sturdy feeling.

The rain was still coming down. For no reason, really, he tilted his head back, opened his mouth, and let a few drops fall in.

He looked down at the muddy spot where they had buried the seed and he imagined it growing, first into a sapling and eventually into a great Tree like they'd had in the Westwood. Just as a way of play-acting his fantasy, he tapped the earth with the base of the staff. If only it were that simple . . .

He was getting very wet now, so he turned to rejoin Padgett, still sitting with his head between his legs under the overhang. But then, his hand, the one that held the staff, began to vibrate, subtly at first, but then faster. A sensation he'd never felt before traveled up his arm before spreading to the rest of his body. The red stone held by the staff began to glow and then change colors. Blue. Yellow. Violet. Green. White. White. White. Blinding, blinding white.

"What did you do?" Padgett called from somewhere behind, but Vorlan didn't know, and if he had, he would have still been too shocked to speak. He felt his arm being pulled down as if by an irresistible force and the staff slammed into the dirt. There was a great rumble, like the earth groaning, and Vorlan was thrown back into the mud.

One night, a few days after the spring equinox, Corinne dreamed of Erlan.

She was still staying at the house in the Mandrakhi Quarter. After everything—all this business with Vorlan, Schumm's murder—she'd told her new supervisor at the library she needed to take some time off. She liked her work there and eventually she'd return, but for now, she needed to be here—amongst Erlan's people—to see what would become of that seed buried beneath the ground not twenty paces from her room.

Since Vorlan's incident with the scepter two weeks earlier, there was nothing they could do but wait.

Perhaps if the seed sprouted, if the Tree came, she might find a way, after so much time, to put the past to rest.

She missed him so much.

The room she slept in had a small window facing the courtyard. In her dream that night, Erlan's floating spirit tapped gently on the windowpane. He didn't appear how he had at the end but instead looked as he had when they were first married, black-haired, healthy, strong.

"Come," he said.

"But I'm tired."

"Come."

She looked through the window and behind Erlan's floating ghost was the silhouette of a full-grown Tree. "Come," he said again.

Sometime during the middle of the night, Corinne woke and looked out the window onto the darkened courtyard, her dead husband's voice echoing in her ears.

She wrapped her blanket around her and went out to the courtyard.

"Are you out here?" she said, but there was no answer.

She sat down in one of the chairs under the overhang. Eventually she fell back asleep.

When she woke again, just as the sun was rising, the courtyard was still mostly dark. She could smell the cooking of meat coming from the kitchen. Still disoriented, she searched for the Tree she'd seen earlier in her dreams.

Nothing. At the center of the grass, the large ring of stones circled only dirt.

Of course, nothing!

Dreams were just our mind's wishful thinking.

There was no Tree and Erlan was dead.

But then... Was that? She squinted her eyes. There. Still covered over by the shadow of the house, she saw, not a full-grown Tree, but the tiniest of green sprouts.

All day, bells sounded throughout the Mandrakhi Quarter and huge crowds of Mandrakhar began gathering outside the house. They all wanted to see the sapling.

Sera was happy for them, but the whole situation gave her an anti-climactic feeling. Like, what was she going to do now?

That night, there was celebrating and dancing and music in the streets. Sera couldn't walk ten steps without someone handing her sweets or a skewer of chicken. Everyone was laughing and happy. Sera even saw some of those gray-cloaked weirdoes who never seemed to make facial expressions smile a little. Nob would have loved it. True, there was no wine since the Mandrakhar didn't drink, but maybe she should drink a little less anyway.

That night as she was eating what must have been her eleventh sweet fig pastry and watching a troupe of adorable, fat-cheeked Mandrakhar kids dance, Padgett came up to her and they talked for a time. Now that they'd figured out how to make the seeds germinate, Padgett and Vorlan, along with a dozen or so other sorcerers were going to travel to the other Mandrakhi settlements all throughout the Continent to plant new Trees.

"When do you leave?" Sera said.

"Perhaps in another day or two," he said. "Some of my Brothers are staying here to make sure that no one disturbs this new Tree. The Redcloaks have also committed to help stand guard."

Sera popped the rest of the pastry in her mouth and wiped her face with her sleeve. She'd lived a pretty interesting life but had hardly traveled anywhere outside the cesspool that was the capital.

Maybe it was time for *her* to close up shop and see the world a little bit.

"Is there room for one more on your grand arborist expedition?"

"I wouldn't have imagined you'd want to come along." Padgett said.

"When else am I going to get an opportunity to run around with a bunch of sorcerers?"

"Fair enough. But you don't ride a horse, do you?"

Sera hadn't thought of this. "That's right," she said, disappointed.

"But I am not so big a man. Perhaps then you can ride with me?"

She thought about it. She was known to ride with Nob from time to time. To tell the truth, she didn't love it. But perhaps it was time for her to get over all that.

Artist, Executive, Philanthropist, Friend and Mother. Sarah M. Fitzroy (D'Albero) died at home in Rowayton, CT on January 14, 2066 following a complication related to her two-decade-long battle with Alzheimer's. Sarah is survived by her daughter, Margaret "Maggie" Fitzroy, who was deeply involved as a caregiver and comforter during the last years of Sarah's life and was at her side at the time of her final passing. Sarah is also survived by her brother, Paul D'Albero and his wife April (Selma), their two children (Phillip and Arwen), and five grandchildren. Sarah was born on October 28, 1982 in Cincinnati, Ohio and lived there until age nine, before moving first to Northern California then Connecticut. Sarah was predeceased by her husband, Henry Fitzroy, sister, Emily D'Albero (who died when Sarah was 11), and her parents (Anthony D'Albero, a successful businessman and CEO of three publicly traded companies, and Alice Eklund D'Albero, a concert pianist in her twenties and later a marketing executive). Sarah attended Fairfield High School (2000), where she was an all-state basketball player and later, Duke University (2004), where she graduated with a dual degree in Graphic Arts and Economics. After college, Sarah met and married her first husband, author Jack Ampong, and the couple was married for six years. Through her twenties and thirties, Sarah was an accomplished artist and illustrator and worked as a designer for Princeton Collectibles in New Jersey before becoming a freelance illustrator, during which time she illustrated nearly a dozen children's books. It was while at an artist's retreat, finishing her first book *Titus and Ronica's Escape from*

Magic-Land, that Sarah met her second husband, Henry Fitzroy, in 2017. The couple married two years later and stayed together until Henry's death in 2049. In 2025, Sarah combined her passions for art and commerce to found The D-Fitz Group, an award-winning advertising agency and interaction design studio that worked on a wide range of campaigns for technology companies like Tesla Rails and Bethesda Interactives, as well as the successful 2032 Chelsea Clinton presidential campaign. Sarah was deeply involved in charitable giving and served as trustee for the Anthony and Alice D'Albero Foundation, started by her parents in 2014. Throughout her life she also served on the boards of a number of other charitable and arts-related non-profits, including The Brooklyn Academy of Music and later, The Fairfield County Women's Group. Sarah had great love for the natural world and actively cultivated a sense of wonder; she was an avid hiker (she twice hiked the Appalachian Trail and completed a number of challenging treks around the world) and loved sailing with her family and friends (countless excursions in the Long Island Sound, longer trips to Cape Cod, Nova Scotia, and Ireland). Sarah had boundless energy, deep intelligence, an eye for the sublime, and tremendous warmth. She believed that life presented endless opportunities to learn, even during moments of tragedy. In an executive profile, she once remarked regarding the death of her sister: "Emily's death was incredibly hard on me, but it also opened up a wellspring of strength—and a realization that there are no guarantees in life, but that we still need to fight like hell for the things that are important to us." Sarah faced her own illness with this same 'fight,' as she had a remarkable amount of independence, even as her illness became quite advanced. Sarah felt a profound duty to embrace everyone she encountered with compassion, and she shared her love of people and life equally with those close to her as well as, through her charitable work, with those she never met. Perhaps the role that Sarah cherished above all else though, was that of being a mother. Said her daughter, Maggie Fitzroy, who Sarah adopted after marrying her second husband, Henry: "I was seven when I first met Sarah, but in all the years afterwards, I never felt like we were anything other than blood relatives. It's a kind of miracle, and a testament to Sarah's love, that though my birth mother tragically died when I was young, I never felt her absence like I might have expected." A celebration of Sarah's life will be held in Norwalk, CT in early March on a date to